t

e onmenta con

in e polar regions, and has taught perative ana

an biological anthropology.

S s the creator of the Matthew

ysteries set in medieval Cambr

has Chaloner books, and now es in Wales with

usband, who is also a writer.

Also by Susanna Gregory

The Thomas Chaloner Series

A Conspiracy of Violence
Blood on the Strand
The Butcher of Smithfield
The Westminster Poisoner
A Murder on London Bridge
The Body in the Thames

The Matthew Bartholomew Series

A Plague on Both Your Houses
An Unholy Alliance
A Bone of Contention
A Deadly Brew
A Wicked Deed
A Masterly Murder
An Order for Death
A Summer of Discontent
A Killer in Winter
The Hand of Justice
The Mark of a Murderer
The Tarnished Chalice
To Kill or Cure
The Devil's Disciples
A Vein of Deceit
The Killer of Pilgrims
Mystery in the Minster
Murder by the Book

THE PICCADILLY PLOT

Susanna Gregory

SPHERE

First published in Great Britain in 2012 by Sphere
This paperback edition published in 2012 by Sphere

Copyright © Susanna Gregory 2012

The moral right of the author has been asserted.

WEST DUNBARTONSHIRE	
D000016431	
Bertrams	17/10/2012
CRI	£8.99
BK	

ISBN 978-0-7515-4428-2

Typeset in Baskerville MT by Palimpsest Book Production Limited,
Falkirk, Stirlingshire

Printed and bound in Great Britain by Clays Ltd, St Ives plc

Papers used by Sphere are from well-managed forests
and other responsible sources.

MIX
Paper from
responsible sources
FSC® C104740

Sphere
An imprint of
Little, Brown Book Group
100 Victoria Embankment
London EC4Y 0DY

An Hachette UK Company
www.hachette.co.uk

www.littlebrown.co.uk

For Bernard and Jean Knight

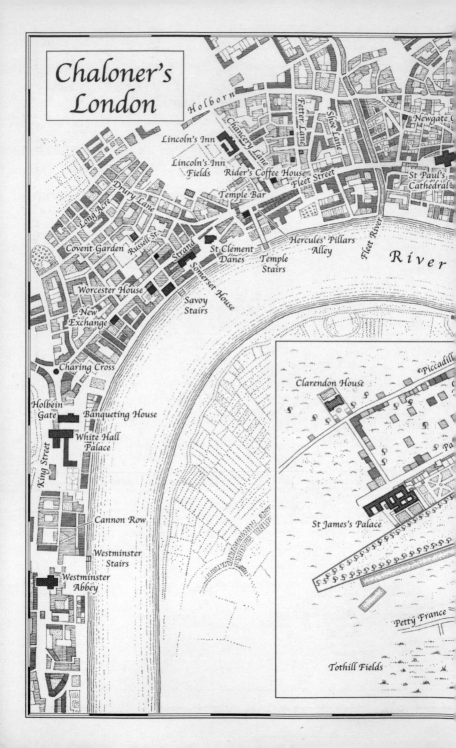

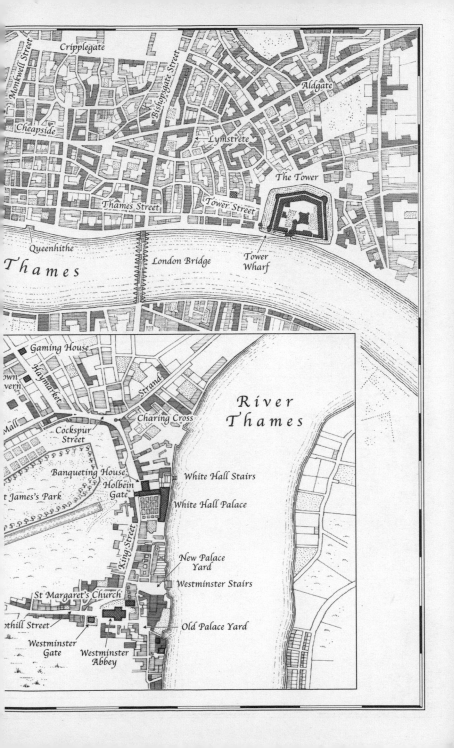

Prologue

William Reyner watched Lord Teviot lead the five hundred soldiers to their deaths. It would be easy to prevent the massacre – just gallop after the column and tell Teviot that more than ten thousand Barbary corsairs were lying in wait ahead – but he made no move to do so. A large amount of money was at stake, and that was considered far more important than the lives of mere warriors. Besides, Reyner had never liked Teviot: the man was a greedy fool, who should never have been appointed Governor of Tangier in the first place.

He glanced around him. Tangier had come to England as part of Queen Katherine's dowry, but it was a paltry place – a few winding streets huddled on a hill, rich with the scent of exotic spices, sun-baked manure and the salty aroma of the sea. It was being fortified, in the hope that it would provide British ships with a secure Mediterranean anchorage, although personally Reyner thought the King should have held out for

1

something better. Tangier's harbour was too shallow and too exposed, while the surrounding countryside was full of hostile Moors.

When the last infantryman had marched through the town gate, Reyner and his fellow scouts followed on horseback. Colonel Harley was in the lead, sullen and scowling as usual, while the impassive Robert Newell brought up the rear. All three were careful to keep their distance: *they* did not want to become entangled in the slaughter that was about to take place.

Teviot's destination was a wood named Jews Hill; a place where corsairs often gathered to harry the town. The three scouts had assured him that it was safe that day – a good time to chop down some of the trees and make it more difficult for raiders to use in the future. The reality was that it had never been more dangerous.

It was not long before the first sounds of battle drifted back on the hot, dusty breeze – the yells of men roaring an attack and the spluttering crack of gunfire. Reyner, Harley and Newell pulled up.

Although Reyner did not care about Teviot, he had always been uncomfortable with sacrificing half the town's garrison into the bargain. Harley and Newell had scoffed at his faint-heartedness, reminding him of the fabulous rewards they would reap when the deed was done, but he could not escape the conviction that the plan was unnecessarily brutal, and that a less bloody way should have been devised to realise their master's plans.

The first skirmish did not last long, and the British cheered when the Moors turned and ran. Reyner stared hard at Harley: there was still time to stop what had been set in motion, to warn Teviot that the first attack was a ruse to lure him and his men deeper into the

2

woods. But Harley ignored him. Oblivious to the peril, Teviot rallied his troops and led an advance up the hill.

The British were jubilant at the enemy's 'flight', and it was clear they felt invincible. They walked a little taller in the wavering heat, the fierce African sunlight glinting off their helmets and weapons. Teviot was at their head, a tall, athletic figure on his white horse. He looked like a god, although Reyner knew he was anything but: the Governor of Tangier was a vain, stupid man, whose incompetence was matched only by his venality.

The corsair commander timed his ambush perfectly, splintering Teviot's column into clusters. There was immediate panic: the British had been trained to fight in a specific formation, and did not know what to do once their orderly line had been broken. Teviot did his best, bawling orders and laying about him like a demon. Grudgingly, Reyner admitted that, for all his faults, the man was no coward.

The battle was short and brutal. Pikes and short swords were no match for ten thousand scything scimitars, and the British were cut down in ruthless hand-to-hand skirmishing. Teviot managed to rally a few men at the top of the hill, where he mounted a brave last stand, but it was hopeless. The Moors advanced in an almost leisurely fashion, and Teviot was hacked to pieces.

Without a word, Reyner, Harley and Newell rode back to Tangier, ready to feign shock when news of the catastrophe reached the town. They did not have long to wait. Miraculously, about thirty soldiers had managed to escape. They stumbled through the gate, shaken and bloody, gasping their tale to the settlement's horrified residents.

Reyner closed his ears to the wails of shock and disbelief, telling himself that the massacre was Teviot's own fault for choosing the wrong side in the struggle for riches and power – his master had had no choice but to order his elimination. But he was uneasy, even so. The order to kill Teviot had been delivered with a ruthless insouciance, and Reyner had sensed a dark and deadly power.

Not for the first time since he had been recruited, he wondered whether he had been right to throw in his lot with such a person. He had been promised a handsome payment, it was true, but what good was a fortune if he was not alive to enjoy it – if it was decided that those who had engineered the atrocity were too great a liability, and should be dispatched themselves?

But what was done was done, and there was no going back. He, Harley and Newell would just have to ensure that no one ever learned the truth about what had transpired on Jews Hill that pretty spring morning. And if that entailed more murders, then so be it.

Queenhithe, early October 1664

It had been a pleasant voyage for the passengers and crew of *Eagle*. The sea had been calm, even across the notorious Bay of Biscay, and the winds favourable. The cargo comprised luxury goods from the eastern Mediterranean, so there were no noxious odours from the holds to contend with, and the journey from Tangier had been made in record time.

Now they were almost home. They had sailed up the River Thames that morning, arriving at London Bridge just as the drawbridge was being raised to let masted ships through. The timing could not have been better, and Captain Pepperell was pleased with himself as he conned his ship towards Queenhithe. Then he glanced at his passengers, who had gathered on deck to watch *Eagle* dock, and felt his good humour slip a little.

An irascible, unfriendly man, Pepperell much preferred those journeys where the guest cabins were empty. Still, he had been paid to monitor these particular passengers, although it had not been easy – they had been almost as reluctant to socialise as he himself, and the information he had gathered was meagre. Of course, that was not to say it was unimportant, and he believed it would be very gratefully received.

They were the usual mixed bag. Reverend Addison was Tangier's chaplain, returning to London for a holiday; Thomas Chaloner was some sort of diplomat; Harley, Newell and Reyner were army scouts – surly, mean-spirited individuals whom the crew disliked; and John Cave was a musician who had been sent to entertain the troops.

The Captain smirked as he recalled the garrison's stunned disbelief when Cave had embarked on a medley of elegant arias. They liked bawdy tavern songs, and excerpts from Italian operas were definitely not what they had wanted to hear. Yet for all that, thought Pepperell, Cave did sing prettily. Chaloner played the bass viol, and even Pepperell – not a man given to foolish sentiment – had been moved by the haunting beauty of some of the duets they had performed on the voyage home.

He gave the last few orders that saw *Eagle* safely moored, then left his second-in-command, Anthony Young, to supervise the unloading, while he went to complete landing formalities with the harbour master. He strode towards the customs building, a little unsteady on legs that were more attuned to the roll of the sea.

He turned when he heard a shout, and saw two men running towards him, one in a brown coat and the other resplendent in a red uniform with a plumed Cavalier hat. He waited, supposing their business with him must be urgent, or they would not be racing about like madmen.

By the time he realised they meant him harm, it was far too late to think of defending himself. The man in brown lashed out with a knife, and Pepperell felt it slice deep into his innards. He gasped in pain and shock as he dropped to the ground, and tried to shout for help. He could only manage a strangled whisper, barely audible over the hammering footsteps as his assailants sped away.

Chaloner heard it, though, and Pepperell could have wept with relief when the diplomat snapped into action, yelling for his fellow passengers to tend the wounded captain even as he vaulted over the rail to give chase. Unfortunately, the others were slower to react, and several long, agonising minutes had passed before they came to cluster at Pepperell's side.

'Thieves!' muttered Young, shaking his head in disgust as he tried to stem the flow of blood with his cap. 'The scourge of every port in Christendom.'

'But the captain still has his purse,' Reverend Addison pointed out, kneeling to lay a comforting hand on Pepperell's shoulder. 'Besides, I recognise the man who stabbed him. He is Josiah Brinkes, a vicious scoundrel who can be hired by anyone wanting dirty business done. This was not robbery – it was assassination!'

'Rubbish!' declared Harley the scout, staring dispassionately at the dying man. 'They intended to steal the purse, but Chaloner was after them too fast – they were forced to run before they could lay hold of it.'

But Pepperell knew the truth. He tried to grab Addison's sleeve, to draw him nearer so he could explain, but there was no strength in his fingers. Then Chaloner arrived back, panting hard from his exertions, and the chaplain did not notice Pepperell's desperate attempts to claim his attention.

'Escaped, did they?' Harley smiled unpleasantly. 'Well, I cannot say I blame you for deciding to let them go. Dockyard felons can be notoriously brutal, and there *were* two of them.'

'Then you should have gone with him,' said Addison admonishingly, still oblivious to Pepperell's weak but increasingly frantic gestures. 'You claim to be a professional soldier.'

Chaloner silenced them with a glare, then leaned close to the captain, straining to hear what he was struggling to say.

'Picc . . . a . . . dilly . . .'

Chaloner regarded him in confusion. 'Do you mean the street?'

Pepperell's world was growing darker as his life drained away. He tried again. 'Tr . . . trade . . .'

'I had better see to the ship.' Young's eyes gleamed as he looked at the vessel that was now his to command. 'Her owners will not let this unfortunate incident interfere with her itinerary – they will still expect her to sail on the evening tide.'

'With you as master?' asked Addison in distaste.

'Why not?' Young shrugged. 'I know *Eagle* and her crew. There is no one better.'

'Damn you!' snarled Pepperell with the last vestiges of his strength.

'Who is he cursing?' asked Addison uneasily. 'Chaloner for failing to catch his killer; Young for taking his ship; or all of us for not knowing what he is talking about?'

'We will never know,' said Chaloner softly. 'He is dead.'

Chapter 1

It had been raining all night, and Thomas Chaloner was cold, wet and tired, so when the workmen arrived he left his hiding place with relief, hobbling slightly on legs that were stiff from staying still too long. Chatting and laughing, the men set about lighting a fire and balancing a pot above it: no self-respecting labourer began the day without a cup of warmed ale inside him. Chaloner would have liked to have joined them at the brazier, but he kept his distance until Roger Pratt arrived.

Pratt was reputed to be one of the country's most innovative architects, although Chaloner was inclined to suspect that 'innovative' was a euphemism for 'overrated and expensive'. He was a haughty, self-important man, who always managed to appear coolly elegant in his Court finery. By comparison, Chaloner was a dishevelled mess. No wig covered his brown hair, and his clothes had suffered from their night under a tarpaulin. Pratt eyed him disparagingly, although Chaloner was tempted to ask what else he expected after such a miserable night.

'Well?' the architect demanded curtly.

Chaloner fought down his resentment at the brusque greeting. 'Nothing. Again. Perhaps your bricks, nails and wood are going missing during the day.'

'Impossible,' snapped Pratt. 'We hire upwards of sixty men here, and thieves would be noticed. The villains come at night, and I am disgusted by your inability to catch them. These thefts are costing your master a fortune, and Clarendon House is not a cheap venture to begin with.'

Chaloner looked at the place he had been guarding since he had returned from Tangier the week before. When he had left London at the beginning of July, the imposing H-shaped mansion had been nothing but foundations, but walls and a roof had flown up in his absence, and windows and doors had been installed. Now, most of the remaining work was internal – plastering, tiling and decorating.

'It will be hailed as the finest building in London,' said Pratt, allowing himself a smile of satisfaction as he followed the direction of Chaloner's gaze. 'I was delighted when the Earl of Clarendon chose me to be his architect. Clarendon House will be the best of all my work, a fabulous stately home within walking distance of White Hall and Westminster.'

'Yes,' agreed Chaloner unhappily. He had always felt the project was a bad idea: it was too sumptuous, too ostentatious and too costly, and he was sure it would bring his employer trouble. 'That is the problem. As most of London is poor, it will attract resentful—'

'No one begrudges the Earl a nice place to live,' interrupted Pratt. 'He is the Lord Chancellor, for God's sake. He *should* have a decent home.'

10

'But Clarendon House is not a "decent home",' argued Chaloner. 'It is a palace – and far more luxurious than any of the ones owned by the King.'

'Do you think so?' asked Pratt, flattered, although Chaloner had not meant it as a compliment.

'His enemies will use it against him, and—'

'The Earl does not have enemies,' snapped Pratt. 'He is a lovely man, and everyone reveres and respects him.'

Chaloner struggled not to gape, because the Earl was neither revered nor respected, and 'lovely' was certainly not a word many would have used to describe him. He was vain, petty and selfish, and Chaloner would have abandoned him for other work in an instant. Unfortunately, opportunities for former Parliamentarian spies were few and far between in Royalist London, and the Earl had been the only one willing to overlook Chaloner's past allegiances and hire him. Thus Chaloner was stuck with Clarendon, regardless of his personal feelings towards the man.

The antipathy was wholly reciprocated. The Earl needed Chaloner's range of unorthodox skills to stay one step ahead of his many rivals, but he made no secret of the fact that he disapproved of Chaloner, his past *and* his profession. He had promoted him to the post of gentleman usher a few months before, but only because Chaloner had married a lady for whom the Earl felt a fatherly affection – an affection that was certainly not extended to her husband.

Yet despite his dislike, Chaloner hoped the Earl would survive the political maelstrom that surged around him, because if he were to fall from grace, then his intelligencer would fall with him. Worse, Chaloner's wife might be dismissed from her post as lady-in-waiting to the Queen, simply because of whom she had married. Chaloner winced. Hannah would be devastated if that happened: she loved her work, her status at Court and Queen Katherine in equal measure.

When there was no reply to his remarks, Pratt strode away to talk to the workmen. Chaloner watched, wondering how many of them knew more than was innocent about the missing materials, because he was sure the thieves could not operate so efficiently without inside help.

One man returned the stare. His expression was distinctly unfriendly, as if he had guessed what Chaloner was thinking. His name was Vere, a woodmonger who had been hired to act as supervisor. He was a thickset fellow with greasy ginger hair, and he continued to glare until Chaloner, too cold and tired for needless confrontations, looked away.

Next to Vere was John Oliver, Pratt's assistant, a gangly, shambling man with a pear-shaped face, sad eyes, and shoulders that seemed perpetually slumped in defeat. When he spoke, his words were often preceded by a gloomy shake of the head, as if to warn the listener that any news *he* had to impart would not be good.

As Pratt told the workmen that their materials had survived another night intact, Chaloner was alert for a furtive glance or a sly nod that might indicate guilt, but he was wasting his time: there was no discernible reaction from anyone. Then Pratt started to issue orders, which had them hurrying in all directions to obey. While the architect was busy, Oliver came to talk to Chaloner.

'It means the villains will come tonight instead,' he predicted morosely. 'Or tomorrow. And you cannot stand guard indefinitely. Is it true that Clarendon ordered you back from Tangier specifically to investigate the matter?'

12

Chaloner nodded. The Earl had hated being the victim of a crime, and the summons to return on the next available ship had been curt and angry, as if it were Chaloner's fault that he had not been to hand when he was needed. Chaloner had been relieved though, because he had been in Tangier disguised as a diplomat for almost ten weeks, and was beginning to think the Earl had forgotten him – that he was doomed to spend the rest of his life in the hot, dirty, dangerous little outpost pretending to be something he was not.

'I doubt you will succeed,' said Oliver, when no other answer was forthcoming. 'It is almost as if they spirit our bricks away by magic.'

'I have succeeded in that nothing has disappeared since I arrived,' said Chaloner defensively.

'Well, yes,' acknowledged Oliver grudgingly. 'That is true. But I worry for you. Your presence may have deterred them so far, but what happens when they get desperate? I imagine they are ruthless villains, and they may do you harm. You are, after all, only one man.'

Chaloner smiled. Before he had been recruited as a spy, he had been a soldier in Cromwell's New Model Army, and was better able than most to look after himself. But no one else had expressed any care for his safety, and he appreciated Oliver's concern.

'Pratt is calling you,' he said. 'It is time for you to begin work, and for me to finish.'

He made one last circuit around the house, and took his leave.

It was still not fully light as Chaloner walked home. The day was unseasonably cold, and a bitter breeze blew from the north, so he strode briskly in an effort to work some warmth into his limbs. Normally, he would have cut through St James's Park to reach his house in Tothill Street, but that would have entailed scaling two high walls, and his hands and feet were far too numb for such antics. He went east instead, along the muddy, rutted country lane named Piccadilly.

He hoped Hannah would still be in bed when he arrived, because sliding between icy blankets held scant appeal that day. It was likely that he would be in luck, because her duties with the Queen meant she often worked late, but even if not, she hated rising early. Or perhaps one of the maids would have lit a fire in the parlour, and he could doze next to it for an hour or two before going to report to the Earl in White Hall.

It was a quarter of a mile before he reached the first signs of civilisation – a cluster of tenements and taverns where Piccadilly met the busy thoroughfare called the Haymarket. The most prominent building was the Gaming House, once a fashionable resort, but like many such establishments, it had been allowed to fall into shabby decline under Cromwell's Puritans.

It was apparently closing time, because a number of patrons were emerging. Some sang happily after a night of freely flowing wine, while others moved with the slouched, defeated air that said their losses at the card tables had been heavy.

Opposite was a tavern called the Crown, and Chaloner was amused to note that *its* customers were using the Gaming House's commotion as an opportunity to slink away in dribs and drabs. An extremely attractive woman was directing people out, timing their departures so they could blend into the throng that staggered noisily towards London. It was natural for any spy to be intrigued by brazenly suspicious behaviour, so Chaloner ducked behind a stationary milk-cart to watch almost without conscious thought.

First to emerge was a man with an eye-patch and an orange beard so massive that its end had been tucked into his belt, presumably to prevent it from flying up and depriving him of the sight in the other eye. He walked with a confident swagger, and when he replied to a slurred greeting from one of the Gaming House's patrons, his voice was unusually high, like that a boy.

Next out was a fellow wearing the kind of ruffs and angular shoes that had been fashionable when Chaloner had last visited Lisbon; the man's complexion was olive, and he had dark, almost black, eyes. His companion wore a wide-brimmed hat that concealed his face, although the red ribbons he had threaded through the lace around his knees were distinctive and conspicuous.

Chaloner was surprised to recognise the next three. They were Harley, Newell and Reyner, the scouts who had sailed home with him on *Eagle*. Rather than aim for the city, they turned north. He watched them go, thinking the surly trio were certainly the kind of men to embroil themselves in dubious business. And there was definitely something untoward going on in the Crown, given the manner in which its customers were sneaking out.

He was about to leave when someone else emerged whom he recognised. It was the fellow who had stabbed Captain Pepperell – Brinkes, the felon said to do anything for money. Chaloner eased farther behind the cart as he recalled Pepperell's dying words: 'Piccadilly' and 'trade'. Had the captain been naming the place where his killer liked to do business?

Chaloner thought back to the murder. It had occurred exactly a week before, but the authorities had made no effort to arrest the culprit, mostly, it appeared, because they were afraid Brinkes might not like it – it had not taken Chaloner long to realise that those in charge of Queenhithe were frightened of the man, and were loath to do anything that might annoy him. Chaloner had done his best to see justice done, but his efforts had been ignored.

Did the fact that Harley and his scouts frequented the same tavern mean that *they* had hired Brinkes to kill Pepperell? But how could they have done, when they had been in Tangier for the last two years? And what reason could they have for wanting Pepperell dead, anyway? The captain had not been pleasant, with his sulky temper and rough manners, but that was hardly a reason to dispatch him. Or, more likely, had they been so impressed by Brinkes's efficiency with a knife that they had hired him for business of their own?

Outside the Crown, Brinkes paused to light his pipe. Chaloner watched, wondering whether to grab him and drag him to the nearest magistrate. Unfortunately, he had no idea where that might be, and Brinkes was unlikely to go quietly. Moreover, given the authorities' reluctance to act so far, he suspected Brinkes would not stay in custody for long, at which point Chaloner would have a vengeful assassin on his trail. With a sigh, he decided to leave matters well alone.

Once Brinkes had gone, the woman withdrew and the Crown's door was closed. It was then that Chaloner glimpsed a flicker of movement in an upper window that told him he had not been the only one watching. A young lady gazed out, and even from a distance Chaloner could see she was troubled. He was aware of her eyes on him as he resumed his walk, and, on an impulse, he waved – the furtive exodus said the Crown's patrons were keen to maintain a low profile, and his gesture would tell her that she needed to be more careful if she intended to spy.

He was somewhat disconcerted when she waved back, and a beaming smile transformed her into something quite lovely – he had expected her to duck away in alarm. Bemused, he went on his way.

He was almost at Charing Cross when he heard someone calling his name. The Earl's Chief Usher was hurrying towards him, waving frantically. Chaloner struggled to keep a straight face. John Dugdale was not built for moving at speed: his arms flapped as though he were trying to fly, and his long legs flailed comically. He was not an attractive specimen, despite the care he took with his appearance. His skeletal frame and round shoulders made even the finest clothes hang badly, and his beautiful full-cut breeches only accentuated the ridiculous skinniness of his calves.

'You heard me shouting,' he gasped accusingly when he caught up. 'But you ignored me so I would have farther to run.'

Chaloner had done nothing of the kind, but there was no point in saying so. Dugdale disliked him for a variety of reasons, the two most important being that he did not consider it right for ex-Parliamentarians to be made ushers, no matter how high the Earl's regard for their wives; and that Chaloner's clandestine activities on the Earl's behalf meant that Dugdale could not control him as he did the other gentlemen under his command.

'Nothing was stolen last night,' said Chaloner,

17

supposing Dugdale had come for a report on their employer's bricks. 'I am not sure Pratt is right to claim they go missing at—'

'I do not want to know,' snapped Dugdale. 'Lying in wait for thieves is hardly a suitable pastime for a courtier, and I condemn it most soundly.'

'Shall I tell the Earl that I cannot oblige him tonight because you disapprove, then?' asked Chaloner, suspecting that if he did, the resulting fireworks would be apocalyptic.

Dugdale did not deign to acknowledge the remark. Instead, he looked Chaloner up and down with open disdain. 'Decency dictates that you should change before setting foot in his presence, but he says he needs you urgently, so there is no time. He will have to endure you as you are. Just make sure you do not put your filthy feet on his new Turkey carpets.'

The church bells were chiming eight o'clock as Chaloner and Dugdale reached Charing Cross. The square was a chaos of carts and carriages, most containing goods that were to be sold in the city's markets or ferrying merchants to their places of business, but others held bleary-eyed revellers, making their way home after a riotous night out.

The noise was deafening, with iron-clad cartwheels rattling across cobblestones, animals lowing, bleating and honking as they were driven to the slaughterhouses, and street vendors advertising wares at the tops of their voices. The smell was breathtaking, too, a nose-searing combination of sewage, fish and unwashed bodies, all overlain with the acrid stench of coal fires. Chaloner coughed. He rarely noticed London's noxious atmosphere when he was in it, but a spell in the cleaner air around Piccadilly always reminded him that his country's capital was a foul place to be.

He started to turn towards White Hall, where the Earl had been provided with a suite of offices overlooking the Privy Gardens – Clarendon worked hard, and was at his desk hours before most other courtiers were astir – but Dugdale steered him towards The Strand instead.

'He is at home today,' he explained shortly. 'Gout.'

Chaloner groaned. The Earl was not pleasant when he was well, but when he was ill he became an implacable tyrant, and the fact that Chaloner had been summoned to his presence did not augur well. He racked his brains for something he had done wrong, but nothing came to mind – he had spent the past week investigating the stolen bricks, so had had scant opportunity to err. Unfortunately, the Earl was easily annoyed, so any small thing might have upset him.

'I imagine he wants you to tell him about Tangier,' predicted Dugdale. 'You have barely spoken to him since you returned, so you cannot blame him for becoming impatient.'

Chaloner regarded him askance. He had written a lengthy report about his findings, and had offered a verbal account on several occasions, but had been given short shrift each time, leading him to assume that the Earl was no longer interested in knowing why Tangier was costing the government so much money. It would not be prudent to say so to Dugdale, though, who would almost certainly repeat it out of context, so he held his tongue.

'You have not told me, either,' said Dugdale coldly. 'And I am your superior.'

Manfully, Chaloner suppressed the urge to argue,

heartily wishing that Dugdale's kindly, genial predecessor had not retired. It had been a shock to find a new chief usher in place on his return, especially one who was determined to subdue the people under his command by bullying. Dugdale sensed his resentment, and his expression hardened.

'It is my duty to keep our master's household respectable, so there will be no more of this running about on your own. You will keep me appraised of your every move.'

'Very well,' said Chaloner, with no intention of complying. He had worked alone for years, confiding in no one, and was not about to change the habits that had kept him alive for so long.

'Then tell me about Tangier,' instructed Dugdale. 'Why is it costing us so much in taxes?'

Chaloner might have replied that he had never seen a place so steeped in corruption, and that for every penny spent on the new defences, another ten were siphoned off by dishonest officials – from the governor down to the lowliest clerk. But Dugdale gossiped, and Chaloner did not want to be responsible for a rumour that said the King made mistakes in his choice of bureaucrats.

'It is under constant attack from Barbary pirates,' he said instead. 'In order to repel them, the settlement needs a sea wall and a fortress. Naturally, these are expensive to build.'

Dugdale narrowed his eyes. 'The Earl said you were involved in several skirmishes there. Such activities are beneath a gentleman usher, and I forbid you to engage in them again.'

'There is nothing I would like more,' said Chaloner fervently. The civil wars that had erupted when he was a child, followed by twelve years in espionage when they were over, made him feel as though he had been fighting all his life, and he was tired of it. 'However, it is not always practical to—'

'Then make it practical. You are said to be blessed with sharp wits, so use them instead of a sword. But tell me more about Tangier. Who is to blame for these escalating costs? The new governor, Sir Tobias Bridge? His was not a sensible appointment.'

Bridge had taken over the running of the desolate little outpost after Lord Teviot's brutal death.

'No?' Chaloner seized the opportunity to sidetrack the discussion. 'Why not?'

'Because he fought for Parliament during the wars, so he is by definition devious and wicked. No one who supported Cromwell can be considered as anything else.'

It was Dugdale's way of telling Chaloner – yet again – what he thought of his former allegiances. Fortunately, there was a flurry of excited yells from the opposite side of the street at that moment, and Chaloner's dubious history was promptly forgotten.

'A swordfight,' said Dugdale, with rank disapproval. 'I see one of the combatants is James Elliot. He works for Spymaster Williamson.'

Williamson ran the country's intelligence network, and Chaloner had expected to continue serving overseas under him when the Royalists had been returned to power – the King needed information on foreign enemies just as much as Cromwell had. But all the old spies had been dismissed, and long-term Royalists appointed in their place. Even so, Chaloner harboured a faint hope that Williamson would see sense one day, and send him to Holland, France or Spain.

'Elliot's opponent is John Cave,' he said, recognising the singer who had sailed from Tangier with him on *Eagle*. 'A tenor from the Chapel Royal.'

It was odd that he should see so many fellow passengers – Harley, Newell, Reyner *and* Cave – within an hour of each other, especially as he had not set eyes on any since disembarking the week before. But London was like that – the biggest city in Europe on the one hand, with a population of some three hundred thousand souls, but a village on the other, in which residents frequently met friends and family just by strolling along its thoroughfares.

Dugdale shot Chaloner another distaste-filled glance. 'I cannot imagine how *you* come to be acquainted with Court musicians. The Earl tells me that you have spent virtually your entire adult life in foreign countries, and that you know nothing of London.'

Chaloner was the first to admit that his knowledge of the capital was lacking – and it was unlikely to improve if the Earl kept sending him to places like Tangier, either – but it was not for Dugdale to remark on it. He scowled, but the Chief Usher was not looking at him.

'You had better intervene,' Dugdale was saying. 'Elliot will kill Cave, and we cannot have members of Court skewered on public highways.'

It was anathema for a spy to put himself in a position where he would be noticed, and the altercation had already attracted a sizeable gathering. Moreover, although Chaloner had accompanied Cave's singing for hours aboard *Eagle*, their association had been confined solely to music: they had not been friends in any sense of the word, and he was not sure Cave would appreciate the interference.

'You just ordered me not to take up arms again,' he hedged. 'And—'

'Do not be insolent! Now disarm Elliot, or shall I tell the Earl that you stood by and did nothing while a fellow courtier was murdered?'

Aware that Dugdale might well do what he threatened, Chaloner moved forward. The argument was taking place outside the New Exchange, a large, grand building with a mock-gothic façade. It comprised two floors of expensive shops, and a piazza where merchants met to discuss trade. It was always busy, and most of those watching the quarrel were wealthy men of business.

As he approached, Chaloner thought that Elliot looked exactly like the kind of fellow who would appeal to Williamson – the Spymaster had yet to learn that there was more to espionage than being handy in a brawl. Elliot was well-dressed and wore a fine wig made from unusually black hair, but his pugilistic demeanour and the scars on his meaty fists exposed him as a lout. By contrast, Cave was smaller, and held his fancy 'town sword' as if it had never been out of its scabbard – and now that it was, he was not entirely sure what to do with it.

'Chaloner!' he cried. 'You can be my witness, because I am going to kill this impudent dog!'

'You can try,' said Elliot shortly. 'Because no man tells *me* not to take the wall.'

In London, 'taking the wall' was preferable to walking farther out into the street, because it was better protected from those who were in the habit of emptying chamber pots out of over-jutting upstairs windows. Disputes about who should have the more favourable spot were frequent and often ended in scuffles. Few drew weapons over it, though, and Chaloner was astonished that Cave should think such a matter was worth his life.

'Cave, stop,' he said softly. 'Come away with me. Now.'

'Never,' flared the musician. 'He insulted me, and I demand satisfaction.'

'Tomorrow, then,' said Chaloner. That would afford ample time for tempers to cool and apologies to be sent. 'In Lincoln's Inn Fields at dawn.'

'He is right,' said a man at Elliot's side. Of burly build, he had a ruddy face and sun-bleached hair that indicated a preference for outdoors living. 'Listen to him. There is no need for this.'

'There is every need, Lester,' snarled Elliot. 'You heard what Cave said. He called me a—'

'For God's sake!' hissed Lester. 'You will kill him, and then not even Williamson will be able to save you from the noose. This little worm is not worth it! Come away before it goes any further.'

With a roar of outrage, Cave surged forward and blades flashed. As it quickly became apparent that Elliot was by far the superior swordsman, Chaloner waited for him to relent – and for Cave to yield when he realised the extent to which he was outgunned. But although the singer was stumbling backwards, struggling desperately to defend himself, Elliot continued to advance, doing so with a lazy grace that said he was more amused than threatened by Cave's clumsy flailing.

Cave's eyes were wide with alarm, and he gasped in shock when Elliot scored a shallow cut on his cheek. Elliot seemed surprised, too, and Chaloner suspected it had been an accident – that Elliot had overestimated the singer's ability to deflect the blow. Hand to his bleeding

24

cheek, Cave darted behind Chaloner, and several onlookers began to laugh.

'Enough,' said Lester firmly, grabbing his friend's arm and jerking him back. 'Think of Ruth. She will be heartbroken if you are hanged for murder, and—'

Suddenly and wholly unexpectedly, Cave shot out from behind Chaloner and attacked not Elliot but Lester. Chaloner managed to shove him, deflecting what would have been a fatal blow, but it was a close call, and there was a hiss of disapproval from the crowd: Lester was unarmed.

Elliot's face went taut with anger, and he advanced with sudden determination. His first lunge struck home, and Cave dropped to his knees, hand to his chest. Blood trickled between his fingers, thick, red and plentiful. With such volume, Chaloner had no doubt that the wound was mortal.

The onlookers were stunned into silence, and the only sound was that of Cave struggling to breathe. Lester quickly disarmed Elliot, who gazed at his victim with an expression that was difficult to read. Chaloner knelt next to the stricken man, but Cave pushed his hands away when he tried to inspect the wound.

'There is no pain. Please do not make it otherwise by attempting to physick me – I know my case is hopeless.'

'You know nothing of the kind,' argued Chaloner, fumbling to unbutton Cave's coat. 'I may be able to stem the bleeding until a surgeon arrives.'

'But a surgeon will do unspeakable things.' Cave grabbed Chaloner's hand and gripped it with surprising strength. 'And I am not brave. Besides, I am ready to die.'

25

'No!' cried Lester, horrified. He turned to the crowd. 'Fetch help! Hurry!'

No one obliged, partly because it was more interesting to watch the situation unfold than to dash away on an errand of mercy, but mostly because any medical man would almost certainly demand a down-payment from the Good Samaritan before answering the summons. Lester was almost beside himself with agitation, while Elliot's face was whiter than that of his victim.

'I want . . .' Cave gasped. His flicked a hand at Elliot. 'Him . . . I must . . .'

Elliot approached reluctantly. He knelt when Cave started to speak, but the singer's words were inaudible, and he was obliged to lean closer. Cave's arm jerked suddenly, and Elliot bellowed in pain. When Elliot recoiled, there was a dagger protruding from his stomach. Chaloner stared at Cave in disbelief, and did not think he had ever seen an expression of such black malice on the face of a dying man.

Groaning, Elliot struggled to his feet, hauling out the blade as he did so. It slipped from his fingers to clatter on the cobbles. He lurched towards Lester, who escorted him away. No one made any attempt to stop them.

'Well,' murmured Dugdale, arms folded. 'I suppose that was a neat end to this insalubrious affair. The King's singer is speared, but at least his killer did not escape unscathed.'

'Is Elliot dead?' asked Cave weakly. 'Did I kill him?'

'Almost certainly,' replied Dugdale, prodding the dropped dagger with the toe of his elegant shoe. It was stained red to the hilt.

'Good,' breathed Cave. Then his head lolled suddenly, and the breath hissed out of him.

Chaloner sat back on his heels, overwhelmed by the stupidity of it all.

As it would not be right to leave Cave in the street, Chaloner paid a carter to transport the body to the Westminster charnel house. He had no idea whether corpses from The Strand would be welcome there, but he was not sure where else to take it. Dugdale was right in that much of London was still a mystery to him, and while he knew exactly how to dispose of cadavers in Amsterdam, The Hague, Paris, Lisbon, Bruxelles, Hamburg, Venice, Madrid and several other major cities, he was not sure what to do with one in his own country.

'We had better make sure the charnel-house keeper will accept him,' he said to Dugdale after the cart and its grim cargo had rattled away. 'As you pointed out, Cave held a royal appointment, so it is our duty to see him treated with respect.'

'I am not setting foot in a place like that,' declared Dugdale with a fastidious shudder. 'You go. I shall return to the Earl, and inform him that you are unavoidably delayed. He will be irked to be kept waiting, but I shall do my best to mollify him.'

Chaloner suspected he would do nothing of the kind, and that the opportunity would be used to blacken his name. But it could not be helped – common decency dictated that he should ensure Cave's body was properly looked after, and that was that.

The Westminster charnel house was located in a narrow lane near the Thames, between a granary and a warehouse where coal was stored. It was an unprepossessing place, in a particularly dingy area. By the time Chaloner

27

arrived Cave had been delivered, and the cart and its driver had gone so the lane was deserted and eerily quiet. He opened the door with some reluctance, grimacing at the damp chilliness and stench of decay that immediately wafted out at him.

The charnel house comprised a mortuary at the back, with two handsomely appointed chambers at the front where the owner went through the formalities of death with the bereaved. John Kersey had made a fortune from dealing with the dead, partly by offering guided tours to wealthy ghouls, but also from the small museum he had established to display some of the more unusual artefacts he had collected over the years. He was a neat, dapper little man, whose elegant clothes were made by bespoke tailors. He did not, as Chaloner had first assumed, deck himself out in items reclaimed from corpses.

That morning, he was entertaining a friend, and Chaloner's heart sank when he recognised the loudly ebullient tones of Richard Wiseman, Surgeon to the King. Kersey kept Wiseman supplied with specimens, some of which were dissected publicly at Chyrurgeons' Hall. It was a grisly business, and may have explained why Wiseman always chose to wear red. Coupled with the fact that he possessed a head of thick auburn curls, and was a large man with an immensely powerful physique, he made for an imposing figure. He considered himself Chaloner's friend, but although the spy respected Wiseman's courage and honesty, he found it difficult to like a man who was so disagreeably arrogant.

'Good morning,' said Kersey with a pleasant smile. 'What can we do for you today?'

'The body that just arrived,' began Chaloner. 'It is—'

28

'Toted in like a sack of onions,' interrupted Kersey disapprovingly. 'By a grubby carter from The Strand. Do folk have no sense of decorum?'

Chaloner wondered how he could ask such a question when he let some of his charges go to a far worse fate than being lugged along a hall. Wiseman guessed what he was thinking.

'I perform anatomies in the name of science,' he declared loftily. 'However, I shall leave that particular cadaver alone, because it is John Cave, one of the Chapel Royal musicians.'

'Do you not dissect musicians, then?' asked Chaloner, a little acidly.

'Not ones with Court appointments. The King attends my Public Anatomies, and I cannot imagine him wanting to watch one where he is acquainted with the subject.'

Chaloner was not so sure about that: the King liked to think of himself as a scientist. He turned to Kersey. 'I arranged for Cave to be brought here. I did not know where else to suggest.'

'You did the right thing,' said Kersey kindly. 'Do not worry: I shall look after him.'

Chaloner nodded his thanks. His journey had been unnecessary: he should have remembered that Kersey was solicitous of his charges, especially the important or famous ones.

'You will have to contact the Chapel Royal choir and ask his colleagues to arrange a funeral, Kersey,' said Wiseman helpfully. 'As far as I am aware, he had no family.'

But Kersey was looking at Chaloner, doing so rather uneasily. 'There was an awful lot of blood. *You* did not kill him, did you? If so, I hope you are not expecting

29

me to disguise the fact, because I do not engage in that sort of activity. Well, not without a very good reason.'

'He died in a brawl,' objected Chaloner, offended. 'I had nothing to do with it.'

'You have no right to sound indignant,' said Kersey. 'Given that you have been associated with so many premature deaths in the past. Indeed, there have been times when my domain has contained nothing *but* folk who have arrived here as a result of your investigations.'

'But not today.' Chaloner felt the accusation was unjust. It was hardly his fault that the Earl was in the habit of ordering him to explore dangerous matters.

'You have only been home a week, but you are already embroiled in something deadly,' scolded Wiseman. 'And it is doing you no good. You glowed with health and vitality when you first returned, but now you are pale and mangy.'

Chaloner was disinclined to tell him how he had been spending his nights. He did not have the energy to deal with the inevitable indignation that would arise when Wiseman learned that the Earl, a man he admired for some inexplicable reason, was being relieved of the bricks and wood intended for his house.

'I should go,' he said instead. 'Clarendon is expecting me.'

Kersey was surprised. 'Do you not want to see Cave? I covered him with a nice clean cloth.'

Chaloner shook his head and made for the door, keen to answer the Earl's summons before the delay saw him in too much trouble. Wiseman and Kersey followed.

'I am sorry Cave is dead,' said the surgeon. 'He had

30

a lovely voice, and everyone was delighted when he returned from Tangier to rejoin the Chapel Royal choir. Henry O'Brien will be especially distressed – since Cave returned, he has refused to sing duets with anyone else.'

'Who is Henry O'Brien?' asked Chaloner.

Wiseman regarded him as though he were short of a few wits. 'He is married to Kitty.'

'Oh.' Chaloner was none the wiser. 'Say no more.'

Wiseman scowled. 'There is no need to be acerbic. O'Brien is an Irish baron who came to London to sell copper from his estates. Even he is astonished by how rich it has made him. His wife Kitty is . . .' The surgeon made an expansive gesture with his hand.

'Beautiful, clever and distantly related to the King,' supplied Kersey. 'Every man in London longs to be in her company, but she already has a lover.'

'She does not!' declared Wiseman. 'She is a decent lady – upright, honourable and kind.'

'Those qualities do not preclude her from taking a lover,' argued Kersey. He turned to Chaloner. 'Suffice to say that O'Brien's wealth and Kitty's beauty means that people are keen to fête them, and soirées are always being held in their honour. He will be grieved when he hears his singing partner is dead. Who killed him, did you say?'

'A man named James Elliot,' replied Chaloner. 'He is one of Williamson's spies, apparently.'

Wiseman pulled a face to indicate his distaste. 'Elliot is married to a sweet girl named Ruth, and she will be heartbroken when he is hanged for murdering a courtier. But she will be better off without him in the long run. He is a greedy, unscrupulous devil.'

'He may not live long enough to hang,' said Chaloner soberly. 'Cave stabbed him.'

'We can but hope,' said Wiseman ruthlessly.

The clocks were striking ten by the time Chaloner left the charnel house. Wiseman walked with him, chatting about all that had happened during the time the spy had been away. Chaloner listened, not because he liked gossip, but because Dugdale's remarks about him being poorly versed in London's affairs had reminded him that he needed to rectify the matter – only foolish spies did not take the time to acquaint themselves with the society in which they were obliged to move.

'O'Brien and Kitty are the King's current favourites,' Wiseman was saying, jostling a beefy soldier out of his way. The surgeon had always been large, but he had made himself even more powerful by a regime of lifting heavy stones each morning. He claimed it was to improve his general well-being, but the practice had given him the arms and shoulders of a wrestler, and meant prudent people were inclined to overlook any insults he might dole out, physical or verbal. Hence the soldier bristled at the rough treatment, but made no other response.

'Why?' asked Chaloner. 'Because they are wealthy, or because she is pretty?'

'Have a care!' Wiseman glanced around uneasily. 'There is no need to announce to everyone that our King is an unscrupulous womaniser with a voracious appetite for his subjects' money.'

'Your words, not mine,' said Chaloner, supposing His Majesty must have reached new depths of depravity, if even a loyal follower like Wiseman voiced reservations about his character.

'Still, at least O'Brien and Kitty are not Adventurers. And as I am sure you have no idea what I am talking about, let me explain. It means they are not members of that shameful organisation of gold-grabbing nobles commonly called the Company of Royal Adventurers Trading into Africa.'

'I have heard of it,' said Chaloner drily. 'In case you did not know, Tangier is in Africa, and the place was full of talk about the Adventurers.'

'What talk?' asked Wiseman curiously.

'Mostly that their charter forbids other Britons from buying or selling goods that originate in Africa. They have secured themselves a monopoly on gold, silver, hides, feathers, ivory, slaves—'

Wiseman's expression turned fierce. 'Slaves?'

Chaloner nodded. 'The Portuguese used to dominate that particular trade – most of their "cargos" go to the sugar plantations in Brazil. But the Portuguese are no longer quite so powerful at sea, and the Dutch now control the best routes.'

'Do they, by God?' growled Wiseman. Britain was on the verge of war with the Dutch, so even mentioning them was likely to provoke a hostile response from most Londoners.

'It is a lucrative business,' Chaloner went on. 'And the British merchants in Tangier itch to join in. But the Adventurers' charter means they cannot.'

'I do not approve of the slave trade,' declared Wiseman hotly.

'No decent person does.'

Wiseman brightened. 'I read in *The Newes* a week ago that a slaving ship named *Henrietta Maria* sank mysteriously in Tangier harbour. It went down before it could be loaded, and the delay allowed many captives to escape.' He stared at Chaloner. 'It happened when you were there. Did *you* . . .'

'I have no idea what you are talking about.'

Wiseman clapped him on the shoulder. 'I might have known! The loss set the Adventurers back a pretty penny, too! They had invested a fortune in fitting it out for transporting humans.'

'It will make no difference in the end,' said Chaloner despondently. 'They will just build another. And another and another, until the sea is full of the damned things.'

'You and I are not the only ones to be repelled. Others will make a stand, and the business will founder. You will see.'

Chaloner said nothing, but thought Wiseman's optimism was sadly misplaced. People probably *would* be appalled by the barbaric way sugar was produced on the plantations, but they would buy the stuff anyway, and that would create a market. The ethics of the matter would be swept under the carpet and quietly forgotten.

Wiseman changed the subject. 'I cannot say I like Roger Pratt the architect, by the way. I am beginning to think you were right when you said Clarendon House will bring our Earl trouble.'

'What made you change your mind?' asked Chaloner, surprised. Wiseman was one of those who firmly believed that Clarendon had every right to an extravagant mansion.

'Pratt himself. He is arrogant and thinks himself some kind of god. I cannot bear such people.'

Chaloner smothered a smile, thinking the description applied rather well to Wiseman himself.

*　　*　　*

The Earl lived in a rambling Tudor palace on The Strand, which he had never liked and that he complained about constantly. Indeed, Chaloner suspected that Worcester House's poky rooms and leaking ceilings were largely responsible for his master's wild extravagance over his new home.

'You missed him,' said a gardener, straightening from his labours as Chaloner walked past. 'He left for White Hall an hour ago.'

'I thought he was ill,' said Chaloner, wondering whether he was destined to spend the entire day traipsing around London. He hoped not: he was cold, damp and wanted to go home.

'He recovered.' The man sounded disappointed; the Earl was not popular with his staff.

'That was fast. Gout usually keeps him in bed for days.'

The gardener grinned evilly. 'He told everyone it was gout, but if you knew what he ate for his supper, you would not be surprised that he spent half the night clutching his innards. But a tonic restored him, and he sent for his coach shortly afterwards. It is not far to White Hall, but the lazy goat never walks. No wonder he is so fat.'

Wearily, Chaloner retraced his steps. White Hall was the King's official London residence, and a number of his ministers had quarters there. It represented power and authority, as well as being the place where the King and his dissipated friends frolicked until the small hours of the morning, doing things that invariably transpired to be expensive for the tax-payer.

The palace was ancient, but had developed in a haphazard manner, depending on when money had been available for building and repairs. It was said to contain more than two thousand rooms, ranging from the spacious apartments occupied by the King and his nobles, to the cramped, badly ventilated attics that housed laundresses, grooms and scullions.

Chaloner was about to walk through the gate when a carriage drew up beside him. A face peered out and Chaloner recognised Spymaster Williamson, a tall, aloof man who had been an Oxford academic before deciding that his slippery talents would be more useful in government. He was feared by his employees, treated with extreme caution by his superiors, and detested by his equals.

'I did not know you were back,' Williamson said without preamble. 'I thought you were still in Tangier, trying to learn why building a sea wall is transpiring to be so costly.'

'Clarendon ordered me home,' replied Chaloner, shortly and not very informatively.

He and Williamson had never liked each other. They had reached a truce of sorts in the summer, after an adventure involving some foreign diplomats, but it was an uneasy one, and Chaloner was acutely aware that it would take very little for the Spymaster to break it.

'What is wrong, Joseph?' came a female voice from inside the coach. Chaloner was surprised: the fairer sex tended to shy away from Williamson. 'Why have we stopped?'

'I want a word with this gentleman,' replied Williamson, turning to her with a brief smile. 'It will not take a moment, and then I shall show you my Westminster offices.'

'Good,' said another voice. It was a man and he

sounded pleased. 'I am looking forward to seeing the place where you spend so much time.'

Chaloner wondered whether the couple were actually being conveyed there so they could be arrested – that when they arrived, they would find themselves whisked into a grim little cell for the purposes of interrogation. It had certainly happened before. But Williamson climbed out of the carriage and began to make introductions. Chaloner was surprised a second time, because the Spymaster had never afforded him such courtesy before. He was immediately on his guard.

'These are my very dear friends Kitty and Henry O'Brien. O'Brien and I were up at Oxford together.' Williamson addressed the occupants of the carriage. 'Chaloner is the fellow I was telling you about, who helped me with that business concerning the Dutch ambassador last June.'

Chaloner was not sure whether he was more taken aback to meet O'Brien and his wife so soon after the discussion in the charnel house, or to be informed that Williamson had friends. The only other man he knew who was willing to spend time in the Spymaster's company was the sinister John Swaddell, who claimed to be a clerk, but whom everyone knew was really an assassin.

He regarded the pair with interest as they peered out. Kitty's beauty was indeed breathtaking. Red hair tumbled around her shoulders, and there was both intelligence and humour in her arresting green eyes. He bowed politely, thinking that Kersey's claims about her loveliness were, if anything, understated.

When he turned his attention to her husband, he thought for a fleeting moment that she had married a child, but O'Brien was just one of those men who had retained boyish looks into his thirties. He had fair curly hair, blue eyes, and the lines around his mouth said he laughed a lot. They were an attractive couple, and Chaloner was not surprised that the King had deigned to grace them with his favour. Their clothes said they were indeed wealthy, and the ruby that gleamed at Kitty's throat was the largest that Chaloner had ever seen.

'O'Brien has just received some sad news,' said Williamson, addressing Chaloner. 'A musician from the Chapel Royal, of whom he was very fond, is dead.'

'Killed by one of your spies, Williamson,' put in O'Brien sourly.

Kitty rested a calming hand on his arm. 'He cannot hire choirboys for the dirty business of espionage, so it is hardly surprising that some transpire to be unruly. Like that odious Swaddell. I am glad *he* is no longer in your service, Joseph. He was downright sinister.'

'Swaddell has left you?' Chaloner was astounded – he had thought the bond between the two men was unbreakable, mostly, he had suspected uncharitably, because neither could find anyone else willing to put up with him.

Williamson grimaced. 'I am afraid so.'

'I shall miss Cave,' O'Brien was saying unhappily. 'He was an excellent tenor, and the only man in London capable of understanding how I like to perform. What shall I do without him? The King liked to listen to us sing, and he will be devastated when he hears what has happened.'

Chaloner doubted the King would care, especially if O'Brien financed some other form of entertainment. He did not usually make snap judgements about people, but there was something about O'Brien that said he lacked his wife's brains, and that he was vain and a little bit silly.

While Kitty murmured soothing words in her husband's ear, Williamson drew Chaloner to one side, so they could speak without being overheard. 'One of my informants witnessed what happened. He told me you tried to prevent the skirmish.'

'But unfortunately without success.'

'It is a pity, especially as the quarrel was trifling. I cannot say I like Elliot, but he is a decent intelligencer.'

'He is still alive?' asked Chaloner, recalling the vicious blow Cave had delivered, and the dagger protruding from Elliot's innards.

'At the moment,' nodded Williamson, 'although his friend Lester fears he may not stay that way for long. And I hate to lose him. He was making headway on a troublesome case—'

'The Earl is waiting,' said Chaloner, unwilling to be burdened with the Spymaster's concerns when he had more than enough of his own to contend with.

'You can spare me a moment,' said Williamson reproachfully. 'And I am having a terrible week, what with Swaddell leaving, Elliot attacking Cave, and more plots to overthrow the government than you can shake a stick at. *And* the Privy Council has cut my budget. Again.'

'Where has Swaddell gone?' asked Chaloner, not liking the notion of such a deadly fellow on the loose. Williamson had never done much to control him, but he had been better than nothing.

'To someone who can pay him what he deserves,' replied Williamson shortly. 'I wish I *could* offer him double, but how can I, when I barely have enough to make ends meet?'

'Perhaps your friend O'Brien can secure you better funding,' suggested Chaloner. 'Ask him to mention it while he warbles for the King.'

'I most certainly shall not,' declared Williamson indignantly. 'It would be ungentlemanly to raise matters of money with a friend. Besides, he is too distressed by Cave's death. I am taking him to see my Westminster offices, as a way to take his mind off it. For something pleasant to do.'

Chaloner regarded him askance. 'You think that is pleasant? A heavily guarded hall filled with labouring clerks, and dungeons below containing God knows what horrors?'

Williamson looked exasperated. 'Then what do you suggest? I am not a man for frivolity, but I feel compelled to offer some sort of diversion.'

'What is wrong with a visit to the Crown Jewels or the Royal Menagerie? Or even a play?'

Williamson nodded slowly. 'Those are good ideas. But I did not stop you to ask for advice about my social life. I want to know why Cave and Elliot fought. My informant's account made no sense.'

Seeing no reason not to oblige him, Chaloner gave a concise account of the squabble. When he had finished, Williamson frowned unhappily.

'But *why* did Cave and Elliot become agitated over so ridiculous a matter? Men do not squander their lives on such trivialities. There must be more to it.'

'Very possibly,' acknowledged Chaloner, glad he was not the one who would have to find out.

'Cave will have a grand funeral in Westminster Abbey,' Williamson went on. 'The Chapel Royal choir will provide the music, and the Bishop of London will almost certainly be prevailed upon to conduct the ceremony. It will be a lofty occasion, and I should not like it spoiled with the taint of suspicion. I do not suppose you have time to—'

'No,' said Chaloner firmly.

Chapter 2

The guard on duty at White Hall's Great Gate that day was Sergeant Wright, a petty, grasping individual who was heartily disliked by those soldiers who took pride in their work; those who were shirkers considered him an icon. He was an unattractive specimen with a bad complexion, stubby nose, and eyes that were too small for his doughy face.

'You cannot come in dressed like that,' he declared, when he saw Chaloner. 'You are wet, dirty and there is blood on your coat. Someone else's, more is the pity. Other gentlemen ushers do not—'

'Let him through,' came a commanding voice from behind them. The interruption was timely, because Chaloner did not take kindly to being berated by the likes of Wright, who was no picture of sartorial elegance himself with his food-stained tunic and greasy hair.

The speaker was Thomas Kipps, the Earl's Seal Bearer, a tall, handsome man with an amiable face. He was dressed in the Clarendon livery of blue and gold, and it was his duty to walk ahead of his master in formal processions. Unfortunately, the Earl liked the ritual, and encouraged Kipps to escort him when he wandered around White Hall, too. Such vanity was ill-advised, because it gave his enemies the means with which to mock him – Chaloner had lost count of the times he had seen the Court rakes mimic the Earl's waddling gait, preceded by another of their own bearing a pair of bellows in place of the seal.

Wright was outraged that someone should presume to tell him his business. 'How dare—'

'Clarendon wants him,' snapped Kipps. 'And you do not have the right to keep *him* waiting.'

Wright stepped aside with ill grace. Chaloner pushed past him rather more roughly than necessary, hard enough to make him stagger.

'He is an odious fellow,' said Kipps, once they were through the gate. 'Do you know why he is not dismissed and someone more competent appointed in his place? Because he once carried an important message to the King during the civil wars. Anyone *could* have done it, but His Majesty remembers Wright, and this post is his reward.'

Chaloner liked Kipps, who alone of the Earl's household had been friendly to him on his return from Tangier. He shrugged. 'White Hall is full of such people.'

'He is corrupt, too,' Kipps grumbled on. 'He hires out the soldiers under his command for private duties, such as acting as bodyguards or minding property. He pays them a pittance and keeps the bulk of the earnings for himself. Unfortunately, the extra work reduces their effectiveness at the palace – they are too tired to fulfil their proper responsibilities.'

Chaloner had never been impressed by White Hall's security. And as the King's popularity had waned since he had reclaimed his throne at the Restoration some four years earlier – mostly because of his hedonistic lifestyle and the licentiousness of his Court – he needed someone a lot more efficient than Wright to ensure his safety.

Chaloner and Kipps crossed the huge, cobbled expanse of the Great Court, which was a flurry of activity as usual. A number of courtiers had just emerged from Lady Castlemaine's apartments, yelling drunkenly and accompanied by giggling prostitutes; the King's mistress was famous for her unconventional parties. Elsewhere, clerks, guards and servants hurried about on more mundane business, and carts lined up to deliver supplies to kitchens, laundries, pantries and coal sheds.

'Watch yourself when you see Clarendon,' advised Kipps, pausing a moment to admire a duchess who was too drunk to realise that she had left the soirée without most of her clothes. More chivalrous men than he rushed to give her their coats, although they regretted their gallantry when she was sick over them. 'Dugdale told him that you insisted on meddling in some fight on The Strand, despite the fact that you knew he was waiting.'

Chaloner groaned. 'It is not true.'

'I am sure of it. I wish Clarendon had not given him such power, because the man is a despot. Every night at home, I marvel that I have managed to pass another day without punching him.'

They were obliged to jump to one side when a caval-cade of coaches rattled towards them, the haughty demeanour of the drivers telling pedestrians that if they did not get out of the way they could expect to be crushed. Most of the carriages bore crests, and it was clear that the occupants considered themselves to be people of quality.

'Adventurers,' said Kipps disapprovingly. 'Here for a meeting with the King who, as you will no doubt be aware, is one of their number. So is the Duke of Buckingham.'

Buckingham, the King's oldest friend, was the first to alight when the convoy rolled to a halt. He was an athletic, striking man whose fondness for wild living was beginning to take its toll – his eyes had an unhealthy yellow tinge, his skin was sallow and he had developed a paunch.

'He looks fragile this morning,' Kipps went on gleefully. 'He must have stayed too late at Lady Castlemaine's soirée. I keep hoping he will debauch himself into an early grave, because his hatred for our Earl grows daily, and he is a powerful enemy.'

'Are all these people Adventurers?' asked Chaloner, staggered by the number of men who were lining up to enter the royal presence.

Kipps nodded. 'They represent White Hall's wealthiest courtiers. You see the short, pasty-faced villain? That is Ellis Leighton, their secretary, said to be the most dangerous man in London.'

'Why?' Leighton did not look particularly deadly, and when he moved, it was with a crablike scuttle that was vaguely comical, although Chaloner supposed there was something unsettling about the man's button-like eyes, which were curiously devoid of expression.

Kipps lowered his voice, although there was no one close enough to hear. 'Because he has amassed himself a fortune, but no one is sure how. And he has friends in London's underworld.'

'Is he a merchant?'

'He calls himself a businessman, which is not the same thing at all.'

'I see,' said Chaloner, not seeing at all.

'They are meeting today because one of their number has gone missing,' Kipps continued. 'Peter Proby has not been seen for a week, and they are worried about him.'

'What do they think might have happened?'

'I imagine they are afraid that he has been murdered.'

Chaloner regarded him askance. 'Is Proby the kind of man to warrant such a fate, then?'

'They all are,' replied Kipps darkly. 'They have cordoned off an entire continent, and decided that no one is allowed to profit from it except themselves. And the aggravating thing is that none of them have the faintest idea of what they are doing.'

'You mean they do not appreciate the depth of the ill-will they have generated?'

'Oh, I imagine they are perfectly aware of that, but being courtiers, they do not care. What I meant was that they have no concept of how to run such a venture. They are a band of aristocratic treasure hunters, whereas they should be a properly organised corporation.'

Chaloner was startled by the passion in Kipps's voice. 'You speak as though you resent their—'

'I *do* resent it!' declared Kipps through gritted teeth. 'I should like to speculate in Africa myself.'

'Join the Adventurers, then,' suggested Chaloner.

Kipps sniffed. 'I would not demean myself by treating with that dim-witted rabble. Besides, they rejected my application, although I have no idea why.'

Chaloner looked at the assembled men, recognising many. 'Could it be that they comprise a large number of the Earl's enemies? They will not want members of his household among their ranks.'

'No,' replied Kipps, 'because his son is an Adventurer, and so is Dugdale. There must be another reason why they elected to exclude me, but I cannot imagine what it might be.'

It occurred to Chaloner that they may have taken exception to Kipps referring to them as a 'dim-witted rabble'. 'If they are as incompetent as you say, their venture will fail. And when it does, you can speculate to your heart's content.'

'Yes, but by then the Dutch will have secured all the best resources.' Kipps sighed and gave a rueful smile. 'Forgive me. I cannot abide ineptitude, and the Adventurers represent it at its worst.'

Eventually, Chaloner and Kipps arrived at the great marble staircase that led to the Earl's domain. It was cold even in the height of summer, so it was positively frigid that day, and Chaloner shivered in his still-damp clothes. Kipps wished him luck and disappeared into the elegantly appointed room he had been allocated, where a fire blazed merrily, and wine and cakes had been set out for him.

Tiredly, Chaloner climbed the stairs, and continued along a passageway to the fine chamber from which the Earl conducted his official business. He smiled at the new secretary, William Edgeman, although his friendly greeting was not returned: Edgeman, a short, disagreeable man, was friends with Dugdale.

When Chaloner reached the door, he heard voices. The Earl's was the loudest, but there were others, too. He knocked, but the room's occupants were making so much racket that no one heard.

'You will be in trouble,' called Edgeman, smirking gleefully. 'The Earl was furious when he heard that you deliberately ignored his summons in order to wander off with a corpse.'

Chaloner was not surprised to learn that he was about to be given a frosty reception – the opportunity to harm him would have been too much of a temptation for Dugdale. He was exasperated, though. Why did the man have to be so petty? Surely someone of his status should be above such antics?

'Lady Clarendon, Henry Hyde and Sir Alan Brodrick have been waiting, too,' Edgeman went on. 'They are also angry with you.'

'Waiting for me?' asked Chaloner in surprise. He had never met Clarendon's wife, Frances, while the son and heir, Henry Hyde, had always made a point of ignoring him, making it clear that ex-Parliamentarian intelligencers were beneath his contempt. Clarendon's cousin Brodrick liked Chaloner, though – a feeling that was reciprocated – because they shared a love of music.

'They will be wanting you to deal with some matter that is too sordid for the rest of us,' predicted Edgeman unpleasantly. 'Why else would they be so keen to meet the likes of you?'

Unwilling to listen to more of the secretary's spiteful speculation, Chaloner knocked again, then jumped back smartly when the door was whipped open rather abruptly. Without conscious thought, his hand dropped to his sword.

The man who stood on the other side of the door was in his mid-twenties, with a catlike face and a long, straight nose. He was dressed in a fashionably elegant silk suit with a profusion of lace. He was Clarendon's eldest son, who revelled in the title of Viscount Cornbury, although most people simply referred to him by his family name of Hyde.

'Good God!' he yelped, when he saw the half-drawn

48

weapon. But he recovered himself quickly, and looked Chaloner up and down in disdain. 'I see you have dressed for the occasion.'

Chaloner felt he could come to dislike Hyde as much as his pompous, overbearing father, and several tart responses flashed into his mind. Fortunately, prudence prevailed, so he said nothing.

'Enter,' ordered Hyde, with an unwelcoming scowl. 'With your blade *inside* its scabbard, if you would be so kind. We have been expecting you these last two hours.'

As usual, the office had been heated to suffocation point – the Earl believed cold air was bad for his gout, and always kept the chamber wickedly hot. For once, Chaloner did not mind, although he was disconcerted when his clothes began to steam.

'Have you discovered who is stealing my father's bricks?' asked Hyde in an undertone, catching the spy's arm to hold him back for a moment. 'Personally, I think he is overreacting. Anyone who builds a house in London should expect a few items to go missing. It is the natural order of things.'

'Yes and no,' argued Chaloner. 'There is a big difference between "a few items going missing" and the regular and sustained pilfering of—'

'You are wasting your time,' predicted Hyde. 'You will not catch the culprit, so you should forget about it and do the job for which you were hired – protecting my father against the many scoundrels at Court who mean him harm.'

'Willingly,' said Chaloner. 'When will you tell him of this decision? Today?'

Hyde glowered. 'Watch your tongue. My father may

49

overlook your insolence because he thinks he needs your services, but I am not so indulgent. Now follow me.'

The Earl was on one side of the spacious hearth, and his wife was sitting opposite him. Brodrick was next to her, slumped with his head in his hands in a way that implied he was suffering from a serious hangover, while Dugdale perched on a stool at the Earl's feet. The Chief Usher looked ridiculous there, like a performing monkey, and Chaloner wondered why he had consented to take such a demeaning position.

'There you are at last,' muttered Brodrick, while the Earl pointedly ignored Chaloner and continued speaking to Dugdale. 'Where have you been? Because of your tardiness, I am missing an important meeting with the King.'

Brodrick was generally regarded to be one of the most dissipated men at Court, although the Earl steadfastly refused to believe anything bad about him and never tired in his campaign to secure him a lucrative post. Fortunately for Britain, others could see Brodrick's failings, and he had so far been denied a government appointment.

'You are an Adventurer?' asked Chaloner. He was not surprised. Brodrick was essentially penniless, but that had never prevented him from enjoying an expensive lifestyle, and investing money he did not have in a badly organised venture was certainly something he would do.

Brodrick nodded. 'On account of the dinners – they are the best in London, and I do like a good evening out.'

'Did the Adventurers meet last night, then?' asked

Chaloner, taking in Brodrick's pale face and bloodshot eyes. 'Or were you at Lady Castlemaine's—'

'No,' interrupted Brodrick, shooting his cousin an uneasy glance. The Earl hated the King's mistress so much that he could not even bring himself to say her name; she was always just 'the Lady'. He would certainly not approve of Brodrick enjoying her soirées, although Chaloner knew for a fact that Brodrick was usually the first to arrive and last to leave. 'I caught a chill at church yesterday.'

'Our cousin is a very devout man,' said Frances. She was a soft, motherly creature who had probably never been pretty, but who had such a kind, generous face that Chaloner instinctively liked her. The wry gleam in her eye suggested that she had Brodrick's measure, even if her husband remained obstinately blind.

'Ah, Chaloner,' said the Earl, pretending to notice his gentleman usher's arrival.

He was a short, plump man, who liked to dress fashionably, which was unfortunate because the profusion of lace, ribbons and ruffles served to accentuate his short neck, ample girth and double chins. That morning he was clad in the sumptuous robes that marked him as the country's Lord Chancellor, and a yellow wig reached almost to his waist. Chaloner regarded him in astonishment, wondering what he wore at state functions if he attired himself so elaborately when at leisure.

'Chaloner has donned his best clothes for you today, father,' said Hyde slyly.

'I know you have been obliged to lurk at my mansion since you came home,' said the Earl, eyeing his intelligencer disapprovingly, 'but Henry is right. Must you dress so shabbily? You look like a ruffian.'

51

'It rained all last night, sir,' Chaloner started to explain. 'And—'

'Never mind that,' interrupted the Earl impatiently. 'I ordered you to come here without delay, but Dugdale says you ran off on another errand.'

'Well, he is here now,' said Frances soothingly. 'And I applaud his actions. Would you have had him leave poor Cave in the street, like so much rubbish? He did the decent thing.'

'If you say so, dear.' The Earl's voice said he did not agree, but knew better than to argue.

'Poor Cave,' said Brodrick. 'Did you ever hear him sing, cousin? It was the stuff of Heaven, and his voice will be sorely missed. I was only remarking to Lady Castle—' He cleared his throat uncomfortably, '—to a friend last night that the Chapel Royal choir has been much improved since he came home.'

'I have often heard him sing,' said Frances, as the Earl, who had not missed Brodrick's slip of the tongue, frowned his puzzlement at it. 'Did his killer escape, or is he arrested?'

'He escaped, but not before Cave stabbed him,' supplied Dugdale. 'I had asked Chaloner to prevent violence, but I am afraid he failed rather miserably.'

Frances regarded him coolly. 'Did he indeed! Then why did *you* not intervene instead?'

Dugdale regarded her uneasily. 'Because I am not quali-fied to meddle in street brawls, My Lady. I am a gentleman.'

'A gentleman who claims to have fought for the King during the wars,' pressed Frances. 'So you cannot be a total stranger to weapons.'

Chaloner watched Dugdale squirm, and found himself liking Frances even more. Of course, Dugdale was likely to remember the humiliation she had inflicted on him, but it would not be her who would pay the price. It would be Chaloner, for witnessing it. The Earl clapped his hands suddenly, causing Brodrick to wince and put a hand to his head.

'We have wasted enough time this morning, so I recommend we get down to business. Go and stand outside, Dugdale, and ensure we are not interrupted.'

'You want me to leave?' asked Dugdale in disbelief. 'But I . . .'

He trailed off when his master pointed to the still-open door. He struggled up from the stool and bowed, although the glance he shot at Chaloner said he was seething. Chaloner, meanwhile, was uneasy. Surely his Tangier report could be of no interest to Frances, Hyde and Brodrick? His disquiet intensified when Hyde followed Dugdale to the door, to ensure his father's instructions were being followed, and then locked it before joining the group at the hearth.

'We learned something terrible this morning, Chaloner,' whispered the Earl, once his son had taken the stool Dugdale had vacated. 'The most dreadful plot . . .'

'He wants you to investigate,' said Hyde. He glared at his father. 'Although I am more than capable of solving the case, and so is Brodrick. There is no need to involve outsiders.'

'I am sure you can, dear,' said Frances. 'But we are talking about a man's life, and Mr Chaloner has skills and experience that you do not. It would be unethical not to seek his assistance.'

'How may I help?' asked Chaloner, thinking that a 'most dreadful plot' and saving someone's life sounded a lot more interesting than watching piles of bricks.

53

'There is a plan afoot to murder my architect,' breathed the Earl. 'Roger Pratt.'

There was silence after the Earl had made his announcement, as he, Hyde, Brodrick and Frances waited for Chaloner to react. The only sounds were the crackling of the fire and a ticking clock. It was an expensive one from France, but although it was baroque art at its finest, it was two hours fast, suggesting its makers considered an elaborate case more important than functional innards.

Chaloner stared at the Earl's family, assuming they had misread whatever intelligence had come their way. Regardless, dispatching an architect was not his idea of a 'most dreadful plot'.

'Why would anyone harm Pratt?' he asked eventually. 'Is it because people think Clarendon House too grand, and murdering its designer might make you reconsider—'

'No!' snapped the Earl angrily. 'That is *not* why. If it were, the villains would have struck while it was being raised. It has walls and a roof now, and most of the remaining work is internal.'

'We told Pratt about the threat, and once he had recovered from the shock, he agreed with us,' added Hyde. 'It cannot be an attack on his creation, or it would have happened months ago.'

'I believe the *real* plot is an attempt to inconvenience me,' the Earl went on. 'My enemies see the house nearing completion, and they want to delay me moving in. For spite. Or jealousy.'

'You may think it is extreme,' said Frances, apparently reading the doubt in Chaloner's face, 'but you do not need us to tell you that there are some very unpleasant people at Court.'

'How did you hear about it?' asked Chaloner, making an effort to take their concerns seriously. 'Was there a rumour?'

'We found a letter,' explained the Earl. He looked at his wife, then at his son, and then at his cousin, before bringing troubled eyes back to Chaloner. 'In the Queen's personal correspondence.'

Chaloner was bemused. 'How did it get there?'

'Because *she* is the one who has commissioned the murder,' stated Hyde baldly.

Chaloner gaped at him. Of all the people in London, Queen Katherine was the last to engage in murky business. She was a shy, convent-raised Portuguese princess who had still not come to terms with the fact that she had married into one of the most sybaritic courts in the world. Chaloner liked her, but she was unpopular with almost everyone else for several reasons: she was Catholic, she spoke poor English, and she had so far failed to provide an heir for the throne.

'She would never involve herself in such a matter,' he said, finally regaining his voice. 'First, I doubt she has ever met Pratt. Second, she is not the kind of lady to kill people. And third, even if she were, she is still a virtual stranger here, and would not know how to go about it.'

'So you say,' snapped Hyde. 'But, as you know, I am her Private Secretary. I found this letter.'

As it happened, Chaloner did not know that Hyde worked for the Queen, and was ashamed of himself for it, because it was the sort of detail spies should know about their employers' families.

'May I see it?' he asked, still sure there had been a mistake.

Hyde looked set to refuse, but the Earl indicated he should hand it over. He did so reluctantly, and Chaloner read what had been written:

Your Majestye is truthfull in her clayme that Clarendone House is an abomination before our most Holie and Catholick God. I will kill Pratt on the Feast Day of St Frideswide, as you ordered. I remayne youre humble and obedient servant in Christ and the Virgin Marye.

'Well?' demanded the Earl. 'How will you prevent this outrage?'

'There will be no outrage, sir,' said Chaloner, wondering what had possessed them to take such a patent piece of lunacy seriously. 'It is hardly Her Majesty's fault that some madman has elected to send her an insane letter.'

'Hah!' exclaimed Brodrick in satisfaction. 'That is exactly what I said.'

'Then you are both wrong,' said Hyde, scowling. 'The threat is genuine.'

'It is not,' argued Chaloner. 'This letter is a transparent and laughable effort to implicate the Queen in something of which she is innocent. I would have thought the clumsy references to her Catholicism would have made that apparent.'

'That is a valid point,' agreed Frances. 'And her English is still poor . . .'

'It has improved,' said Hyde stiffly. 'She is not fluent, but she could certainly comprehend what is written here. And she has a motive for harming you, father: she is hurt that you do not visit her as often as you once did.'

'Because I have no choice,' objected the Earl defensively. 'I chose her as a bride for the King, but it was a terrible mistake, because she is barren. If I do not distance myself, my enemies will use her to destroy me. Surely she understands that?'

Poor Katherine, thought Chaloner. Now even those who had been friends were abandoning her.

'And she wants revenge,' Hyde finished. 'She knows how important Clarendon House is to you, so she means to strike at you through Pratt.'

'No,' said Chaloner with considerable force. The Earl's eyes widened at the tone of his voice, and Hyde bristled, but Chaloner did not care. 'She would never do such things.'

'The evidence is there,' snarled Hyde, pointing at the letter. 'Thank God I intercepted it.'

'Do you really think a co-conspirator would send such a thing?' demanded Chaloner, feeling his dislike of Hyde mount. Surely the man owed his mistress some shred of loyalty? 'Even the most inept of assassins would know not to leave written evidence of his plans.'

'He doubtless assumed the Queen would destroy it after digesting its contents,' snapped Hyde. 'It was only luck that allowed me to find it before she could do either.'

'Do you not see what is happening?' Chaloner was becoming exasperated. 'Someone left it for you to find, with the specific intention of harming her. Only instead of throwing it away, like any rational man, you have played directly into this lunatic's hands by taking it seriously.'

Hyde glowered. 'If that were the case, there would have been other messages of a similar nature. And this is the only one.'

'The only one you have found,' corrected Chaloner. 'Or perhaps this is the first, and more will follow.'

'No!' barked Hyde. 'The explanation is obvious: she should have burned it, but she is a novice in such matters, and she was careless. She left it lying on a desk, where I happened across it.'

'How very convenient,' said Chaloner acidly. 'The instigator of this nasty piece of poison must be delighted that you are making his task so easy.'

'Watch yourself, Chaloner,' breathed Brodrick, shocked. 'Or you will be in trouble.'

'He *is* in trouble,' snarled Hyde. He turned to his father. 'I want him dismissed. He has made no headway with catching the villain who steals our bricks, and now he does not believe the threat against Pratt. I will explore both matters, and you can save yourself the cost of employing him.'

'You cannot, Henry,' said Frances reasonably. 'You do not have the necessary expertise. Besides, you do not believe the theft of our bricks amounts to anything – you tell us to ignore it. How will you investigate something you do not consider to be serious?'

'Because I know about architecture,' replied Hyde loftily. 'I have always been interested in the subject, and Christopher Wren told me only last week that he considers me talented. I know far more about building supplies than Chaloner ever will.'

'But not about theft and murder,' argued Frances quietly. 'And those are the issues here.'

Hyde scowled, and it was clear he resented his mother's interference. Chaloner appreciated it, though, and suspected she might have just saved him from unemployment, because the Earl's eyes had glittered

58

thoughtfully when the prospect of saving money had been raised.

'So what will you do, Chaloner?' asked Brodrick. 'How will you begin?'

'By finding out who sent the message,' answered Chaloner, not bothering to reiterate his belief that the architect was in no danger, but that the Queen might well be. 'And—'

'A waste of time,' interrupted Hyde. 'I have already questioned Her Majesty's household, but no one saw this missive delivered. And I doubt *she* will appreciate being interrogated by you.'

Chaloner suppressed a sigh. Hyde's precipitate actions would have told the sender that the letter had been discovered, thus making the matter that much more difficult to explore.

'Perhaps we should send Pratt away until the would-be assassin is under lock and key,' suggested Frances. 'I shall never forgive myself if he is murdered while working on our new home.'

'The letter says Pratt will not die until the Feast of St Frideswide.' Chaloner calculated quickly. 'That is a week next Wednesday – nine days from now.'

'How do you know?' asked the Earl in astonishment. 'We had to consult an almanac. I sincerely hope you are not a papist. I would not countenance one of those in my household.'

'It is general knowledge, sir.' Chaloner did not feel strongly enough about religion to affiliate himself with any sect, although he suspected that the Earl would dismiss him if he knew that his intelligencer was married to a Catholic – Hannah had converted when she had first been appointed to serve the Queen.

'We shall hire Sergeant Wright to protect Pratt,' determined Brodrick. 'To put Frances's mind at rest.'

It would be a waste of money on two counts, thought Chaloner. By paying guards to mind a man who did not need them, and by employing Wright, who would not know how to repel an assassin if his life depended on it. But before he could say so, there was a knock on the door. Chaloner unlocked it to admit Dugdale, who looked around carefully, as if trying to gauge what had been discussed in his absence. He shot Chaloner a malevolent glance, but masked the expression quickly when he addressed the Earl, unwilling for their master to see the extent of his dislike.

'I have just received a note from Pratt, sir. Apparently, twenty planks of best oak were stolen last night. How extraordinary that Chaloner did not notice.'

Fortunately for Chaloner, Kipps arrived shortly after Dugdale's announcement, to inform Hyde and Brodrick that their presence was required at the Adventurers' meeting immediately. Neither man could ignore a summons from the King, and they disappeared without another word. Chaloner was grateful, suspecting that Hyde would have used the missing wood to resume his campaign to have him dismissed – and he might have succeeded, because the Earl was clearly livid about their loss. Lady Clarendon frowned.

'I do not like Henry mixing with Adventurers,' she said, once everyone had gone, and only she, the Earl and Chaloner remained. 'He is easily led, and I have not heard good things about Secretary Leighton. The other members leave much to be desired, too. Henry told me only yesterday that they transported more than three thousand slaves to Barbados last year. Slaves! How *can* he associate with such vileness?'

The Earl sighed unhappily. 'We cannot dictate his behaviour for ever – he is twenty-six years old. But we should not discuss this now. I am more interested in my planks.' He glared at Chaloner.

'I watched your supplies all night, sir,' said Chaloner tiredly. 'And I checked them before I left. They were all there then.'

'But this particular wood was stored *inside* the house,' explained the Earl shortly. 'And I know for a fact that every door is secured at dusk, so no one should have been able to get in.'

'No one did, sir. So these planks must have been stolen after I left this morning, when the doors were unlocked for the workmen.'

'Without anyone seeing?' asked the Earl archly.

'Without anyone raising the alarm,' corrected Chaloner. 'As I have said before, I suspect the thieves have accomplices among the workforce.'

'Nonsense! My labourers are above reproach.' The Earl held up his hand when Chaloner started to point out that such a large body of men, none of whom were very well paid, was likely to contain at least one rotten apple, and probably a lot more. 'You let your attention wander, and these cunning dogs seized the opportunity to climb through a window. They cannot have gone through a door, because my locks are tamper-proof.'

'Are they now?' murmured Chaloner. He had not met a lock yet that could keep him out.

'They are the best money can buy.' The Earl's eyes shone, as they always did when he was boasting about his new home. 'And one key opens them all.'

Chaloner had never heard of such a thing. 'Really?'

The Earl rummaged in his clothing and produced a key that hung on a cord around his neck. 'There are only two copies in existence. I have one, and Pratt has the other – his will eventually go to Frances. It means we shall be able to lock whichever rooms we like without having to sort through vast mountains of keys.'

'I see,' said Chaloner, resisting the urge to ask what would happen if one was mislaid.

'The only door it cannot open is the one to the vault.' The Earl grinned. 'And that is clever, too – it is designed to be airless, so if ever there is a fire, my papers and other valuables will be safe.'

'Airless?' asked Chaloner uneasily. 'But what if someone is shut inside?'

The Earl looked smug. 'That will never happen to an innocent person, and thieves deserve to be suffocated. Pratt is a genius for inventing such clever measures. My new home is impregnable.'

'Except for the fact that someone broke in and stole your planks,' Chaloner pointed out.

The Earl scowled. 'That was *your* fault. You failed to ensure all the windows were closed, and then you were asleep when the burglars arrived to take advantage. And it obviously happened during the night, because thieves never operate in broad daylight.'

'Do not rail at him, dear,' said Frances mildly. 'And thieves *do* operate in broad daylight. Indeed, they probably prefer it, because they will be able to see what they are doing.'

Chaloner wished she were present during all his interviews with the Earl. 'The only way to catch the culprits – or to deter them – is to put the house under continuous surveillance. But I cannot do it, sir, not if I am to look into the threat against Pratt.'

'True,' acknowledged the Earl. 'So Pratt and his assistant Oliver can take responsibility during the day, and I shall hire Sergeant Wright to do it at night – he has more than enough men to protect Pratt *and* guard my house. That should leave you plenty of time to unmask the assassin – and to lay hold of these wretched burglars before they steal anything else.'

'Very well, sir.' Chaloner turned to leave.

'Wait,' said the Earl. He grimaced. 'Much as it pains me to admit it, Henry is wrong, and you and Brodrick are right – the Queen would never conspire to kill my architect, not even to repay me for neglecting her these last few months. But that does not mean Pratt is safe. You *must* learn who sent that letter and prevent something dreadful from unfolding – Pratt dead and the Queen blamed.'

'I shall do my best, sir.'

Chaloner was preparing to take leave of his employer when Edgeman the secretary arrived to remind the Earl that it was time to attend a meeting of the Tangier Committee. The Earl indicated Chaloner was to help him up – gout and an expanding girth meant he was not as agile as he once was – and Frances rose to leave, too, unwilling to linger in her husband's place of work when he would not be there.

'I suppose you had better tell me what you learned in Africa,' said the Earl, waddling towards the door. 'I know you wrote me a report, but I could not be bothered to read it.'

'I did, and it was very interesting,' said Frances, making

Chaloner warm to her even more. 'Your assertion that Tangier is a hard posting, miles from the centre of power at White Hall, does explain why honest men refuse to accept jobs there. Only the dross, who cannot get anything else, are—'

'A hard posting?' interrupted the Earl uneasily. He turned to Chaloner. 'Do you think the Portuguese cheated us when they gave it as part of the Queen's dowry, then?'

As the man largely responsible for negotiating the royal marriage contract, he was the one who would be blamed if that transpired to be true. And Chaloner thought it was – he strongly suspected the Portuguese had been rather glad to be rid of it.

'The harbour is not all that was promised,' he hedged. 'It is too shallow for warships, and is open to northerly gales. But the garrison is building a mole to protect it, which should help.'

'A mole is a sea wall,' interposed Frances, eager to show off the knowledge she had gleaned from reading Chaloner's commentary. 'And when it is finished, it will provide British ships with a safe haven in the Mediterranean. This will re-establish us as the greatest maritime nation in the world, by letting us control the Straits of Gibraltar.'

'The problem is that only a fraction of the money we send is spent on the mole,' explained Chaloner. 'Most is siphoned off by corrupt officials. The new governor, Sir Tobias Bridge—'

'A damned Parliamentarian,' grated the Earl. 'I argued against appointing him, but he was the only person willing to do it.'

'What happened to his predecessor?' asked Frances of Chaloner. 'Lord Teviot? We heard rumours about his death of course, but I felt we never had the truth of it.'

'He took five hundred soldiers to chop down a wood,' Chaloner replied, thinking that she was right to be suspicious: there had definitely been something odd about what had happened that fateful day in May. 'His scouts told him it was safe, but in fact a large enemy force was waiting. Teviot repelled the first wave, but then he made a fatal mistake.'

'He skulked back to the town?' asked the Earl, his interest caught. 'Instead of pursuing them, and showing the devils what British infantry can do?'

'The opposite. He thought he had managed a rout, when it should have been obvious that he was being lured into a trap. All but thirty of his men were killed.'

'And Teviot died too,' sighed the Earl. 'I did not like him personally – he was arrogant, greedy and stupid – but no one can deny his courage.'

'The fact that his scouts told him it was safe bothers me,' said Chaloner, more to himself than his listeners. 'I raised the matter with them when we travelled home together on *Eagle*, but they refused to discuss it.'

'Then perhaps you had better look into that affair, too,' said the Earl. 'As you point out, good men are not exactly queuing up to accept duties in Tangier, and if rumours about dangerously incompetent staff start circulating, no one will ever volunteer again.'

'You want me to go back?' asked Chaloner, heart sinking. He had hoped to be home for a while.

'Not before you have caught my thieves and exposed whoever plans to kill Pratt. But if these scouts are in London, then there is no need for foreign travel. You can question them here.'

'But I have questioned them, sir. They were unwilling to talk.'

'Then try harder. I am sure you have cracked tougher nuts in the past. That gives you three different assignments, which is a lot, but I am sure you will manage. However, remember that the most important one is catching the villains who keep raiding my house.'

'No, most important is the plot involving the Queen and Pratt,' countered Frances. 'I do not want our architect murdered by an assassin. Or the poor Queen held responsible for it.'

'He will give all three equal attention,' said the Earl, although the tone of his voice made it clear that there would be trouble if his own concerns were not given priority. Chaloner bowed again, thinking unhappily that none of the enquiries filled him with great enthusiasm, and he would be lucky if he solved one of them to the Earl's satisfaction.

In the corridor outside, the Earl's retainers were waiting to escort him to his meeting. His seal bearer stood ready to lead the way, and his secretary and gentlemen ushers had lined up to process behind him. All wore his livery of blue and gold, and made for an imposing sight.

'You cannot join us, Chaloner,' said the Earl, looking pointedly at the spy's soiled and crumpled clothing. 'So you may escort my wife home instead.'

'Not yet, though,' said Frances. 'I should like to see the great lords of the Tangier Committee make their appearance. I adore a spectacle.'

But she was to be disappointed. Her husband was the only man who stood on ceremony, and the other members arrived in a far more modest fashion. Most had not even bothered to don wigs, and badly shaven heads were the order of the day.

One person had taken care to look his best, however.

66

He was Samuel Pepys, an ambitious clerk from the Navy Board. Because Chaloner was standing with Lady Clarendon, Pepys deigned to acknowledge him, although his eyes widened in shock at the spy's dishevelled appearance.

'Tangier's residents say Teviot was the best of all their governors,' he was informing the man at his side. 'But to my mind, he was a cunning fellow.'

'He died gallantly, though,' replied his friend. 'But never mind him. Tell me why you object to paying what Governor Bridge has demanded for the mole.'

'Because of the casual way he presents his expenses,' explained Pepys. 'We should demand a better reckoning. Lord! How I was troubled to see accounts of ten thousand pounds passed with so little question the last time the Committee met. I wished a thousand times that I had not been there.'

'Perhaps my husband was right to ask you to look into Teviot's death,' said Frances, after Pepys and his companion had entered the building. 'If such vast sums really are being sent to Tangier with so little accounting, then it will be easy for the unscrupulous to line their pockets. And to some villains, five hundred lives is a small price to pay for personal profit.'

'If so, then I shall do all I can to avenge them,' promised Chaloner.

'But not today,' said Frances kindly. 'You were only married a month before sailing to Tangier, and you have been desperately busy since you returned. Spend the rest of the day with Hannah.'

Chaloner woke before it was light the next morning, aware that he had a great deal to do. He lay still for a moment, working out a plan of action, and decided that he would begin by hunting down Harley, Newell and Reyner, on the grounds that the deaths of so many soldiers was a rather more serious matter than missing planks and the lunatic letter about Pratt.

He was not sure what time Hannah had returned from her duties with the Queen the previous night, but she did not stir as he slipped out of bed and dressed in the dim light of the candle she had forgotten to extinguish before she had retired. He bent to kiss her as he left, but she chose that moment to fling out an arm, catching him on the shoulder. With a squawk of pain, her eyes flew open.

'What are you doing?' she demanded, wringing her knuckles and eyeing him accusingly.

She was a small, fair-haired lady with a pert figure and an impish grin. She was not pretty, but she possessed a strength of character and an independence of thought that he had found attractive. They had married before they really knew each other, but it had not taken them long to learn that each possessed habits the other did not like. Chaloner disapproved of the company Hannah kept at Court and was appalled by her surly morning temper; Hannah deplored Chaloner's inability to express his feelings and hated the sound of his bass viol.

Music was important to Chaloner. It soothed him when he was agitated, cleared his mind when he was dealing with complex cases, and there was little that delighted him more than a well-played recital. He could not imagine a world without it, and felt incomplete when deprived of it for any length of time. Unfortunately, Hannah did not like him playing in the house, and ignoring her and doing it anyway negated any enjoyment he might have gained from the exercise. As far as he was concerned, it was a serious impediment to their future happiness together.

His frustration with the situation had led him to rent a garret in Long Acre the previous week. All spies kept boltholes for those occasions when returning home was inadvisable, but Chaloner needed one for the sake of his sanity, too. He had taken his best viol, or viola da gamba, there immediately, along with the clothes Hannah had parcelled up for the rag-pickers – she also hated the fact that his work meant he was sometimes obliged to dress in something other than courtly finery. His second-best viol was stored in a cupboard under the stairs, and was only played when she was out.

'I am just leaving,' he whispered. 'Go back to sleep.'

'Leaving?' Hannah cast a bleary eye towards the window. 'In the middle of the night?'

'It is nearly dawn.'

'Exactly! Dawn is the middle of the night. Come back to bed, or you will wake the servants.'

The servants were yet another bone of contention. Chaloner accepted that his post as gentleman usher and Hannah's as lady-in-waiting demanded that they keep one, but he had returned from Tangier to find she had hired three. None were women he would have chosen, because they were brazenly curious about their employers, and watched them constantly. Even if he had not been a spy, obliged to keep a certain number of secrets, being under constant surveillance in his own home would have been an unwelcome development.

'I will not wake them,' he said, wishing he had abstained from reckless displays of affection and that she was still asleep. 'But you might, if you continue to bawl.'

'Do not tell me when I can and cannot speak,' snapped Hannah, displaying the sour temper that invariably afflicted her when she first awoke. It was so unlike her personality during the rest of the day that he wondered whether he should take her to a physician. 'I shall shout if I want to.'

He sat on the side of the bed and took her hand in his, speaking softly in the hope that it would soothe her back to sleep. 'I am sorry I disturbed you.'

'You are improperly dressed again,' said Hannah, wrenching her hand free and struggling into a sitting position. 'That old long-coat is not fit for a beggar, while your shirt does not have enough lace. People will think I married a ruffian if you go to White Hall looking like that.'

'You did marry a ruffian. The Earl said so only yesterday.'

That coaxed a reluctant smile. 'Then I retract my words, because I refuse to agree with anything that pompous old relic says.'

Although the Earl was fond of Hannah, the affection was not reciprocated, partly because he disapproved of most of her friends, and partly because she disliked the fact that he kept sending her husband into dangerous situations. She also objected to the fact that Chaloner spent more time away from London than in it – since being employed by the Earl, he had been sent to Ireland, Spain and Portugal, Oxford, Wimbledon, Holland and most recently Tangier.

'Did you catch whoever is stealing his bricks?' she asked, grinning suddenly. 'Everyone at Court is laughing about it, and I cannot help but wonder whether they are being removed as a prank.'

70

'It is possible. Do you have any idea who the culprit might be?'

'Of course! Do you have three hours to spare while I write you a list? His overbearing manners and priggishness have alienated virtually everyone at White Hall, and his only cronies are bigoted old churchmen who share his prudish views.'

Chaloner nodded unhappily, perfectly aware that the Earl would have been more popular had he been of a more tolerant disposition.

'Wait,' instructed Hannah, as he stood to leave. 'I have hired another servant, and you should speak to him before you go out.'

Chaloner was horrified. 'Another? But we already have two maids and a housekeeper.'

'We have our status to consider,' said Hannah coolly. 'And I do not want to live like a pauper, even if it suits you. Besides, we need these people. Susan is my waiting-woman, Nan is the cook-maid, and we would be lost without Joan as housekeeper.'

Chaloner said nothing, but thought they 'needed' nothing of the kind. He considered the trio who now occupied the back half of the house. Joan was an old friend of Hannah's family, which afforded her considerable leeway in dealing with the household, and also prevented Chaloner from sending her packing for her dour manners. Meanwhile, Susan and Nan were sly girls who never missed an opportunity to side with Joan against him. He supposed he would be spending more time in Long Acre if a fourth member were added to their ranks, because he already felt outnumbered.

'His name is George, and he will be your footman,' Hannah continued.

'But I do not want a footman!' cried Chaloner in alarm, imagining the fellow dogging his every step, obliging him to take increasingly inventive measures to avoid being monitored.

Hannah grew petulant. 'I do not understand this peculiar objection towards hired help. Your family had dozens of retainers to help run their huge estates in Buckinghamshire, so you must be used to them. Of course, that was before the Royalists returned to power and confiscated everything of value from Roundheads. I suppose your brothers do not engage many servants now?'

The Royalists had indeed avenged themselves on anyone who had supported Cromwell, and unlike many, Chaloner's family had declined to pretend that they had really been on the King's side all along. As a consequence, great tracts of their land, items of furniture and even cutlery had been seized in lieu of crippling taxes they could not pay. He made no reply to her remark.

'Talk to George before you leave,' she ordered. 'He is a Black Moor, and it is currently in vogue to have one. Do not look so dismayed! He is quite respectable, or I would not have taken him.'

'It is not his respectability I am worried about.' Chaloner *was* dismayed, and made no effort to hide it. 'It is him. It is not right to snatch people from their homes and sell them to—'

'What odd notions you have! I did not snatch him from his home, and nor was he sold to me.'

Chaloner struggled for patience. 'You may not have done, but someone else—'

'George is not a slave, Thomas,' interrupted Hannah sharply. 'He is a sailor who has decided he would rather have a life ashore.'

'And what happens when it is not "in vogue" to employ a black footman?' Chaloner was unappeased by her reply. 'Shall we exchange him for one of a different colour?'

'You know we will do nothing of the kind – I abhor the traffic in human beings as much as you do. However, George is *not* a slave.'

'But by following this repellent fashion of hiring black retainers, we are encouraging the trade. I want no part of it, Hannah.'

Hannah was silent for a moment, then nodded slowly. 'Yes, I see your point, and you are right. But what can we do about it now? We cannot turn him out – he needs employment.'

Chaloner could see no answer, and left the bedroom wishing Hannah had thought through the consequences of her actions before following such an objectionable fad.

Another change that had taken place when Chaloner had been in Tangier was Hannah renting a larger house. He would have dissuaded her had he been home, because it and the servants took too much of their income. However, by the time he returned she had been in residence for weeks, and her move from the pretty little cottage three doors down was a fait accompli. The two maids slept in the attic, while the kitchen and its adjoining parlour, sculleries and pantries were the domain of the formidable Joan. That left Chaloner and Hannah with a bedchamber, a drawing room and a hall-like space for eating. All three were large, chilly places with a marked paucity of furniture – they had not owned much when they had lived in the cottage, and there was certainly not enough to fill the cavernous rooms of a much larger house.

Although it was early, the servants were up. Joan was

a stooped, pinched woman with a large nose and a penchant for loosely fitting black clothes. She had reminded Chaloner of a crow when he had first met her, and her grim visage and sharp little eyes had done nothing to dispel the illusion since.

Susan was sitting in a corner, darning a stocking, while Nan was stirring something in a pot over the fire. Chaloner had trouble telling them apart, because they were both disagreeable young women with bad complexions, whom Joan dressed in identical uniforms. They stood as he entered, and he nodded to indicate that they should return to their duties.

'May I help you?' asked Joan coolly. 'If so, perhaps you would wait in the drawing room.'

It was her way of informing him that he should confine himself to those parts of the house that she considered his. He was tempted to retort that he would go where he pleased in his own home, but he had already learned that arguing with her was more trouble than it was worth. He forced himself to smile as he explained.

'Hannah asked me to speak to George.'

Nan and Susan exchanged a glance that Chaloner found difficult to interpret.

'He is in the scullery,' said Joan. She scowled. 'You should have told me you wanted a footman. It was thoughtless to have gone out and hired one yourself without consulting me or the mistress.'

So there it was, thought Chaloner. Hannah had sensed Joan's disapproval, and rather than admit that it was her idea, she had decided to let Joan assume it was his. He was tempted to tell her the truth, but suspected it would not be believed: Joan was nothing if not loyal to the family she had served all her life.

'You have created a very welcoming atmosphere here,' he said, unable to resist toying with her. 'I am sure he will soon feel at home.'

'Have I?' asked Joan, clearly thinking something would have to be done about it. She eyed him beadily. 'Will you be wanting something to eat? You do not usually bother us with demands, but Nan can whisk you up a raw egg. Or there are cold kidneys left over from last night's dinner.'

'It is a tempting offer,' said Chaloner, perfectly aware that *she* would not be starting her day with raw eggs and cold kidneys. 'But I shall speak to George instead.'

All three women watched him leave. Joan's expression was openly hostile, while Nan and Susan exchanged a smirk. They had understood his sarcasm, even if Joan had not.

He walked along the tiled corridor to the scullery, and pushed open the door. A man sat there, polishing boots. He stood abruptly, making Chaloner take an involuntary step backwards. He was huge, with muscular arms and powerful legs. His face was smooth and chestnut brown, and his hair so dark as to be almost blue. His eyes were black, and carefully devoid of expression.

Chaloner closed the door behind him, not because he planned to say anything that should not be overheard, but to deprive Joan of a chance to eavesdrop. He heard her sigh of annoyance just before it clicked shut, which gave him no small sense of satisfaction.

'Good morning.' George spoke in a sour, resentful way that said servitude did not come readily to him.

Chaloner nodded acknowledgement of the greeting, for the first time wondering what Hannah expected him to say. He was not going to give George a list of duties for three reasons. First, because there was nothing he wanted done; second because it would imply that she had been right to hire a footman; and third because any instructions he gave would be circumvented by Joan anyway, and then George would be in the unenviable position of choosing which of them to obey.

'Where were you before you came here, George?' he asked pleasantly.

'I spent the last ten years with Colonel Fitzgerald. At sea, mostly.'

'Ten years is a long time. Why did you leave?'

'Because he was obliged to reduce the size of his staff, to save money,' replied George tightly, giving the impression that he resented finding himself unemployed in a city so far from home. 'My testimonials are excellent, though, if you would care to see them.'

Chaloner shook his head. 'I do not know Colonel Fitzgerald.'

George raised his eyebrows. 'But you have heard of him?'

'No,' replied Chaloner shortly, piqued by the fact that now even foreigners showed themselves to be unimpressed by his knowledge of London and its inhabitants.

George did not seem discomfited by the curt tone. He met his new master's gaze with a steadiness that bordered on insolence. 'He is a pirate.'

Chaloner regarded him askance. 'You think I will be impressed by testimonials from a pirate?'

'Perhaps *privateer* would be a better word. He made his fortune by attacking Parliament-owned ships during the Commonwealth. I was his steward.'

'I assume he lost this fortune, or he would not have been obliged to reduce the size of his household,' said

Chaloner, supposing that the maids had not yet had a chance to gossip to George about their employer's past allegiances, or the footman would have found another way to describe how he had spent the past decade.

George nodded. 'His biggest and best ship sank, which bankrupted him. It was fortunate that he and I were ashore at the time, or we would have drowned.'

'So you are actually a sailor,' said Chaloner. 'Not a footman.'

George shrugged. 'A steward's duties at sea are not so different from a footman's on land.'

'Where is your home?' asked Chaloner, not sure he agreed.

The ghost of a smile crossed George's face. 'Somewhere you have been – Tangier. A fine place, do you not agree?'

'It has its advantages,' hedged Chaloner, struggling to think of one. His abiding memories of the place were of uncomfortable heat, dust, flies and a locust jumping on his dinner plate one night.

'Indeed it does,' said George softly.

Chapter 3

Chaloner's most pressing duty that day was to begin his investigation into the Tangier massacre by questioning the three scouts. He did not know where they lived, but the Crown in Piccadilly was as good a place as any to start making enquiries, given that he had seen them leaving it the previous morning. But the tavern was closed, and rather than waste time waiting for it to open, he decided to visit Clarendon House first, to see whether any more bricks had been stolen.

He approached with his usual stealth, and was unimpressed when Sergeant Wright and his White Hall soldiers did not notice him until he was standing next to them. Several were rubbing sleep from their eyes, while others reeked of ale. He doubted they had done much in the way of surveillance, and the best the Earl could hope was that their presence had been a deterrent to thieves.

Wright was regaling them with a story of his courage during the civil wars, when he had single-handedly defeated an entire regiment of Parliamentarians and had come close to dispatching Cromwell in the process. They looked bored and disbelieving in equal measure as they huddled around a brazier, waiting for a pot of ale to warm through.

'Did anything happen last night?' asked Chaloner, cutting into the tale. He was normally tolerant of men who embellished the truth about what they had done during those uncertain times, when both sides had had their flaws and no one wanted to admit to backing the loser. But there was a difference between exaggeration and brazen lies.

The dough-faced sergeant regarded him frostily, disliking the interruption. 'No.'

'You saw and heard nothing?'

'I said no,' snapped Wright. 'Obviously, the villains knew we were here and dared not strike. *We* are not foppish Roundheads, who would not know what to do if a robber came up and bit him.'

His men sniggered obligingly, and Wright preened, revelling in the role of wit.

'So the Earl's supplies are all present and correct?' pressed Chaloner, rather flattered to hear himself described as foppish. He would have to tell Hannah.

'Of course,' replied Wright, with calculated insolence. 'Where else would they be?'

Chaloner grabbed his arm in a grip that was not only painful, but was difficult to break, and marched him to where the materials were piled. The soldiers watched uneasily, but made no effort to intervene.

'Count the bricks,' Chaloner ordered, releasing Wright so abruptly that he stumbled.

Wright's small eyes took on a vicious cant, and he reached for his knife. Chaloner smiled lazily as he did likewise, and Wright promptly turned to do as he was told, unnerved by the spy's calm confidence. He was soldier enough to know who would win that confrontation.

The sergeant finished his inventory with some consternation, then started reckoning again. Chaloner waited patiently for him to finish. *He* had not needed to count to know the pile was lopsided in a way that it had not been the previous day.

'Some are gone,' Wright breathed, appalled. Then his expression hardened. '*You* took them when we were in the tav— when we were patrolling the back of the house. To get us into trouble!'

'I assure you, I have better things to do.'

'We could not be everywhere,' another man bleated. 'It is a huge site, with gardens as well as a massive house. That makes it easy for thieves. It is not our fault!'

'How long were you here before you went to the Crown?' asked Chaloner, not bothering to point out that he had done it for a week on his own.

'Of course we visited the Crown!' snarled Wright. 'That is where Mr Pratt the architect lodges, and we are hired to protect him. We did both duties.'

Chaloner tried another tack. 'Then how many men guarded Pratt, and how many stayed here?'

'It varied,' replied Wright tightly, leaving Chaloner to suspect that most if not all had elected to sit in the tavern. No one was wet and cold, as he had been the previous morning, indicating none had been outdoors for very long.

'I am telling Clarendon that *you* pinched his bricks,' declared Wright, eyeing Chaloner defiantly. 'You did it for malice, because we are better guards than you. And then you sold them.'

Chaloner did not grace the accusation with a reply, confident in the knowledge that the Earl would not believe it. Clarendon might have a generally low opinion of his intelligencer, but he had never doubted his honesty.

'He did not steal them,' said one of the others. 'Look at his clothes – they are too clean.'

Wright swallowed uneasily. 'Maybe they are just mislaid, then. We will search the site. You lot look, while I stay here and keep the fire going.'

Muttering resentfully, the guards shuffled away, although Chaloner knew they were wasting their time. He had conducted a thorough search when he had first returned from Tangier, and there was no indication that the missing supplies were being stored in the house or its grounds.

'We will find them,' predicted Wright confidently. 'So you had better not go braying to the Earl about them being gone, because it will not be true.'

'I have no intention of telling him. He does not react well to bad news.'

Wright glowered, but said no more.

'It is curious, though,' said Chaloner, more to himself than the sergeant. 'These thefts started *after* the walls and roof were finished – when the bulk of the building was completed, and the materials available were considerably reduced. Moreover, it is easy to pilfer items that are stacked outside, but some – like the planks yesterday – disappeared from *inside* the house.'

'Supply and demand, mate,' shrugged Wright. 'Maybe the villains had no market when the house was in its early stages.'

Chaloner supposed he would have to explore the city with a view to learning who else's home was being made from fine bricks and oaken planks. It would not be easy, but it represented a lead, and he decided to follow it as soon as he had a free moment.

*　　*　　*

It was not long before Pratt arrived, his gloomy assistant Oliver in tow. Reluctantly, Wright confessed that a number of bricks were gone, although he was careful to reiterate that he could not be expected to monitor such a large site *and* protect the architect with only ten men.

'Chaloner managed,' Oliver pointed out. 'Well, he did not have Pratt to mind, too, but—'

'And he was just as ineffective,' interrupted Pratt angrily. 'Is no one in London capable of doing his job? I have been invited to submit a design for rebuilding St Paul's Cathedral, but I do not think I shall bother. Not if it entails labouring amid thieves and men who cannot deter them.'

'Ignore him, Chaloner,' said Oliver kindly, once the architect had stalked away. 'He is in a bad mood today, because a lot of carousing in the Crown kept him awake last night. He is thinking of going to stay with a friend in Charing Cross tonight, just to get some sleep.'

'I found the Crown rather tame, personally,' said Wright, thus indicating the probable source of the disturbance.

Supposing he had better ensure the rest of the house was in order, Chaloner walked with Oliver towards it. Yet again, he was seized with the notion that it would bring the Earl trouble. It towered above them, as grand as anything owned by the extravagant kings of France, and the doors in the showy portico would not have looked out of place on a cathedral. Pratt was in the process of opening them with a key that, not surprisingly, was identical to the Earl's.

'Is it a good idea to have all the locks on the same key?' asked Chaloner, sure it was not.

Pratt scowled. 'Do not presume to tell me my business.

And anyway, all the locks are *not* on the same key. The strongroom has one of its own.'

'Have we told you about the strongroom?' asked Oliver, his morose visage breaking into what was almost a smile. 'It is designed so that no air can get inside once the door is shut. In that way, if there is ever a fire, its contents will be protected. It might even save lives, because Clarendon himself could use it, to escape being incinerated.'

'Yes, but only if he does not mind being suffocated instead,' Chaloner pointed out.

Oliver's lugubrious face fell. 'I had not thought of that.' He turned to Pratt in some alarm. 'What *does* happen if someone is trapped in there?'

Pratt opened his mouth once or twice but did not reply, which told Chaloner that the notion of safety had not crossed his mind, either. Then the architect shrugged. 'He will yell for help, and someone will come to let him out. However, if it is a villain who is shut inside, then he will die and it will serve him right. Would you like to see it?'

'No!' Chaloner had not meant to sound sharp, but he had a deep and abiding horror of cell-like places, which had afflicted him ever since he had been imprisoned in France for espionage.

'As you please,' said Pratt stiffly, offended. 'Are you coming in today, or does the rest of my creation fill you with revulsion, too?'

He turned away before Chaloner could think of a tactful response.

When Chaloner had first been given the task of guarding Clarendon House and its supplies, he had taken the opportunity to explore it thoroughly. It was rigidly symmetrical. There were two rooms to the left, which led to a huge staircase that swept up to the Earl's bedchamber, and an identical arrangement to the right, which would be used by his wife. Chaloner supposed they should be grateful that they already had all the children they intended to produce, because it would be something of a trek to meet each other in the night. Other rooms on the ground floor were graced with such grand names as the Great Parlour, the Room of Audience, My Lord's Lobby and the Lawyers' Library.

The upper storey was equally majestic, although wood panelling and tapestries meant the bedchambers and dressing rooms would be cosier than the stark marble monstrosities below. The attics were above them, with rooms already earmarked as sleeping quarters for the sizeable retinue that would be needed to run the place.

But it was the basement that was the most confusing, and Chaloner had counted at least thirty rooms in it, ranging from kitchens, pantries, butteries and sculleries to laundries and tack rooms. There were also places where servants could work and eat out of sight of the more lofty company above. All were connected by a maze of corridors and hallways. Beneath them were the strong-room and a range of dark, cold cellars.

'Are you sure you will not see the vault?' coaxed Oliver, as Chaloner followed him inside. 'You will be impressed.'

Chaloner was about to decline a second time, when he reconsidered. How much longer were his experiences in France going to haunt him? Determined to overcome what he knew was a foolish weakness, he nodded agreement. Obligingly, Oliver lit a torch and led the way down one flight of steps to the basement and then another to the cellars, chatting amiably as he went. Chaloner was grateful for the monologue, because it concealed the fact that his own breathing was ragged, and that he had to steady himself with one hand against the wall.

At the bottom, there was a long corridor with a floor of beaten earth, which had chambers leading off it, all low-ceilinged, dark spaces that would be used for storage. Two rooms were different, though. One was the purpose-built cavern where the Earl would keep his wine; the second was the vault.

Oliver pushed open the door of the latter to reveal a chamber that was no more than ten feet long and six wide. The door was unusually thick – wood encased in metal – and the internal walls had been lined with lead, which had the curious effect of deadening sound; as Oliver described how the place had been constructed, his voice was strangely muted.

'The door locks automatically when it is slammed shut. Then it can only be opened with a key.'

'No,' said Chaloner quickly, as Oliver started to demonstrate.

Oliver's sad face creased into a grin. 'The operative word is *slammed*. If you close it gently, it can be opened again. Besides, Mr Pratt has the key, and will rescue us if we inadvertently lock ourselves in. All we have to do is yell for help.'

'You think he will hear us, do you?' said Chaloner, stepping outside before Oliver could give him a demon-stration. 'If this room really is airtight, we will suffocate long before he realises we are missing.'

Oliver smiled again, to indicate that he thought Chaloner was being melodramatic, and led the way back towards the stairs. Chaloner was silent, wrestling with the uncomfortable notion that he might have to become much more familiar with the strongroom when the Earl was in residence. His duties did include safeguarding his employer's property, after all.

Once Oliver had finished showing off the vault, Chaloner hunted Pratt down in the Lawyers' Library. This room was already finished, with shelves and panelling in place, and a functional hearth. Pratt was using it as an office from which to work on the rest of the house. It was cold, though, and Oliver immediately set about lighting a fire.

'What time did you finish work last night?' asked Chaloner, wondering whether it was possible to glean clues about the thieves by identifying what time they struck.

It was Oliver who replied. 'Early. Mr Pratt had been called away, but shortly afterwards a question arose about the cornices, which meant we had to stop work to await his decision. Rather than keep the men hanging around idle, I sent them home at three o'clock.'

'I left at noon,' said Pratt, adding smugly, 'Christopher Wren wanted to show me his designs for a new St Paul's, you see. He values my opinion.'

'What did you think?' asked Chaloner curiously. He had seen Wren's plans, and had been appalled: the architect intended to tear down the iconic gothic building and replace it with a baroque monstrosity of domes and ugly pediments.

'That without me, he will make some terrible mistakes,' replied Pratt haughtily. 'No one has my skill with Palladian porticos.'

Chaloner found the prospect of a cathedral with Palladian porticos vaguely sacrilegious and considered telling Pratt so, but he knew he should not waste time on a debate when he had so much to do. Reluctantly, for he would have liked to denounce Wren's flashy notions, he turned the discussion back to the thefts. 'So the supplies could have been stolen yesterday afternoon?'

'It is possible,' acknowledged Oliver. 'All we can say for certain is that they were there when we left. Personally, I do not believe *common* thieves are responsible. Clarendon has enemies at Court, and I think some of them are doing the pilfering. To annoy us and inconvenience him.'

Chaloner was about to ask if he had any specific suspects, recalling that Hannah believed much the same thing, when Vere shuffled in to announce that the labourers were ready to begin work. The sullen wood-monger regarded Chaloner with disdain.

'You did not last long as nightwatchman,' he said. 'I see real soldiers are doing it now.'

'Chaloner is still investigating, though,' said Oliver, endearingly loyal. 'The Earl just wants him free to do more questioning than watching. He will catch these villains, never fear.'

'I hope so,' growled Vere. 'Because at the moment he suspects my lads of helping the thieves. But he is wrong, and when he has the real culprits in custody, he will owe us an apology.'

'We shall work on the Room of Audience today,' announced Pratt, uninterested in what his staff thought about Chaloner's suspicions. 'So I shall need all the cherry-wood panels, and as much plaster as you can mix.'

Oliver left to supervise the operation, and Vere followed him out only after shooting Chaloner a glower-ingly resentful glare. When they had gone, Pratt closed the door.

'I suppose you are here about the threat against my life,'

he said. 'The Earl told me about it yesterday, but there is no need for alarm. It means I have reached an apogee.'

Chaloner regarded him uncertainly. 'I do not understand.'

'I mean that ignorant fools often take exception to my buildings, because they do not possess the intelligence to appreciate how exquisite they are. You are probably one of them, which is why you think Clarendon House is too grand. But threats against me are a *good* thing. They tell me that I have succeeded in making people notice what I have done.'

'I see,' said Chaloner cautiously. He had met people with inflated egos in the past, but none who interpreted threats to kill them as a welcome form of flattery. 'Are you saying that this is not the first time someone has offered to deprive you of your life?'

Pratt shrugged. 'It *is* the first time, but it will not be the last. You see, the culprit will be someone who does not understand that my creations are not just a case of hurling up a few bricks, but an *expression* that is French in inspiration. In other words, the equal proportions of my floors represent a new innovation, compared to the Palladian manner of emphasising a *piano nobile*.'

Chaloner had no idea what he was talking about. 'Can you be more specific? About people who have taken against you, I mean, not about a *piano nobile*.'

'I built three stately homes before this one,' replied Pratt loftily. 'Doubtless there are philistines galore who fail to appreciate my perfect classical lines and I could not possibly list them all.'

'Are any in London at the moment?' pressed Chaloner, determined to have a sensible answer.

'Not that I am aware,' replied Pratt. He grinned

suddenly. 'I told Wren that there is a plot afoot to kill me, and he was *very* impressed. No architect can ever say that he has fulfilled his potential until he has designed something that makes people want to kill him.'

Chaloner blinked. 'Surely you should strive to produce buildings that people will like?'

'Why? The masses should keep their sorry opinions to themselves, and leave architecture to those of us with the wit and skill to devise great masterpieces.'

'Modestly put,' said Chaloner drily.

The sun was beginning to show its face as Chaloner walked towards the cluster of buildings where Piccadilly met the Haymarket. It was heartening, because it was the first time that he had seen it since he had returned from Tangier. Unfortunately, it was obliged to shine through a layer of haze, which lent the city a dirty, slightly yellowish cast that rendered it distinctly seedy.

He reached the junction and looked around. There were perhaps two dozen homes, some detached and others terraced, along with the Gaming House, three taverns and a windmill. As in most of London, dirty, insalubrious hovels rubbed shoulders with edifices that looked as though their residents were comfortably wealthy.

He knocked on the door to the Crown but there was no answer, and he could only suppose that its landlord was still asleep. He raised his hand to rap louder, but a picture of Hannah suddenly came to mind: *she* would not answer questions if dragged out of bed so soon after dawn. He could force the taverner to cooperate, of course, but it would be more pleasant for everyone if it was done willingly, so he decided to wait until the inn showed some signs of life.

To pass the time, he went to the Gaming House, where he ordered a cup of wine that he had no intention of drinking – it was far too early in the day for strong beverages. The place was comparatively empty, although a game of cards was underway in a corner. The tense faces of the participants, and the thick fug of pipe-smoke that enveloped them, indicated that they had been there for some time and that the stakes were high.

When the wine arrived, Chaloner settled at a table overlooking the street. It was busy now, with carts rolling in from Kensington and Knightsbridge bearing country produce for the great markets at Smithfield and Covent Garden. There were also coaches taking wealthy merchants to business in the city, and a variety of riders, ranging from farmers on plodding carthorses to elegant courtiers on prancing stallions.

Chaloner watched for a while, then picked up the latest government newsbook, which had been left for patrons to peruse. *The Intelligencer* was published on Mondays and *The Newes* on Thursdays, to keep the general populace abreast of foreign and domestic affairs. Unfortunately, the government did not like its people knowing what it was up to, lest there was another rebellion, so news tended to be selective, biased and well larded with lies.

He began to read, learning with some bemusement that the Portuguese ambassador had enjoyed having supper with the King, and that Mr Matthew's Excellent Pill was very efficacious at slaying fluxes and expelling wind. Overseas intelligence was in even shorter supply, the most significant being that nothing very exciting was happening in Venice. Finally, there was an advertisement for a book that claimed it would teach him 'how to walk with God all day long'.

He tossed the publication away in disgust, but at that point something began happening across the street: people were converging on the Crown. He recognised several he had seen leaving the previous morning – the jaunty Cavalier with the red ribbons in his boot hose; the Portuguese; the fellow with the orange beard, eye-patch and voice of a boy; and lastly, the pugilistic man named Brinkes, who had murdered Captain Pepperell.

The Portuguese and Brinkes glanced around furtively before slipping inside, but the Cavalier and One Eye entered confidently, indicating they did not care who saw them. They were followed by a couple wearing the kind of hats that were popular in The Hague, and whose clothes were more sober than those currently favoured by Englishmen.

Chaloner was pleased to see the scouts arrive, too. Harley was in the lead, walking with a confident swagger, while Newell slouched behind. Reyner was last, his shoulders hunched and a hood shadowing his face. They had emerged from a house several doors up, leading Chaloner to surmise that one of them – or possibly all three – lived there.

The remainder of the gathering was a curious mix of well-dressed people and ruffians, and once they were all inside, the door was firmly closed. Chaloner glanced upwards and saw the pale face of the woman he had seen the previous morning. His warning wave had evidently gone unheeded, because she was watching the arrivals with undisguised interest.

He waited a moment, then left the Gaming House, determined to find out what was going on.

*   *   *

Like many tenements, the Crown fulfilled a variety of functions. Its lower chamber served as a tavern, while the upper floors were rented to lodgers – Sergeant Wright had mentioned earlier that Pratt had rooms there, presumably because it was close to Clarendon House. In addition, the yard was leased to a coach-maker, while the stable had been converted into a pottery.

The tavern comprised a large, airy chamber crammed with tables and benches. It boasted a massive fireplace, although only embers glowed in it that morning. The ruffians were sitting around it, talking in low voices. Brinkes was with them, but he stood when Chaloner entered, his manner unfriendly. There was no sign of the well-dressed people.

'We are closed,' said the landlord, who had hurried from the back of the house when he had heard the door open. He wore a clean white apron and his sleeves were rolled up to reveal arms that were red from the cold – he had been washing his tankards. He was middle-aged, with thick grey hair and eyes like an inquisitive chicken.

'You are not,' countered Chaloner, nodding towards the men around the hearth.

'Private party.' The landlord shot them a nervous look. 'Try the Feathers, down the road.'

'I have a bad leg,' said Chaloner, truthfully enough. It had been injured by an exploding cannon at the Battle of Naseby, and had not been right since. 'I cannot walk any farther.'

The man regarded him sympathetically. 'Gout, is it? I suffer from that myself, and I would not wish it on my worst enemy. Come to my parlour at the back, then, and sit with me while I rinse my pots. My name is John Marshall, by the way, owner of this fine establishment.'

'It *is* fine,' said Chaloner, remembering to limp as he followed Marshall down the corridor. It was true: the Crown was a good deal nicer on the inside than it looked from the street.

Smiling amiably, Marshall directed him to a chair while he filled a tankard with ale. 'You are better off in here than with Brinkes, anyway. The man is a brute, and I am sure he has killed people. He has that look about him.'

'Then why do you let him in?'

Marshall's expression was pained. 'Because he is with them upstairs. He and his cronies act like guard dogs, and oust anyone who tries to come in while they are here – I do my best to reach visitors first, to eject them more politely, but I do not always succeed.'

Chaloner was intrigued. What dark business had Harley and his cronies embarked upon that entailed hiring a killer to keep it from prying eyes and ears? He doubted it would have anything to do with what had happened in Tangier, but he was keen to find out anyway. If nothing else, it might enable him to force them to answer questions, something he had been unable to do on *Eagle*.

'Who are "them upstairs"?' he asked.

'They call themselves the Piccadilly Company,' replied Marshall. Like many taverners, he loved to gossip. 'They rent the rooms on the first floor, and often gather to chat.'

'To chat about what?'

Marshall spread his hands. 'Who knows? I used to eavesdrop when that lovely Mr Jones was in charge – he is the one with the red boot-ribbons – although all he and his friends ever talked about was exporting glassware to New England. It was rather dull, to be frank. But then

93

others joined the Company, and *they* hired Brinkes to keep listeners away. So I have no idea what they discuss now.'

'What others?' asked Chaloner, a little taken aback by the taverner's bald admission that he liked to spy on his tenants.

Marshall lowered his voice. 'Well, a Dutch couple called Margareta and Cornelis Janszoon made an appearance today. I heard Margareta inform Mr Jones that her country will win the war we are about to wage.'

Chaloner was surprised: Hollanders tended to keep a low profile in London, on the grounds that they were currently Britain's most hated adversary. They certainly did not go around speculating on who might triumph in the looming confrontation.

'But they are not the worst by a long way,' Marshall went on. 'Last week, Harley, Newell and Reyner appeared. Now, I know Harley is a colonel, but he is no better than that monster Brinkes.'

'Why do you say that?' asked Chaloner, hoping that Marshall's loose tongue would not land him in trouble. Brinkes might reward him with the same fate as Captain Pepperell if he knew he was the subject of chatter, while Harley was unlikely to appreciate being discussed either.

'Because he is evil. Have you seen his eyes? They are like the devil's – blazing with hate and malice. But even *he* is not the worst. About a month ago someone even more dreadful joined. Namely Mr Fitzgerald.' Marshall hissed the name in a way that made it sound decidedly sinister.

'Not Fitzgerald the pirate?' asked Chaloner. Could this be George's last employer?

'He prefers the term privateer.' Marshall glanced around, as if he was afraid the man might appear and take umbrage. 'He lost a lot of money recently, and word is that he is working on plans to get some more. I am surprised at Mr Jones for letting the likes of *him* join the Piccadilly Company – Mr Jones is such a *nice* gentleman.'

'I do not suppose Fitzgerald is the one with the beard and the eye-patch, is he?' asked Chaloner, amused. The fellow could not have moulded himself more to the popular image of a pirate had he tried. He was lacking only the gold earrings.

Marshall nodded earnestly. 'And he has an unusually high voice. Listen, you can hear him now, singing. I wish he would not do it. It is horrible!'

As a lover of music, Chaloner had to agree. The sound that came from upstairs was redolent of tortured metal. It was treble in range, but there was a grating quality to it that was far from pleasant.

'You mentioned him losing a lot of money,' he said, eager to talk so that he would not have to listen. 'Do you know how?'

'His best ship sank during a storm. It was full of French gold, so King Louis arrested him and offered him a choice: repay every penny or execution. Fitzgerald had to sell everything he owned, and it broke him financially. *That* is why he is in London now – to recoup his losses by embarking on another business venture.'

At that moment there was a clatter of footsteps as the Piccadilly Company took its leave. Uncharitably, Chaloner wondered whether Fitzgerald's singing had brought the meeting to a premature end, because *he* would certainly not have wanted to be in the same room with it – it was bad enough from a distance. He leaned forward in his chair, so he could look up the hall and watch them file out.

They left in ones and twos again, with the Dutch woman – Margareta – directing who should go when.

Some elected to leave by the back door, which had Chaloner huddling towards the fire to conceal his face; but he need not have worried: no one gave him a second glance.

When everyone had gone, Chaloner claimed his gout had eased and he could walk. Marshall nodded genially and invited him to visit again, but preferably not in the mornings, which tended to be when Fitzgerald and his cronies were in conference. Evenings, he assured his visitor, would see him in far more conducive company.

For a moment, Chaloner thought the three scouts had disappeared, but then he saw them walking north. He assumed they were returning to the house from which they had emerged earlier, but they ducked into another tavern, with broken windows and a sign outside that said it was the Feathers. He followed, then went through an elaborate charade intended to make them think the encounter was coincidence.

'How nice to see you!' he exclaimed amiably. 'I did not think we would meet again.'

His cordiality was not reciprocated. Colonel Harley's pale 'devil' eyes were full of suspicion and Newell fingered his dagger. Reyner smiled, but it was a wary expression, devoid of friendliness.

'Neither did we,' said Harley, making it clear that he wished they had not.

'Well, I suppose it is no surprise to run into you here,' Chaloner blustered on, pretending not to notice their hostility. 'I distinctly recall you saying that you hailed from Piccadilly.'

He remembered no such thing, but his gambit worked. Pride suffused Reyner's face.

'I was born here, and my mother owns this tavern,' he said, and the smile became genuine. 'Meanwhile, Harley and his sister have taken up residence next door, and Newell lives across the street. We prefer Piccadilly's cleaner air to the foul vapours of the city.'

'Understandable.' Sensing the other two were on the verge of sending him packing, Chaloner sat down and began to talk quickly. 'There was a meeting of the Tangier Committee yesterday.'

Harley regarded him coldly, and Chaloner began to understand what Marshall had meant about the disconcerting quality of his eyes. 'So what? That town is no longer of interest to us.'

'The matter of Teviot's death was raised.' Chaloner hoped they were not in a position to know he was lying. 'There is going to be an official inquiry.'

Harley's gaze did not waver, although Reyner gulped hard enough to be audible. There was a thump, and Reyner leaned down to rub his leg – Newell had dealt him a warning kick under the table. Chaloner continued to meet Harley's gaze, but he had learned two things already: that Reyner was the weak link in the trio, and that they had reason to fear such an eventuality. It was more than he had gleaned during all the time he had spent on *Eagle* with them.

'What will such an inquiry entail?' asked Newell, when the silence following Chaloner's announcement had extended to the point where it was uncomfortable.

Chaloner shrugged. 'It will be conducted by lawyers from the Inns of Court, so you can be certain it will leave no stone unturned.'

Reyner groaned, then winced when Newell kicked him a second time.

'We have nothing to fear,' said Newell, more to Reyner than to Chaloner. 'Jews Hill was clear of Barbary corsairs when we surveyed it, but everyone knows how fast they can move. They waited until we left, and then they crept forward. What happened to Teviot was not our fault.'

'Impossible,' said Chaloner immediately. 'Jews Hill is surrounded by miles of open countryside, and ten thousand men could *never* lurk there without being seen. Ergo, they were in the woods when you said they were not, and anyone looking at a map will know it. The inquiry will want to know why you lied – why you killed Teviot and half his garrison.'

Harley's eyes flashed, and his hand went to the hilt of his sword. 'You play a dangerous game, accusing us of wilful murder.'

Chaloner smiled lazily. 'I have powerful friends at the Inns of Court – men who owe me favours. I may be able to influence the outcome of the inquiry. Would you like me to try?'

'In return for what?' asked Reyner, thus reinforcing Chaloner's suspicion that they had indeed given the hapless Teviot a deliberately misleading report.

'I will need to know the whole truth,' he went on, ignoring the question. 'Clearly, you had a reason for doing what you did. Explain it to me, and I will advise you how to—'

'We asked what you want in return,' interrupted Harley. His hand was still on his sword, but the knife that Chaloner always carried in his sleeve was at the ready, and it would be in the colonel's heart before his weapon was halfway out of its scabbard. Of course, he would be in trouble if the other two attacked at the same time.

'Information,' he replied, more to keep them talking than because it was true. 'Specifically the names of the thieves who are stealing Clarendon House's supplies. The culprits must use a cart, so the chances are that you have seen them passing.'

'We have not,' declared Reyner, before the others could speak. 'All Piccadilly is talking about those burglaries, but none of us have seen anything. It is a mystery. The villains must travel down St James's Street, because they certainly do not come this way.'

Newell sneered. 'I would not tell you even if we did know their names, because I cannot abide that fat, greedy old Clarendon, and his palace is an abomination. Besides, we have nothing to fear from the Teviot affair, because Fitzgerald said—'

This time it was Harley doing the kicking under the table, and Chaloner frowned. He had assumed that the curious happenings in the Crown were unrelated to the Teviot massacre, but Newell's remark made him reconsider. Fitzgerald was a pirate, and they operated by the dozen around Tangier, so perhaps there *was* a connection.

'If you cannot give me information, I will settle for an introduction instead,' he said, improvising wildly. 'To Fitzgerald. He may be interested in a certain business proposition I have to offer.'

'He will not,' stated Harley firmly. 'And you would be well advised to keep your mouth shut about Tangier, because you know nothing about it. If you start spreading rumours, all I can say is that you will regret it most bitterly.'

Chaloner could think of no way to prolong the discussion further, so was forced to take his leave. He went back to the Gaming House and stood in its doorway, hidden in the shadows. It was not long before the three scouts emerged from the Feathers. They were arguing, Harley and Newell muttering in fierce whispers at Reyner, who kept shaking his head. Eventually, they parted: Harley and Newell turned north, while Reyner began to walk towards the city alone.

Chaloner followed Reyner and caught up with him near Charing Cross, hauling him into a narrow alley that ran between two tall houses. Reyner scowled when he saw who had ambushed him, but the sly, calculating expression in his eyes said he was not particularly surprised to have been waylaid.

'Who are you really?' he asked. 'Newell thinks you work for Spymaster Williamson, while Harley says you are just a greedy opportunist out for his own ends. But I suspect you are from the Tangier Committee, and that you have been charged to learn the truth about Teviot.'

'Then you had better be honest,' said Chaloner, deciding to let him assume what he liked. 'The murder of five hundred soldiers is a serious matter. A hanging matter.'

'Four hundred and seventy-two,' countered Reyner, as if it made a difference. 'But why does the Tangier Committee care? Everyone knows that Teviot was a corrupt fool who should never have been made governor, and all the men have been replaced. Besides, it happened months ago.'

Chaloner regarded him with contempt. 'They can never be "replaced". Nor did they deserve to be hacked to pieces.'

Reyner looked away. 'It was not our fault that Teviot allowed himself to be ambushed.'

'Of course it was your fault! He relied on you to provide him with accurate information, and you betrayed that trust by feeding him lies. What I cannot understand is why – *why* did you arrange the slaughter of your own countrymen?'

Reyner had the decency to wince. 'It is complicated, and will take a long time to explain.'

'Then you had better make a start.'

'I cannot – at least, not now. Harley will be suspicious if I am gone too long.'

'I do not care whether he is suspicious or not.'

'Well, I do,' snapped Reyner, regaining some of his composure. 'So meet me in the Gaming House gardens at ten o'clock tonight. I will tell you everything then. But in return I want a written pardon from the government – someone from the Tangier Committee should be able to organise it – and two hundred pounds in gold coins.'

Chaloner raised his eyebrows. 'Anything else?'

Reyner glowered. 'Do not judge me, Chaloner. I will not be safe once I tell my story – I shall be a marked man, and a lot of powerful people will want me dead. I need that money to disappear.'

'Why should—'

'I will explain everything tonight. But bring the pardon and the money, or I am not telling you anything. And for Christ's sake, make sure you are not followed.'

Chaloner drew his dagger. 'I do not like this plan. You will tell me your story now.'

Reyner's gaze was defiant. 'What will you do? Kill me? Then you will never have the truth. And I am not doing this for myself, anyway – my mother is old and I need to protect her, which I cannot do without funds. Now let me go before you put both our lives in danger.'

He shoved Chaloner away and marched towards the end of the alley. He looked carefully in both directions before slipping out and resuming his journey towards the city.

Chaloner was thoughtful as he walked down King Street, trying to imagine what plan could have required the murder of so many men. Newell's slip in the Feathers said Fitzgerald was involved, which in turn said the Piccadilly Company warranted further investigation. But what could its members be doing? How had the deaths of Teviot and his garrison benefited them? No answers came, and he supposed he would have to wait until he met Reyner later.

He turned his mind to the Queen's letter, and went directly to her apartments. He was pleasantly surprised when he was refused entry – security was so lax at White Hall that he was under the impression that anyone could gain access to anywhere he fancied.

'Her Majesty is vulnerable,' explained the captain. His name was Appleby, a grizzled veteran with a beard. 'People do not like her because she is Catholic and barren, but the King will be vexed if she is harmed, so we cannot let anyone inside unless he has an appointment.'

'How do I make an appointment?' asked Chaloner.

'*You* do not! She is the Queen, man! People cannot wander in off the streets to pass the time of day with her. Besides, she has ladies in there, and the Court rakes are always trying to slip past me to get at them. It is quite a task to keep them out, I can tell you!'

Chaloner knew he could gain access to the Queen if he wanted. Fortunately for her, most people did not possess his particular array of talents – or a wife who was one of Her Majesty's ladies-in-waiting, for that matter. Prudently, he changed the subject, and asked what happened when letters were delivered. Appleby explained that he handed all such missives to the Queen's private secretary. Hyde opened everything she received, and although he claimed to stay out of her personal correspondence, it was a lie.

'He likes to know what is going on in every aspect of her life,' said Appleby disapprovingly. 'I cannot bear the odious prig. He is worse than his father for overbearing manners.'

From what little he had seen of Hyde, Chaloner was inclined to concur.

'Have you heard the news?' Appleby asked, changing the subject abruptly. 'About Proby?'

'Peter Proby?' asked Chaloner, recalling what he been told the previous day – that the Adventurers had been obliged to call an emergency meeting because Proby had disappeared.

'He has been found,' said Appleby. 'Well, *most* of him has been found.'

Chaloner regarded him uneasily. 'What do you mean?'

'He threw himself off the roof of St Paul's Cathedral, and landed with such force that parts of him have yet to be discovered. What is the world coming to, when such terrible things happen?'

'What indeed?' murmured Chaloner.

When he had finished with Appleby, Chaloner spent the rest of the morning and the first part of the afternoon questioning other members of the Queen's household, but learned nothing he did not know already – that Her Majesty was unpopular, and so any number of people might have sent malicious letters to see her in trouble. It was a depressing state of affairs, and when he eventually left White Hall he was tired and dispirited.

His gloom intensified when he visited St James's Fields, an area that had been open countryside at the Restoration, but that was now the domain of developers. There were several such sites in the city, but this was the nearest to Clarendon House. It did not take him long to realise that even if the Earl's bricks were finding their way there, he would never prove it. Dozens of carts kept the workforce supplied with materials, from hundreds of different sources. Moreover, each house had been tendered out to a different builder, and it would take weeks – perhaps months – to track down the provenance of all their supplies.

He persisted, though, and the sun was setting when he was finally compelled to admit that he was wasting his time. As he walked along The Strand it occurred to him that he had not eaten all day, so he stopped to buy a meat pie from a street vendor. It was cold, greasy and filled with something he supposed might have once belonged to a cow, although he did not like to imagine what part. He ate it, then heartily wished he had not when it lay dense and heavy in his stomach.

Feeling the need to dislodge it with something hot, he went to his favourite coffee house – the Rainbow on Fleet Street – entering its steamy fug with relief after the chill of outside. Most of the regulars were there, enjoying a dish of the beverage that was currently very popular in London. He sat on a bench and listened to the chatter around him, breathing in deeply of the comfortingly familiar aroma of burned beans, pipe smoke and wet mud trampled in from the road.

'What news?' called Farr, the owner, voicing the usual coffee-house greeting.

'The Portuguese ambassador enjoyed having dinner with the King,' offered Chaloner, repeating what he had read in the newsbook earlier. No one looked very impressed, so he added, 'Afterwards, he skipped all the way from White Hall to St Paul's, and one member of the Privy Council was so impressed by his elegance that he has engaged him as a dancing master.'

He expected everyone to know he was being facetious, but Farr nodded sagely. 'The Portuguese are a strange nation. I am not surprised that one of them knows how to gyrate over long distances.'

'*The Intelligencer* did not report the prancing, though,' said a young printer named Fabian Stedman, who spent so much time in the Rainbow that Chaloner wondered whether he had a home of his own – or a place of work, for that matter. 'I do not know how it dares call itself a newsbook, because it never contains anything interesting.'

'Well, what do you expect?' asked the Rector of St Dunstan-in-the-West. Chaloner liked Joseph Thompson, a kindly, liberal man with a conscience. 'The government is afraid that we will embark on another civil war if it tells us too much – this time to rid ourselves of King *and* Parliament, given that neither have proved themselves worthy to rule.'

'There was a fascinating piece about a fish caught in the River Severn last week, though,' said Farr. 'Apparently, it was of great size and uncouth shape.'

'Does that count as foreign news or domestic?' mused Stedman. 'The Severn is in Wales, which is a distant land full of heathens.'

'Nonsense,' argued Thompson. 'I have been to Wales, and it is very nice.'

'The farthest I have ever been is Chelsey,' confided Farr. 'And that was more than foreign enough for me! I was worried about being set on by footpads every inch of the way. Life is very dangerous outside the city.'

'Have you ever travelled, Chaloner?' asked Stedman. 'You hold very controversial opinions, so I imagine you have. For example, you are always telling us that it is wrong to go to war with the Dutch, when the rest of the country cannot wait to start fighting.'

'Hear, hear!' cheered Farr. 'I am thoroughly looking forward to trouncing the Hollanders at sea, and stealing all their trade routes.'

'War with the Dutch is not a good idea,' said Chaloner tiredly. He had lost count of the times he had tried to explain the reality of the situation to them. 'They have faster ships, better-trained sailors, and mountains of materiel that will allow them to stay at sea for months. We do not.'

'He is right,' agreed Thompson. 'Fighting Hollanders would be madness. Besides, they are a Protestant nation that was kind to the King when he was in exile. What purpose will conflict serve?'

'They are taking slaves from Africa to work on their sugar plantations,' argued Farr. 'When we defeat them, *we* can do it instead, so *we* shall have cheap sugar – as much as we can eat.'

'Excellent!' declared Stedman. 'Coffee is a lot nicer with sugar.'

Chaloner wondered whether that was why he had yet to acquire a taste for coffee: he did not use sugar, as a silent protest against the plantations. He knew his self-denial made no difference to the slaves, and it was impossible to avoid sugar in all its forms, but he persisted anyway.

'The slave trade is a vicious, despicable business, and any good Christian should agree with me,' declared Thompson, uncharacteristically vehement. 'It is evil.'

'It is a matter of commerce,' argued Farr. 'We need affordable sugar, and slaves are the best way to get it. Morality has nothing to do with—'

'Of course it does!' cried Thompson. 'How can you condone snatching men, women and children from their homes, and forcing them to work for no pay, just so you can have sweet coffee?'

'If I were an African, I would accept it as my lot,' declared Farr. 'The wealthy and powerful have always dominated the weak. God made us that way.'

'He most certainly did not,' yelled Thompson, outraged. 'And if you ever say such a wicked thing again, I will . . . I will . . . well, I do not know what I shall do, but you will be sorry.'

Everyone stared at him. Thompson had never lost his temper with Farr before.

'He is right,' said Chaloner in the silence that followed. He rarely joined coffee-house debates, because he disliked the attention it earned him. However, this was a matter about which he felt strongly. 'The slave trade is an abhorrent business.'

'How do you know?' pounced Stedman. 'You appeared last week all brown and healthy after months of absence – which you still have not explained. You were clearly in warmer climes, so where did you go? Barbados? Jamaica? Is that why you hold forth about the slave trade?'

Chaloner was aware that everyone was regarding him with interest, and wished he had held his tongue.

'Tangier,' he replied, supposing there was no harm in telling them. His mission had not been secret, and an evasive answer might be more trouble than it was worth.

'How unpleasant,' shuddered Farr. 'I understand it is a vile place, full of snakes and swamps.'

'No, that is New England,' countered Stedman. 'Tangier is in the middle of a desert. The Portuguese were delighted to foist it on us, because it is hot and nasty. Is that not right, Chaloner?'

'It is certainly hot,' replied Chaloner, wondering how the Rainbow's patrons came by such wildly inaccurate information. How could Stedman think Tangier was in the *middle* of a desert when it was being fortified a sea port?

'I have been told it will be a useful slaving centre one day,' said Farr. 'But Thompson is glaring, so we had better discuss something else. How about this Collection of Curiosities near St Paul's, which is the talk of the city? Has anyone been to see it? Apparently, it has an "Ant Beare" from Brazil on display. Where is Brazil, exactly? Is it anywhere near China?'

While Stedman obliged him with a lesson in geography, Thompson gave Chaloner a strained smile. 'I am glad *one* of my acquaintances has proper views on the slave trade. I preached against it in my sermon on Sunday, but I do not think anyone listened. I have a bad feeling that we will follow the Portuguese into the business, simply because there is money to be made.'

'Portugal is not a major factor in the trade any longer. Holland has supremacy now.'

'But the Portuguese *do* continue to take slaves to Brazil,' countered Thompson. 'You should not ignore their role in this evil simply because the Dutch have surpassed them in wickedness. More to the point, did you know that the Adventurers transported more than three thousand people to Caribbean plantations last year? It is disgraceful, barbaric and . . . and *wicked*! And it is not as if the Adventurers need more money. They are all fabulously rich already.'

'Wealth seems to be one of those commodities that no one ever admits to having enough of,' said Chaloner. 'The more someone has, the more he itches to acquire.'

'Yes,' said Thompson caustically. 'In my line of work, we call it greed.'

Night had fallen by the time Chaloner left the coffee house, a set of carefully forged documents in his pocket for Reyner – he had borrowed pen and paper from Farr, although it had not been easy to dissuade the other patrons from trying to see what he was doing. Many other pedestrians had hired linkmen – carriers of pitch torches – to light their way, especially north of Charing Cross, where fewer houses meant it was much darker. Chaloner did not bother, although it meant he was in danger of stumbling in potholes or treading in something unpleasant. There was another peril, too: two louts approached him with the clear intent of demanding his purse, but they backed away when his hand dropped to the hilt of his sword and they saw he was able to defend himself.

He reached the Crown and spent a few moments studying it from the shadows cast by the Gaming House opposite. Lights blazed on the ground floor, and a lamp was lit in the attic, but the rooms in between were in darkness. He crossed the road and entered the tavern. It was full and very noisy; Landlord Marshall moved between the tables with a genial smile and amiable conversation.

Still happy to gossip, Marshall informed Chaloner that the Piccadilly Company had permanent hire of the first floor, while the two storeys above it were rented by tenants, namely Pratt and a woman for whom he seemed to hold a fatherly regard. Chaloner sat for a while, watching and listening, and when he was sure no one was looking, he slipped up the stairs.

The Piccadilly Company's chambers were locked, but it did not take him long to pick the mechanism and let himself inside. He lit a candle from the embers of the fire, shielding it with his hand so it would not be seen from outside.

The first room was an elegantly appointed parlour, with wood-panelled walls and a finely plastered ceiling. Its only furniture comprised a large table of polished oak, with benches set around it. He examined them minutely, then did the same for the panelling, floorboards and chimney, but if there were secret hiding places for documents, then he could not find them. The only evidence that papers had been present was in the hearth, where some had been reduced to ashes.

The second room was a pantry, indicating that refreshments were sometimes served, but a search of it yielded nothing. He returned to the parlour and sat on one of the benches, wondering what it was that Fitzgerald the pirate, the Dutch Janszoons, the nice Mr Jones, the Portuguese man, the three scouts and their cronies discussed. It was clearly something they wanted kept secret, or they would not have hired Brinkes to stand guard downstairs.

Could they be plotting rebellion? There had been dozens of uprisings since the King had reclaimed his crown – by Parliamentarians unwilling to accept that the

Republican experiment was over, and by fanatics who believed the throne should have been offered to Jesus instead. They occurred so frequently that the newsbooks no longer bothered to report them, and the only person remotely interested was Spymaster Williamson, whose duty it was to suppress them.

But Chaloner did not think Harley and his fellow scouts were the kind of men who would care about politics – they were too selfish to risk themselves for a principle. However, Fitzgerald had lost his fortune in a storm, and Landlord Marshall believed he intended to make himself wealthy again. Somehow, money seemed a far more likely explanation than insurrection. But what were they planning, exactly? And how did the Tangier massacre fit into it?

As sitting in the parlour was not providing answers, Chaloner stood to leave. He glanced at the ashes in the hearth and, out of desperation, poked among them until he recovered a fragment that had escaped the flames. He tweaked it out, but it had been written in cipher:

iws	ubj	kwy	jvv	rzv	wiy	evj
jvb	rdi	xlp	ell	qcm	ftq	xds
cmr	zva	knt	elq	pad	dpm	znx
pdk	yto	jgw	pup	qpj	rbh	tjo
ufz	moq	iqq	ylz	hjh	ibj	wiq
iaq	oqi	jhn	rtr	shw	qsi	jbx
egq	yin	udh	azd	hag	fcm	dyp
ivy	am					

He shoved it in his pocket, thinking it told him one thing for certain: that if the Piccadilly Company was sending or receiving coded messages and then burning

111

them, it *was* embroiled in something untoward. It was not something that honest people tended to do.

He relocked the door and was about to walk down the stairs when he heard someone coming up them. The person was carrying a lamp, and it cast a shadow on the wall. Chaloner froze in alarm when he recognised the unmistakable bulk of Brinkes – he was about to be caught prying by a man who made his living by violence and murder.

Chapter 4

Chaloner was reluctant to fight Brinkes, because he did not want the Piccadilly Company to know it was being monitored. Unfortunately, there was no time to pick the lock on the door again, so he ran silently up the stairs to the next floor. Not surprisingly, Pratt's rooms were locked, and as he bent to try the handle, his sword scraped against the wall. It was a careless mistake, and he heard Brinkes falter on the floor below. There was a brief pause and then footsteps as the man came to investigate.

With no other option, Chaloner continued upwards to the attic. Luckily, that door was open, so he stepped through it quickly.

The woman sitting in the window spun around in alarm. She was pretty, with brown hair and clear skin, and she recognised him as the man who had seen her watching the street because she smiled. He interpreted it as a sign that she would be willing to help him, so he put his finger to his lips, and had only just managed to duck behind the bed before the door flew open.

Brinkes stood there, one meaty hand clutching a lamp and the other holding a dagger. When he began to stride towards the woman with barefaced menace, Chaloner swore softly, seeing he would have to do battle after all. He started to stand, but sank down again when she began to speak.

'Do you have a dog?' she asked in a curiously childish voice. She beamed at Brinkes, an expression that bespoke vacuity, and Chaloner realised with a start that there was something amiss with her wits. 'James has a dog. A black one. Have you seen it? It is missing.'

'Your husband is dead,' said Brinkes, stopping in his tracks to regard her warily. 'And so is his dog. Do you not remember being told? But never mind that. Did anyone just come in here?'

'I like visitors,' declared the woman, rocking back and forth. 'But I do not have many.'

'Christ,' muttered Brinkes. Like many folk, he was unsure how to deal with disturbed minds. Unsettled, he began to back away. 'Lock the door when I have gone. There are a lot of unpleasant people in this part of the city, and you do not want them coming in.'

The door closed, but Chaloner waited until Brinkes's footsteps had gone all the way to the ground floor before moving. He stood and smiled gratefully at the woman.

'I like visitors,' she announced brightly. 'My name is Ruth Elliot, and my husband is called James. He has a dog, and it is missing. Have you seen it?'

Chaloner frowned. James Elliot was the name of the man who had fought and killed Cave. 'When did your husband die, mistress? Yesterday?'

'He has not been to see me all day, and my brother told me he was dead.' Then her troubled expression lifted, and she laughed. 'But it cannot be true, because he was alive on Sunday.'

A miniature line-engraving had pride of place on the table, so Chaloner picked it up. The likeness had been made when Elliot was younger, but the eyes and black wig were the same. Also, Lester had mentioned a Ruth who would be heartbroken if Elliot were harmed, although Chaloner doubted it was the shock of her spouse's death that had turned her wits: the array of medicines on the cabinet, and the dolls lined up on the bed, suggested they had been awry for some time.

He regarded her thoughtfully. It was a curious coincidence that Elliot's wife just happened to live in the place that was the object of one of his three investigations. Or was it? There was a connection of sorts, in that Elliot had killed Cave, a man who had travelled home from Tangier on the same ship as the three scouts. And Harley, Newell and Reyner were involved with the Piccadilly Company, which met downstairs.

'You watch the people who use the rooms below you,' he said, coming to kneel next to her and trying to gauge her level of intelligence. 'What do you see?'

'I do not like them,' she declared. 'James said he will stop them from coming, but he forgets.'

'What do they do?'

'They talk,' replied Ruth, pouting. 'They discuss gravel.'

'Gravel?' echoed Chaloner warily.

'I do not like gravel. I fell over in some once, and it hurt my knee. Look.'

She whipped up her skirts and showed Chaloner a minute scar. Gently, he pulled them down again, hoping she would not do the same to Brinkes, because the leg was shapely.

'Who are the people you watch? Do you know their names?'

'Oh, yes! Mr Fitzgerald the pirate. And Mr Jones with the red ribbons. And Mr Harley. And Mr Reyner. And Mr Newell.' She sang the names rather oddly.

'What about the others?'

Ruth shook her head and shrank away from him, her expression darkening. 'They frighten me, and my brother told me that they killed James's dog. But I do not believe that people would kill dogs – it must have run away. Have you seen it?'

'Do not look out of the window any more,' advised Chaloner, standing up. 'These people will not like being monitored.'

'But James told me to do it,' said Ruth, wide-eyed. 'He told me it was important.'

Chaloner was disgusted that Elliot should have encouraged such a dangerous habit, and wondered what he had been thinking. He took his leave, first ensuring that she locked the door after him, then exited the Crown by its back door, to avoid Brinkes, who was lurking at the front one.

Once outside, he aimed for the Gaming House. It was far earlier than the appointed ten o'clock, but he wanted to watch Reyner arrive, to ensure he was alone. He fingered the papers he had forged earlier, which he hoped would be convincing enough to persuade Reyner that a pardon and two hundred pounds would be his in exchange for information. He felt no guilt over the deception: anyone complicit in the deaths of Teviot's garrison – and considered them 'replaceable' – deserved no better.

Because it was a cold night, the grounds were deserted. Moving silently, Chaloner made his way to the line of trees that divided the bowling green from the formal gardens, intending to use them as cover while he awaited Reyner's arrival.

He was almost there when he saw a dark shape lying in one of the rose beds. Abandoning all efforts at stealth, because he knew it no longer mattered, he ran towards it. He reached the inert form and felt for a life-beat, not surprised when there was none. He rolled the body over. Reyner's throat had been cut.

A brief search of the grounds revealed that Reyner's killer had long gone, so Chaloner returned to stare at the body, disgusted with himself for not pressing the scout to talk earlier. He wondered how he was going to find out what had happened to Teviot now, because Harley and Newell would be far more difficult to crack. He sighed, supposing he would have to pursue the charade of the fictitious official inquiry.

Unwilling to answer the questions that would arise from informing the Gaming House owner that there was a corpse among his roses, Chaloner left, assuming the body would be found the following morning. He was wrong.

He had taken only a few steps along the Haymarket, eager now for home and bed, when there was a shrill shriek, followed by a lot of shouting. Because it would have looked suspicious to continue walking in the opposite direction, he joined the throng that poured into the garden. The alarm had been raised by a serving maid who had gone for a tryst with a card player, and had been distressed to find her favourite flower bed occupied by a cadaver.

By the time Chaloner arrived, torches had been lit,

allowing the full extent of Reyner's injury to be seen. Whoever had cut his throat had used enough force almost to sever his head from his body. It was a vicious attack, and Chaloner wondered who had done it. Harley or Newell, because they knew their comrade was about to betray them? Or Brinkes?

The two scouts were among the crowd. The faces of both were white, and Newell was leaning heavily on Harley's shoulder. Chaloner eased back into the shadows, reluctant for them to see him, lest they assumed he was responsible. They did not linger long, though, and slouched away when the spectators began to reveal what they knew of the victim.

'His name is Reyner, and he lives in that shabby old Feathers tavern,' the serving wench was saying. She added rather sneeringly, 'With his mother.'

Chaloner brightened. Perhaps Reyner's dam would know what her son had embroiled himself in. He loitered a while longer, hoping to learn more by listening to the excited speculations, but it soon became clear that no one knew anything useful. He left and aimed for the decrepit Feathers, arriving to see lamps lit: Mrs Reyner already had visitors. He crouched down outside and pretended to fiddle with the buckle on his shoe, pleased when he heard the discussion within emanating through several conveniently cracked and broken windows.

'Reyner was a good man,' Newell was saying, his voice tight with fury. 'We will hunt down who killed him, and slit *his* throat.'

'Thank you kindly.' Mrs Reyner's voice was slurred, but Chaloner did not think it was from shock at the news she had just received. 'Pour me another drink, will you? My nerves are all aquiver.'

'It was Chaloner,' said Harley softly. 'It is too much of a coincidence that he should start asking questions about Teviot, and within hours Reyner is dead. He must have thought Reyner was a soft touch and slit his throat when he discovered otherwise.'

'Chaloner wants to gain our favour, not kill us,' argued Newell. 'He is not the culprit. And it cannot be anyone from the Piccadilly Company, so that only leaves one set of suspects: our old adversaries. They killed Reyner because of what happened to Proby.'

'You may be right,' conceded Harley. 'They certainly hate us.'

'They do,' said Newell tightly. 'And when I find out which of them was responsible, I will kill him. I swear it on Reyner's soul.'

At that point Mrs Reyner knocked over her cup, and there was a fuss as the mess was mopped up. Chaloner frowned his confusion. The only Proby he knew was the Adventurer who had recently jumped from the roof of St Paul's Cathedral. Was Newell referring to him? But why would he be an enemy of the Piccadilly Company? And who were the 'old adversaries'?

He continued to listen, but the scouts and Reyner's mother had repositioned themselves after the spillage and he could no longer hear them clearly. As there was only so long he could pretend to be adjusting his shoe, he stood and began to walk home. He would have to interview Mrs Reyner the following day, when she was alone.

He was relieved that Newell had convinced Harley of his innocence, because it would have been inconvenient to dodge murderous attacks when he had so much else to do. But Reyner's death was a blow, and he could not

119

escape the feeling that it was his fault. He turned south when he reached Charing Cross, but it had been a frustratingly trying day, and he felt the need to be alone, away from the inquisitive stares of the servants in Tothill Street. He retraced his steps, intending to sleep at Long Acre instead.

Long Acre had once been a fashionable part of the city, with residents that included Oliver Cromwell and the poet John Dryden, but standards had slipped since the Restoration. Most of the elegant people had moved to more salubrious lodgings, and the place was now given over to coach-makers and brothels. It suited Chaloner perfectly. First, it was usually busy, even at night, which meant he was less likely to be noticed – always an important consideration for a spy. Second, it was convenient for White Hall. And third, Landlord Lamb only cared about the rent being paid on time, and never asked questions about his tenants' business.

The house was a four-storey affair with a cellar, and was neither respectable nor notably seedy. The ground floor and rear garden were occupied by a coach-maker, while the first floor was home to Lamb and his wife. An old Cromwellian major named John Stokes lived in the rooms above, and Chaloner was right at the top.

The attic comprised three tiny chambers, and had the advantage of being reached by two separate staircases. It was also possible to climb out of the windows to the roof next door, further reducing his chances of being trapped. There was a bed and a chest in one chamber; the second was a cosy parlour where he kept his best bass viol; and the third was a cupboard-like pantry.

He was too restless to sleep, so he took his viol and began to play, a sad, lilting melody by Schütz, which matched his mood. He felt the music begin to calm him, and although he knew he should work on the cipher he had found, he continued to play until he could barely keep his eyes open. Then he lay on the bed, fully clothed, and fell into a deep, dreamless sleep.

A loud clatter in the street below woke him the following morning. He was off the bed with his sword in his hand before he was fully cognisant, but soon learned that the noise was nothing to concern him. Red kites liked to range themselves along the roof, from where they swooped down to pick juicy morsels from the filth of the road, and one had dislodged a tile. It had landed on a glazier's cart, making short work of the finished wares. Needless to say, the glazier was furious, and an argument ensued when he began to demand compensation from an indignantly defensive Landlord Lamb.

Chaloner ignored the clamouring voices as he fetched water from the butt in the hallway. He washed and shaved, then donned a heavily laced shirt, breeches with enough ribbon to satisfy even the most particular of critics, and a green long-coat with buttons to the knees. A white 'falling band' – a piece of linen that fell across the chest like a bib – completed the outfit.

He went to White Hall first, to report to the Earl. The dough-faced Sergeant Wright was on duty at the Great Gate, bags under eyes that were rimmed red with tiredness.

'Bad night?' asked Chaloner, as Wright stepped in front of him to prevent him from passing.

Wright spat. 'Your Earl has a vicious tongue. He refused to pay me for the night before last, just because his bricks went missing. It meant I had to stay awake all

121

last night, to make sure it did not happen again. It was damned hard work!'

'Doing the job you have been paid for can be taxing.'

'Too right,' agreed Wright, the irony sailing over his head. 'I usually find somewhere to snatch a doze, but I did not dare last night, not after what he said to me. Still, I shall manage a nap later this morning. Have you heard the latest news, by the way? About the missing Adventurer?'

'I thought Proby had been found,' said Chaloner. 'After he jumped off St Paul's Cathedral.'

Wright leaned closer, treating Chaloner to a waft of second-hand onions. 'They are worried about another of their members now. Mr Grey set out to visit the Hercules' Pillars Alley brothel last night, but he never arrived.'

'Perhaps he found somewhere better to take his pleasure along the way.'

'There is nowhere better.' The sergeant sighed ruefully. 'Not that the likes of you and I will ever see it, of course. It is an exclusive establishment, open only to barons or the extremely wealthy.'

Chaloner did not tell him that he had visited that particular bordello on numerous occasions, because he was friends with its owner.

'I suppose I can let you pass,' said Wright, looking Chaloner up and down critically, although he was deluding himself if he thought he could stop him. 'You are almost respectable today.'

Once inside, Chaloner walked across the Great Court towards the Earl's offices. In the Privy Garden a group of drunken courtiers, which included the Earl's debauched kinsman Brodrick, were throwing pebbles at Lady

122

Castlemaine's windows, hoping to secure her attention. There was a cheer when she appeared in a dangerously low-cut robe.

'I am going to tell my father about Cousin Brodrick. His behaviour is disgraceful!'

Chaloner turned to see Hyde standing there, although he could not help but wonder whether the younger man's disapproval stemmed from jealousy – the Lady was obviously delighted to flirt with Brodrick, but she had not included Hyde in her sultry salutations.

'I was hoping to catch you today, Chaloner,' Hyde went on, reluctantly tearing his attention from the Lady's generous display of bosom. 'I found another letter yesterday. This time it was in the hearth, and you can see it is singed. Obviously, the Queen tried to burn it but failed to ensure it was done properly.'

Chaloner took it from him and saw the edge was indeed charred. The writing was identical to the previous missive, and confidently informed the recipient that Pratt would die on St Frideswide's Day, when the whole Catholic world would rejoice at his demise. Chaloner handed it back.

'Let me guess: it was placed at the front of the hearth, where it would be seen. And it happened to be there at a time when you were the one most likely to notice it.'

'It was in a prominent position,' Hyde acknowledged stiffly. 'And being a man of habit, I always go to the hearth the moment I arrive at work. But it was *not* put there for me to find. The Queen is dabbling in dark business, and the sooner we dissuade her from such foolishness by catching her confederates, the sooner she will be safe. Have you unveiled them yet?'

'No,' replied Chaloner. 'But—'

'Then I suggest you refrain from regaling me with unfounded opinions and do your job,' interrupted Hyde coldly. His glower intensified. 'My father should never have appointed a spy – especially one with Parliamentarian leanings.'

He stalked away before Chaloner could inform him that he no longer had leanings one way or the other, being heartily disillusioned with both sides.

The new letter was worrying. It suggested that someone was determined to see the Queen in trouble, and that whoever it was had slipped past Captain Appleby to put his nasty note in a place where he knew it would be discovered by the credulous Hyde. But there were still seven days before the Feast of St Frideswide, so there was ample time to explore the matter. At least, Chaloner hoped so.

When Chaloner arrived at the Earl's offices, it was to find Chief Usher Dugdale there, rifling through the drawers of a cabinet. Edgeman the secretary was sitting at the desk, also rummaging, while Kipps stood in the window. The Seal Bearer had placed himself so as to secure an unimpeded view of the Lady in her flimsy gown.

'Where have *you* been?' Dugdale demanded, using anger to mask his chagrin at being caught pawing through his master's belongings. 'I told you to report to me every day, and you failed to appear yesterday.'

'Actually,' countered Chaloner, 'what you said was that you wanted to know my every move. It is not the same thing.'

'You insolent dog!' snarled Dugdale. 'How dare you talk back to me! Do you—'

Chaloner stepped towards him, fast enough to make

him cower involuntarily. 'Please do not call me names. Unless you want to repeat them on the duelling field?'

'Duelling is illegal,' blustered Dugdale. 'And I do not break the law.'

'It is only illegal if you are caught,' said Kipps, tearing his eyes away from the Lady and turning towards them. 'Do you need a second, Chaloner?'

'No, he does not,' cried Dugdale, alarmed. 'The Earl expects high standards of his gentlemen, and you will never coerce *me* into behaving disreputably.'

Chaloner looked pointedly at the recently searched cabinet. 'You need no coercion from me.'

'Tell me what you intend to do today,' ordered Dugdale, immediately going on the offensive. 'I shall then decide whether to give my permission.'

Chaloner had no intention of confiding his plans. 'It depends on what the Earl says after he has heard my report. Where is he?'

It was Edgeman who replied. He smirked spitefully. 'You have had a wasted journey. He will come late today, because he is going to watch the King dine at the Banqueting House. I might join him there. It is always an entertaining spectacle.'

'Is it?' Chaloner had been once, but had failed to understand the attraction in watching someone else eat. It was not as if His Majesty hurled food around or told clever jokes while he feasted. But it was a popular pastime for many, and the Earl rarely refused an invitation.

'You are incapable of appreciating the finer things of life,' sneered Edgeman. 'Because—'

'The same might be said of you two,' interrupted Kipps sharply. 'I invite you to spend an evening at the best brothel in London, and what do you do? Decline!'

125

'Because *we* do not indulge in sordid wickedness,' said Edgeman loftily. 'Do we, Dugdale?'

'No,' agreed Dugdale piously. 'Only low-mannered scum frequent brothels.'

'The King is a regular at this one.' Kipps smiled rather wolfishly. 'Shall I tell him your opinion then? I am sure he will be interested to hear what you think of him.'

He spun on his heel and stalked out. Chaloner followed, wondering what it was about White Hall that seemed to attract such dreadful people. He was sure the foreign courts in which he had worked had not housed such a profusion of them.

'Baiting them gives me great pleasure,' confided Kipps, once they were out of earshot. 'Yet I cannot help but wonder whether it is expensive fun. We shall never have the better of a man like Dugdale, because he is so damned slippery.'

'Why were they searching the Earl's drawers?' asked Chaloner.

'Were they? I did not notice. I try not to look in their direction whenever possible, especially Dugdale's. The very sight of him stirs me to violent impulses.'

'You like him well enough to invite him to brothels.'

'Only because I knew he would never accept,' replied Kipps, with a conspiratorial wink.

The first thing Chaloner did after leaving White Hall was to visit Mrs Reyner. It was a pleasant day, and the sun had turned the sky pink in the east. He breathed in deeply, then coughed as grit caught at the back of his throat. As always, London was swathed in a yellow-black haze, from its citizens lighting sea-coal fires for heat, hot water and cooking.

When he reached the Feathers, he listened carefully outside, to ensure Harley and Newell had not kept her company overnight. When he was sure she was alone, he knocked, and when the door was answered, he was hard-pressed to prevent himself from recoiling at the stench of wine on her breath. Clearly, she was a woman who liked to give her sorrows a good dousing.

'My son is dead,' she said, sharply. 'And if he owed you money, then that is too bad, because I am not responsible for his debts.'

'I heard what happened to him,' said Chaloner gently. 'I am sorry.'

She softened at the kindness in his voice. 'Well? What do you want? It is cruel to keep an old woman on her doorstep in the chill of the morning.'

'Then I had better come in,' said Chaloner, stepping past her and entering a dingy hall.

She made no complaint, and only shuffled to a pantry, where she poured herself a generous measure of wine. Her movements were uncoordinated, which he supposed was to his advantage: if she were drunk, she was less likely to wonder why he was interrogating her.

'You must have been very proud of your son,' he began. 'Being a scout in Tangier.'

'Spying on people was what he did best.' She nodded. 'He was always good at it, even as a child. But he did not come home a happy man. He was frightened.'

'Frightened of what?'

'He would not tell me, although he did mention that we were going to be rich. Of course, that will not happen now.' Bitterly, she took a gulp from her mug.

'No? Surely Harley and Newell will see you are looked after – for his sake?'

'Those scum! They are furious that he is dead, and promised vengeance. But vengeance does not put wine on the table, does it? I want money!'

'He belonged to a group called the Piccadilly Company,' said Chaloner, a little taken aback by her brazen rapacity, especially as Reyner professed to have been fond of her. Naively, he had expected the sentiment to have been reciprocated. 'Do you know what—'

Mrs Reyner sneered. 'That Brilliana is a member! She is Colonel Harley's sister, and an evil witch. The others I do not know. Well, there is Fitzgerald – the one-eyed sailor with the large orange beard – but we do not talk about him, of course.'

'Why not?' asked Chaloner, aware that her voice had dropped to a whisper.

'Because he is a pirate. And he visits brothels, like the one in Hercules' Pillars Alley.'

'I see. Is that the best place to find him, then?'

'No one "finds" Fitzgerald. And you had better hope he does not find you, either.'

Chaloner changed the subject, thinking he would rather have answers about Fitzgerald from the man himself, anyway. 'Did your son tell you what happened in Tangier the day Lord Teviot died?'

'He said he was paid handsomely to facilitate an ambush, although I never saw any of the money.' Mrs Reyner sighed mournfully. 'And now I never will.'

'Did he tell you that this ambush resulted in the deaths of almost five hundred men?'

She shrugged. 'What of it? They were soldiers, and soldiers are supposed to fight. It was hardly my boy's fault that they were not very good at it.'

There was no point in embarking on a debate about the ethics of the situation, and Chaloner did not try. 'What else did he tell you about it?'

'Nothing, except that it plagued his conscience.' She grimaced. 'He always was a weakling.'

'Who do you think killed him?' asked Chaloner, fighting down his revulsion for the woman.

'His enemies – the deadly horde that Harley and Newell kept talking about last night. You see, there is the Piccadilly Company, and there are their foes. They hate each other. You should watch yourself, Mr . . . what did you say your name was?'

'Thank you for your time,' said Chaloner. 'But if this "deadly horde" is as dangerous as you say, you might be wise not to speak to anyone else about your son's activities in Tangier.'

'The horde will not harm me,' stated Mrs Reyner confidently. 'Because I have this.'

She reached under her skirts, and there followed several moments of rather unseemly rummaging. Chaloner was on the verge of leaving – there was only so much he could be expected to endure for the sake of an inquiry – when she produced a piece of paper with a drunken flourish.

'It is a list of names, but it is in code, so no one can read it. My son gave it to me, and said it would protect me if his enemies come.'

She brandished it again, but the movement caused her to teeter, obliging Chaloner to grab her arm before she fell. He settled her in a chair, then turned his attention to the paper. On it were written about fifty words, all in cipher. Pen and ink stood on the table, so he began to make a copy.

'Here!' she demanded belligerently. 'What are you doing?'

'Saving your life. If this horde comes, and you are forced to give them the list, you can tell them there is a duplicate – one that will be made public should anything happen to you.'

'Who shall I say has it?' she asked blearily. 'You have not told me your name.'

Chaloner smothered his exasperation. 'That is the point! If they do not know me, they cannot order me to hand my copy over, too. They will have to leave you alone, or risk being exposed.'

Such a complex explanation took a while for Mrs Reyner to grasp, but when she did, she grinned. 'Hurry up, then. But be warned – my boy said the code is impossible to crack, because it came from vinegar.'

'Vinegar? Do you mean Vigenère?'

She snapped her fingers. 'That is the man! Do you know him?'

'No,' said Chaloner, although his heart sank. The polyalphabetic cipher adapted by Vigenère was said to be unbreakable. He handed the scroll back to Mrs Reyner, reminded her what she should say if her son's enemies came calling, and took his leave. It was time to visit his friend John Thurloe, who had a rare talent for decoding messages not intended for his eyes.

Chaloner took a hackney carriage to Chancery Lane, not because he was tired, but because he was bored with the journey between Piccadilly and the city. Unfortunately, he was not in the coach for long before it rolled to a standstill, and he peered out to see The Strand was in the midst of one of its 'stops' – carts, carriages and horses in a jam so dense that nothing was moving.

With a sigh, he clambered out and began to walk, dodging through the traffic until he reached Lincoln's Inn, one of London's four great legal foundations. He waved to the duty porter as he stepped through the wicket gate, then made his way to Chamber XIII. He tapped softly on the door, and let himself into the one place in London where he felt truly safe, a comfortable suite of rooms that were full of the cosy, familiar scent of old books, wax polish and wood-smoke.

John Thurloe was sitting by the fire. He was a slight man with large blue eyes, whose unassuming appearance belied the power he had wielded when he was Cromwell's Secretary of State and Spymaster General. There were those who said the Commonwealth would not have lasted as long as it had without Thurloe's guidance – he had run a highly efficient intelligence network, of which Chaloner had been a part. He had retired from politics at the Restoration, and now lived quietly, dividing his time between London and his estate in Oxfordshire.

'Tom!' he exclaimed. 'Come in! It is a bitterly cold day, and you must be freezing.'

Chaloner laughed. 'It is a pleasant morning, and I am hot from walking.'

'Then you had better take one of these,' said Thurloe, offering him a tin. 'We cannot have you overheating. One of Mr Matthew's Excellent Pills should put you right.'

Thurloe was always concerned about his own health, and declared himself to be fragile, although there was a strength in him that was unmatched by anyone else Chaloner had ever met. He swallowed all manner of cure-alls in his search for one that would make him feel as he had when he was twenty. Chaloner was sure they could not be good for him.

'Good for slaying fluxes,' he said, shaking his head as he recalled what he had read about the tablets in *The Intelligencer*. He did not mention the bit about expelling wind: Thurloe was inclined to be prudish.

'If you will not accept a pill, then have a sip of this instead,' said Thurloe, proffering a brightly coloured phial that declared itself to be Sydenham's Laudanum.

Chaloner shook his head a second time, then watched in alarm as Thurloe drained it in a single swallow. 'Easy! There might be all manner of unpleasant ingredients in that.'

'Almost certainly,' agreed Thurloe blithely. 'But if essence of slug or tincture of quicksilver can restore the spark of vitality that has been missing in me since Cromwell died, I shall not complain.'

'You will complain if they kill you. Quicksilver is poisonous. I know – I have seen it used.'

'I doubt there is quicksilver in this. Indeed, it imparts a wonderful sense of well-being, and I feel as though I could raise mountains after my daily dose.'

'Then do not do it in Lincoln's Inn. Your fellow benchers would not approve.'

Thurloe gave one of his rare smiles. 'It is good to see you, Tom. Is this a social call, or have you come to ask what I know about certain happenings in Piccadilly?'

Chaloner gaped at him. Thurloe had inspired deep loyalty among his intelligencers, and many continued to supply him with information, even though he was no longer active in espionage – fortunately, as it happened, because it was what allowed him to stay one step ahead of those who still itched to execute him for the role he had played in the Commonwealth. But even so, Chaloner was startled that the ex-Spymaster should know what he was currently investigating.

Thurloe smiled again. 'It was a guess, Tom, based on logic. It is obvious that the Earl would order you to find out about his missing bricks, while he cannot be happy with what is happening in the Crown, a place that is virtually his neighbour.'

'What do you know about the Crown?' asked Chaloner.

'Very little, other than that it rents rooms to a group that calls itself the Piccadilly Company. Word is that Spymaster Williamson is trying to probe their business, but with no success. Perhaps his failure is because Swaddell is no longer with him – he has gone to work for the Adventurers.'

'The Adventurers?' asked Chaloner, startled. 'You mean the wealthy but inept aristocrats who have declared a trading monopoly on Africa? Why would they need an assassin?'

'I do not know. However, it is not they who meet in the Crown, and whose gatherings are so carefully guarded that no one can eavesdrop. The Piccadilly Company worries me.'

'I searched their parlour last night and found this.' Chaloner handed him the singed paper.

Thurloe took it. 'It looks like a substitution code. You should be able to break it yourself. It will not be difficult, merely time-consuming.'

'Apparently, the Piccadilly Company has some deadly enemies. These are their names.' Chaloner passed him Mrs Reyner's list. 'They are written in Vigenère's cipher.'

Thurloe frowned. 'This represents more of a challenge, so I suggest I tackle it, while you work on the

133

document from the Crown. It will take me too long to do both, and I am busy with an errant kinsman at the moment – one of my wife's brothers, who has always been recklessly wild.'

'Do you need help?'

'I can manage, thank you. Besides, you will have enough to do if you plan to break through the secrecy surrounding the Piccadilly Company.'

'I think they might have something to do with what happened to Teviot in Tangier.' Briefly, Chaloner outlined all he had learned and reasoned, including about Reyner's murder.

'It sounds as though you are right to make a connection between the massacre and the Piccadilly Company,' mused Thurloe when he had finished. 'But I cannot imagine what it might be.'

'Do you know anything about them? Rumours about their plans? The identities of their members? I know some of them – for example, the three scouts and Harley's sister Brilliana. But "Mr Jones" is probably an alias, and I suspect the same is true of "Margareta and Cornelis Janszoon". They are the Dutch couple who attended a meeting in the Crown yesterday.'

'Why would you think they are using false names?' asked Thurloe, puzzled.

'Because they are the Dutch equivalent of John and Mary Smith. They might be genuine, but I seriously doubt it. Fitzgerald is not an alias, though. He is—'

'Fitzgerald?' asked Thurloe in horror. 'Not John Fitzgerald the pirate?'

'He prefers the term privateer, apparently. Do you know him? He has a ridiculous orange beard, one eye and an extremely peculiar voice.'

Thurloe's expression was suddenly haunted. 'Of all the enemies I faced as Spymaster, he was the one I most wish I had bested. His flagship sank recently. I had hoped he was on it.'

'Why?' asked Chaloner in alarm. Thurloe did not usually wish death on his opponents, and the reaction was deeply unsettling. 'What did he do?'

'He destroyed a number of Commonwealth vessels and butchered their crews. You must take more than your usual care if he is involved. In fact, you will stay away from him. Do you promise?'

'No.' Chaloner did not want his hands to be so tied. 'He cannot be—'

'If you tackle him alone, he will kill you. And if you take reinforcements, but lack the evidence to destroy him, he will wriggle free of the charges – and *then* he will kill you. You must hold back until we understand *exactly* what he is doing. Do you understand?'

'But I need to question him—'

'Please, Tom,' said Thurloe quietly. 'I ask you for very little, and I would be grateful if you would oblige me in this. Will you swear to stay away from him? On your mother's soul?'

Chaloner tried to think of a way to avoid making the promise, but nothing came to mind. 'I will,' he agreed reluctantly. 'But—'

'Good,' said Thurloe, cutting across him before conditions could be attached. 'I think I must emerge from retirement if he has returned. We shall work together on this case.'

'No, we will not.' Chaloner was even more alarmed. 'He is not your only enemy – others will attack you if you start meddling with—'

'I shall meddle where I please, Thomas,' said Thurloe, rather dangerously. 'Moreover, I fail to understand your persistent conviction that I need protecting. I do not. Have you forgotten that I was once Spymaster General?'

'Spy*master*, not spy,' countered Chaloner. 'There is a world of difference. You organised missions and interpreted information gathered by others. You did not go out and do it yourself.'

Thurloe was silent for a moment. 'Perhaps you are right. So I shall act as a spymaster again, deciphering what you bring me and collating it with snippets I shall commission from others. Will that satisfy you, or shall we work separately and less efficiently to bring Fitzgerald to task?'

'We can try to work together,' agreed Chaloner cautiously. 'And see how we fare.'

Thurloe wasted no time, and immediately set about writing to old contacts, to see what shreds of information might be gleaned about the Piccadilly Company. Chaloner was detailed to return to the Crown, and engage Landlord Marshall in conversation again.

'The man loves to gossip,' Thurloe said. 'Which means he probably watches the Company very closely. See what else he can tell us.'

It was raining outside, which surprised Chaloner, because the sun had been shining earlier. He was hungry, so he stopped at an 'ordinary' – an eating house that sold meals at set prices – on Fleet Street, and ate a venison pastry that was well past its best, although the baker assured him that the meat had spent the previous night in the ground, a popular cure for game that had been allowed to over-ripen. Afterwards, feeling slightly queasy, he took a hackney to Piccadilly.

'Do you know William Reyner – one of the Piccadilly Company members?' Marshall asked excitedly when he saw Chaloner, positively bursting with the need to talk. 'Well, he was murdered last night. Harley and Newell are livid about it – they have vowed to catch the culprit and kill him.'

'Do they have any suspects?'

'Not that they told me,' said Marshall ruefully. 'But that is not my only news. Reyner's mother is dead, too. She was found not an hour ago.'

Chaloner stared at him. 'How did she die?'

'Throat cut, same as her son,' replied Marshall with ghoulish glee. 'Perhaps Reyner told her some secret, and she was dispatched to ensure she never revealed it to anyone else – she drank, you see, so was not discreet. Or perhaps Harley or Newell killed her for not being much of a mother to their friend – he doted on her, but she was indifferent towards him.'

'You are not safe here.' Chaloner's stomach churned, and he had the sickening sense that *he* had sealed Mrs Reyner's fate just by visiting her. 'Dangerous people meet in your tavern, and—'

'Nonsense.' Marshall raised a hand when Chaloner began to argue. 'I complained to Mr Jones about the Piccadilly Company's odd habits this morning, and he explained everything. He said he and his friends still export glassware, but they just do it on a larger scale, which is why they are so keen on secrecy. It is a lucrative business, apparently.'

Chaloner wondered how Marshall could have believed the tale. 'But Fitzgerald is a—'

'Mr Jones says Fitzgerald is a changed man now the Royalists are in power,' interrupted Marshall with a smile.

'He has given up piracy, and will make his fortune honestly instead.'

'I seriously doubt—' began Chaloner.

'It is true,' insisted Marshall earnestly. 'He is respectable now, and has even been granted audiences with the King – he preyed on Cromwell's ships during the Commonwealth, you see, which is considered patriotic these days. Indeed, he is in the Banqueting House at this very moment, invited there to watch the King devour his dinner.'

Chaloner was astounded. 'A pirate is welcomed at Court?'

'The King considers him a hero for what he did to the Roundheads,' said Marshall. 'He is a pirate no more. He took Harley and Newell with him, to cheer them up after losing their friend.'

Chaloner tried again to warn him about the danger he was in, but Marshall declined to listen, and there was nothing Chaloner could do to make him. He took his leave and began to walk to White Hall, wishing Thurloe had not shackled him with the promise to stay away from Fitzgerald, because an interview with the man might answer all manner of questions. However, while he was forbidden to approach the pirate, he could still speak to his cronies – and it was high time he had a serious discussion with Harley and Newell.

The Banqueting House was a large, airy building with huge windows and a ceiling painted by Rubens. It was never easy gaining access to it when the King was eating, because it was a popular event and places were limited. Surprisingly, the solution came from Chief Usher Dugdale, who ordered Chaloner to don a liveried hat and coat, and take his place in the Lord Chancellor's retinue. Chaloner obliged happily, and Dugdale's eyes narrowed in instant suspicion.

The procession set off, Kipps at the front bearing the seal. Clarendon and his wife were next, followed by their son Hyde, while the gentlemen ushers brought up the rear. All eyes were on the Earl, because he was wearing expensively fashionable shoes that were far too tight, and he waddled outrageously, more of a caricature of himself than anything his cruel mimics could ever manage.

They had not been settled for long in the gallery that overlooked the main hall before the King arrived. He sat at the table that had been set ready for him, his Queen on one side, and his mistress on the other. Poor Katherine was dark and dowdy compared to the glorious Lady Castlemaine. She looked miserable, and it was clear she wished she were somewhere else.

A blaring fanfare heralded the arrival of the food, which not surprisingly was a good deal more appetising than rancid venison pastry. There were huge pieces of roasted meat, elegantly decorated pies, whole baked fish and sweet tarts. The King fell to with an enthusiasm that was heartening, watched intently by spectators who must have numbered in the hundreds. Because it was hot in the Banqueting House with so many of them crammed together, and because best clothes had been donned for the occasion, the air was thick with the reek of sweat and moth-repellent.

Chaloner looked for Fitzgerald, Harley and Newell, but they were nowhere to be seen. He wondered whether they had spun Marshall a yarn, and the pirate was no more welcome at Court than any other man with a brazenly criminal past would be.

There were plenty of other people he recognised, though. They included Leighton, the Adventurers' secretary, whom Kipps had described as the most dangerous man in London. Was it true? There was definitely something compelling about the fellow, with his button-like eyes and unsettlingly bland face.

Leighton was next to O'Brien and Kitty, whose newly acquired wealth was evident in their fine but tastefully understated clothes. Chaloner recalled being told several times that they were the King's current favourites – although apparently not enough to be asked to join him at his feast. Kitty looked especially lovely in a green dress that matched her eyes, her auburn hair in tight ringlets around her face. O'Brien's obvious excitement with the occasion made him seem more boyish than ever, his fair curls bobbing and his eyes flashing with unbridled delight.

Leighton kept tapping O'Brien's arm to claim his attention, but O'Brien was more interested in the King's feast, and Chaloner could see them growing exasperated with each other. Meanwhile, Kitty had been cornered by Brodrick, who had a dark, sinister figure at his side – John Swaddell, who had worked for Spymaster Williamson until seduced away by the prospect of better wages. Surely, thought Chaloner uneasily, *Brodrick* had not hired the man? He doubted the Earl's cousin could afford him, and he wondered whether there would be a murder to investigate when Swaddell learned he was never going to be paid what he had been promised.

After a few moments, Hyde and Dugdale joined them, and Leighton began to address the whole ensemble, although O'Brien and Kitty were obvious in their preference for watching the King instead, and it was not long before he gave up. Brodrick took up the reins, relating some tale that had them rocking with laughter, and Leighton promptly moved away, his expression difficult to read.

Eventually Chaloner spotted Fitzgerald, Harley and Newell in the opposite gallery, and supposed they must have told Marshall the truth after all. They were with several others he had seen in the Crown, all members of the Piccadilly Company. Chaloner abandoned the Earl and edged towards them, aiming to come close enough to eavesdrop. As he did so, he studied Fitzgerald carefully, curious about the man who had bested Thurloe.

The pirate was wearing a fine blue suit with a matching eye-patch, and his red beard had been allowed to flow free, so it covered his chest and a good part of his stomach. In all, it made for an arresting appearance. His peculiarly high voice was audible over the general hubbub, as he told a sullen Harley a tale about a chest of silver.

Newell was with the swarthy man whose clothes had led Chaloner to assume he was from Lisbon. When a trumpet blast announced the beginning of another course, the fellow jumped in alarm and blurted a curse in Portuguese. Chaloner nodded his satisfaction: he had been right.

A short distance away, 'the nice Mr Jones', complete with red ribbons in his boot hose, was chatting to Margareta and Cornelis Janszoon, although people were scowling at them, disliking Hollanders in their midst when the two countries might soon be at war. At first, Chaloner did not rate their chances of escaping the event in one piece, but then he saw that they were accompanied by several burly soldiers. Clearly, they were aware of their unpopularity, and had taken measures to protect themselves.

141

Chaloner did not think he had ever seen a couple more obviously Dutch. Janszoon looked as though he had stepped directly out of a painting by van Dyck, with a wide-brimmed hat and the kind of collar popular among Amsterdam's burgomasters. There was a vivid scar on one cheek, which made Chaloner wonder whether an assault had prompted the hire of bodyguards. Margareta's clothes were dark and sombre, with a maidenly wimple of a kind never seen in England. Perhaps as a sop to London fashions, both had used liberal amounts of face-powder and rouge.

'The King eats with his fingers,' she remarked to Jones in heavily accented English. 'How curious. In Amsterdam, we use forks.'

Her voice had not been loud, but the comment coincided with a lull in other conversations, and those around her heard it quite clearly. There was a collective murmur of indignation, and Jones moved away sharply, his handsome face burning with embarrassment.

'The Queen's manners are delicate,' said Janszoon quickly, also in the clipped, uncertain way of the non-native speaker. He smiled benignly. 'Not like the . . . what is the word? Strumpet? Yes, strumpet. The Queen is more delicate than the common *strumpet* on the King's left.'

Chaloner winced on his behalf, suspecting that someone had taught him the word as a joke. Then Fitzgerald stepped forward and whispered something. Janszoon was patently puzzled, but nodded agreement, and all three left, the guards at their heels. Chaloner tried to follow, but the press was too great, and he gave up when he realised they would be gone before he could reach the door.

'Lord!' came a familiarly peevish voice. 'I cannot say I approve of that sort of judgement being passed about Lady Castlemaine. She is hardly a *common* strumpet.'

It was Roger Pratt, and his comment broke the uncomfortable tension that had followed the Janszoons' departure, because people started to laugh. The architect looked bemused: he had not intended to be droll.

'They are Dutch,' explained Jones to the people who still regarded him uncertainly. 'With poor English, so they cannot be expected to know how to behave in polite society. Unlike the Portuguese.' He smiled ingratiatingly at the man in black.

Another bray of bugles interrupted any more that might have been added, and then there were coos of wonder, because one of the dishes comprised an enormous gelatine castle, wobbling precariously on a tray of live eels. The King plunged a spoon into one of the towers, accompanied by an encouraging cheer from the audience, but its taste apparently did not equal its appearance, because he pulled a face and did not take any more.

Feeling he should at least try to glean some useful information that day, Chaloner approached Harley and Newell.

'So you are Clarendon's creature,' Newell said in disgust when he saw Chaloner's uniform. 'I might have known. The man has a reputation for meddling where he is not wanted.'

'Reyner is dead,' said Harley, his devil-eyes boring into Chaloner's. 'And if I learn you had anything to do with it, I will slit *your* throat.'

'Why would I want Reyner dead?' asked Chaloner with quiet reason. 'I barely knew him.'

'You had better be telling the truth,' said Harley in a low, menacing voice. 'I dislike liars.'

'So do I,' said Chaloner, returning the scout's hard stare. 'Have you thought about my proposal, by the way? The Tangier Committee is now certain to order an inquiry, and—'

Harley moved suddenly, and shoved him against the wall. The knife from Chaloner's sleeve dropped into his hand, but he did not use it.

'We do not need your good auspices, because there are others who will protect us,' the colonel snarled. 'Now leave us alone, and do not bother us again.'

He released Chaloner and stalked away. Newell followed, and Chaloner saw he would have to find another way to make them tell him what had happened that fateful day on Jews Hill.

The King did not take long to demolish his nine courses, and was leaping up from the table by the time Chaloner returned to the Earl. The entertainment over, people began to file out of the Banqueting House. Clarendon claimed his feet hurt, and sent his Seal Bearer and ushers to find him a sedan chair. As other courtiers wanted them, too, the commission was likely to take some time, so Dugdale ordered Chaloner to wait with him – a number of his enemies were nearby, and Chaloner was the only member of the retinue wearing a sword.

'Who has cornered my wife?' asked the Earl, perching on a plinth and slipping his feet out of his tight shoes to waggle his plump toes in relief. 'Does she look as if she needs rescuing?'

'That is Ellis Leighton, sir,' replied Chaloner. 'The Adventurers' secretary.'

'So it is.' The Earl grimaced, then pointed rather indiscreetly. 'Do you see that portly man and his skinny companion, talking near the door? They are Sir Edward Turner and Lord Lucas – also Adventurers, and two of the richest men in London. I cannot imagine why *they* elected a man like Leighton to be their leader. He is said to be a criminal.'

Turner was enormously fat, while Lucas was painfully thin, and they made for a curious pair as they stood together. Both had the smug, self-satisfied air of men who had done well for themselves.

'They are particular friends,' the Earl went on. 'Look! Other Adventurers are going to join them now – like moths around a flame.'

Chaloner recognised most. They were either wealthy or had positions at Court, and he eyed them with distaste, aware that here were the people who owned the nation's monopoly on the slave trade.

'Frances is probably asking Secretary Leighton not to lead our son astray,' said the Earl, his attention snapping back to his wife. 'But she is wasting her breath. Damn! She is bringing the fellow over, and there is something about him that has always made me uneasy.'

'My Lord,' drawled Leighton as he approached. Despite the elegant bow he effected, there was something that said he was anything but submissive, and when the Earl nodded back, it was he who seemed the lesser of the two. 'I trust you are well?'

'No, actually,' replied Clarendon shortly. 'I am in pain, and my ushers are taking an age to summon me a sedan chair. I knew I should have brought my personal carriage.'

'Then you must join me in mine,' said Leighton graciously. He turned to Turner and Lucas, who were

145

suddenly at his heels, clearly eager for an opportunity to ingratiate themselves with the Lord Chancellor. 'There is room for another, is there not?'

'Of course,' gushed Turner, multiple chins wobbling as he nodded. 'I hope it arrives soon, though. I have not eaten in more than an hour, and the sight of all that food . . .'

'It made *me* feel sick,' countered Lucas, clutching his concave middle. 'I think I shall stay with you tonight, Turner. I do not feel equal to riding home after that display of gluttony.'

'Gluttony?' asked Turner, startled. 'They left half of what was provided. Personally, I would not have moved until every last crumb was consumed. It looked far too good to waste.'

Leighton smiled at them, although it was a curious expression and one that made even Chaloner uncomfortable, although he could not have said why. 'I shall summon my coach.'

The Earl started to decline, but Leighton was already moving towards the gate, using the curious scuttle Chaloner had noticed the first time he had seen him. When Lucas and Turner had gone, too, the Earl shot his wife a pained glance.

'Leighton is said to treat with felons, and now I am obliged to sit in his coach! I would sooner walk, but I dare not offend him. He might make me disappear, like he has some of his enemies.'

'Nonsense, dear,' said Frances mildly. 'Mr Leighton is perfectly genteel. And he has agreed to ensure that Henry does not fall by the wayside at the Adventurers' dinners, too. I know you have asked Cousin Brodrick to oblige, but that is rather like putting a fox in charge of the hen coop.'

'I do not know what you mean,' said the Earl, offended on his kinsman's behalf. He started to add more, but was interrupted by the arrival of the son and heir himself, puffed up with importance and towing Kitty and O'Brien in his wake. O'Brien was grinning widely, informing the world at large that watching the King eat had been one of the most delightful experiences of his life. Chaloner could only surmise that he did not get out much.

'I would like you to meet my new friends, father,' said Hyde, openly thrilled to have secured the company of the King's favourites. 'Kitty and Henry O'Brien.'

'Upstarts,' muttered the Earl unpleasantly. 'Made wealthy from the sale of a bit of copper.'

It was rude, and Chaloner was not surprised when O'Brien looked offended. The nobleman opened his mouth to respond, but was apparently not someone with the intellect for witty ripostes, so he closed it again. Kitty stepped forward and took his arm. Her pretty face was flushed, although with anger or mortification was difficult to say.

'It has been a long day,' she said with quiet dignity. 'And we are all tired, blurting things without thinking. Good afternoon to you, My Lord Chancellor.'

'The King has invited us to his apartments tomorrow,' called O'Brien, over his shoulder as she tugged him away. 'It is to be a small affair for his *close friends*.'

Chaloner was fairly sure O'Brien was only trying to convey to the Earl that not everyone at Court shunned him because he was newly rich, but the reality was that there were few remarks that could have been more wounding. Clarendon's prissiness and tendency to nag meant he was losing the King's affection, and it had been a long time since *he* had enjoyed a private soirée in the

147

royal apartments. It was the Earl's turn to flounder for a response.

Meanwhile, Hyde was livid at his father's lack of courtesy. He spoke through gritted teeth.

'They may be upstarts, but the King likes them, and it is foolish to alienate people who have his ear. Moreover, Leighton is trying to get them to invest their fortune with the Adventurers, and if they do, we can buy another ship. We shall all be richer if they join, and we have been asked to do what we can to persuade them. That does *not* include having them insulted by our sires.'

The Earl's face was puce with fury at being challenged, and to prevent a family spat in a public place, Frances asked before he could speak, 'Are they resisting, then, Henry?'

Hyde pulled a face. 'Yes, because they dislike the fact that we trade in slaves. But such scruples have no place in commerce, which they should accept if they are going to join the ranks of the wealthy. Please do not offend them again, father. I do not want Leighton vexed with me.'

He trotted after them, leaving Clarendon spluttering with impotent rage. He caught up with them just as they stopped to exchange words with their friend Spymaster Williamson. Chaloner tuned out the Earl's furious diatribe, and watched O'Brien greet Williamson with a happy grin; Kitty approached in such a way that her fingers brushed the Spymaster's thigh. Chaloner gaped in astonishment, but then Kersey's words flashed into his mind: that Kitty had taken a lover. But surely it could not be Williamson? O'Brien was his oldest friend!

'We have been asked to the King's private apartments,' O'Brien announced with open delight. He was clearly a man for whom invitations were important. 'What fun!'

'You will soon have your wish of being accepted into high society,' said Williamson warmly. 'God knows, you deserve it. There is no better company in England than you.'

O'Brien laughed his pleasure, but then Hyde grabbed his arm and steered him and Kitty towards a gaggle of Adventurers, leaving Williamson to continue alone. The indulgent smile had been replaced by grim determination by the time the Spymaster reached Chaloner.

'I need to see you urgently,' he whispered. 'Come to my Westminster office tomorrow.'

Chaloner nodded, although he had no intention of complying. They might have reached a truce, but he was not such a fool as to step willingly into Williamson's lair.

'Do not go,' ordered the Earl, when the Spymaster had gone. The whiteness of his lips said he was still seething. 'His assassin has abandoned him, and word is that he is looking for a replacement. And you work for *me*.'

Frances cleared her throat, claiming the attention of both of them. She beamed at Chaloner who began to smile back, although he stopped when he saw the Earl's immediate scowl.

'No, Frances,' said Clarendon angrily. 'He is busy with work *I* have set him to do.'

Frances ignored him. 'I appreciate your kindness in dealing with Cave's body the other day, Mr Chaloner. Or may I call you Thomas? I was fond of him – he often sang at Worcester House.'

'He had a fine voice, ma'am,' agreed Chaloner cautiously.

'Very fine. I questioned Dugdale about his death. He said Cave spat insults until Elliot retaliated with his sword. And Cave cheated, too – he tried to murder Elliot's unarmed friend.'

'Yes,' acknowledged Chaloner carefully, recalling the wild swing at Lester.

'He was not himself when he came home from Tangier, and I want to know why.' Frances raised her chin and regarded her husband defiantly. 'Indeed, his death sounds almost like suicide to me. Will you ask a few questions on my behalf, Thomas, and discover what really happened?'

The Earl shook of his head vehemently behind her back.

'The dispute was about who should take the wall, ma'am,' explained Chaloner gently. 'Insults were traded, and both parties lost their tempers. That is all.'

He did not mention the curious and suspicious connections he had uncovered since, or the fact that Williamson believed there had been something odd about the altercation.

'No,' said Frances. 'The whole affair is peculiar, and I want the truth. I know you are busy, but you can spare me a few hours. Will you do it?'

Short of an outright refusal, Chaloner had no choice. He nodded reluctantly.

Chapter 5

Recalling that Mrs Reyner had mentioned Fitzgerald's liking for the brothel on Hercules' Pillars Alley, Chaloner decided to visit it that evening. Unfortunately, it was still too early, so he started to walk towards Tothill Street, thinking it was a good opportunity to spend an hour or two working on the cipher. He was just passing the Westminster Gatehouse when he saw Lester.

Chaloner had not paid him much attention during the spat between Cave and Elliot, but he studied him now as their paths converged. Lester was a burly fellow, with a ruddy face and the slightly rolling gait of a sailor. His clothes were fine but practical, with enough lace to say he was a gentleman, but not enough to interfere with his comfort or movement.

'Elliot died,' Lester stated bluntly. 'I took him to a surgeon, but the wound was too severe.'

'I am sorry,' said Chaloner. 'You were friends?'

Lester's face clouded. 'We served on several ships together, when I was master and he was my first officer. He had his faults, but there was no better man in a battle.'

'Do you know what started the argument between

151

him and Cave?' asked Chaloner, supposing he may as well begin Lady Clarendon's investigation, given that a witness was before him.

'Brilliana Stanley,' replied Lester bitterly. 'She was Cave's mistress before he went to Tangier, and Elliot took her on while Cave was away. I told Elliot no good would come of such a dalliance, but he would not listen. And then Cave returned . . .'

Chaloner supposed that jealousy might have led to a quarrel. He frowned as he recalled where he had heard the unusual name before. 'Colonel Harley has a sister called Brilliana.'

Lester nodded. 'Harley is a malevolent brute, and it would not surprise me to learn that *he* told Cave his sister's affections had gone to another man.'

'I had better visit her,' said Chaloner, more to himself than Lester.

Lester raised his eyebrows. 'Why? Are you thinking of taking up where Elliot and Cave left off? I would not recommend it. She might be pretty, but she is as unsavoury as her brother.'

'I am married,' said Chaloner shortly.

'So was Elliot,' Lester shot back.

Chaloner did not say that he knew this already, although it occurred to him that Elliot might have dallied with Brilliana because Ruth was feeble-minded.

'Brilliana lives near the Feathers tavern in Piccadilly,' Lester went on. 'And it is rumoured that she engages in some very dubious business.'

Chaloner frowned. 'Elliot was one of Williamson's spies. I do not suppose he was ordered to inveigle himself into Brilliana's affections in order to monitor this "dubious business", was he?'

Lester gaped at him. 'How in God's name did you know that? *I* had no idea what Elliot did in his spare time until he confided it to me on his deathbed.'

'Why did he agree to work for a man like Williamson?'

Lester looked pained. 'I invested the money we made from capturing Dutch prizes at sea, but his went to the gaming tables. He needed a way to pay his debts.'

'Did Williamson recruit you, too?'

Lester was affronted. 'No, he did not! I have no desire to meddle in the affairs of landsmen – they are always complex and sordid. Nothing like being on a ship.'

Chaloner laughed. 'I have spent time at sea myself, and people are people whether they are afloat or on solid ground.'

'Which vessels?' asked Lester keenly. 'Navy or merchantmen?'

Chaloner waved the question away. Instinctively, he liked Lester, but he was not in the habit of divulging his past to men he barely knew. 'There was something odd about the fight between Cave and Elliot. Cave was not a man to challenge battle-hardened mariners to swordfights.'

Lester nodded. 'Others have told me the same. Of course, Cave was in love with Brilliana, and men act oddly when in Cupid's grip. But I must go. There is a meeting of sea-officers who object to transporting slaves today. Someone must make a stand against that foul business, and we hope that the trade will founder if we refuse to accept human cargo.'

Chaloner was heartened. 'How many of you are there?'

'Four. But we aim to recruit more. I was on *Henrietta Maria*'s maiden voyage, and it was . . . Suffice to say that

I believe God sank her because He was appalled by the venture.'

'For every one of your four officers, there will be ten willing to take such commissions.'

'More like a hundred,' said Lester gloomily. 'But it is a start, and I cannot stand by and do nothing while greedy villains profit from the misery of others. Call me naive if you will, but it is a matter of conscience.'

'Then go,' said Chaloner. 'You should not be late.'

Chaloner was tired when he reached Tothill Street, and half hoped Hannah would be out. But as soon as he opened the door, he could tell by the acrid stench of burning that not only was she home, but that she was baking. He coughed as smoke seared the back of his throat, and approached the kitchen with caution, knowing that to do otherwise might result in bodily harm – she was not averse to hurling her creations across the room if they did not turn out as she expected. And as her loaves had the shape and consistency of cannonballs, being hit by one was no laughing matter.

She was at the table, peering at a smouldering tray. Joan was next to her, a bucket of water at the ready, while Nan and Susan were scrubbing a wall that looked as though something had exploded up it. All were uncharacteristically subdued. George, resplendent in new clothes of which any courtier would be envious, lounged by the fire, peeling an apple. He glanced up when Chaloner entered, but made no move to stand. Hands on hips, Hannah glared at her husband.

'I hope you did not go to White Hall dressed like that, Thomas.'

154

Chaloner looked down at himself. He was perfectly respectable. 'Why?'

'Because no one is wearing green this year. And you should have donned a wig. We have been through this before. Dress is a gesture of class consciousness, and an inability to conform means either a slovenly display of bad taste, or a provocative demonstration of nonconformity.'

'I am not a nonconformist,' said Chaloner, obliquely referring to the fact that she, as a Catholic, was far more of one than he would ever be.

Hannah's eyes flashed. 'Do not take that tone with me. I have had a terrible day.'

'Have you?' Chaloner tried to sound sympathetic. 'Then tell me about it.'

'Just as long as you promise not to fall asleep, like you did last time. God only knows how long I was talking to myself.' Finally, it dawned on Hannah that railing at him in front of the servants was unedifying. She grabbed his hand and hauled him towards the door. 'Put my cakes on a plate, Joan,' she ordered crisply. 'And bring them to the drawing room. Tom would like one.'

Normally, Joan, Nan and Susan would have smirked at this notion, and Chaloner was surprised when there was no reaction. He was also aware of George settling himself more comfortably in his chair, at the same time tossing the apple core on to the floor. Nan swooped forward to pick it up.

'He seems to have settled in,' Chaloner observed, as he was bundled along the corridor.

When they reached the drawing room, Hannah closed the door and lowered her voice. 'You made a mistake when you hired him. He is a bully, and our women are terrified of him.'

'Perhaps they will resign, then,' said Chaloner hopefully. 'And I did *not* hire him, Hannah. You did, no matter what you have led Joan to believe.'

Hannah had the grace to look sheepish, but declined to apologise. 'You must dismiss him. He will find another post if we give him decent testimonials. He is big, strong and intelligent. Rather alarmingly so.'

'What do you mean?'

'I caught him reading some of our papers today. They were only deeds about the lease of the house, but it made me uncomfortable even so. He was *spying*, Tom.'

'So do Joan, Nan and Susan,' Chaloner pointed out. 'All the time.'

'Yes, but they have never worked for Fitzgerald the pirate, have they.'

Chaloner stared at her. 'You think Fitzgerald ordered him to watch us?'

'Yes – because I work for the Queen and have influential friends, while you are embroiled in God knows what unsavoury business for your horrible Earl. It is common knowledge that Fitzgerald is short of money, so he probably intends to blackmail us.'

'Then he will be disappointed, because there is nothing to blackmail us about.' Chaloner shot her an uneasy glance. 'Is there?'

'Not on my account. But even if George is not under Fitzgerald's orders, I do not want him in my house. You must get rid of him.'

'No,' said Chaloner firmly. 'I am sorry, but he is not like the other servants. He is a stranger in our country, and it would not be right to turn him out. You wanted a fashionable household, so you must live with the consequences.'

He expected her to argue, but she only sighed, reminding him that under her sour temper was a decent woman. 'Then the only way to be free of him is to find him another post. I will start making enquiries tomorrow. Perhaps the Duke will take him.'

She referred to Buckingham, with whom she had developed a rather unfathomable friendship: Chaloner failed to understand what she saw in the man, but she was fond of him and the affection was fully reciprocated. She knew Chaloner disapproved, but maintained that her acquaintances were her own affair, and not to be dictated by a mere husband.

'Is George the only reason you have had a terrible day?' he asked with polite concern.

'No. We had hopes that the Queen might be with child, but it was another false alarm. She was bitterly disappointed, and cried all afternoon. Ah! Here is Joan with your cakes.'

'They are sure to be delicious,' said Joan, placing the platter of singed offerings on the table. She smiled maliciously. 'You will certainly want several.'

As she knew he would not, Chaloner could only suppose it was yet another attempt to create friction between him and his wife. When he hesitated, Hannah slapped one in his hand. It was still hot, obliging him to juggle it, and a tentative gnaw made him wonder whether she wanted him toothless. He tried again, while she waited for a compliment.

'Very nice,' he lied, when he had eventually managed to bite a piece off. In truth, it tasted like all her efforts in the kitchen – of charcoal. Disappointed, Joan left, slamming the door behind her.

'I omitted the sugar on principle,' said Hannah,

tellingly declining to eat one herself. 'Have you ever been to a sugar plantation? You once mentioned visiting the Caribbean.'

Chaloner nodded, but did not elaborate. It had shocked him, and he was not sure how to begin describing the horrors he had witnessed.

Hannah sighed. 'It is a good thing I usually have plenty to say, or we would spend all our time together in silence. Is it so much to ask that you tell me about your travels? *Talk* to me, Tom!'

'Sugar is made by extracting syrup from a certain type of cane, which—'

'No! I want your *opinion* of these places, not a lesson in botany. No wonder I sometimes feel as if we do not know each other at all. You are wholly incapable of communicating your feelings.'

Chaloner knew the accusation was true, because even thus berated, he struggled for the right words. Then, when he thought he had them, Hannah grew tired of waiting and changed the subject.

'I am going out this evening. You are invited, too, but I imagine your Earl expects you to lurk under more tarpaulins. It is a pity, because there will be music.'

'Music?' asked Chaloner keenly.

Hannah nodded. 'Henry and Kitty O'Brien are holding a soirée for select courtiers. Have you met them? They are great fun and extremely rich, so everyone wants to be in their company. Everyone except your Earl, that is. Apparently, he thinks they are upstarts.'

Somewhat disingenuously, Chaloner informed Hannah that it would be rude for him to ignore the O'Briens' invitation, strenuously denying the accusation that he was only interested in the music. It would be better to visit the Hercules' Pillars Alley brothel later anyway, he told himself, when it would be busier and Fitzgerald was more likely to be there.

Hannah was pleased to have his company, although she made him change first. Once clad in their best clothes, they walked to the O'Briens' mansion in Cannon Row, just south of White Hall. George preceded them, toting a pitch torch, although he held it for his own convenience, and Chaloner was obliged to tell him several times to adjust it so that Hannah could see where she was going.

'Would you like me to carry her?' asked George, the fourth time it was mentioned.

Chaloner peered at him in the darkness, not sure whether the man was serious or being insolent. 'We will settle for you holding the torch properly,' he replied curtly.

George must have heard the warning in his voice, because he did not need to be told again. But Hannah's suspicions about his spying were still in Chaloner's mind, and it seemed as good a time as any to question the man – better, in that Joan, Nan and Susan were not there to eavesdrop.

'Why were you reading our papers this morning?' he asked, opting for a blunt approach. He felt Hannah stiffen beside him, and supposed she had not wanted George to know that she had tattled.

'I was looking for tobacco,' replied the footman curtly. 'I smoke.'

Even Chaloner was taken aback at the bald admission that George felt entitled to rummage among his employers' possessions in search of a commodity that, if found, would effectively be stolen. Hannah gasped her disbelief.

'Did you hunt for tobacco among Fitzgerald's belongings, too?' asked Chaloner coolly.

'Of course,' replied George, unruffled. 'What else was I to do when I wanted a pipe?'

'Even if we did smoke,' said Hannah, 'we would not keep tobacco among our legal documents.'

'So I have learned. I shall not look there again.'

Chaloner gaped at the man's unrepentant audacity, but when he stole a glance at Hannah, he saw she was laughing.

'Lord!' she whispered. 'Perhaps we had better buy him some, or who knows where he might pry next. Unfortunately, Joan disapproves of smoking . . .'

'I will bring him some tomorrow,' said Chaloner, thinking it would kill two birds with one stone: relieve George's cravings and annoy the housekeeper. Of course, he thought, as he watched George pause to see Hannah over a rutted section of road, the man still might be a spy.

The O'Briens had rented a pleasant house with attractive gardens, and their great wealth was reflected in the number of lights that blazed from their windows. As they entered, Hannah was immediately claimed by Buckingham, who whisked her away to meet some of his friends.

Chaloner loitered at the edge of the gathering, aware that it included a lot of very well-connected individuals, many of them Adventurers. There was, however, no one from the Piccadilly Company. He was not sure what it meant – perhaps just that the two groups were drawn from different sections of society, with the Adventurers comprising the uppermost echelons, and the Piccadilly

Company admitting men like Fitzgerald the pirate and the Tangier scouts.

Secretary Leighton was by the fire, surrounded by fellow Adventurers. They included a man with an exceptionally large nose named Congett. Congett was a drunk, who had earned himself a certain notoriety by mistaking a French cabinet for the King at His Majesty's birthday party, and informing it of his undying loyalty. Only the fact that he was immensely wealthy had saved him from being laughed out of Court.

'Turner and Lucas promised to be here,' Leighton was saying. He sounded annoyed, and Chaloner was under the impression that the pair would be in trouble when he next saw them. 'I wanted them to work on O'Brien, and persuade him to join us.'

'I hope no harm has befallen them,' slurred Congett worriedly. 'Especially after Proby . . .'

'A vile business,' said Leighton, with a marked lack of feeling. His button eyes glittered. 'And now poor Grey is missing, too. He disappeared en route to a brothel.'

'If I did not know better,' whispered Congett, 'I would say someone is targeting Adventurers.'

'Why would anyone do that?' Leighton's face was impossible to read.

'Well, I do not believe Proby threw himself off St Paul's,' replied Congett. 'I think he was pushed – murdered. And I think there will be more deaths to come.'

'Nonsense,' snapped Leighton. 'There is no evidence to suggest such a thing, and we all know he was upset when his wife died. But this is no subject for a fine evening. Let us talk of happier matters. Have you heard that the price of gold has risen again? It is good news for our company.'

161

Once the discussion turned fiscal, Chaloner wandered away. He went to where a quartet of musicians was playing. They invited him to join them, and he was soon lost in a complex piece by Lawes. He came back to Earth abruptly when he became aware that he was the subject of scrutiny.

'I had no idea you were so talented,' said Spymaster Williamson.

'It is a pastime, no more,' lied Chaloner, standing and nodding his thanks to the musicians. He was horrified to have exposed such a vulnerable part of himself to a man he did not like.

'Personally, I have never cared for music,' said Williamson. 'I prefer collecting moths.'

'Do you?' asked Chaloner, startled. 'There are plenty in the curtains. Shall I shake them out?'

Williamson smiled. 'It is a kind offer, but I am more interested in the rarer varieties. You will not forget to visit me tomorrow, will you? There is something important we must discuss.'

'There you are, Joseph!' came a voice from behind them. It was Kitty, radiant in a bodice of blue with skirts to match. Something sparkled in her auburn hair – a delicate net with tiny diamonds sewn into it. 'We have been looking for you.'

She grabbed the Spymaster's hand, and they exchanged a look of such smouldering passion that Chaloner was embarrassed. He was amazed, not only that a fine woman like Kitty should have such poor taste in men, but that Williamson should unbend enough to embark on a liaison. Or had it been Kitty who had done the seducing? Then O'Brien arrived, and she tugged her hand away.

'I was just telling Chaloner about my moths,' said Williamson smoothly. 'He is very interested.'

'Is he?' O'Brien flung a comradely arm around the Spymaster's shoulders, addressing Chaloner as he did so. 'Williamson always enjoyed peculiar pastimes, even at Oxford. Now those were good days! It was just one invitation after another.'

'It was,' agreed Williamson, although with considerably less enthusiasm. 'Of course, Chaloner was at Cambridge. Perhaps that explains his unaccountable liking for music.'

'I *adore* music,' said Kitty warmly. 'Especially Locke. He is my favourite composer.'

He was one of Chaloner's, too, and he felt himself losing his heart to Kitty. Then she and O'Brien began a lively debate about the best compositions for the viola da gamba, while Williamson listened with an indulgent smile. It was obvious that he was fond of both, and Chaloner wondered what would happen when O'Brien learned about their betrayal.

As the evening progressed, Kitty showed herself to be vivacious, intelligent and amusing, with a talent for making people feel at ease. It was clear that her servants worshipped her, while her guests positively fawned. O'Brien encouraged her to shine, and Chaloner soon understood why: the man wanted to be accepted into high society on the basis of their popularity, not because they were rich. It was pitiful, yet there was something charming about his eager naivety, and Chaloner hoped he would not be too badly savaged by the ruthless vultures of Court.

'Thank you, Leighton,' he was saying, clapping his hands in unbridled pleasure. 'We should *love* to attend a reception on a ship next week. However, you must promise that you will not spend the entire evening trying to convince us to become Adventurers.'

'It would be to your advantage,' said Leighton immediately. 'You could double your money.'

'And what good would that do?' asked O'Brien, laughing. 'We already have more than we can spend. Besides, the Adventurers deal in slaves, and we do not approve of that.'

'No,' agreed Kitty vehemently. 'It is a wicked business. But I firmly believe that the trade will founder eventually, and then anyone who participated in it will live in shame.'

Chaloner, listening in the shadows, felt himself warm to her more than ever.

'It is a very small part of our operation,' said Leighton coaxingly. 'We also trade in gold, ivory, nuts, gum and feathers. Africa is dripping with riches just for the taking. You should let me show you our accounts. I promise you will be impressed.'

'Oh, probably,' said O'Brien, with careless indifference. 'But we should not talk about commerce when we are supposed to be enjoying ourselves. Who would like to dance?'

Williamson and Kitty were the first couple to take the floor, encouraged by a delighted O'Brien. Chaloner felt sorry for him – a man prepared to challenge the likes of Leighton on a question of ethics deserved better. But it was getting late, and time for him to leave the merry comfort of O'Brien's home to be about his work for the Earl.

Temperance North had once been a prim Puritan maid, but the death of her parents two years before had prompted a change in her outlook on life. She had used her inheritance to found a 'gentleman's club', an establishment that catered to the needs of very wealthy clients. It earned her a fortune, and was frequented by royalty and other influential people. It was located in Hercules' Pillars Alley, a lane named for a nearby tavern, and the hours between ten and dawn tended to be its busiest time.

Because it was popular and fashionable, it had been necessary to hire a doorman to exclude undesirable elements. A nonconformist fanatic called Preacher Hill had been hired for the job, a post he loved, because it left his days free to deliver public sermons on the dangers of licentious behaviour. He did not like Chaloner, and as getting past him was invariably a trial, the spy climbed over a wall and entered the brothel via the back door. He was greeted by bedlam.

The temperamental French cook was standing in the middle of his domain, shrieking orders in an eclectic array of languages, none of which were English. The scent of fresh bread and roasted meat vied with the less appealing aroma of burning, where things had not gone according to plan.

'You used too much oil,' translated Chaloner, as he weaved his way through the chaos.

There was a collective sigh of understanding, and the assistants hurried to rectify the matter. Chaloner walked along a hall to the club itself, where a different frenetic activity was in progress.

The club comprised an enormous parlour on the ground floor, where its patrons could enjoy fine wine, good food and popular melodies played by members of the King's Private Musick. If a gentleman wanted a lady, he would inform one of the scantily clad girls who flounced around the place, and his request would be passed to Maude, the formidable matron who guarded the foot of the stairs. When the woman of his choice was ready, he was escorted discreetly to an upstairs chamber.

When the club's doors first opened, the conversation was genteel and the violists played to an appreciative audience, but it was nearing midnight by the time Chaloner arrived, and any pretensions of civility had long since been abandoned. The atmosphere was debauched, and the place reeked of spilled wine and vomit. The musicians had been provided with far too much free claret, and only two of the quartet were still conscious – and it was probably fortunate that cheers and raucous laughter drowned out their efforts.

As Chaloner stepped into the parlour, he was obliged to duck smartly when a decanter sailed through the air to smash against the wall behind him. It was closely followed by a jelly, which slid gracefully down the plaster leaving a trail behind it, like a slug. He was barely upright again before coming under assault from a battery of fruit tarts, forcing him to take refuge behind a statue.

He looked for Fitzgerald, recognising as he did so several members of the Privy Council, two admirals and three prominent clerics. Then there were the Court debauchees, men who had nothing better to do than amuse themselves in increasingly wild ways.

He was astonished to see Dugdale and Edgeman there, though, given that they had so vigorously denounced such places earlier that day. The Chief Usher's eyes were glazed, while the secretary was singing at the top of his voice. They seemed at home, suggesting they were regular visitors. Chaloner wondered where they got their money, because the club was expensive and the Earl was not exactly generous with his retainers' salaries.

They formed a distinct party with several other men who looked prosperous and important. Chaloner surmised that they were Adventurers when he recognised one as the missing Grey – the man who had 'disappeared' en route to the brothel the previous night.

The group also included Swaddell the assassin, who despite the gaiety of the occasion was clad in his trademark black. His restless eyes were everywhere, and it was not long before they spotted Chaloner. He left his companions and sidled towards him.

'I was relieved to discover Grey alive and well,' he said in a pleasantly conversational voice that belied his true nature as a vicious, dispassionate killer. 'People were beginning to fear that he had met an unpleasant end. Like Proby.'

'Where has he been?' asked Chaloner. 'Did he say?'

Swaddell smirked. 'With a woman. Where else?'

'It was not you who pushed Proby off the cathedral, was it?'

A pained expression crossed Swaddell's face. 'No, and I am getting tired of people asking me that. Just because I have dispatched one or two worthless individuals in the past does not mean I am responsible for every death in London. Proby committed suicide – he was an unhappy man.'

'I see,' said Chaloner, supposing he was telling the truth. Besides, Swaddell's preferred method of execution was throat slitting. He recalled what had happened to Reyner and his mother.

'Were you anywhere near Piccadilly last night?'

'I was with Congett and Leighton from six until midnight, standing guard while they went over the Adventurer account books. Why? Did someone die there, too, and you think to blame me?'

'It does not matter.' Chaloner believed him: his alibi was one that could be checked, and the assassin was too experienced an operative to concoct stories that would show him to be a liar.

'Have you heard that I am no longer in Williamson's service?' Swaddell asked casually. 'I work for Leighton now – he is secretary of the Adventurers, and a very wealthy man.'

'I cannot imagine Leighton having much use for an assassin. Besides, he looks as though he can manage that side of the business himself.'

'I do more than just kill people, you know,' said Swaddell irritably. 'Do not underestimate me, Chaloner. Men have done it before, and lived to regret it.'

Or *not* lived to regret it, thought Chaloner. He was not afraid of Swaddell, although there was no disputing that the assassin was an unsettlingly sinister individual. But there was no point in making enemies needlessly, and he had enough to do without dodging attempts on his life by professional killers. He nodded an amiable farewell and moved away.

The revellers on the far side of the parlour were wearing masks, although Chaloner was not sure why – perhaps as part of some exotic game. It was easy to identify Fitzgerald, though, despite the grinning crocodile-head he had donned; his massive red beard had been carefully fluffed up for the occasion and it stood out like a beacon.

Chaloner stole a mask from someone too intoxicated

to notice, found a corner where he could pretend to be slumped in a drunken stupor, and settled down to watch the pirate at play.

His earlier assumption that Adventurers and the Piccadilly Company did not mix was wrong, because members of both were in Fitzgerald's party. The Adventurers were represented by Brodrick, safe in the knowledge that his prim cousin would never believe anyone who told on him; and by Congett, who had apparently not consumed enough wine at O'Brien's house earlier and was busily rectifying the matter. Both wore visors, but Chaloner recognised them by their clothes. Then Dugdale and Edgeman tottered across to join them, disguised as an ape and a toad, respectively.

Several Piccadilly Company members were also readily identifiable, despite their elaborate headdresses. 'The nice Mr Jones' was wearing his trademark red boot-ribbons, while Cornelis Janszoon appeared brazenly foreign in his sombre Dutch suit. Chaloner glanced around quickly and saw three henchmen lurking in the shadows near the door; Janszoon was still taking no chances with his safety.

There were two others he recognised, too, although he doubted they were Adventurers or from the Piccadilly Company: Pratt the architect was betrayed by his haughty bearing, while his assistant Oliver still contrived to look morose despite the merrily beaming imp that concealed his face.

Everyone was laughing uproariously, because Jones was encouraging Pratt to describe the mansions he had designed before Clarendon House. Jones was making much of the fact that Pratt could only lay claim to three, which should not have been sufficient for him to have formed such an elevated opinion of himself. Pratt did not know he was being practised upon, and his bragging replies unwittingly emphasised his foolish vanity.

'Clarendon House is effluence,' declared Janszoon suddenly, cutting across Pratt's declaration that his buildings were the best in the country. 'And all London's architects are repulsive and bald.'

Chaloner knew the revellers were far too drunk to understand that the Hollander was remarking on Clarendon House's affluence, and the impulsive boldness of the capital's builders. He braced himself for trouble, and saw the guards do the same.

'British architects are the greatest in the world, sir,' slurred Congett indignantly. 'Whereas you Dutch never build anything except warehouses in which to store butter.'

'Or cheese,' added Brodrick, while Oliver nodded at his side.

'I like Dutch cheese,' said Janszoon gravely. 'But England's is odious.'

Chaloner suspected he had confused 'odious' with 'odoriferous', and was merely commenting on the fact that British cheeses tended to smell riper than their milder Dutch counterparts. But eyes were immediately narrowed at the perceived slur.

'Nonsense,' snapped Dugdale. He struggled to enunciate the next sentence. 'There is nothing odious about England. God save the King!'

The cry was taken up by others, and the atmosphere turned raucously genial again, indignation forgotten. One of the guards slipped up to Janszoon at that point, and whispered in his ear. Janszoon nodded to whatever was said, and aimed for the door, his protectors at his heels.

'Good,' said Dugdale viciously, watching them go. 'That butter-eater did nothing but abuse us from the moment he arrived, and I might have punched him had he persisted.'

'Would you?' asked Fitzgerald softly, his one eye gleaming oddly beneath his mask. 'You sat back all night and let him bray all manner of insults about our country, our King and our food. I imagine he will always be perfectly safe from your fists.'

His voice dripped scorn, and Chaloner sensed he was more disgusted with the Chief Usher for failing to defend their nation's honour than with Janszoon for uttering the remarks in the first place.

'We came here for fun,' objected Dugdale defensively. 'Not to trounce impudent foreigners. Besides, Temperance does not approve of fighting in her parlour, and I do not want to be ousted while the night is still young.'

Pratt spoke up at that point, eager to reclaim the attention. 'Have you heard that *I* am the subject of a planned assassination?' he enquired smugly. 'Someone hates my work enough to kill me.'

'Congratulations,' came an unpleasantly acidic voice from a man wearing the face of a dog. Chaloner recognised it as Newell's, and supposed the hawk next to him was Harley. 'No architect can claim notoriety until at least one person itches to dispatch him for the hideousness of his creations.'

Pratt frowned as he tried to gauge whether he had just been insulted. Newell opened his mouth to add more, but Fitzgerald was there first, laying his hand on the scout's shoulder.

'Stop,' he ordered. 'Pratt is our friend – a member of our Company. It is unkind to tease him.'

Chaloner was surprised to learn that the architect was a member of the Piccadilly Company, but supposed he should not be – Pratt lived in the place where it met, and would have money to invest. Of course he would be recruited to its ranks.

'He deserves to be jibed,' said Newell sullenly. 'He is an arrogant dolt. Besides, Janszoon is a friend and a member of the Company too, but you just castigated that courtier for not hitting him.'

'I did nothing of the kind,' said Fitzgerald, and although his voice was mild, there was a definite warning in it. 'I merely dislike people who make casual reference to violence. If they mean it, they should carry it through. *I* have never made an idle threat in my life.'

Newell was clearly unsettled by the remark, because he flung off his mask, grabbed a jug of wine from a table and began to drain it. When they saw what was happening, the other revellers egged him on with boisterous chants. Fitzgerald turned away, but the crocodile head prevented Chaloner from telling whether he was angry, amused or disgusted by the scout's antics.

When the jug was empty, Newell slammed it on the table and slumped into a chair. Chaloner homed in on him when the revellers drifted to another part of the room, and tried to rouse him, but it was hopeless – the scout would still be sleeping off his excesses at noon the following day.

Meanwhile, the Portuguese man had seized another jug and looked set to follow Newell's example, but once again, Fitzgerald was there to intervene.

'No, Meneses,' he piped, removing it firmly. 'You have much to do tomorrow, and you will need a clear head. Allow me to summon a carriage to take you home.'

Meneses opened his mouth to argue, but Fitzgerald gripped his arm and began to lead him towards the door. Meneses tried to pull away, but was far too drunk for a serious struggle, and he desisted altogether when Harley came to take his other arm. Chaloner followed, staying well back and hiding as the trio reached the hall and Fitzgerald sent Preacher Hill to fetch a hackney.

'What do you think, Fitzgerald?' asked Harley in a low voice, propping Meneses up against a wall while they waited for the coach to arrive. 'How do we fare?'

'Well, enough,' replied the pirate. 'Our master will be pleased, because tonight I have achieved two things: avenged Reyner's murder, and let those who oppose us know that we are a potent force. Killing Reyner and his mother in revenge for Proby was rude, and I have taught them a lesson.'

Harley nodded slowly. 'Do you know who killed Reyner, then?'

'No, but he will not live long, I promise – our St Frideswide's Day plans will take care of him. Next Wednesday, our master will show everyone that *he* can organise noteworthy events, too.'

In the shadows, Chaloner frowned his bemusement. St Frideswide's Day was when Pratt was supposed to be murdered, but Fitzgerald had just saved him from ridicule and described him as a friend and a fellow Piccadilly Company member. Surely, he – or his mysterious master – could not be the author of *that* plot? Or was Fitzgerald actually saying that there was a second unpleasant event planned for the same day, one that would outshine the other in its viciousness?

'Good,' said Harley. 'Then let us hope we succeed, because it has been months in the planning, and I am eager for it to be finished. But what exactly did you do tonight?'

'You will see. Our enemies and all London will be agog with the news tomorrow.'

The coach arrived at that point, and they manhandled Meneses into it. As the hackneyman declined to take a near-unconscious man unaccompanied, Harley went, too, while Fitzgerald returned to the parlour.

Chaloner mulled over what he had heard, wondering who the pirate considered to be his enemies. Frustrated, he realised he had a list of them from Reyner's mother, but until Thurloe broke the code, their names would remain a mystery. He hoped the ex-Spymaster would not take long, because they were obviously in danger, and needed to be warned. He cursed the promise that Thurloe had forced out of him, because the obvious way forward was to corner Fitzgerald and demand some answers, most particularly the name of his master.

His musings were interrupted suddenly when the hall filled with laughing, shrieking courtiers, all involved in a riotous game of chase. The curtain behind which he had taken refuge was hauled from its rail by someone struggling to stay upright, and he only just managed to hurl himself into the mêlée in time to prevent being exposed as someone who hid behind the draperies – and while most patrons were too drunk to notice or care, it was not a risk he was willing to take.

As he scrambled to his feet, pretending to totter as he did so, a figure materialised in front of him. It was Fitzgerald. He itched to initiate a conversation, sure he could extract some information from the pirate without arousing his suspicions.

'Allow me to help,' Fitzgerald said, reaching out to

steady him. 'Mistress North's wine has flowed very freely tonight, and not everyone can take it.'

'But you can?' slurred Chaloner.

'I am a sailor,' replied Fitzgerald, intensifying his grip to the point where it hurt. Chaloner was not sure whether the pirate was genuinely trying to hold him up, or whether there was a warning in the steel-like fingers. 'We are more used to powerful brews than the average man. Indeed, we are a breed to be respected in many ways.'

He escorted Chaloner to a nearby chair, where the spy pretended to fall asleep. Fitzgerald watched him for a moment, then turned and made for the door, apparently deciding that he had had enough of the club and its entertainments. Chaloner found himself inexplicably relieved when he had gone – there was definitely something unsettling about him, and he was beginning to understand why Thurloe considered him such a daunting opponent.

Back inside the parlour, the merrymaking continued unabated, and all manner of food was still flying through the air. Pratt was lying on the floor, liberally splattered with custard, and an inanely grinning Oliver – an expression that did not sit well on his naturally melancholy face, now devoid of its mask – was sitting astride the architect, rummaging in his clothes.

'I am looking for the key to Clarendon House,' he explained, as Chaloner approached. 'Pratt usually keeps it round his neck, see.'

Chaloner helped him search with the express intention of taking it – he did not think Oliver or Pratt should have possession of it that night. It was not there, indicating either that the architect had been sensible enough to leave it at home, or someone else had got to it first.

'Damn,' said Oliver, reeling as he sat back on his heels. 'He always gives it to me when he knows he is going to be late for work. And he will be late tomorrow, because he will still be drunk.'

'Does he often come here?' asked Chaloner.

'Oh, yes – he is always waxing lyrical about it. Usually it is barred to the likes of me, but the King is being entertained elsewhere tonight, so Mistress North said her regulars could bring a friend. Just this once. And Mr Pratt invited me, which was nice.'

He sounded ridiculously pleased, giving Chaloner the impression that it would be the highlight of his year. Then the grin slowly disappeared, and he mumbled something about needing to close his eyes for a moment, before sinking down on top of Pratt and beginning to snore.

Chaloner was about to go home when he saw Jones pouring himself more wine. The man was perfectly steady, and was one of few sober people in the room.

'Temperance is canny,' Jones said affably, wincing as he sipped. 'The claret was excellent earlier in the evening, but now few are in a position to savour quality, she has brought out the slop.'

'You are a member of the Piccadilly Company,' said Chaloner, deciding the environment was right for a frontal attack – everyone else was blurting whatever entered their heads, so why should he not do likewise? 'May I join?'

Jones blinked. 'You are very direct! How did you find out about us?'

It was on the tip of Chaloner's tongue to say that Harley and Newell had told him, but he remembered what had happened to Reyner, and baulked. He did not

176

want another death on his conscience, not even theirs. 'I listen,' he said instead.

Jones smiled apologetically. 'Personally, I would love a new member, because our meetings are tedious and you might liven them up. Unfortunately, my colleagues have decided that our business has reached its optimum size of thirty investors, and they will not enrol anyone else.'

'Should I ask Fitzgerald to make an exception?'

Jones considered the question carefully. 'You could try, although I am told he is not always very friendly. I have never found him so, but there you are.'

'What is the Piccadilly Company, exactly?'

Jones raised his eyebrows. 'You do not know its nature, yet you want to enlist?'

'I have heard it is a lucrative venture,' lied Chaloner.

Jones laughed and clapped his hands. 'Then you heard right! It is very profitable. We export fine glassware to New England, and we bring gravel back.'

'Gravel?' echoed Chaloner. Ruth had mentioned gravel, too.

Jones shrugged. 'No ship wants to travel one way empty, and there is always a great demand for gravel. It is useful for building roads, apparently.'

'Who is in charge of your company?' asked Chaloner. 'The man Fitzgerald calls his master?'

Jones looked puzzled. 'He does not have a master. What are you talking about?'

Chaloner could only surmise that Jones was not trusted to the same degree as Harley. 'What is your name?' he asked. 'And do not say Jones, because we both know that is an alias.'

'Do we indeed?' Jones seemed more amused than

offended as he raised his cup in a salute. 'People really *are* called Jones, you know – there are dozens of us in London alone.'

Once Jones had gone, Chaloner aimed for the hall again, bored with wealthy hedonists and their secrets, and keen to go home. His hand dropped to his dagger when someone intercepted him, but it was only Lester. Chaloner smothered a smile when he saw the captain had chosen to wear a mask of delicate silver lace, which had been intended for a woman. It would have made him conspicuous if anyone had been sufficiently sober to notice.

'Everything here costs a fortune,' Lester said disagreeably, watching the antics in the parlour with prim disapproval. He winced and ducked as a syllabub missed its intended target and flew through the door towards him. 'I hope Williamson reimburses me.'

'So you *are* working for him?' Chaloner was unimpressed. 'You told me you were not.'

Lester grimaced. 'I was a free agent when we spoke this morning, but he has since learned of a certain weakness of mine, and holds me to ransom over it.'

'A weakness?'

Lester shot him a cool glance. 'One I am not prepared to discuss. However, the upshot is that he thinks there was more to Elliot's death than a fight over a woman, and has ordered me to look into it. I do not suppose you would help, would you? I am rather out of my depth.'

'So would I be,' said Chaloner shortly.

'Not according to Williamson. He says you are the most resourceful man he has ever met.'

'Does he?' Chaloner was uneasy to learn that the Spymaster talked about him to all and sundry.

'I suspect he is right to order an investigation into the Cave–Elliot affair, though,' Lester went on soberly. 'I have been considering the matter, and I believe it may be connected to the murder of one Captain Pepperell. Have you heard of him? He was stabbed in Queenhithe two Mondays ago.'

Chaloner stared at him. 'What makes you think that?'

'Because it is odd that *two* sea-officers should die in suspicious circumstances within a week.'

'London is a big place. People are unlawfully killed here every day.'

'But the matter stinks! I have already learned that Cave sang duets with O'Brien, who seems a decent fellow, and Fitzgerald, who is a damned pirate! I cannot abide the breed. Privateers should be hanged at the yardarm, and—'

'What else do you know about Fitzgerald?' Chaloner headed off what promised to become a rant.

'Is being a pirate not enough?' demanded Lester. Then he relented. 'Tonight, I heard him say that something terrible was going to be common knowledge tomorrow. He also mentioned gravel.'

Chaloner regarded him narrowly. 'What is gravel?'

Lester's eyebrows shot up. 'Small bits of stone, man! How much claret have you had?'

'It must mean something else, too. Fitzgerald is in London to recoup his losses after losing a ship full of treasure. He will not do that by trading in grit.'

'If it is code for another commodity, then it is one I do not know.'

'Have you heard whether Fitzgerald is working for anyone else?' asked Chaloner.

Lester shook his head, but was more concerned with

his own enquiries than in answering questions. 'I suppose I shall have to visit all Elliot's old haunts to ask whether Pepperell was ever with him, because I am sure I shall discover a connection between them. It will not be easy, though. I do not have a way with words, and both were average men, difficult to describe.'

Chaloner had taken a liking to Lester, although he could not have said why. Perhaps it was his hearty, bluff manner, or the stance he had taken over the slave trade. Regardless, he sensed a decency in him that was missing from virtually everyone else at Temperance's club.

'I will send you something that might help. It will arrive tomorrow.'

'What is it?'

Chaloner smiled. 'You will have to wait and see.'

Lester drew him into an alcove when Brodrick lurched past. Behind the Earl's cousin, clinging drunkenly to his waist, was Dugdale with Edgeman clutching him, all three in a state of semi-undress. Chaloner was sure the Earl would be appalled if he could see them. Then came several Privy Councillors and five Members of Parliament, singing a popular tavern song at the tops of their voices as they danced along in a single, weaving line. They jigged out of the front door, took a turn around the courtyard, and trotted back in again before aiming for the kitchens. The screech of outrage from the French cook would have been audible in Chelsey.

'It is good to know our country is in such capable hands,' said Lester contemptuously. 'God save us! Is this why I risk my life in the navy? So these monkeys can sit in authority over us?'

'Easy! It is hardly sensible to bawl treasonous remarks when half the government might hear.'

Lester rubbed his eyes. 'My apologies. Incidentally, Williamson said that if I saw you, I was to urge you to go to his office. Normally, I would tell you where to put such an invitation, but I have a bad feeling about whatever is unfolding in Piccadilly. I recommend you oblige him.'

Chaloner nodded, but had no intention of following the advice as long as Thurloe was helping him. If the ex-Spymaster proved lacking, then he might see whether Williamson was prepared to trade information, but he was certainly not ready to go down that road yet, aware that there would be a price for collaboration – and he was not sure whether it was one he would be willing to pay.

Chaloner was about to leave the club and go home when he remembered that he had not paid his respects to Temperance, and while they were not the close friends they once were, he was loath to hurt her feelings. He found her in an antechamber with Wiseman. The surgeon was asleep, and she was in the process of covering him with a blanket.

'He is exhausted, poor lamb,' she whispered, although if Wiseman could slumber through the drunken revels in the parlour, then she had no need to lower her voice. 'Because of that terrible business with Sir Edward Turner. Richard was the first *medicus* on the scene, you see.'

Temperance was a large young woman, who should not have worn gowns designed for those with slimmer figures. She had once owned glorious chestnut curls, but had shaved them off to don a wig, which was seen as more fashionable. The upshot was that she was fat, plain and bald, although Wiseman did not seem to mind, because they had been lovers for months.

'What terrible business?' asked Chaloner, recalling how he had seen the obese Adventurer not many hours before, watching the King dine in the Banqueting House. The spectacle had made Turner hungry, he recalled, while his thin friend Lord Lucas had been sickened by the sight of such plenty.

'You will hear about it tomorrow. All London will be appalled by the news.'

Chaloner stared at her. Could this be what Fitzgerald had mentioned? 'Tell me about it.'

Temperance smoothed Wiseman's hair back from his face in a gesture of infinite tenderness. Chaloner felt a mild twinge of envy; Hannah was never so loving with him.

'Turner's house caught fire, and he and his household were roasted alive.'

'How many?' asked Chaloner, his stomach churning.

'Turner and his wife, their three children and six servants. Lucas was staying with him, so he was caught in the inferno, too. Still, we should not be surprised. The last time Turner came here, he quarrelled with Fitzgerald, and only a fool does that.'

'Are you saying Fitzgerald is responsible?' Chaloner wondered whether the man had set the blaze himself, or whether he had hired a minion to do it while he cavorted at the club.

Temperance glanced around in alarm. 'Not so loud, Tom! I do not want him coming after *me*.'

'You cannot be afraid of him – he is one of your patrons. You would not admit him if—'

'I wish I could refuse him entry, but I do not dare. He is a pirate, and you cannot be too careful with those. They are depraved monsters, who love to kill and maim.'

'If he did set Turner's house alight, he will be punished for it. Spymaster Williamson—'

'Will never get the evidence he needs to make a case. And if you do not believe me, ask Mr Thurloe. That is why *he* never managed to bring Fitzgerald down.'

'I do not suppose you have heard rumours about Fitzgerald working for someone else, have you?' asked Chaloner hopefully. 'That another man dictates his actions in London?'

Temperance shook her head. 'But if there is such a fellow, I should not like to meet him. He would have to be very evil and powerful to control a pirate.'

The food-fight in the parlour was getting out of hand. The ceiling and walls were now heavily splattered, and so were most of the guests. Chaloner saw Congett pick up a huge pot of brawn, and quickly pulled Temperance out of harm's way, wincing when the bowl crashed into the wall behind them and dented the plaster. There was a wild whoop of glee at the resulting mess.

Smiling indulgently, as if she considered these foolish, middle-aged men her unruly children, Temperance led Chaloner to the small room near the kitchen where she and Maude counted their nightly takings. There were already several full purses on the table, and their ledger registered more money than Chaloner earned in a month. She flopped into one of the fireside chairs, removed her wig and reached for a pipe. She was not yet two years and twenty, but the eyes that studied Chaloner through the haze of smoke were far older.

'Have you been away, Tom? I do not recall seeing you for a while.'

There was a time when Chaloner would have been

hurt by the fact that she had not noticed an absence of three months, but he had learned to accept that he was no longer very important to her.

'Tangier,' he replied.

'What were you doing there? Learning Arabic? I know you have a talent for languages, but you should not bother. Every civilised person speaks English these days. Except that evil Queen.'

'She is not evil,' said Chaloner coldly. 'And she is learning as fast as she can.'

Temperance shot him a sour look. 'I had forgotten your unfathomable liking for the woman. I cannot imagine why, when the rest of the country wishes her gone to the devil. She will never give the King an heir, and it is all your Earl's fault. He deliberately picked a barren princess.'

'He could not have known—'

Temperance cut across him. 'Of course he knew! It is common knowledge in Lisbon that she is infertile. Did you know that she plans to buy a child, and pass it off as her own?'

Chaloner raised his eyebrows. 'I imagine even the dim-witted rabble currently destroying your parlour would be suspicious if she produced a baby without being pregnant first.'

Temperance shrugged. 'I am only repeating what Count Memphis of America told me.'

'That is his real name?' asked Chaloner doubtfully.

'Or something similar. I rarely pay attention to foreigners. They are not worth my notice.'

Chaloner gazed at her, wondering whether she had purposely set out to shock him. He had come to terms with her smoking, drinking, shaven head and relationship with Wiseman, but she had never displayed a streak of xenophobia before. And he did not like it.

She smirked at his response, then changed the subject. 'Why did you come here tonight? To hear the latest gossip about my clients so you can repeat it to your horrid Earl?'

'No,' said Chaloner, standing abruptly. He was too tired for a spat. 'I came to see you.'

'I am sorry, Tom,' she said quickly. When he hesitated, she reached out to take his hand. 'Please stay. I am upset about Turner and Lucas, and it has barbed my tongue. And I will never tell anyone else, but I think Fitzgerald had the atrocity planned before he came here tonight.'

'How do you know?' asked Chaloner, sitting again.

Temperance stared at the embers of the dying fire. 'Because I heard him tell Harley that Turner would not be a problem for much longer at about nine o'clock tonight, and Richard told me the fire started at ten – a whole hour later.'

'Then you must inform Williamson what—'

'No!' Temperance looked genuinely frightened. 'Peter Proby challenged Fitzgerald, and look what happened to him. And you must not tackle him, either. I would not like to think of *you* smashed into pieces outside St Paul's Cathedral.'

'At least someone would not,' sighed Chaloner.

'Hannah?' asked Temperance sympathetically. 'I could have told you not to marry her.'

'You could?' asked Chaloner, taken aback by the turn the discussion had taken.

Temperance nodded. 'She is a nice lady, but you are ill-matched. I wish you had asked my advice before you agreed to wed her, because you will make each other very unhappy.'

'Oh,' said Chaloner, not sure how else to respond, at least in part because he knew she was right.

'Will she be attending Cave's funeral?' asked Temperance, tactfully changing the subject. 'It will be the social event of the month, and everyone at Court plans to be seen there. People have already started to buy new black clothes, as is the fashion. I imagine it will be next week, because it will take some time to organise such a grand occasion. Richard will go, and I shall accompany him.'

'You knew Cave?'

'He came here on occasion, although I never liked him much – he was never very friendly.'

As Temperance and Chaloner rarely shared the same opinions, he was surprised that her assessment of Cave was the same as his own – the singer had made no effort to be pleasant on the voyage from Tangier, and had endured Chaloner's company only because he played the viol. It had suited Chaloner, though; he had not extended himself to be sociable, either.

'What else do you know about him?'

'Nothing, because he only ever talked about music. He was a bore, to tell you the truth.' She smiled suddenly. 'The Chapel Royal choir are going to sing at his burial, and that alone will encourage many to come. They are extremely good.'

'The best in the country,' agreed Chaloner, deciding to do whatever was necessary to secure a place at the ceremony. He told himself it was to explore Cave's peculiar death, even though he knew nothing could be accomplished while the service was underway.

'Do not worry about Hannah,' said Temperance kindly a short while later, as she was accompanying him to the front door. 'I know many couples who dislike each other, yet still function perfectly well together in society. You will soon work out rules and boundaries.'

'I do not dislike Hannah,' exclaimed Chaloner, startled.

'No,' said Temperance softly. 'Not yet.'

Chaloner did not feel like returning to Tothill Street after Temperance's bleak remarks, and found himself walking towards Piccadilly instead. It was cold after the muggy heat of the club, so he strode briskly to keep the chill at bay. He soon left the city behind, and then the only sounds were the hoot of owls and the whisper of wind in the trees.

When he reached the hamlet, he made for the back of the Feathers, and let himself in through a broken window. There were two coffins in the parlour, mother and son lying side by side. Chaloner struggled to mask his distaste as he lifted Mrs Reyner's skirts to hunt for the encrypted paper. He was not surprised to find it gone, especially when he saw her lip was swollen. He could only suppose she had handed it over when violence was used, although it had not saved her – the wound to her throat was every bit as vicious as the one that had killed her son.

He stared at her. She reeked of wine, and it occurred to him that she might not have been sober enough to tell her attackers that the list had been copied. Or had they not cared, because it was not as important as Reyner had believed? Chaloner supposed he would not know until it was decoded, which needed to happen now as a matter of urgency.

Carefully leaving all as he had found it, he made for Clarendon House, unimpressed to find not a single guard on duty, although a banked fire indicated that they intended to return at some point during the night. He checked the supplies that were stored outside, and then approached the building itself, idly counting the number of ways he could get in – four doors, two loose windows and a badly secured coal hatch. He entered through the grand portico because it represented the biggest challenge, and he felt like honing his burgling skills.

Once inside, he wandered aimlessly. It seemed especially vast in the dark, like a church. It smelled of damp plaster and new wood, and he felt his dislike of it mount with every step. Why did the Earl have to build himself such a shameless monstrosity?

He left eventually, but rather than cut across St James's Park towards home, he took the longer route via Piccadilly and the Haymarket. As he passed the Crown, all was in darkness except Pratt's room, in which several lanterns blazed. It had not been so when he had gone by earlier, and afraid something was amiss, he decided he had better investigate.

There were no lights in the tavern, but there were snores, and it did not take him long to see that Wright and his men had bedded down near the embers of the fire. There were eight of them, and he wondered what tale Wright would spin if materials went missing again.

Disgusted, he climbed the stairs, treading on the edges, which were less likely to creak and give him away. When he reached Pratt's door he listened intently but could hear nothing. He tried the handle and was alarmed to find it unlocked. He opened it to see Pratt lying fully clothed on the bed with his mouth agape. Certain he was dead, Chaloner felt for a life-beat, then leapt away in shock when the architect's eyes fluttered open.

'Snowflake!' Pratt purred, raising his arms enticingly. Then he became aware that he was not at Temperance's brothel. 'Chaloner? What are you doing here?'

Heart still pounding, Chaloner began to douse the lamps, unwilling to leave so many burning when he left, lest Pratt knocked one over in his drunken clumsiness and started a fire. The thought reminded him of what had happened to the two Adventurers.

'Did you hear about Turner and Lucas?' he asked.

'One wants me to design him a stately home, but I cannot recall which. Lord, my head aches! I should have stayed with Lydcott in Charing Cross tonight. I wish I had, because then you would not be looming over me like the Angel of Death.'

'Who is Lydcott?'

'A dear friend. He was a Parliamentarian in the wars, but is a Royalist now – *he* knows how to survive turbulent times! He is an excellent horseman, too. Did you hear that someone thinks enough of my work to threaten me with death, by the way? Not even Wren has achieved that accolade!'

'How do you know Harley and Fitzgerald?' asked Chaloner. The architect was far too haughty to converse with him when he was sober, so it made sense to do it while he was intoxicated.

'They are members of the Piccadilly Company,' replied Pratt drowsily. 'As am I. We trade in glassware and gravel. I have invested heavily, and it will make me richer than ever.'

'How can gravel be lucrative?' asked Chaloner. 'Or glassware, for that matter. There cannot be a massive demand for it in New England, because none of the colonies are very big.'

But Pratt was asleep. Chaloner tried to shake him awake, but he responded only by mumbling more incoherent nonsense about Lydcott. When he began to mutter about Snowflake, too, Chaloner decided it was time to leave.

He was passing the table when he saw the key to Clarendon House, the silken cord still attached. He considered pocketing it, but common sense prevailed – Pratt might remember his visit the following morning, and he did not want to be accused of theft. So, working quickly, he melted a candle into a pill box, and waited for it to set. While it was still malleable, he pressed both sides of the key into it, then eased it out. He cleaned it, put the mould in his pocket, and left as silently as he had arrived. He could not steal Pratt's key, but he could certainly make one of his own.

Downstairs, he gave Wright the fright of his life by sneaking up behind him and putting a knife to his throat. He kept the sergeant's cronies at bay by brandishing his sword.

'You are supposed to be guarding Pratt,' he informed them shortly. 'So why is no one outside his door? And who is watching Clarendon House? I have just been there, and it is deserted.'

'If it is deserted, then there is no need to watch it,' argued Wright. 'Let me go, Chaloner, or I will tell Dugdale that you picked a fight with me. He offered to pay me for any bad tales about you.'

Chaloner released him with a shove that made him stagger. 'Go to the house, or the Earl will learn that he is paying you to sleep in a tavern all night.'

Wright started to draw a knife, but thought better of it when Chaloner pointed the sword at him. Glowering, he slouched out, five of his men at his heels. The others reluctantly abandoned the fire, and went to take up station outside Pratt's door, although Chaloner doubted they would stay there long once he had gone.

He went home, where the hour candle said it was three o'clock, but although he was tired, he did not feel like going to bed. He went to the drawing room, intending to doze for an hour before resuming his enquiries, but his mind was too active. He took the cipher from his pocket and began to work on it. Unfortunately, while he was too restless for sleep, he was not sufficiently alert for such an exacting task, and it was not long before he gave up. He stared at the empty hearth, then whipped around with a knife in his hand when he became aware of someone standing behind him.

'I came to light the fire,' said George, eyeing the blade with a cool disdain that told Chaloner he was more familiar with such situations than was appropriate for a footman in a respectable house.

Chaloner indicated with an irritable flick of his hand that he was to carry on. 'Please do not creep up on me again. You might find yourself harmed.'

'I doubt it. Fitzgerald was much freer with weapons than you, and I survived him.'

'If he attacked you, why did you stay with him for ten years?'

The sour expression on George's face said Chaloner had touched on a sore point. 'Ten years! And he dismissed me like so much rubbish.'

If George had behaved as sullenly with the pirate as

he did in Tothill Street, then he was lucky he had not suffered a worse fate, thought Chaloner. He changed the subject, sure he would not be given an answer, but supposing there was no harm in trying.

'What is the nature of Fitzgerald's current business in London?' By means of a bribe, he passed George a plug of tobacco he had palmed in Temperance's club, where the stuff had been lying around for its patrons to enjoy.

George almost snatched it from him, and set about tamping the pipe he pulled from his pocket. 'He did not tell me, but it will involve death and destruction, because he was singing about it. At sea, he always sang before he attacked another ship.'

'Can you be more specific?'

'I am afraid not,' replied George, through a haze of smoke.

'Does he have any powerful friends here? Ones he might refer to as his master?'

George regarded him oddly. 'Not that I am aware.'

'You cannot name any of his London acquaintances?'

'No.' George regarded Chaloner thoughtfully, then reached inside his shirt and produced an old leather pouch. 'But if you intend to go after him – as your questions suggest you might – take this.'

'What is it?' asked Chaloner, disconcerted that George should read him so easily.

'Dust from Tangier, which contains something that always sets him to uncontrollable sneezing. It should not affect you, but it will render him helpless.'

Chaloner did not take it. 'And what am I supposed to do with it?'

'Throw it in his face, should he decide to come at

you.' George tossed the pouch into Chaloner's lap. 'It works, believe me.'

Chaloner was thoughtful as George busied himself at the hearth. He had not forgotten Hannah's conviction that the footman had been ordered to spy, and George's inept fiddling with the fire said he was not skilled at the duties that usually went with being a footman. Or a captain's steward, for that matter. If that were the case, why had he given Chaloner something with which to defeat his former master? Or was it a ploy that would see him in danger?

He doubted a direct enquiry would yield a truthful response, so he sat at the table instead and, recalling his promise to Lester, began to make sketches of Captain Pepperell and Elliot. He had a talent for drawing, and had been trained to remember faces, so it was not long before he had reasonable likenesses. He folded them in half, and as he did not know where Lester lived, told George to take them to Williamson's offices in Westminster.

'The Spymaster?' asked George uneasily. 'You want me to visit *him*?'

'Just his clerks. Why? Have you done something to excite his interest?'

'No more than any other man in London.' George glanced out of the window without enthusiasm. 'Shall I go now? It is still dark.'

'Take a torch,' said Chaloner shortly.

Chapter 6

An hour before dawn, Chaloner began to feel the effects of his sleepless night. He would have gone to bed, but Joan was crashing around in the kitchen, and he knew he would never sleep through the racket. He wondered how Hannah could, but a visit to the bedroom showed him that she had stuffed her ears with rags.

Lethargically, he walked to the Rainbow Coffee House, hoping a dish of Farr's poisonous brew would sharpen his wits. The only customer at that hour was Grey, the Adventurer who had caused such consternation by disappearing with a woman. He was sitting in the corner, crying softly.

'Weeping for Turner and Lucas,' explained Farr in a low voice. 'They died in a fire last night, along with Turner's family and servants. Twelve people in all. A terrible tragedy.'

To give Grey privacy, Chaloner picked up *The Newes*, just off the presses that morning, and began to read. Home news comprised two main reports: that Dover expected to be invaded by the Dutch at any moment because the wind was in the right direction, and that a purple bed-cloth had been stolen from Richmond. Foreign intelligence revolved around the fact that the Swedish ambassador was expected at White Hall the following Tuesday, where he would attend a feast.

In smaller type were the advertisements. One promoted the exhibition that Farr had mentioned the last time Chaloner had visited the Rainbow:

At the Mitre near the *West-end of St Paul's* is to be seen a rare Collection of Curiosities much resorted to, and admired by Persons of great Learning and Quality: among with, a choyce *Egyptian Mummy with hieroglyph-icks* and the *Ant Beare* of Brasil; a *Remora*; a *Torpedo*; the huge Thigh-bone of a *Gyant*; a *Moon Fish*; a *Tropick Bird &* C.

Although intrigued by the torpedo in particular, Chaloner doubted he would have the time to see the display. He finished the coffee, nodded a farewell to Farr, and set off for Chancery Lane.

Lincoln's Inn's grounds had recently been replanted, and had gone from a pleasantly tangled wilderness to a garden of manicured precision. Chaloner was still not sure he liked it, but Thurloe did, and spent a lot of time there. It was usually deserted at dawn, a time the ex-Spymaster spent in quiet contemplation before the day began.

'I have been expecting you,' Thurloe said, as Chaloner materialised out of the gloom and fell into step beside him. It was not raining, but the garden had endured a good soaking during the night, and the paths were soggy under-foot. 'I want you to purchase a handgun for yourself.'

'Why?' asked Chaloner suspiciously.

'Because this case has a dangerous feel, and a sword is no defence against firearms. Here is a purse. No, do not refuse it – it is not my silver, it is Fitzgerald's. He did not best me *every* time I tackled him, and I have been saving it for a time when it might be used against him. Which is now.'

Chaloner accepted reluctantly. Not only did he dislike taking money from friends, regardless of its provenance, but he had never been comfortable with the unpredictability of guns. They were, however, obscenely expensive, and he certainly could not have afforded to purchase one on his own salary.

'Tell me what you have learned,' instructed Thurloe, after they had walked in silence for a while, their footsteps alternately crunching and squelching.

'That Fitzgerald has a master. Unfortunately, no one seems to know who he is.'

Thurloe nodded. 'I suspected as much. I shall ask my old spies for a name. What else?'

'He said he had scored a great victory over his "enemies" – presumably the men who oppose the Piccadilly Company – in revenge for Reyner, and it seems he arranged the deaths of Turner and Lucas. He probably tossed Proby off the roof of St Paul's, too. Certainly, he believes that Reyner was killed in retaliation. And Proby, Turner and Lucas were Adventurers . . .'

'So Fitzgerald's foes – listed on the Vigenère cipher – are Adventurers? I thought the Adventurers were respectable men, not the kind to engage in tit-for-tat killings with pirates.'

'Secretary Leighton is not respectable! He is alleged

to have accrued vast wealth by criminal means. Moreover, most Adventurers are courtiers, and the words "courtier" and "respectable" are mutually exclusive. However, we shall know for certain when you decode the cipher.'

'I am afraid I cannot. I worked on it all night, but it is beyond me. So I sent a copy to John Wallis, who was my code-breaker during the Commonwealth. If he cannot crack it, no one can.'

Chaloner hoped it would not take long. 'So we have two commercial operations at war with each other – the Adventurers and the Piccadilly Company. The Adventurers have lost three of their number, and the Piccadilly Company has lost one.'

Thurloe was thoughtful. 'The Adventurers comprise wealthy courtiers and merchants, and include men such as the Duke of Buckingham, Congett, Secretary Leighton and several members of your Earl's household – Hyde, Brodrick, Dugdale and Edgeman. They have declared a monopoly on trading with Africa, and are greedy but inefficient.'

'Meanwhile, the Piccadilly Company comprises a pirate, a Dutch couple, a Portuguese, two Tangier scouts, Harley's sister, Pratt and the enigmatic Mr Jones. They send glassware to New England and bring gravel back – a venture that necessitates hiring Brinkes to ensure secrecy.'

'Their sea-routes lie in opposite directions,' mused Thurloe. 'And they deal in different commodities. They should not be rivals, yet they are killing each other. It makes no sense.'

Chaloner's mind wandered to the mysteries he had been ordered to solve, and the way the two organisations featured in them. 'I have four cases – Cave's death, the Tangier massacre, the Queen's letters about Pratt, and the stolen bricks. They are so different that they should be unrelated, yet there are strands linking each one to the others.'

'Explain,' ordered Thurloe.

'First Cave. He and Elliot stabbed each other in a duel over Brilliana. She is Harley's sister, and they live in Piccadilly. So does Pratt, whose latest house is the victim of stolen supplies, and who himself may be the target of an assassination.'

'And Pratt is a member of the Piccadilly Company,' mused Thurloe. 'As is Harley.'

'Harley is also one of the scouts whose intelligence sent Teviot to his death. Moreover, Elliot was Williamson's spy, and his duties entailed monitoring the Crown. His wife – his *deranged* wife – lives in the Crown's garret. And Cave sang duets with Fitzgerald, another member of the Piccadilly Company. Then there is the connection between Elliot and Pepperell.'

'Who?'

'The captain of *Eagle* – Elliot's friend Lester thinks it suspicious that two sea-officers should die within such a short space of time of each other. Pepperell was murdered by Brinkes – the man charged with ensuring that Piccadilly Company meetings are not disturbed. I will hunt down Brilliana today, to see what she can tell me about her dead lovers – and about her brother, too. Lester is also looking into it, on Williamson's behalf.'

'Lester,' said Thurloe disapprovingly. 'Stay away from him. I distrust him intensely.'

'Do you? I rather like him.'

'Oh, I am sure he is charm itself. However, do not forget that he was present at the beginning of the spat that saw Elliot and Cave dead.'

'He tried to stop them from fighting, and was almost killed when Cave lunged at him.'

'And that is suspect in itself. I sensed something devious about him the first time we met – years ago, when we were both much younger. Do not trust him, Tom.'

Chaloner nodded, but although he usually respected Thurloe's insights, he was inclined to dismiss this one. Of all the people he had met since returning from Tangier, Lester was by far the most personable.

'The second case is Teviot,' he went on. 'He and his garrison died because Harley, Newell and Reyner gave him misleading information. All are members of the Piccadilly Company, but Reyner was murdered within hours of agreeing to tell me what happened at the ambush on Jews Hill. He gave his mother that list of the Piccadilly Company's enemies.'

'Which probably comprises the names of specific Adventurers,' surmised Thurloe.

'Then Reyner's mother was murdered, and her list stolen. Fitzgerald says the killer will have his just deserts next Wednesday – St Frideswide's Day – because his master has a plan.'

'Pratt's murder?' asked Thurloe. 'Or are we talking about a different plot?'

'It must be a different one. I had the feeling that he expects something truly catastrophic, and the death of an architect – no matter how valuable Pratt thinks himself – is hardly that. But this is the third case: the letters. I have questioned the Queen's staff, but learned nothing useful. However, Pratt hobnobs with the Piccadilly Company *and* the Adventurers. And he lives in the Crown.'

'How will you proceed with that particular investigation?'

'Spend time in White Hall, asking more questions of more people. The last case is the Earl's stolen bricks – connected to the others by virtue of its architect and its location in Piccadilly. I have no idea who the culprits might be, and I suspect his materials will continue to go missing until the damned place is finished.'

'Pity,' said Thurloe. 'Because I imagine that is the one your Earl would most like solved. You must visit the place as often as possible, and interview Pratt, Oliver and their workmen. Something will occur to you eventually, you will see.'

Chaloner was not so sure, but felt it was the least of his worries. 'Perhaps you should tell Williamson to arrest Fitzgerald, on the grounds that his master might not be able to put this diabolical plot into action if his chief henchman is unavailable.'

'Lawyers would have him free within the hour – suspicion and rumour is not solid evidence. No, Tom. It is better to leave him alone, because if he goes to ground, we will never thwart him.'

'If you say so,' said Chaloner unhappily.

The day that followed was not very successful. Chaloner arrived at White Hall to find Dugdale waiting. The Chief Usher looked decidedly fragile, with bloodshot eyes and a sallow complexion. So did the Earl's secretary Edgeman, who was sipping some sort of tonic as he sat at his desk.

'Good,' Dugdale whispered when he saw Chaloner. 'When you have finished telling me what you have learned about the stolen supplies, you will go to the Tennis Court. The Duke of Buckingham has challenged Mr O'Brien to a bout, and the Earl wants a representative from his household to be there.'

'I suspect he would rather I hunted the brick-thief.' Chaloner spoke deliberately loudly.

'That is why he wants you to go to the game,' said Dugdale, wincing as he put a hand to his head. 'All his enemies will be there, and you will eavesdrop, to learn which of them is the culprit. This order comes directly from him, so you *will* obey it.'

'But it is a bad idea,' objected Chaloner. 'First, the Tennis Court is too open for eavesdropping. And second, most of his enemies know me, so will watch what they say when I am near.'

'Then you will have to find a way around it.' Dugdale smirked unpleasantly. 'But do not take too long – if you fail, you may find yourself jobless.'

'Leave him alone, you two,' said Kipps, arriving suddenly, and as bright and energetic as the Chief Usher and secretary were seedy. 'I am tired of you baiting him all the time.'

Dugdale ignored him. 'Make your report to me, Chaloner, and then be about your duties.'

'Significant headway has been made,' lied Chaloner vaguely.

'Good,' said Kipps, before the Chief Usher could remark that this was insufficient. He regarded Dugdale coolly. '*I* shall pass the news to the Earl – we do not want it garbled in the retelling, do we?' He turned back to Chaloner. 'Have you uncovered anything about the villain who sent those letters to the Queen? That is the most serious matter, as far as I am concerned. I like the woman.'

'Really?' asked Dugdale scathingly. 'I thought your tastes ran more towards Lady Castlemaine.'

'Did you enjoy yourself at the brothel last night,

Dugdale?' asked Chaloner, speaking loudly again, this time in the hope that the Earl would hear. 'You and Edgeman?'

Edgeman regarded him in alarm, while Kipps's eyebrows shot up in astonishment.

'You spied on us?' demanded Dugdale, shocked. 'How dare you! Get out, before I commission some of my friends to teach you a lesson.'

'Friends like Fitzgerald the pirate?' asked Chaloner, unmoved. 'Or Harley, the scout whose faulty intelligence saw five hundred men dead? You were certainly in their company last night.'

'We do not know them,' said Edgeman quickly, while Dugdale spluttered with outrage. 'But your remarks suggest that *you* were in this brothel, and I am telling the Earl. He will not believe that Dugdale and I frequent such places, but you are another matter entirely.'

He was right, and Chaloner suspected that his attempt to combat their bullying had just misfired. He had only mentioned Fitzgerald and Harley in an effort to disconcert them, but Edgeman's denial made him think again: *could* the secretary and Chief Usher be associated with the Piccadilly Company? As most of its thirty members wore disguises, it was impossible to say who attended its meetings. Or did being Adventurers preclude them from joining, on the grounds that the two groups were at loggerheads?

He bowed a curt farewell, and started to walk to the Tennis Court, although he stopped abruptly when an uncomfortable thought occurred to him: should he be wary of Kipps? The Seal Bearer had admitted that his application to join the Adventurers had been rejected, so had he promptly thrown in his lot with their rivals?

202

Moreover, he should not have known about the Queen's letters, because the Earl – in a rare display of discretion – had kept the matter within his family. Did that imply Kipps had another reason for knowing, namely that he was involved in the matter himself?

The notion was not a happy one, and Chaloner was grateful he had Thurloe's friendship, because he was otherwise quite alone.

As Chaloner had anticipated, eavesdropping was hopeless at the Tennis Court. It was dangerous, too, because the Earl's enemies had gathered in force, and Chaloner was jostled, pinched and poked but did not dare retaliate, because at least twenty men with swords would have been delighted to fight him if he had. Individually, they posed no threat, but en masse they were a distinct menace.

The bullies included the big-nosed Congett, who was either still drunk from the night before, or had started imbibing afresh that morning; he 'accidentally' trod on Chaloner's foot. Lady Castlemaine and the Duke of Buckingham confined themselves to verbal abuse, while others fingered the guns they wore in their belts or pretended to inspect their knives.

Then Kipps appeared, and although he explained in an undertone that he was there to help Chaloner eavesdrop, he promptly took himself off to sit in a corner with the Adventurer Grey, who seemed to have recovered from his earlier grief and was smiling.

'Stop!' cried O'Brien, hurrying forward when Congett elbowed Chaloner hard enough to make him stumble. 'It is not his fault that Clarendon is an ill-mannered brute. Leave him be.'

'Especially as he plays the viol like an angel,' said

Kitty, smiling first at Chaloner and then at his tormentors. The spy suspected he was not the only one whose heart melted. 'In fact, we must organise another soirée, so all our talented friends can exhibit their musical skills.'

There was a smattering of applause, although Chaloner imagined her admirers would prefer something more rambunctious; most of them had been at Temperance's club the previous night.

'Speaking of invitations, the King has asked us to a drama in the Banqueting House,' said O'Brien, clearly delighted. 'A Turkish one. What fun! I can hardly wait! I shall wear a pair of—'

'Never mind that,' interrupted Buckingham briskly. He turned to Chaloner with a malevolent grin. 'Is it true that Clarendon has taken to spending his nights under a tarpaulin, guarding his bricks and nails?'

'No,' replied Chaloner, once the spiteful laughter had died down. 'He pays others to do it for him. His supplies are now extremely well protected, and anyone raiding them will be caught.'

There were several uneasy glances, and he wondered whether his remark would be enough to see the thefts stop. If so, then at least something would have been gained from his trying day.

'I do not believe they were stolen in the first place,' said Lady Castlemaine. She was wearing a gown cut tight at the waist to show off her shapely figure, and careful application of face-paints almost disguised the fact that her wild lifestyle was beginning to take its toll. 'I think Pratt underestimated what he needed, and is covering his incompetence with false accusations.'

Chaloner stared at her, wondering whether she might

be right. It was certainly possible – Pratt was not the sort of man who would admit to making mistakes.

'I dislike Pratt,' declared Congett, clinging drunkenly to a pillar. 'He is odious for an architect.'

'Odious enough to warrant being assassinated?' asked Chaloner. He winced: the question had just slipped out. Fortunately, no one seemed surprised by it, leaving him with the impression that those deserving of timely demises was a regular topic of conversation at Court.

'Dugdale would like Pratt dead,' mused the Lady, her eyes gleaming with spite. 'Because he is jealous of Clarendon's admiration for the fellow. Dugdale knows he will never be Pratt's equal, you see.'

'Or that sly secretary – Edgeman,' added Buckingham. 'I do not think I have ever encountered a more reprehensible individual. He positively *oozes* corruption.'

There was a general murmur of agreement, and Chaloner thought wistfully how satisfying it would be if Dugdale and Edgeman *were* responsible for the threatening letters. Moreover, it would show that Hyde had fallen for a hoax, which would make him look both ridiculous and disloyal to the Queen. But Chaloner knew better than to let prejudices lead him astray, so while he would bear the notion in mind, he would not let it influence his conclusions.

'Kipps does not like Pratt, either,' added the Lady in a low voice, glancing to where the Seal Bearer was still muttering to Grey. 'And he is a very dark horse with his—'

'I do not like this kind of talk,' interrupted O'Brien in distaste. 'Let us play tennis instead!'

Buckingham obliged, but transpired to be a much better player than his opponent, and the spectators soon

205

lost interest in what quickly became a rout. They began talking among themselves again, and their first topic of conversation was the fire.

'It is almost as if someone has declared war on Adventurers,' said Kitty with a shudder. 'Because first there was Proby, and now Lucas and Turner. And those poor children . . .'

'Do you think Fitzgerald did it, Secretary Leighton?' asked Congett, tossing back a cup of wine as though it were water. 'We all know he disapproves of our monopoly on African trade.'

'No,' replied Leighton. 'Because he is a pirate, and monopolies are irrelevant to those who operate outside the law. I cannot see him wasting his time with us. Indeed, I am under the impression that he is in London because he has bigger fish to fry.'

'What fish?' asked Chaloner.

'Fitzgerald is not a pirate!' exclaimed Kitty, while Leighton treated Chaloner to a contemptuous glance and declined to answer. 'He came to our house. Cave brought him, and he sang with my husband. He is not nice – and neither is his voice – but I do not see him incinerating babies.'

'He prefers to be called a privateer, anyway,' added Kipps. 'Or a patriot.'

'I disagree with you, Leighton,' slurred Congett. 'I believe that Fitzgerald killed Turner and Lucas to avenge his friend Reyner. He probably killed Proby, too.'

'Nonsense!' declared Leighton dismissively. 'Reyner died in the Gaming House, which is full of gamblers. Obviously, one of them cut his throat in a quarrel over money.'

'Reverend Addison – who is Tangier's chaplain, and

206

who came back to London on a ship named *Eagle* a couple of weeks ago – told me that Reyner was not a very nice man,' confided Kipps. 'He said he was not surprised the fellow had died violently.'

More wine was served at that point, and the discussion moved to other matters, leaving Chaloner supposing he had better track Addison down.

As Kitty's mention of Cave made him wonder whether *she* might have any insights into why the singer had died, he set about cornering her and her husband alone. It was not easy, because Leighton stuck to them like a leech, muttering in O'Brien's ear about the many invitations that would come his way if he invested his fortune with the Adventurers. But Chaloner managed eventually, and steered the discussion around to the dead singer.

Kitty's face clouded. 'Poor Cave. He had such a lovely voice.'

'It is a damned shame,' agreed O'Brien, red-faced and sweaty after his exertions on the court. 'He was the best tenor in London. Have you heard that the Chapel Royal choir will perform at his funeral? We shall go, of course.'

'I cannot imagine why he was chosen to organise music for Tangier's troops, though,' said Kitty. 'I doubt he knew any of the songs that soldiers like.'

'I suppose it was a peculiar appointment, now you mention it,' mused O'Brien. 'And I think he was relieved to be home. Until he was murdered by Elliot, of course.'

'Did he ever mention Elliot to you?' asked Chaloner.

O'Brien frowned. 'You know, I think he did. At least, he mentioned running into an old friend, who had been a sailor, but who now worked for Williamson. I imagine it is the same fellow. But he only alluded to it in passing, and I doubt it is important.'

But Chaloner was not so sure.

The games dragged on interminably, but Chaloner dared not leave, sure the Earl would be told if he did. He chafed at the lost time, and was disgusted when he emerged to find dusk had fallen. He was weary from fending off sly prods and shoves, and wanted only to go home, but as he aimed for King Street, he met the Earl. Clarendon was surrounded by his ushers, and Hyde was at his side.

'You stayed all day, then,' the Earl said, pleased. 'I thought you would sneak out.'

'I should have done,' said Chaloner, too tired to be politic. 'It was a waste of time.'

The Earl's expression darkened. 'In other words, you have failed to identify the brick-thief, even though you spent the entire day in his company?'

'He is worthless, father,' said Hyde, before Chaloner could point out that even if the culprit had been at the Tennis Court, he was unlikely to stand up and reveal himself. 'He probably has no idea who wants to kill Pratt, either, and we are paying him for nothing.'

'I have several suspects,' said Chaloner, goaded into saying something he should not have done.

'Good,' said the Earl. 'Because if you do not identify the villain by St Frideswide's Feast – six days hence – Pratt might pay with his life. And as a deadline will serve to concentrate your mind, I shall expect answers to your other enquiries by then, too.'

Chaloner fought down the urge to say that he might have had them if he had not been forced to waste an entire day at the Tennis Court. 'I doubt Pratt is in danger, sir. However, the Queen is a different matter. She will be harmed badly if the tale of—'

'Yes, yes,' interrupted the Earl impatiently. 'I know. What about Cave? Frances keeps asking for news of him. What shall I tell her?'

'That she is right: his death probably is suspicious. Williamson has ordered an investigation.'

'Then leave the matter to him,' ordered the Earl. 'Concentrate on my bricks. And on catching the author of the Teviot massacre and the villain who sent those three horrible letters to the Queen.'

'*Three* letters?' asked Chaloner sharply.

'I came across another this afternoon,' explained Hyde.

'What did it say?' asked Chaloner.

Wordlessly, Hyde handed him a piece of paper, which Chaloner scanned quickly in the gathering gloom. The handwriting was the same as the last one, and so was the tenor of the message – that the Queen's plan to dispatch Pratt would meet with the approval of all downtrodden Catholics. It was so clumsily executed that Chaloner felt a surge of anger – not towards its writer, but towards Hyde for giving it credence. He tore it into pieces.

'Hey!' cried Hyde, trying to stop him. 'That was evidence.'

'Not any more,' said Chaloner, shoving the bits in his pocket to put on the next fire he saw. 'And I strongly advise you to destroy the others, too. Where did the culprit leave it this time?'

'In one of the Queen's purses,' replied Hyde sullenly.

Chaloner regarded him askance. Purses contained

ladies' intimate personal items, and not even a private secretary should have had access to the Queen's. 'What were you doing in that?'

Hyde scowled. 'It looked overly full, so I investigated. And it was a good thing I did!'

Unhappily, Chaloner watched the Earl and his party continue on their way. Letters on a desk and half-burned in a hearth were one thing, but in a purse were another. Had he been wrong, and the Queen *was* embroiled in something deadly, not from malice, but from ignorance?

He took his leave of White Hall in a troubled state of mind and began to walk home. He stopped once, at a potter's shop, where he purchased a large piece of clay.

By the time Chaloner reached Tothill Street, he was despondent, feeling he had learned nothing new that day, except the possibility that Pratt might be responsible for the disappearing materials and that Reverend Addison might be a source of information on Teviot's scouts. He decided to explore both lines of enquiry the following morning, after he had interviewed Brilliana.

He arrived to find Hannah preparing to go out. She was wearing a new bodice and skirt, the latter of which was cut open at the front to reveal delicately embroidered underskirts. In accordance with fashion, she wore a black 'face-patch' on her chin, although he was relieved that she had confined herself to one; it was not unknown for people to don up to thirty in an effort to be stylish.

She was in the kitchen, which reeked powerfully of burned garlic. Lounging in a chair, George puffed on his pipe, feet propped on the wall where they left black marks on the plaster. Nan had just poured him a cup of ale, which she delivered with a curtsy before fleeing behind

Joan; Susan was sewing him another shirt. All three women were subdued, and Chaloner wondered whether George's bullying had gone beyond mental intimidation to something physical.

'Stand up in your mistress's presence,' he snapped, sweeping the footman's legs off the wall.

George came to his feet fast, and Chaloner braced himself for a fight, but the footman only bowed an apology and stood to attention. Nan and Susan exchanged a startled look, while the flicker of a smile crossed Joan's dour face. Hannah nodded her approval, then turned to the mirror, assessing the way her hair fell in ringlets around her face.

'You should not be leaving the house at this hour, mistress,' chided Joan, glancing out of the window at the darkness beyond. 'It is not seemly.'

'Thank you, Joan,' said Hannah crisply. 'I shall be home late, so there is no need to wait up. Take the evening off. All of you.'

Susan and Nan did not need to be told twice, and were away before she could change her mind, jostling to be first out of the door. Joan followed more sedately, head held high to indicate her annoyance at being so casually dismissed. George started to sit back down, but saw Chaloner's look and went instead to fetch Hannah's cloak. Chaloner escorted her to White Hall himself, not liking the notion of her being out alone after dark.

'You were right, and I was wrong,' said Hannah, once they were out of the house. She sounded as dispirited as he felt. 'George is a brute, Joan is bossy, Susan is spiteful and Nan is insolent. She just told me that I cannot cook.'

'Did she?' Chaloner hoped he would not be called

upon to dispute it; he was too weary to tell convincing lies.

'But I *can*,' said Hannah, obviously hurt. 'I made you a lovely stew. With lots of garlic.'

'Thank you,' said Chaloner weakly. 'Have you found anyone willing to hire George yet?'

'Unfortunately, his reputation goes before him, so no one will oblige. I wish you would take him with you when you go out. Then I would not feel like an unwelcome interloper in my own home.'

Chaloner had visions of trying to blend into courtly functions with the surly ex-resident of Tangier in tow. 'Impossible. Do you want my company this evening, or only as far as White Hall?'

Hannah grimaced. 'I wish you could come, because it would make the occasion bearable – her Majesty is entertaining Meneses, the Conde de Almeida, again, and it is my turn to act as chaperon.'

'Meneses?' asked Chaloner sharply. Was this Temperance's 'Memphis, Count of America', and the Portuguese member of the Piccadilly Company?

'I cannot abide the man,' Hannah went on. 'Unfortunately, the Queen can.'

'What is wrong with him?'

'He pretends to know no English, but he understands it when it suits him. Personally, I think he is here to see what he can get from her, but he will be disappointed.'

'Why?' asked Chaloner. Hannah was right about the language: Meneses had spoken perfectly passable English at the club.

'Because the Queen has nothing to give. Personally, I think the Court will keep her poor until she produces an heir. Of course, *that* will never happen. She is like me:

212

we both have dutiful husbands, but there is no sign of a baby. Surgeon Wiseman told me that some women simply never conceive.'

'You want children?' asked Chaloner, startled.

'Of course I do! I thought I was just unlucky with my first husband, but it is the same with you, too. And as you had a son with your first wife, the fault must lie with me.'

Chaloner was not sure what to say. He had lost his first wife and child to plague, and since he had arrived in London, he had come to believe that it would be unwise to start another family when his own life and future were so uncertain. He was astonished to learn that Hannah thought otherwise, and it underlined again how little they knew each other.

'The Queen's failure is rather more serious than mine, though,' Hannah went on. 'So I am toying with the notion of acquiring a baby, and passing it off as hers.'

'Please do not,' begged Chaloner, recalling uncomfortably that there was a rumour about that very possibility. 'Royal surgeons will need to be present during the birth, and—'

'Surgeons can be bribed.'

'If they can be bribed, then they are likely to be treacherous. They will betray you.'

'I will not recruit anyone dishonourable,' declared Hannah, in the kind of statement he had once found endearing but that now made him wonder whether she was in complete control of her wits.

'Your plan will see the Queen accused of treason.' Chaloner hesitated, but then forged on – Hannah should know her mistress was in danger. 'Letters have been found

213

that implicate her in a murder. Obviously, she is innocent, but it shows that someone is keen to harm her.'

Hannah paled. 'Who has been murdered? And who found these letters? Do not tell me – Hyde! That treacherous little beast! He told his father and the Earl ordered you to look into it. Am I right?'

Chaloner nodded. 'We know the Queen is innocent of wanting Pratt dead, but—'

'But others will not care whether it is true or not,' finished Hannah angrily. 'They will use it against her, regardless. You must exonerate her immediately.'

'I shall try my best. Hyde discovered these messages in her apartments. Do you know how they might have arrived there?'

'It would not be easy,' replied Hannah, still livid. 'But *you* might see how it was done if I show you her quarters. Meet me there tomorrow . . . No, I shall be busy tomorrow. Come the day after – Saturday – late in the afternoon. And dress nicely, Tom, because she might be there.'

Back in Tothill Street, Chaloner burned the ripped-up letter on the kitchen fire. Then he took a bowl of Hannah's stew, but the reek of charred garlic was so strong that it made him gag. He poured it on the flames, leaping back in alarm when something in it produced a great billowing blaze that almost set him alight. There was bread and cheese in the pantry, along with a jug of milk, so he took them to the drawing room, and started to work on the cipher he had found in the Crown.

Unfortunately, he was no more alert than he had been that morning, and it was not long before the letters blurred in front of his eyes. He tossed down the pen, feeling the need for the restorative effects of music. His best viol was at Long Acre, but he kept another one in the cupboard under the stairs at Tothill Street. There was no Hannah to complain, and no female servants to make disparaging remarks, so he went to retrieve it.

As he played, the tensions of the day drained away. He closed his eyes, allowing the music to take him to its own world, and did not hear the knocking at the door until it was loud enough to be impatient. He was alarmed – that sort of inattention saw spies killed.

'Are you deaf?' demanded Surgeon Wiseman, when Chaloner opened the door. 'I have been hammering for an age, trying to make myself heard over your private recital.'

'What do you want?' asked Chaloner, resenting the return to Earth and its attendant problems.

'To bring you some news,' said Wiseman, equally brusque as he pushed past Chaloner and made for the drawing room. He sat, and warmed his hands by the fire. 'About Cave's funeral.'

'Has a date been set?'

'Yes,' replied Wiseman. 'It took place on Tuesday – two days ago.'

Chaloner regarded him in surprise. 'But I thought it was to be the "social event of the month" with music by the Chapel Royal choir and the Bishop of London presiding.'

'So did everyone else. But it was discovered this evening that he was quietly buried in St Margaret's churchyard on Tuesday morning. It might have gone unrealised for longer, but the curate who conducted the ceremony happened to mention it in passing to the Bishop. Needless to say, a lot of people feel cheated.'

'Who arranged for him to be buried? I thought he had no family.'

'We all did, but we were wrong – he had an older brother named Jacob. However, I cannot imagine what possessed him to shove Cave in the ground with such unseemly haste.'

'Can you not? The ceremony planned by the Chapel Royal choir would have cost a fortune – an expense that Jacob would have been obliged to bear.'

'Cave was comfortably wealthy. He probably had enough money to cover it.'

'But he might not, and the fact that he never mentioned Jacob to his friends means they were not close – no one wants to be bankrupted by the funeral of an unloved sibling. Besides, if Cave did have money, I imagine Jacob would rather keep it for himself.'

'You might be right,' acknowledged Wiseman. 'Are you drinking *cold* milk, Chaloner? Surely, you know that is dangerous? Have you no wine? I shall accept a cup, if you do.' He watched Chaloner go to pour it, then resumed his report. 'A lot of people are upset by what Jacob has done, including a woman named Brilliana Stanley. And we do not want *her* annoyed, believe me. She is a very disreputable character.'

'So I have heard.' Chaloner decided to make use of the surgeon, as he was there. 'Do you know a minister named Addison? I need to talk to him, but I do not know where he lives.'

'Tangier's chaplain? He has taken rooms on The Strand, near the Maypole. Why? Surely you do not suspect him of being complicit in Cave's shameful send-off?'

'It relates to another matter.'

216

'Teviot's fate?' Wiseman shrugged at Chaloner's surprise. 'The Earl told me that you were looking into it, although it seems unreasonable to expect you to find answers so long after the event. Still, I suppose Addison might have a theory; he is an observant fellow. Incidentally, did you hear what happened in the Theatre Royal earlier today?'

Chaloner shook his head.

'*The Parson's Dream* is playing there. It is one of the bawdiest plays ever written – *I* was mortified, and I am an anatomist. But that is beside the point, which is that a Dutch couple were in the audience, and misunderstood something said by the character Mrs Wanton, with rather embarrassing consequences.'

'I do not suppose they were the same Dutch couple who revealed their shaky English in the Banqueting House yesterday, were they?'

'Very possibly. Unfortunately, people are not very forgiving of Hollanders with a poor grasp of our language, and the increasing dislike for this particular couple will do nothing for the cause of peace. Fortunately, someone defused the situation before they could be harmed.'

'Who? And how did he do it?'

'He escorted them outside before they could be assaulted. I believe their saviour was Fitzgerald the pirate. Or should I say Fitzgerald the privateer?'

They were silent for a while, Wiseman sipping his wine and Chaloner pondering how Fitzgerald fitted into his various enquiries. Eventually, the surgeon spoke again.

'The Earl said you were looking into his stolen bricks, too.'

Chaloner wished his master would not gossip about his investigations. He trusted Wiseman to be discreet – for

217

all his faults, the surgeon was sensible of the fact that talking out of turn might endanger lives – but the Earl tended to be loose-tongued with a lot of people.

'You should accuse Oliver of the crime,' Wiseman continued. 'I do not like him. He hired me to cure his bunions, but then refused to pay, just because my lotion made them worse.'

Mention of Clarendon House reminded Chaloner of something else he needed to do. 'Do you recall inventing a substance for immobilising broken limbs? You tried it on me once, and I thought I might have to wear it on my arm for the rest of my life.'

'I have perfected it since then,' said Wiseman coolly, not liking to be reminded of a venture that had been less than successful. 'It now works extremely well. Why?'

'May I have some?'

Wiseman regarded him suspiciously, but mixed him a batch from the supplies he carried in his bag. When it was ready, Chaloner used it and the clay he had bought to produce an accurate mould of the key-impressions he had made the previous night. It did not take long, and when he had finished, all that remained was to take the moulds to a forge and commission a copy in metal.

'Should I ask whose house you intend to give yourself unlimited access to?' asked Wiseman.

'No.'

'Well, perhaps I am better off not knowing, anyway.' Wiseman stood. 'Oh, I almost forgot. The Earl wants you to go to Woolwich tomorrow.'

Chaloner groaned. 'He orders me to solve these mysteries by Wednesday, but then wastes my time by sending me on futile errands. I might have had some answers today had he left me alone.'

'Very possibly, but do not antagonise him by refusing to comply. Apparently, a new ship, *Royal Katherine*, is to be launched, and a lot of his enemies will be there. He wants you to monitor them.'

'What does he expect me to do?' asked Chaloner waspishly. 'Sink it and drown them all?'

Wiseman raised his eyebrows. 'Now there is an idea.'

The following dawn was cold, wet and windy, so Chaloner dressed in clothes suitable for a day outside in foul weather, and trotted down the stairs to spend an hour on the cipher before he left. He had left it in his pen-box, and was troubled to note that it had been moved since the previous night.

He stared at it. The table had been polished that morning, because there were streaks of wax where it had not been buffed properly. Had Joan or one of the maids knocked the box as they had worked, so the disturbance was innocent? Or had they looked inside to see whether it contained anything interesting? Or, more alarmingly, had George?

Chaloner could see no way to find out – he doubted direct demands would yield truthful answers – and supposed he would just have to be more careful in future. As it was raining, he could not take the cipher with him lest the ink ran, so he knelt and slipped it in the gap between the wall and the skirting board. He stood quickly when someone entered the room. It was Hannah.

'What are you doing down there?' she demanded. 'I hope we do not have mice again. George told me he had poisoned them all.'

'Perhaps he missed one.' Chaloner did not like the idea of George in charge of toxic substances, and when

219

the footman marched into the room with a breakfast tray, he declined to take any.

'Eat something, Tom,' instructed Hannah brusquely. 'You are already thinner than when you came home from Tangier.'

Chaloner refrained from saying that her cooking was largely responsible for that, because he could tell from her scowl that her morning temper was about to erupt. He accepted a piece of bread, but spoiled the ale and oatmeal by 'accidentally' knocking one so it spilled into the other; he did not want his wife poisoned by their footman, either.

'Why are you awake?' he asked. 'It is not long past dawn – the middle of the night for you.'

'Do not be facetious with me, Thomas,' she snapped. 'I have to go to Woolwich, because the ship named after the Queen is to be launched today. We are travelling there by barge, God help us. The last time I went on one of those, I was sick the whole way.'

'Then perhaps it is as well the breakfast is spoiled. You cannot be sick with an empty stomach.'

'Spoken like a man who has never suffered from *mal de mer*,' retorted Hannah crossly. 'Because if you had, you would know you could abstain from food for a week and still find something to vomit.'

On that note, Chaloner took his leave.

As he left the house, it occurred to him that it was time he followed Thurloe's orders and purchased a handgun. There was only one place he knew where such weapons could be bought with no questions asked – given their potential for assassination, the government liked gunsmiths to keep records – and that was from the Trulocke brothers on St Martin's Lane. Before he entered their shabby, uninviting premises, he bought a piece of meat, donned an old horsehair wig, and covered his face with the kind of scarf men wore to keep London's foul air from their lungs.

Outside the shop was a fierce dog, which snapped at the ankles of passers-by. Chaloner tossed it the meat, then stepped around it when it leapt on the offering. It wagged its tail as he passed, and he wondered whether it remembered him feeding it on previous occasions.

Inside, the place reeked of gunpowder and hot metal. It was also busy, and all three brothers were dealing with customers. Like Chaloner, the other patrons had taken care to conceal their faces, but unlike him they did not appreciate that a disguise was more than just donning a hat and a scarf. He recognised Secretary Leighton from his scuttling gait, and although Harley knew to change his walk, his blazing devil-eyes gave him away.

Chaloner edged towards Harley. It was not a good place to accost the scout, because it would expose them both to recognition, but he could certainly ascertain what the man was doing in a place where illegal firearms could be purchased. Unfortunately, Harley's business was just concluding.

'It will be ready this evening,' Edmund Trulocke was saying. 'Come back at dusk.'

Harley nodded, and was gone without another word. Thwarted, Chaloner sauntered towards Leighton, pretending to inspect a nearby musket.

'Are you sure?' William Trulocke was asking worriedly. 'It will render the trigger unusually light. If you stick it in your belt and touch it accidentally, it will blow off your—'

'I am sure,' interrupted Leighton shortly. 'The damned thing is so stiff at the moment that I need both hands to set it off. I need a much more sensitive mechanism.'

Trulocke nodded, and a vast amount of money changed hands. Leighton gave instructions for the finished product to be delivered to his Queenhithe home, and left. Chaloner could only suppose that he was taking precautions to ensure he did not suffer the same fate as his fellow Adventurers – Proby, Turner and Lucas.

When Leighton had gone, Trulocke turned to Chaloner, who pointed to the gun he wanted. By the time they had negotiated a price, and Chaloner had been furnished with enough ammunition to blast away half of London, the shop had emptied and the other two brothers had retreated to their workshop. Chaloner laid the mould on the table.

'We do not cut keys,' said Trulocke immediately. 'It would be illegal, not to mention treading on the toes of our colleagues the locksmiths.'

'How much?' asked Chaloner.

Trulocke named a sum, Chaloner halved it, and they agreed on an amount somewhere in the middle. Trulocke took the mould, and disappeared. The item was ready in record time, and it was not long before Chaloner was stepping around the dog with a gun in his belt and a key in his pocket.

Next, Chaloner went to see Thurloe. Unusually, the ex-Spymaster was not strolling in the gardens, but preparing to go out, swathed in a hat and cloak that rendered him incognito.

'It is no day to be travelling.' Thurloe looked at Chaloner's coat. 'You are already drenched, and the day has barely begun. I hope I do not catch a chill from this escapade.'

'Where are you going?' asked Chaloner. 'Home to Oxfordshire?'

'And leave you to deal with Fitzgerald alone? No. I am off to see *Royal Katherine* launched.'

'Because you think Fitzgerald will be there? If he is as slippery as you say, your presence will put him on his guard, and you will be wasting your time.'

'Probably,' sighed Thurloe. 'But it would be remiss not to try.'

'The Earl has ordered me to go, too. He says his enemies will be there, and he thinks the culprit will be braying to all and sundry about the missing bricks.'

'Then we had better listen carefully,' said Thurloe with a smile. He glanced up at the grey clouds that scudded overhead. 'I am not going by boat, though. There is a stiff wind, which will blow directly against the current. It will make for a most unpleasant journey.'

Poor Hannah, thought Chaloner. 'Shall we hire horses?'

'In this weather?' Thurloe was aghast. 'I think not! I have asked the porter to fetch me a hackney carriage. It will scarcely be comfortable, but it will have to suffice.'

Woolwich lay on the south bank of the river, dominated by the largest and oldest of the Thames shipyards. It employed some three hundred workers, whose cottages crouched along muddy lanes behind the dry docks. Cannons boomed as the hackney approached, and Chaloner tensed. He had been wary of artillery ever since the Battle of Naseby.

'They are announcing His Majesty's arrival with a

royal salute,' explained Thurloe. 'There will be another when the Queen disembarks, so do not let it startle you.'

They alighted to find the dockyard already full. Most of the Court was there, many looking as though they had come straight from whatever wild entertainment they had enjoyed the night before. They mingled with officials from the admiralty, including Samuel Pepys, who had inveigled himself a choice spot near the King and the Duke of York.

Royal Katherine was the centre of attention. She was a three-masted warship of eighty-four guns, attractively painted in black, red and gold. Vast windows at her stern indicated that whoever commanded her would be very comfortably accommodated.

'We shall separate,' determined Thurloe. 'We will learn more that way.'

They headed in opposite directions, and the first person Chaloner met was Williamson, who had donned a disguise so bad it was laughable – a landsman's idea of what a sea-officer would wear, complete with an empty coat-sleeve to denote an amputated arm. The Spymaster was gazing at someone with open yearning, and Chaloner followed the direction of his gaze to Kitty. She and O'Brien were with Brodrick, whose company they seemed to be enjoying, and Secretary Leighton, whose presence was obviously unwelcome.

Williamson reddened when he saw that Chaloner had witnessed a look that should never have been given in public, and moved forward to speak.

'You did not visit me yesterday,' he snapped, concealing his mortification by going on the offensive.

'I was busy.'

Williamson glared. 'Then come tonight at six o'clock.

Do not be late – I am invited to O'Brien's home after-wards, before he attends some public event in Westminster.'

Chaloner was about to inform him that he had other plans when the Spymaster hurried away abruptly, and he turned to see Kitty and O'Brien approaching. The amused gleam in Kitty's green eyes said she had not been fooled by the Spymaster's disguise, although Chaloner was fairly certain O'Brien remained in ignorance. Leighton was still with them, and so was Brodrick.

'Chaloner!' O'Brien cried in obvious delight. 'I was just telling Brodrick here about your remarkable talent on the viol.'

'I have heard him play many times,' said Brodrick. 'He is especially good at Ferrabosco and Schütz, whose arpeggios are notably demanding. Their interludes require an exacting sense of rhythm, which separates the integral harmony from the . . .'

He trailed off as Leighton, eyes glazed, scuttled away.

'At last!' exclaimed O'Brien, laughing. 'I did not believe you when you said you could *bore* him into leaving us alone, Brodrick, but you have succeeded admirably. Personally, I thought we were going to be stuck with him all day, and there is something about him I cannot like.'

'Nor I,' agreed Kitty. 'He makes me shudder, although I would be hard-pressed to say why. Perhaps it is because he is an advocate of the slave trade.'

'Actually, it is because he is innately evil,' supplied Brodrick matter-of-factly. 'But speaking of evil, there is Fitzgerald. Come away quickly before he engages us in conversation. We have our reputations to consider, and they will not be enhanced if we are seen conversing with a pirate.'

Chaloner had no reason to flee, so he held his ground

as Fitzgerald approached. The pirate was wearing exquisitely made clothes, but they were slightly worn, indicating that the gossips were right: he probably was a wealthy man who had recently fallen on hard times.

'I know you,' he said in his oddly high voice, although his single eye was fixed on the retreating figures of Brodrick and the O'Briens. 'We met at the bawdy house. I recognise your eyes.'

'Did we?' Chaloner smiled, although he was disconcerted that the man had managed to see beneath the mask he had worn, especially as his eyes were not particularly distinctive. 'I am afraid I recall very little from my evenings there.'

'Wine is a treacherous thing,' said Fitzgerald softly. 'It puts a man out of his wits, and that is never wise when there are so many dangerous individuals at large.'

Leaving Chaloner wondering whether he had just been threatened, Fitzgerald sauntered away. People gave him a wide berth, including several Adventurers and Swaddell, all of whom looked pointedly the other way as he passed.

Some sixth sense told Chaloner he was being watched, and he turned to see Leighton, who was regarding him with a blank expression that was nevertheless unsettling. He returned the stare, and it was the secretary who broke it, because Margareta Janszoon collided heavily with him.

'I retard your impotence,' she said breezily. Her guards immediately tensed nervously.

'Impetus, madam,' said Leighton stiffly, as several courtiers began to laugh. 'It means forward movement. Impotence, on the other hand, has a rather different sense.'

'You correct my speech?' asked Margareta indignantly. 'How rude!'

Chaloner felt his jaw drop as she removed a piece of cheese from her purse and began to eat it. Did she *want* to perpetuate the stereotype of the dairy-produce-loving Hollander?

'I wonder if her husband has a pat of butter on his person,' murmured Thurloe in Chaloner's ear. He sounded amused. 'Incidentally, I saw you break your promise to me just now. Fitzgerald.'

'He approached me,' objected Chaloner defensively. 'And all he did was mutter about dangerous men.'

Thurloe regarded him uneasily. 'What did he mean?'

'I have no idea, but I do not believe he is as deadly as everyone claims.'

'Do not underestimate him, Tom. He . . . Oh, heavens! He is going to sing. I hope *Royal Katherine* does not have much in the way of expensive glassware, because if so, it is in grave peril.'

He was not the only one with a low opinion of Fitzgerald's talents. O'Brien promptly began to run, aiming to put as much distance between him and the performer as possible; Kitty and Brodrick trotted after him, both struggling to mask their laughter. Then the first notes of an aria began to waft around the shipyard.

The sound was indescribable. The notes were mostly true, but had a curious, metallic quality that was deeply unpleasant. They did not sound human, and had Chaloner not been able to see Fitzgerald opening and closing his mouth, he might have assumed they derived from an artificial source. The hubbub of genteel conversation died away.

There was a general a sigh of relief when the great guns roared an interruption. They heralded the arrival of the Queen, whose barge was rowed ashore with great ceremony. Her Majesty alighted jauntily enough, but Hannah was green, and so were several other ladies. Cruelly, the King released a bellow of mocking laughter.

'It was horrible,' Hannah whispered, when Chaloner went to help her. 'The wind blew the river into great waves, and I seriously considered throwing myself overboard, just to end my misery.'

'I will take you home by land when you have recovered.'

Hannah gave a wan smile. 'I wish you could, but Meneses has attached himself to our party, and I am not leaving the Queen alone with *him*.'

Chaloner looked to where she pointed, and saw Meneses had indeed fastened himself to the Queen, a fawning, oily presence that deterred anyone else from greeting her. Hannah snagged the Duke of Buckingham's arm as he passed.

'Come and tell the Queen you like the ship that is being named in her honour,' she ordered. The Duke looked as if he would decline, but Hannah tightened her grip. 'It will please her.'

With no choice, Buckingham went to oblige, leaving Chaloner alone again. Thurloe joined him, and started to speak, but was distracted by a commotion on the other side of the dockyard. Apparently, one of the Janszoons had made another faux pas.

'But *Royal Katherine is* a dog,' Margareta was objecting crossly. 'Many sailors have told us so.'

'It means she has fast legs and strong teeth,' elaborated Janszoon, clearly nervous as he glanced around to ensure his henchmen were to hand. 'There is nothing wrong with dogs.'

'Perhaps I should call *Katherine* a fish,' said Margareta waspishly. 'Is that a better epitaph?'

'Epithet,' corrected Leighton, unable to help himself.

Margareta scowled, but the King prevented a spat by announcing that he intended to go aboard. There was an immediate scramble as everyone tried to accompany him, and Chaloner was sure the great ship listed from the weight that suddenly descended on her. The Janszoons followed with rather more dignity.

'Do they work at being so stupid?' muttered Janszoon. He spoke English and Chaloner wondered why he did not revert to his native tongue, given that his words were intended for Margareta's ears only. 'Or does it come naturally to them?'

Chaloner did not hear her reply, because he was suddenly aware of someone close behind him. It was Lester, who was more soft-footed than Chaloner would have expected for a man of his size.

'They must have eavesdropped on a conversation between seamen,' Lester explained. '*Katherine is* a dog, but the description has nothing to do with speed and strength. Rather, it means she sails like a bucket, and will wallow like the devil in a swell. I should not like to command her.'

'Then perhaps it is as well that you are unlikely ever to do so,' said Thurloe coolly.

'Thurloe?' said Lester, peering at him. 'Good God! I almost did not recognise you in that dreadful old cloak. How are you? It must be eight years since we last met. Now where was it?'

'Dover,' replied Thurloe promptly and without a hint of friendliness. 'You were about to travel to Portugal. Fitzgerald was among your crew, if I recall correctly.'

'Yes!' Lester exclaimed, seemingly unperturbed by Thurloe's icy tone. 'That was before he turned to privateering, of course.' He turned to Chaloner. 'Thank you for the drawings of Pepperell and Elliot, by the way. They have already proved useful.'

'How?' asked Chaloner, wondering why Lester had not mentioned sailing with Fitzgerald when they had discussed him at the club two nights before.

'By allowing me to prove for certain that they knew each other *and* that they had argued,' replied Lester. 'I am not sure what about, but I will tell you when I find out.'

'I had not remembered until now that he and Fitzgerald were crewmates,' said Thurloe, when the captain had walked away. 'It makes me more wary of him than ever.'

'I imagine they have both sailed with lots of people if they have spent most of their lives at sea,' said Chaloner, instinctively defensive. 'It almost certainly means nothing.'

'We are wasting our time here,' said Thurloe, declining to debate the matter. 'You were right: Fitzgerald is far too clever to let anything slip in public, while I suspect most of the Piccadilly Company has no idea that he is taking orders from a higher authority.'

'I have heard no rumours about what is planned for next Wednesday, either,' said Chaloner gloomily. 'Or so much as a whisper about the Earl's bricks. Shall we go home?'

'Not yet. Someone may drink too much wine and become indiscreet. We can but hope.'

Thurloe and Chaloner remained at Woolwich long after the King had galloped away on a fine stallion, his more

230

athletic courtiers streaming at his heels. Meneses was still with the Queen when she clambered on her barge for the homeward journey, and thus so was Hannah. The other ladies-in-waiting were nowhere to be seen, though: they had secured themselves rides in coaches, unwilling to endure a second ordeal on the turbulent Thames.

When they had gone, Chaloner saw Harley and Newell standing near the place where wine was being served, and tried to start a conversation. They turned away, and did not react even when he made provocative remarks about Reyner's murder. Faced with such taciturnity, he was forced to concede defeat and wandered to where Fitzgerald was talking to several people, all of whom were so well wrapped against the weather that it was impossible to tell who they were. When he moved closer, intending to eavesdrop, Brinkes blocked his way.

Chaloner retreated, then started to approach from a different direction, but Thurloe appeared at his side and shook his head warningly. Frustrated by their lack of progress, Chaloner was inclined to ignore him, but a flash of steely blue eyes told him he would be in trouble if he did.

Heartily wishing he had never made the promise, Chaloner watched Fitzgerald and his companions disperse, wondering whether anything would be served by whisking one down a dark alley and demanding answers at knifepoint. Of course, there would be hell to pay if his victim transpired to be someone influential. One of the gaggle walked jauntily towards them, and Chaloner glimpsed red ribbons in the lace around his boots, all but hidden under a long, thick cloak.

'Robert!' the ex-Spymaster exclaimed in astonishment. 'What are you doing here?'

'I move in auspicious company these days,' replied Jones with an engaging grin, once Thurloe had removed his hat to reveal his face. 'The glassware trade is thriving, as I explained to my sister in the letters I wrote.'

Thurloe turned to Chaloner. 'This is my wife's brother. Robert Lydcott.'

'Lydcott,' repeated Chaloner flatly. 'I knew it was not Jones.'

Lydcott shrugged. 'If you were kin to an ex-Spymaster, you would change your name, too. No one wants to know a Lydcott these days. It is almost as bad as being a Cromwell.'

Chaloner was not unsympathetic: he shared his name with a man who had signed the old king's death warrant, and it was awkward to say the least. But using an alias was not Lydcott's only crime.

'He is a member of the Piccadilly Company,' he said to Thurloe. 'In fact, he founded it.'

'He did what?' exploded Thurloe, shocked.

'Where lies the problem?' asked Lydcott, bemused. 'Exporting glassware to New England is a perfectly legitimate venture. Profitable, too. At least, it is now. It was rocky before Fitzgerald came along and offered to invest, but now it is doing splendidly.'

'Robert!' cried Thurloe, appalled. 'Will you never learn? You know what kind of man Fitzgerald is. How can you have been so reckless as to go into business with him?'

'It was a sound commercial decision,' objected Lydcott, stung. 'My company was on the verge of bankruptcy, but he made it viable again. We have been doing well for weeks now. And in case you were wondering, I did not tell you because I knew how you would react. I wrote to Ann about my change in fortunes last month, and she will be proud of me, even if you—'

'On the contrary,' snapped Thurloe. 'You frightened her, and I have been trying to find you ever since. I should have known you were involved in another wild scheme.'

'It is *not* wild. I know what you think of Fitzgerald, but this is honest business. He charters a ship to transport our glassware to New England, and he arranges a different cargo for the return journey. Gravel, mostly.'

'Gravel,' said Thurloe flatly.

'It is a useful commodity. I *swear* there is nothing devious or dubious about the Piccadilly Company. Our membership includes several noblemen and a number of wealthy merchants. Of course, I do not know their names . . .'

'If it is legal, why does Brinkes keep people away from its meetings?' asked Chaloner.

'To prevent spies from learning our business secrets,' explained Lydcott earnestly. 'And because Fitzgerald earned a lot of enemies when he was a pirate. You are one of them, Thurloe, although he has not broken the law since you fell from power. He says it has not been necessary now the Royalists are in control.'

Thurloe did not look convinced, and neither was Chaloner, but Lydcott clearly believed his own tale. He was not overly endowed with wits, thought Chaloner, so was exactly the kind of fellow to be used by more devious minds. But there was nothing to be gained from questioning him further, and Thurloe indicated he could go. Lydcott escaped with relief.

'He always was a fool,' said Thurloe in disgust. 'And I have bailed him out of more trouble than you can imagine, only for him to land himself in yet another scrape. But to throw in his lot with Fitzgerald! All I can hope is that he will escape this foolery unscathed, because Ann will be heartbroken if anything happens to him.'

Chaloner summoned a hackney carriage, and he and Thurloe rode back to Lincoln's Inn in silence. The ex-Spymaster promptly hurried away to see what messages had been left for him by informants while he had been absent, and Chaloner decided to check Clarendon House.

He arrived as dusk was falling. Wright's soldiers had not yet deigned to appear, but Pratt, Oliver and Vere were there, inspecting the newly installed gateposts at the front of the drive – four times the height of a man, and topped with carvings that bore a marked resemblance to winged pigs.

Chaloner considered tackling Pratt about possible errors in his estimates, but decided against it: he was more likely to secure a confession when there was not an audience of minions listening. The same went for Vere and Oliver – they were not going to expose mistakes in their employer's reckoning when he was standing next to them. So Chaloner sank back into the shadows, and waited to see whether the opportunity would arise to accost one of them alone. Unfortunately, all three set off in the direction of the Haymarket together, clearly with the intention of enjoying a post-work drink in the company of each other.

Once they had gone, he approached the house and tried his key in the door. It did not work, but he was expecting that. Using a file he had filched from the Trulockes' shop, he sawed at it until it did, then spent another hour in patient honing until it turned smoothly and silently.

When he was satisfied, he entered the house and lit a lamp, using a tinderbox he found in the library. He prowled the main floor, instinctively memorising lengths, distances and dimensions, and testing his key in other doors as he went. Then he climbed to the next storey, wondering maliciously who would sleep in all the bedrooms, given that the Earl had a small family and very few friends.

Of course, he thought with a pang, the Earl had a lot more friends than *he* did. Other than Thurloe, there was only Wiseman whom he did not much like, Temperance who did not much like him, and Hannah. Most of the friends he had made while spying were dead, and the few who had survived had retired under false names, and would not take kindly to a reminder of their past lives.

Sobered by the thought, he ascended to the top floor, where smaller chambers would provide accommodation for the Earl's retinue and less important guests. One was marked with Kipps's name, and Chaloner unlocked it to see the Seal Bearer had already started to decorate. It was sumptuous, and indicated that either Kipps had paid for some of the fitments himself, or he had persuaded the builders to make a special effort on his behalf.

Eventually, Chaloner descended to the basement, noting that the laundries had been supplied with copper vats since he had last been there. He glanced at the stairs that led to the cellar, and bent to inspect some muddy footprints. They were wet, indicating they had been made not long before, and included human feet and animal claws. It was curious, but he was disinclined to investigate, given that to do so would mean entering a place that was far too similar to a prison to be comfortable. He was about to leave when he heard a sound.

He stood stock still, listening. Had Wright arrived and seen his lamp, so had come to find out who was prowling when the house should be empty? Or, more likely, given that Wright was not a conscientious man, was it the thieves?

Gritting his teeth, he forced himself to walk down the stairs, fighting the clamouring voice in his head that told him to race back up them and run away from Clarendon House as fast as his legs would carry him. At the bottom, he raised the lamp, but saw nothing other than the hallway disappearing into darkness. He moved along it cautiously.

When he reached the strongroom he saw that a large chest had been placed inside it, at the far end. The light from his lantern picked up a flash of white – a piece of paper was on top of the box. He walked toward it and scanned the message:

Behold the smalle jawes of Death and Darknesse

He regarded it in incomprehension, and lifted the lid. Then three things happened at once. First, there was a frantic flurry of movement and he saw the box was full of rats. Second, there was sound behind him, startling him into dropping the lamp. And third, the door slammed closed, leaving him in total darkness.

Chapter 7

Cursing his own stupidity, Chaloner groped his way towards the door, furry bodies scurrying around his feet as he went. Agitated squeaks and the sound of scrabbling claws came from all directions, curiously muffled by the lead-lined walls. He reached the door and tried to open it, but was not surprised when it refused to budge.

He experienced a pang of alarm when it occurred to him that he might not be released until the workmen returned the following morning, but that was nothing compared to what he felt when he remembered that Pratt had designed the room to be airtight.

He did panic at that point, and pounded on the door with all his might, feeling his breath come in agonised bursts, and aware that his fear was transmitting itself to the rodents, because they nipped at his ankles and scratched at his legs. The chest had been full of them, and they would use up the air, reducing the time any of them would survive. How long would they wait before beginning to eat him alive? And how was he to fend them off when he could not see them?

But he had been trained to think rationally in dire

situations, and the debilitating wave of terror did not last long. He forced himself to stand still and think. He would not suffocate immediately, because there was still plenty of air, and the hapless rats were probably more interested in escaping than in devouring their cellmate. While he waited for his heart to slow to a more normal pace, he set his mind to working out who might want him dead.

Was it Fitzgerald or his master, because he had been asking questions about the Piccadilly Company? Harley and Newell, because they resented his interference over the Teviot affair? What about Leighton, who was sinister by any standard, and who almost certainly had something to hide? Or was it the brick-thieves, because he was a nuisance?

There was also a possibility that the culprit was someone nearer home. Chief Usher Dugdale would not hesitate to dispatch him, and neither would his crony Edgeman, but were they sufficiently bold to contrive and act out such a diabolical plan? Kipps was, but Chaloner had received nothing but kindness from him, and could not believe that the Seal Bearer meant him harm. And then there was Hyde, who deplored the fact that his father's household included a spy.

He turned his thoughts to escape. He could not relight the lamp, because he had no tinderbox, so whatever he did would need to be done in the dark. He began to run his fingers over the door, recalling that the vault was the only room in the house that could not be opened with the master key. But it was still secured with a lock, and locks could be picked.

He was just beginning to fear that there might not be one on the inside, when he found it. It was covered by a slip of metal, designed to prevent air from blowing in.

He prised it aside with his knife, ridiculously relieved when he detected air on his fingertips. At least he could kneel there and inhale it if the worst came to the worst. He took his probes from his pocket, inserted them into the hole, and began to fiddle.

He soon learned it was a type he had never encountered before, equipped with a strong spring that was beyond his probes' capabilities. He lost count of the times when he nearly had it turned, only to hear it snap back again. Moreover, the air in the room seemed to be getting thinner, making him light-headed. At one point he sank to the floor, feeling despair begin to consume him, but the sharp teeth of a rat in his hand drove him to his knees again, to start tinkering afresh.

When the lock eventually gave way he wondered whether he had imagined it, but he pushed the door and felt it swing open. The corridor beyond was as dark as the vault, and he still could not see his hand in front of his face. The rats sensed freedom, though, and he heard them surging around him as they retreated to the deeper recesses of the cellars.

Then followed a nightmarish period during which he lurched blindly, trying to locate the steps. When he eventually found them, he ascended as fast as he could, and made for the portico. It took several attempts to insert his key in the front door, and when it opened, he staggered out with a gasp of relief. He leaned against the wall and took a deep breath, relishing the cool, fresh scent of night. By the time he had recovered his composure, he hated Clarendon House more than ever.

The experience had shaken him badly, and he wanted no more than to spend what was left of the evening by a fire with a large jug of wine. He considered going to Long Acre, but the prospect of a cold garret did not appeal: he craved human company. However, he wished he had chosen somewhere other than Tothill Street when he opened the door to his house and immediately sensed an atmosphere.

George was in the kitchen, a picture of serenity with his long legs stretched comfortably towards the hearth and a flagon of ale in his hand. He was in the chair Joan liked to use, and she had been relegated to a far less pleasant seat near the window. Susan was positively cowering, while Nan looked as though she had been crying. George did stand when Chaloner entered the room, but so slowly it was only just on the right side of respect.

'The mistress will be late tonight,' said Joan, coolly aloof as always. 'She baked you a pie, but it is no longer available.'

It was an odd thing to say. 'Why?' Chaloner asked. 'What happened to it?'

'*He* fed it to the neighbour's pig,' said Susan, regarding George through eyes that were full of nervous dislike. George stared back at her, his expression disconcertingly neutral. 'He said he thought it was meant for the slops.'

'What a pity,' said Chaloner, wondering whether George expected him to be grateful. If so, then he was going to be disappointed, because Chaloner was not about to be disloyal to his wife. 'But you all seem merry here together, so I shall leave you in peace.'

He turned to leave but Joan seized his arm, and it was fortunate for her that she was a middle-aged woman, or she might have found herself knocked away with considerable vigour. Chaloner was not in the mood for being manhandled.

'We are not merry at all,' she hissed. 'Indeed, we have not been merry since you hired that horrible footman. If you want to keep Nan, Susan and me, you will dismiss him.'

'Rat bites,' said George, making them both jump by speaking close behind them. Chaloner had not heard him approach, and was disconcerted that so large a man should move with such stealth. 'You should see to that hand, sir. They can be dangerous if left untended.'

Chaloner regarded him sharply. Was there more to the words than concerned advice?

'Rat bites?' Joan's voice was a mixture of revulsion and disapproval, while the maids smirked at this latest evidence of their master's eccentricity. 'I shall not ask how you came by them.'

'Good,' said Chaloner shortly, and stalked out. He had done no more than slump wearily by the drawing room fire when there was a knock on the front door. He smothered a sigh of annoyance when Wiseman was shown in moments later by a spiteful-faced Joan.

'He will berate me tomorrow, for not asking whether he was available to receive you,' she said snidely to the surgeon. 'But it does him no harm to be sociable on occasion.'

Chaloner shot to his feet. There was only so far he could be goaded by surly servants, but Joan ducked behind Wiseman in alarm, and was gone before he could do more than step towards her.

'If ever you dismiss that gorgon, I am sure Temperance would take her on,' said Wiseman, pouring himself a cup of claret from the jug on the table. 'To keep the club in order.'

'Take her with you tonight, then,' said Chaloner, adding pointedly, 'When you leave.'

Wiseman laughed, wholly unfazed by Chaloner's sullen temper. 'Having impudent servants serves you right. Now you know how the Earl feels when you are disrespectful to him.'

'What do you want, Wiseman?'

The surgeon sat, and stretched his hands towards the flames. 'Must I have a reason to visit a friend? But perhaps it is as well I came, because you seem unwell. Do you need my services?'

'No, thank you,' said Chaloner shortly.

Wiseman reached out and grabbed his wrist. 'Is that a rat bite?'

Chaloner tried to pull away, but Wiseman's grip was powerful, and he did not want to free himself at the expense of broken bones. Wiseman rummaged in his bag and produced a pot.

'Smear that on me, and it will be the last thing you do,' warned Chaloner. He had learned to his cost that the medical profession invariably did more harm than good, and although Wiseman was generally better than most, he did have a propensity to experiment.

'It is a salve containing ingredients to combat infection,' said Wiseman sternly. 'Any fool knows rat bites can kill. Did you not hear what happened to poor Congett this evening?'

Chaloner regarded him uneasily as the healing paste was slapped on – the big-nosed Adventurer had been in good health at Woolwich earlier. 'What?'

'He was found dead by the river tonight, and the only

mark on his body was a rat bite on his foot. He must have trodden on it while he was strolling along the shore.'

No self-respecting merchant 'strolled' along the banks of the Thames, on the grounds that all manner of filth was washed up on them, not to mention the fact that they were muddy. Chaloner could only assume that Congett was the latest victim in whatever war was raging.

'His heart must have been weak,' Wiseman went on. 'And he died from the shock of it.'

'He will have been murdered,' predicted Chaloner. 'Although I would not recommend opening the corpse to prove it. That would almost certainly put you in danger.'

'Then I shall abstain,' said Wiseman, packing away his salve and standing to leave. He hesitated. 'I do not want to know what is currently occupying your time – not if it involves murder and rats – but it would make me happier if you accepted this. It is the scalpel I use for dissecting eyeballs. No, do not try to pass it back with such a look of revulsion!'

But Chaloner *was* repelled – the tiny blade was not very clean. 'I do not need it.'

'Yes, you do,' stated Wiseman firmly. 'It is more easily hidden than the rest of the arsenal you tote around with you, and considerably more discreet. Take it, Chaloner. It may save your life.'

Chaloner doubted such a minute thing would do anything of the kind, but he slid it into the waistband of his breeches, nodding his thanks – he had neither the energy nor the inclination to engage in a battle of wills with Wiseman. When the surgeon had gone, he went upstairs and lay on the bed, where he endured nightmare after nightmare about the strongroom and Congett.

* * *

243

Chaloner snapped awake a few hours later to find himself clutching a dagger. A creak on the stair confirmed that his return to consciousness had not been natural. He bounded off the bed and was about to pounce on the person who came creeping into the room when he realised it was Hannah.

'What are you doing?' she demanded suspiciously, seeing him behind the door.

He shrugged sheepishly, dropping the weapon on to the pile of clothes behind his back before she could see it. 'I heard a sound.'

'I was trying to be quiet,' declared Hannah, loudly and on an accompanying waft of wine. It was still dark outside, although a paler glimmer in the east said dawn was on its way. He surmised that she had just enjoyed one of White Hall's infamous all-night parties.

'Whisper, Hannah, or you will wake the servants. Where have you been?'

'Westminster. There was a reception to celebrate the launch of *Katherine*. The whole Court was there. Indeed, I am surprised you stayed away, as it was a good opportunity to eavesdrop.'

Chaloner ignored the censure inherent in her words. 'Who was there?'

'Everyone,' replied Hannah unhelpfully, twirling around happily and then staggering. 'It was very lively, especially once the sober, boring types had gone. Such as your Earl and his retinue – with the exception of Kipps, who knows how to enjoy himself. I am sorry for you, having to endure the likes of Hyde, Dugdale and Edgeman day in and day out.'

'Our paths do not cross very often. Although Dugdale—'

'Leighton from the Adventurers left early, too,' Hannah

went on, cutting across him in the way she always did when she was not very interested in what he was saying. 'So did Grey. Well, I suppose we can excuse Grey, because he still mourns Turner and Lucas.'

Chaloner wondered whether that was true. Grey had wept in the Rainbow Coffee House, but had seemed in perfectly good spirits at the Tennis Courts later, when he had chatted and laughed with Kipps. And why had Hyde, Dugdale, Edgeman and Leighton left early? To lock irritating intelligencers in Clarendon House's strong-room? Chaloner said nothing, and Hannah chattered on.

'Turner and Lucas were decent men. A little preoc-cupied with commerce, perhaps, but that is deemed a virtue these days. They were Adventurers, like the King, the Duke and the Queen.'

'The Queen is not an Adventurer,' said Chaloner, startled.

'Yes, she is. Go and look on the charter if you do not believe me. Of course, I imagine she did not know what she was signing, and if any profits do come her way, they will be siphoned off by dishonest officials. Like Leighton and Hyde.'

'You think Hyde is dishonest?'

Hannah pulled a face. 'Perhaps dishonest is too strong a word. *Slimy* is better. Swaddell was there, too, and so was Williamson, although they ignored each other. Williamson asked after you.'

'Did he?' asked Chaloner uneasily.

'He gave me a message for you.' Hannah rummaged in her purse. 'Here it is. He was all courtesy and kind-ness, quite unlike his usual self. And I like his new man, Lester. Lester left early, too, which was a pity, because he plays the flute like a cherub. Of course, he dances like an ox, but a man cannot have every courtly grace at his fingertips.'

She prattled on while Chaloner unfolded the letter. It had been scrawled in a hurry, and said nothing other than that he should visit Williamson without delay. He screwed it into a ball and tossed it away, recalling that he had been ordered to visit the Spymaster's offices the previous evening too, and Williamson was doubtless piqued with him for failing to arrive.

'You should go,' said Hannah, still speaking far too loudly. 'I told him you were currently investigating four different cases, and he said he might have clues for you.'

Chaloner was horrified that she should have discussed his work with Williamson. 'It is not—'

'The first part of the evening was extremely tedious,' interrupted Hannah, not really caring what he thought. 'Meneses latched himself on to the Queen again, and I dared not leave her. I could only relax and enjoy myself once she had gone.'

'What made you uneasy?' Chaloner swallowed his irritation: berating her for her loose tongue while she was tipsy was unlikely to prove productive. 'I doubt she would have come to harm in a room full of people.'

'No physical harm, perhaps, but she is growing fond of him, and I know he will abandon her when he learns she is poor. When he does, she will be terribly hurt.'

'Then arrange for someone to tell him her status before she becomes too attached,' suggested Chaloner. 'Your friend Buckingham will oblige, I am sure.'

'He tried, but Meneses pretends to have no English. Clearly, he does not appreciate that we are only trying to save him a lot of futile sycophancy. So *you* can do it. You speak Portuguese.'

246

'It is not my place to dispense that sort of advice to foreign barons.'

'But you will do it nonetheless,' stated Hannah. 'Do not worry if the Queen is angry with you – her tempers rarely last long. Damn it! Here comes Joan. You must have woken her by yelling.'

'I wondered who had slammed the front door and startled us all out of our beds,' said Joan, regarding Chaloner coldly. 'Just come home, have you?'

'He has,' replied Hannah cheerfully. 'He arrived a few moments before me.'

'Well, before you go out again, perhaps you would have a word with George,' said Joan stiffly. 'He has eaten the pie Nan baked for today's dinner. I challenged him about it, but he was quite unrepentant. Horrible man!'

Remembering that Hannah had arranged for him to visit the Queen's apartments later, Chaloner dressed with more than his usual care that day, selecting a dark-blue long-coat and matching breeches. The shirt had some lace around the neck and wrists – it was impossible to buy them plain in an age where the degree of frill was virtually equivalent to a man's social status – but not enough to hinder his movements. He added his weapons, including Wiseman's scalpel, and then was ready for whatever that Saturday might bring.

'Cut off all your hair and wear a wig,' advised Hannah, watching him. 'Few men of fashion keep their own locks these days.'

'That is because most men of fashion are either grey or bald.'

Hannah snorted with laughter – a sound she would never have made while sober. 'True. But you will have to conform sooner or later, or you will be the only man at Court with real hair. And then people might think you are poor.'

'God forbid!' muttered Chaloner, determined to postpone the inevitable for as long as possible.

He took his leave of her and aimed for the front door, but found his path barred by Joan. She evidently considered him less intimidating than his footman, because she pointed wordlessly to the servants' parlour, where George was enjoying the newly lit fire. Suspecting it would be quicker to do as she asked than to argue, he went to oblige. He closed the door behind him – he might have been coerced into doing what she wanted, but he was damned if he was going to let her listen.

'The pie was undercooked,' said George, coming slowly to his feet. His shoulders rippled as he moved, and there was a definite gleam of defiance in his dark eyes.

'We will never know, will we? You have ensured that no one else is in a position to say.'

'Shall I leave you a piece next time, then?' asked George with calculated insolence.

Chaloner declined to be baited. 'Or you can be wise and leave them alone. Nan might poison them if she thinks they will only end up inside you.'

The glowering expression lifted. 'I had not considered that possibility. And she *is* knowledgeable about toxins – it was she who taught me how to deal with the mouse problem.'

'Have you seen Fitzgerald since you came to work here?' asked Chaloner, wondering whether he could make George admit to being a spy.

'Of course, but we do not talk. He does not deign to acknowledge minions.'

'He does not enquire after your well-being? That seems harsh, after ten years of service.'

George looked away. 'He is not a sentimental man.'

It was like drawing teeth, and while Chaloner enjoyed a challenge, he could not in all conscience waste the day playing games of cat and mouse with his footman. He turned abruptly, opening the parlour door so suddenly that he was obliged to put out a hand to prevent Joan from tumbling in on top of him.

He left quickly after that, thinking about all he had to do. First, talk to Pratt, to assess whether there was any truth in the allegation that he was fabricating the tales of theft from Clarendon House to cover badly calculated estimates. He needed to speak to Oliver, too, and perhaps corner one or two labourers, to see what they knew about the matter. And perhaps more importantly, he wanted to see whether anyone might know who had locked him in the vault.

Next he would tackle Brilliana, to hear what she had to say about one lover killing another, and also ask about her brother's activities in Tangier. He would then visit St Margaret's Church in Westminster, in the hope that someone there would know where Cave's brother lived – perhaps Jacob would be able to shed light on Cave's quarrel with Elliot. And finally, he would call on Reverend Addison, to assess what he knew about the scouts' role in Teviot's death.

And Williamson? The Spymaster might well have information to impart, but it would come at a price. He elected to stay well away from the man. At least for now.

Because he was wearing his best clothes, Chaloner took a hackney carriage to Piccadilly, but even then, he was not entirely protected from the elements. A drenching drizzle caught the soot in the air from the tens of thousands of sea-coal fires that had been lit to start the day, and when he brushed a drop of water from his cuff, it left a long, black smear.

The Crown was in darkness when he alighted. He crept up the stairs to Pratt's chambers, intending to catch the man before he was fully cognisant, but when he opened the door, it was to find that the architect's bed had not been slept in. He was just wondering whether he should be concerned, when he heard a sound in the hallway outside. He drew his sword, but it was only Ruth Elliot, pale and white in billowing nightclothes.

'You should not be out,' he said, taking her hand and leading her back to her own garret. 'It is cold.'

'My husband had a dog,' she whispered, watching as he knelt by the hearth to build up the fire. 'My brother says they are both dead, but I do not believe him. I miss them.'

'He fought a man called Cave,' said Chaloner, feeling something of a scoundrel for raising the subject with a woman who was so obviously disturbed. 'Did you know him?'

She shook her head. 'My brother says he was a singer, though.'

'Cave has a brother – Jacob. I do not suppose you have ever met him, have you?'

'No, but I met Mr Fitzgerald last night. He said he would kill me if I kept watching him, so now I have to hide under the bed when he comes. He is a mean man. So are all of them, except Mr Jones, who is kind and smiles a lot. He brings me an apple sometimes.'

'Stay away from them all,' advised Chaloner, deciding

that nothing would be gained from questioning her further. 'And lock the door after I have gone.'

It took considerable willpower for Chaloner to approach Clarendon House, and when he did, it was to find it was too early for the workmen, although a solitary guard shivered next to the brazier. The man was making no effort to monitor the premises, but at least he was awake, which was an improvement on previous mornings. Chaloner was about to take shelter under the portico until the labourers arrived when he saw someone was already there. Instinctively, he melted into the shadows until he could ascertain the fellow's identity. Unfortunately, a cloak and large hat obscured everything except for his general shape. Then a second person appeared.

'Where have you been?' the first demanded in a furious hiss. 'I have been lurking here for ages, and I am chilled to the bone. You have no right to keep me waiting.'

Chaloner eased forward to listen, grateful they were amateurs – professionals would not have conversed in a place that could be approached by eavesdroppers from so many different directions.

'I had to be sure no one was looking when I arrived,' snapped the second. 'As you will appreciate, neither of us can afford to be caught.'

Even though the site was deserted save the soldier, the pair spoke in whispers, and while Chaloner had no trouble hearing their words, he could not identify their voices. And that was a pity, because there was something about both that said he knew them.

'There is no need to worry,' the first was breathing. 'Wright's guard is hopelessly incompetent. We could make off with the roof and *he* would not notice.'

'It would have been better if the thefts had gone undetected altogether,' said the second curtly. 'A lot less trouble, and much safer for everyone concerned.'

'It is Dugdale's fault. He told Edgeman to monitor the building accounts, and the inconsistencies are obvious once you know what to look for.'

'I know,' said the second shortly. 'But never mind this. Did you bring what I wanted?'

The first handed him a sheaf of papers. 'I can buy a few bricks, if you think stealing will attract more unwanted attention. As you have already pointed out, neither of us can afford to be caught.'

'No!' exclaimed the second. 'That would tell anyone with half a brain that something untoward is unfolding here. Let me manage this side of matters. I do not want to be hanged just yet.'

'Do not be so melodramatic!' said the first disdainfully. 'We will not be hanged.'

'For stealing several hundred pounds' worth of supplies from the Lord Chancellor? I assure you, not even your lofty station will save you – from the disgrace, if not the noose.'

Chaloner strained forward, desperately trying to see or hear something that would tell him who they were, but they had shrouded themselves too effectively. He consoled himself with the fact that at least he would not have to conduct an uncomfortable interview with Pratt about his estimates: the discussion told him that the materials were definitely being pilfered.

Without another word, the second man tucked the papers under his arm and began to walk towards the nearby woods, leaving Chaloner debating which of the pair to confront. He opted for the first, the one whose station was 'lofty'. He knew he had made the right decision when the fellow opened the door with a key – presumably, one of the only two official copies in existence.

Once inside, the man moved confidently, despite the fact that it was dark. Chaloner followed, but trod on a piece of wood, and the crack it made as it broke caused his quarry to whip around in alarm. The fellow started to run and Chaloner lost sight of him as he ducked around a corner. Chaloner ran too, following the sounds of footsteps in the blackness. Eventually, they reached the Lawyer's Library – the room Pratt was using as an office. Chaloner hurtled towards it and flung open the door.

'Clarendon will be delighted to know the identity of the man who has been stealing from him,' he panted, watching the man who was standing inside spin around in shock.

It was Roger Pratt.

'Have you solved the crime, then?' asked Pratt, hand to his chest to indicate that he had been given a serious start. 'Congratulations. But please do not burst in on me like that again. The Earl is keen to keep me alive until his house is finished, and he will not thank you for terrifying me to death.'

He was standing by the desk, and Chaloner was puzzled to note that not only was he not breathless from the chase, but he was not wearing the hat and cloak that had swathed him, either. Nor were the garments in the room. What had he done with them? Chaloner was sure he had not had time to throw them off while running.

'It is you,' he said. 'Although I cannot imagine why. You are paid a handsome salary to—'

Pratt's jaw dropped. 'You think *I* am the thief? In God's name, why? As you say, I am being well paid for my labours, and have no need to soil my hands by stealing.'

'I just heard you talking to another man in the portico.'

'Then you are mistaken,' snapped Pratt. 'I have been in here all night, because there was a problem with the Great Parlour's cornices that needed to be resolved by this morning. I have been nowhere near the portico for hours. And if you make accusing remarks again, I shall—'

Chaloner did not wait to hear the rest. He turned and tore back through the house, intending to catch the accomplice instead. He saw him near the wood, identifiable by the sheaf of papers under his arm, and began to race towards him.

'Hey!' screamed Pratt, who had followed. 'How dare you insult me and then race off in the middle of a sentence! I am reporting you to Clarendon!'

Alerted by the tirade, the accomplice fled. Chaloner sprinted after him, but the man had too great a start and quickly disappeared in the undergrowth. Chaloner ran harder, feeling his lame leg burn with the effort, but the wood was an almost impenetrable jungle of saplings and brambles, and he had no idea which direction the fellow might have taken.

He stopped, listening for telltale rustling, but there was only silence. Chaloner had lost him.

Disgusted by his failure, Chaloner made his way back to Clarendon House, where Pratt was briefing the labourers on the work that was to be done that day. Chaloner watched them carefully, but it was impossible to say whether any were the man he had chased through the house. They stared at him with blank faces when he explained what had happened.

'We saw nothing amiss,' said Vere. 'Did we, lads?'

There was a chorus of denials, and Chaloner sensed that even if they had, they would not tell him. They were not well paid, and would almost certainly side with the thief. He persisted, though.

'These crimes reflect badly on all of you. Who will hire you, when it becomes known that you worked on a site where so many materials have been spirited away?'

'That is why we have trade guilds,' said Vere insolently. 'To protect us from that sort of accusation. We know nothing about anything, and you would do well to remember it.'

There was another growl of agreement. Chaloner started to ask who might have locked him in the strong-room the previous night, but then changed his mind. They were unlikely to confide any suspicions they might harbour, and worse, it might prompt them to try it themselves, seeing it as a convenient way to be rid of a man who posed offensive questions.

When they moved away to begin their work, he turned to Oliver, recalling how Wiseman had castigated Pratt's gloomy assistant for failing to pay his medical bills. Oliver looked particularly mournful that morning, because he was wearing a hat with a sagging brim that matched his droopy face. Rain poured off it directly down the back of his neck, which may have accounted for at least some of his obvious misery.

'What about you?' demanded Chaloner, frustration making him uncharacteristically short with a man who did not deserve it. 'How can you work here and have no idea of what is happening?'

'Because I am engrossed in my labours all day,' replied Oliver, stung. 'This is a large site and we employ dozens of men – masons, carpenters, plasterers, tile-layers, glaziers. We cannot possibly monitor them all. Besides, the truly amazing fact is that not more has disappeared. It is lonely and isolated at night. A thief's paradise.'

'So you have no idea who these felons might be?' pressed Chaloner.

'I only wish I did,' said Oliver fervently. 'Because I am tired of hearing about them, and would do almost anything to help you lay hold of them – just for some peace.'

The guard was the next to feel the brunt of Chaloner's exasperation, although the man steadfastly maintained that he had heard and seen nothing of the two men and the ensuing chases, even though Pratt's indignant yells must surely have been audible. Chaloner caught him out in several inconsistencies, but it made no difference: the soldier was not about to admit that he had witnessed thieves being pursued but had made no effort to help. When Chaloner eventually let him go, Pratt approached, bristling with indignation.

'Are you going to apologise for calling me a thief?' he demanded.

Chaloner nodded slowly. Pratt could not be the culprit, because Chaloner would have noticed if the architect had removed hat and cloak during the chase, so the only place he could have divested was the library. But there had been no garments there, so logic dictated that Pratt was innocent, and the real villain must have hidden in an alcove while Chaloner had flown past. Moreover, the chase had left Chaloner breathing hard, but Pratt had not been panting.

On the other hand, it had been Pratt's furious diatribe that had warned the accomplice to run, and his occupation probably kept him reasonably fit, so there was nothing to say he would be reduced to a wheezing wreck after a short sprint.

'Where are your bodyguards?' asked Chaloner, his mind a confused jumble.

'They left at dawn. Incidentally, I often work here at night, because it gives me an opportunity to *feel* the house – to assess whether its proportions are correct.'

'In the dark?' asked Chaloner sceptically.

'Of course. Or do you imagine Clarendon will only live here when it is light? The ambience of a house at night is just as important as its looks during the day.'

Chaloner supposed the claim was plausible. Just. Irritably, he shoved past Pratt and walked to the library. With the architect grumbling acidly behind him, he searched the rooms and the corridors he had run through, but there was no discarded hat and cloak.

'Satisfied?' demanded Pratt. 'Perhaps you would like to inspect each panel, to see whether this mysterious intruder hid himself in one of the knots. Or perhaps he wriggled though a crack in the plaster on the ceiling.'

Chaloner rubbed his head. 'I am sorry. I was sure I had cornered him in here.'

Pratt glared at him. 'When Wednesday comes, I do not want *you* guarding me against the assassin. I want someone efficient.'

'Why? I thought you were pleased by the threat to kill you, because it means you have succeeded in designing something unpopular.'

'I am,' said Pratt stiffly. 'But that does not mean I want to die in four days' time.'

'I doubt you are in any danger.' Chaloner was still sure the plot was aimed more at the Queen than the conceited architect. 'There is no need to be concerned.'

'Easy for you to say,' retorted Pratt. 'You are not the intended victim.'

Still thinking about what had happened, Chaloner walked towards the Haymarket, wondering whether he was losing his touch. He replayed the incident in his mind again and again, but although the evidence indicated that Pratt probably was innocent, there was a niggling doubt at the back of his mind that made him reluctant to dismiss the architect as a suspect just yet.

When he reached the Crown, a Piccadilly Company meeting was just ending, and yet again people were being ushered through the door in ones and twos, timed to blend in with the horde disgorging from the Gaming House. The person doing the shepherding was the beautiful woman who had undertaken the task on Monday – a lovely creature with dark eyes, a heart-shaped face, and a figure that surpassed even Lady Castlemaine's.

Chaloner picked up a soggy pamphlet from the ground, and pretended to read it while he watched, wondering at the Company's penchant for gatherings that took place so early. Was it because its members had demanding daytime jobs, so could not manage a more conducive hour? Or because it was hoped that spies would be less attentive at dawn than late at night?

Meneses was first out, although someone must have remarked on the foreignness of his clothes, because he wore a cloak to conceal them. Lydcott was next; Thurloe's disapprobation had made no impression on him, because he was whistling happily and it was clear that he intended

258

to ignore his kinsman's warnings. He was followed by Harley and Newell, both grim-faced, as if whatever had been discussed had displeased them. Or perhaps they were still smarting because Reyner's killer remained at large. Then came a lot of people Chaloner did not know, although their clothes indicated they were wealthy, and he suspected they were merchants.

One of the last to emerge was Fitzgerald, his piratical beard tucked inside his coat and a hat pulled low to disguise his eye-patch. Once everyone had gone, the woman stared across the street, directly at Chaloner. He tensed as she began to walk towards him.

'You have had more than enough time to peruse that wet pamphlet,' she said softly. 'Have you come to hire my services, but cannot pluck up the courage to come to my home?'

'Possibly,' hedged Chaloner, angry with himself for not being more circumspect. He wondered what services she had in mind, although the way she ran her fingers down his sleeve did not leave him pondering for long.

'My name is Brilliana,' she said. 'But I imagine you already know that.'

Chaloner bowed, noting that her clothes were of very high quality, and that she positively dripped jewellery. Here was no lowly strumpet, but a courtesan of some distinction, and he could only suppose she had deigned to approach him because he was dressed for visiting the Queen. Fortunately, his race to the woods had not damaged or soiled anything – at least, nothing that was noticeable on a morning where rainclouds and soot-laden smog meant the light was poor.

'You had better come to my boudoir, then,' she said. 'It is too cold to do business out here.'

Wondering whether it was wise to enter her lair – he had intended to tackle her on neutral ground – Chaloner followed her across the street. Her house, which he recalled was shared with her brother Harley, was a large building on three floors. She conducted him to a pleasantly airy room at the rear, graced with furniture that would not have looked out of place in a French palace.

She sat on an embroidered chair and rang a bell that stood on a table to one side. Immediately, a footman appeared, bearing a tray with a jug of chocolate and two goblets. He poured a little of the dark liquid into each, and from the smell Chaloner suspected it had been fortified with sack.

'I have told you my name,' said Brilliana, when the servant had withdrawn and she and Chaloner were alone again. Her smile was coy. 'What is yours?'

'Do you require names from all your clients?'

Brilliana tilted her head. 'It helps, should I want to address them with any intimacy. Sugar?'

'No, thank you.'

Brilliana raised her eyebrows. 'Do not tell me you are one of those tedious fellows who thinks abstaining makes a difference to the slaves on the plantations? You will have to change your tune soon, or you will find yourself left behind, like those poor fools who still hanker after the lost Republic. But you are not here to discuss commerce and politics. Are you?'

The sharp intelligence in her eyes told Chaloner that she knew exactly who he was, and what he wanted. Seeing no point in playing games, he decided to be blunt.

'No, mistress. I thought we might discuss your brother and his work in Tangier.'

She regarded him coolly. 'He will not need your help

in the event of an official inquiry, because he has done nothing wrong. He did not see the Moors waiting in ambush on the day that Lord Teviot died, and no one can prove otherwise.'

'That will not satisfy the lawyers,' warned Chaloner. 'Teviot is popular now he is dead, and they are looking for a scapegoat. Your brother fits the bill perfectly, so if you do not want him hanged, you should encourage him to cooperate with me.'

It was impossible to read Brilliana's thoughts, although a gleam in her eye said her mind was working fast. 'I shall pass the message on, but I am not his keeper. He may not listen.'

'Then tell me when the Piccadilly Company is next meeting, and I will talk to him myself.'

'The Piccadilly Company is certainly not your concern,' said Brilliana icily. 'Now drink your chocolate and then we shall both be about our own business.'

Chaloner lifted the cup, but did not put it to his lips. 'Cave was on the ship from Tangier, too. I was with him when he died, and he mentioned you.' It was a lie, but she was not in a position to know it.

'Poor John,' she said softly. 'His death was a wicked shame, and I miss him dreadfully.'

'Did you attend his funeral?' He knew she had not, because Wiseman had told him as much.

'No,' she replied shortly. 'Because his brother Jacob shoved him in the ground before his friends could object. I was very upset – I would have liked to say goodbye.'

'Do you know where Jacob lives?'

'If I did, I would visit him and give him a piece of my mind. He had no right to act so precipitately. And damn

James Elliot, too! John might have started the quarrel, but James should never have fought him. Personally, I think *he* encouraged Jacob to opt for a hasty funeral.'

'He cannot have done,' said Chaloner, startled. 'He is dead.'

'Have you *seen* his body?' she demanded. 'No? Then how do you *know* he is dead? I wager anything you please that he is alive and well and telling Jacob what to do.'

'Why would he want Cave buried quickly?' asked Chaloner doubtfully.

'Because he is dangerous and unpredictable,' declared Brilliana. 'I wish I had never bestowed my favours on him. I did it because his wife is insane, and I felt sorry for him. But it was a mistake.'

'I have taken enough of your time,' said Chaloner, his mind full of questions he knew Brilliana was unlikely to answer. 'Thank you for the chocolate.'

'You have not touched it. At least take a sip before you leave. It is expensive.'

'You have not touched yours, either,' said Chaloner, glad a career in espionage had taught him never to partake of anything his host had not tasted first.

She smiled, although it was not a pleasant expression. 'You must come to see me again. I always have chocolate waiting for guests like you.'

Chaloner was sure she did.

It was not far from Piccadilly to St Margaret's Church in Westminster, but the journey yielded little in the way of information. The young curate who had conducted Cave's funeral burst into tears when Chaloner started to ask questions about the musician's hasty send-off.

'I did not know! I thought he was just another pauper

262

from the rookeries – we get lots of them in here, and it is my job to deal with them quickly so they do not distress our wealthier parishioners. His brother never said he was a courtier, and now everyone at White Hall thinks me a villain for depriving them of music by the Chapel Royal choir and a homily by the Bishop . . .'

'Did Cave's brother look like a pauper himself?' asked Chaloner.

The curate shook his head. 'But I did not think anything about it at the time.'

Still sniffling, he led the way to a mound in the church-yard, one in a line of several, which suggested he was telling the truth about the number of cheap and nasty interments he conducted.

'What did Jacob look like?' asked Chaloner, staring down at it.

'He wore decent clothes and an oddly black wig, but there was something of the lout about him. However, he said and did nothing that made me suspect he was trying to avoid paying for a grand funeral. I assumed he just wanted his brother buried quickly because he was busy.'

Chaloner supposed he would have to visit the charnel house, to see whether Kersey knew where Cave's brother lived – Jacob would have had to supply an address when he had collected the corpse. He started to walk there but then changed his mind and aimed for Lincoln's Inn instead. He listened outside Chamber XIII for a moment, where the scratch of a pen on paper told him his friend was alone, then tapped softly and entered.

Thurloe was still in his nightclothes, his hair flowing from beneath a cap that might have looked comical on a man with less natural dignity.

'I am writing to my wife about Robert,' the ex-Spymaster said tiredly. 'The man is a fool.'

Chaloner nodded. 'But a wealthy one. He lodges in the Mews on Charing Cross, which is sufficiently grand that Pratt likes to stay with him when his own rooms in the Crown are too noisy. Fitzgerald seems to have made him very rich.'

Thurloe looked pained. 'I am tempted to order him away from London for his own good. Unfortunately, I doubt he would go.'

Chaloner hesitated. 'Are you fond of him?'

'He is family – fondness is immaterial. Why?'

'Because if you do not mind placing him in danger by "turning" him, he could be useful to us. For a start, he could tell us what Piccadilly Company meetings entail, and why they take place at odd times. Like early this morning.'

Thurloe sighed. 'I interrogated him for hours last night – for so long that I overslept this morning, which is why I am still in my nightclothes.'

'What did he tell you?'

'Nothing, because he is entrusted with nothing. He believes his business is legal, and there was no persuading him otherwise. He is being used – his glass-exporting venture provides a legitimate front for something else. They do not invite him to all their meetings, and he is sent to prepare refreshments when anything significant is discussed at the ones he is permitted to attend.'

Chaloner was sorry that Thurloe was distressed, and disappointed to learn that even knowing a member of the Piccadilly Company was going to be of no use to them.

'It is a pity,' Thurloe went on. 'Robert is a superb

horseman and could have used that talent to earn a respectable living. Instead he prefers to dabble in silly commercial ventures that always fail.'

'This one is not failing,' Chaloner pointed out.

Thurloe sighed. 'I imagine it is – or the legal side of it is, at least. But never mind Robert: he is my problem, not yours. Tell me what has happened to you. It was something unpleasant, because you have the look of a man who did not sleep well, and your hand has been injured.'

Chaloner told him about Clarendon House, unfolding the piece of paper that had been left on the chest. 'The trap may not have been meant for me, though, because these words mean nothing.'

'On the contrary – they mention death, darkness and small jaws, which neatly sums up the fate you were meant to suffer. I suspect it is Fitzgerald's work, because he has always enjoyed inventing unusual ways to dispatch his victims. And if you do not believe me, then look at what happened to Proby, Turner, Lucas and Congett.'

'Wiseman told me about Congett. He suggested shock as a cause of death, but I imagine it was poison. The rat probably bit him after his body was left on the banks of the Thames.'

Thurloe nodded slowly. 'But it was a kinder end than the one devised for you.'

Chaloner did not want to dwell about his time in the strongroom, and changed the subject. 'Have you heard from Wallis about Reyner's cipher yet? We need those names – enemies of the Piccadilly Company may be friends to us. But even if not, we should warn them. We might have been able to save Congett, and perhaps Turner and Lucas, too, had we been able to translate it.'

'I disagree. If they have pitted themselves against

Fitzgerald, they will need no advice from us to be on their guard. They will know it already.'

'We cannot take that chance. However, as all four victims were Adventurers, perhaps we should assume that Fitzgerald considers *all* Adventurers to be his enemies, and warn the lot of them.'

'That would entail notifying the King, the Queen and other members of the royal family, and I doubt *they* have decided to challenge a viciously ruthless pirate. Fitzgerald's adversaries will not be the Adventurers as a whole, but a particular section.'

'But—'

Thurloe held up his hand. 'The only way to be certain is to decode that list. Wallis is working as fast as he can, but that particular cipher is fiendishly difficult to break. How are you managing with the other one?'

'Not well.'

'Send me a copy. We shall both study it in our free moments.'

Chaloner told Thurloe about his failures that morning – losing the thieves, accusing Pratt, and entering Brilliana's lair but gaining nothing except the sense that she had tried to poison him.

'And it is barely ten o'clock,' he concluded morosely. 'I suppose I should visit Kersey next. Then I should ask Lester whether Elliot might still be alive – and if he is, track him down and ask whether he encouraged Jacob to bury his brother with such indecent haste.'

Thurloe winced at the mention of a man he did not trust. 'If Elliot did survive Cave's attack, then Lester will be complicit in a hoax. I doubt Lester will admit to lying.'

'I was not planning to ask if he lied,' said Chaloner, a little irritably. 'Just whether he might have been mistaken. It is not always easy to tell the living from the dead.'

Thurloe nodded, but his expression said he thought Chaloner was wasting his time. 'What will you do about Teviot? How will you persuade Harley and Newell to break their silence and talk?'

'I will visit Revered Addison today and ask what he knows about the matter.'

Thurloe nodded approvingly. 'However, if you do decide to tackle the scouts directly again, you might mention *Jane*. She may loosen their tongues.'

'Who is she?'

'*Jane* is a ship that traded in Tangier when Teviot was governor. I was reliably informed last night that Harley and Newell were hired to guard her when she docked there. My spies were unable to ascertain the precise nature of the cargo, but they heard some of the crew talking. Yet what they overheard makes no sense, so perhaps we should not take it into account.'

'What did they hear?'

'That *Jane* was carrying gravel.'

By the time Chaloner reached the charnel house, Kersey was busy with the morning's trade. Several corpses were awaiting his attention, and the chambers at the front of his premises were full of mourners. Chaloner was impressed to note that he afforded the same gentle sympathy to the poor as to the rich, offering medicinal wine to those in genuine distress, served in exquisite crystal goblets.

'Jacob came here on Monday night and asked for his brother's body,' the charnel-house keeper reported angrily, taking Chaloner's arm and pulling him towards the mortuary so they would not be overheard. 'I assumed he was taking it home, so that friends and acquaintances could pay their last respects. But then I heard the day before yesterday that Cave was shoved in St Margaret's churchyard with an appalling lack of ceremony. I am livid, because it reflects badly on me.'

'How?' asked Chaloner, puzzled. 'You are not responsible for the arrangements.'

'Cave was in my care, and I always take it upon myself to act as adviser to my clients' kin,' explained Kersey shortly. 'People might think *I* recommended this unseemly course of action.'

'I am sure they do not,' said Chaloner soothingly. 'What can you tell me about Jacob?'

'A bit loutish – not like Cave at all. There was a dullness in his eyes that made me suspect he was not overly intelligent, and he looked as though he would enjoy a brawl. He wore nice clothes and had donned an especially black wig.'

Chaloner rubbed his chin. Kersey's description, like the curate's, sounded uncannily like Elliot. Was it possible that Brilliana was right? That he had survived Cave's attack and was avenging himself by shoving Cave in the ground without the pomp and ceremony that was his due? If the quarrel *had* been about her, and not about taking the wall as they had claimed, then it was certainly possible that their antipathy towards each other was powerful enough to result in petty spite.

'Can you remember anything else about Jacob?' he asked.

'He listened attentively to all I said about the grand ceremony that was being arranged, and then shoved his brother in the ground first thing the following morning, employing a novice curate to say the prayers so that no questions would be asked. It was sly, mean-spirited and niggardly.'

'Did he tell you where he lives?'

'Near the sign of the Sun in Covent Garden. Or so he claimed. I would pay him a visit myself and give him a piece of my mind, but I am too busy.'

'Was Cave the only subject you discussed?'

'No, actually,' replied Kersey, and Chaloner was surprised to see hurt and anger in his face. 'He looked at the table on which Cave lay, and told me it was disgraceful. No one has ever complained before and it offended me. I want you to look at it and tell me whether he was right.'

Chaloner had no desire to inspect mortuary furniture, but Kersey was clearly upset, and he liked the man. He allowed himself to be led into the hall, recoiling at the powerful stench of burning that assailed his nostrils the moment the door was opened.

'Turner's family and servants,' explained Kersey. 'And Lord Lucas. A terrible tragedy.'

He aimed for a table that looked no different to any of the others – it was sturdy and had been scrubbed so often that the wood was almost white. It was already occupied by someone else, and although Chaloner tried to prevent Kersey from whipping away the blanket – he did not want to see charred cadavers – he was too late.

But it was not a blackened specimen that lay there. It was Newell, dead of a gunshot wound.

Chaloner stared at the scout, his thoughts in turmoil. Newell was wearing the clothes he had sported when he had left the Piccadilly Company meeting with Harley and Lydcott at dawn, and was still slightly warm to the touch. He had not been dead for long.

'He came in a few moments ago,' explained Kersey. 'An accident in St James's Park – you know how people meet there to show off their new firearms. Well, he was demonstrating one to a party of interested onlookers, and he shot himself by mistake.'

Chaloner seriously doubted it. 'Newell was an experienced soldier. He would not have—'

'There are witnesses: Secretary Leighton, Hyde, Mr O'Brien and the lovely Kitty to name but a few. These accidents are not uncommon, because firearms are notoriously capricious.'

'But Newell was a professional scout. He would not have killed himself by accident, no matter how temperamental the gun.'

Kersey shrugged. 'Yet here he is, lying on my table. Tell me what you think of my furniture, Chaloner. Should I invest in new stock?'

But all Chaloner's attention was on Newell. Experience told him that the scout had probably been looking down the barrel when he had squeezed the trigger, and the ball had taken him in the throat. There were two possibilities. Either Newell had committed suicide because he was losing his nerve over Teviot and whatever other dark matters he had embarked upon with the Piccadilly Company, or the gun had been fitted with an unusually fine firing mechanism.

'The table,' prompted Kersey worriedly. 'Can you see anything wrong with it?'

'No,' replied Chaloner. 'I suspect Jacob made the remark to disconcert you – and to prevent you from asking him too many questions.'

'Well, it worked,' said Kersey bitterly. 'It stopped our conversation dead, and I have been distressed ever since – about the entire episode.'

'Cave was killed by a man named James Elliot, who is supposed to have died of his wounds shortly afterwards. I do not suppose you had him in here, did you?'

'No,' replied Kersey with absolute conviction. 'I have not had a stabbing victim for almost three weeks now.'

Chaloner left the charnel house aware that he now had even more to do. He had to ask Leighton, O'Brien, Kitty and Hyde about what had happened to Newell; interview Addison about Tangier; visit the Sun in Covent Garden to speak to Jacob – assuming he was not Elliot, of course; and talk to Lester about the possibility that his friend was still alive. Then he was due to visit the Queen's apartments, and he wanted to track down Harley – it was even more urgent that he cornered the scout now, given that he was the only one of the three left alive.

His thoughts were so full of how to fit everything in that he failed to pay attention to his surroundings, and he was halfway down the lane before he became aware of several men walking towards him. They were advancing with grim purpose and it did not take a genius to see that they were there for him. There were too many to fight, so he turned, and had just broken into a run when he was faced with more men coming from the opposite direction. There were at least a dozen, all rough-looking types with cudgels.

Was *he* going to have an 'accident' now? Was someone disappointed that he had escaped suffocation the previous night, and intended to rectify the matter? He looked around quickly but either by chance or design the men had chosen a part of the alley with walls that were too high to climb, and there were no windows or doors. He would have to fight.

He drew his sword with one hand and the gun with the other, and stood with his back to the wall, waiting to see which side would strike first. He could not win against so many, but if he was going to die, then he would not be the only one to meet his Maker that day.

'There is no need for that,' said the man in the lead, faltering. Behind him, his fellows drew an assortment of swords and knives. 'We only want a word.'

Chaloner indicated with a gesture that he was to speak.

'Not here,' said the man. 'Come with us.'

'No.' Chaloner levelled the gun at him.

'We have orders to take you somewhere,' said the man, eyeing it uneasily. 'And it will be a lot more pleasant for everyone if you put down the weapons and come quiet, like.'

'Orders from whom?' demanded Chaloner.

'We cannot say, but if you come with us, you will find out.'

'Then I decline.'

The man sighed and indicated that his cronies should advance. They obliged, slowly at first, but then in a rush when a puff of smoke told them that Chaloner's dag had misfired. Cursing the thing, Chaloner used it as a club, bruising at least two of his assailants, while three others reeled away from his sword. But it was an unequal contest and it was not long before he went down under a hail of cudgels, fists and feet. A sack was pulled over his head and tugged so tight that it was difficult to breathe. He managed to free one hand, though, and heard a yelp of pain as he lashed out with it.

'Tie him,' ordered the leader urgently. 'Quickly, before he injures anyone else.'

'Easy for you to say, Doines,' someone grumbled. 'Standing there, giving orders, while we do battle with the devil.'

Chaloner continued to struggle long after he was rendered helpless by an array of ropes, desperately seeking a weakness in his bonds. There was none, and he felt himself lifted and tossed into the back of a cart. Doines clicked his tongue to a horse, which began to trot.

He was not sure how many men piled themselves on top of him, but he could not ever recall a more uncomfortable journey. He tried to ask whether their orders entailed him arriving dead, but the sack muffled his words, and the sound he made encouraged someone to hit him. He felt himself grow light-headed from lack of air, and soon lost any sense of where he was being taken.

Chapter 8

By the time they arrived at their destination, Chaloner was dizzy and disoriented. He was aware of being carried, but did not have the strength to resist. He heard a swirl of voices as the sack was hauled off, but kept his eyes closed, to see what might be learned about his captors by feigning unconsciousness. The ropes were removed, and he was dragged forward.

'What have you done to him?' Chaloner's heart sank when he recognised Williamson's voice. 'I specifically told you to invite him nicely.'

'We did,' came Doines's aggrieved reply. 'But he started to fight, and injured five of us. You cannot blame us for taking him down before he could do any more damage.'

'I can and I do,' snapped Williamson. 'I need his help, and he is hardly going to agree to work with me now you have knocked him senseless, is he!'

'I told you to let me fetch him,' came another voice. It was Lester, and he sounded angry. 'You should have listened.'

Chaloner felt himself laid gently on a bench. Then a cloth began to wipe his face. He opened his eyes a fraction and saw the ministering angel was Lester, his ruddy face full of concern.

'He would not have obliged you,' argued Williamson. 'I asked him to come here several times, and even sent a polite note with his wife. All were ignored. He does not like me, although I cannot imagine why. I have graciously overlooked all manner of injustices, insults and violations in the past – ones I would have killed another man for committing against me.'

'This is not *my* fault,' said Doines sullenly. 'You said not to mention that it was you who wanted to see him, but he got suspicious when we refused to answer. It was—'

'Leave,' snapped Williamson. 'Before I decline to pay you.'

Footsteps crossed the floor, then a door opened and closed. Chaloner opened his eyes a little more, and saw he was in Williamson's Westminster office. Lester was still looming over him, but the Spymaster had gone to sit at his desk. As far as he could tell there was no one else in the room, but in order to get free he would have to incapacitate both, and make an escape from a building that was full of Williamson's clerks, spies and ruffians. Could he do it?

'Perhaps we should summon a surgeon,' said Lester worriedly. 'Wiseman is the best. He is expensive, but I will bear the cost. This should not have happened.'

Chaloner knew then that it was time to pretend to regain his wits, because Wiseman would not be fooled by his act. He sat up.

'Thank God!' exclaimed Lester. 'I thought they had done you serious harm.'

'He is awake?' asked Williamson, coming to stand over them. 'Good. Can he speak?'

'Give him a moment to recover,' snapped Lester. Then his voice softened. 'Sit quietly for as long as you like, Chaloner. We shall talk only when you are ready.'

'I am ready now,' said Chaloner, unwilling to prolong the experience. 'What do you want?'

'I am sorry violence was used to bring you here,' said Williamson stiffly. 'But a situation has arisen that means we must put aside our differences and work together. As we did in June.'

'What situation?' asked Chaloner, hoping he was not about to be given another mystery to unravel. He was struggling with the ones he had already.

'One involving powerful men,' replied Williamson soberly. 'Members of government, wealthy merchants, and several less salubrious characters. Such as Fitzgerald the pirate. Do you know him?'

'Not personally.'

'He is an extremely dangerous individual,' Williamson went on. 'And I have reason to believe that he is behind the tragic deaths of Sir Edward Turner and Lord Lucas.'

'Then arrest him,' suggested Chaloner.

'I cannot – I do not have evidence that will secure a conviction in a court of law.'

'That has never stopped you before.'

Williamson had cells for people whose trials would not win a verdict that he deemed to be in the public interest, and assassins available should he decide on a more permanent solution.

'He is too prominent and well connected,' explained Williamson. 'And if you do not believe me, then ask your friend Thurloe. He was as wily a spymaster as ever lived, but even *he* could not defeat Fitzgerald. The man is not a normal criminal.'

'I overheard him talking,' said Chaloner. He spoke hesitantly, because it went against the grain to share information with someone he distrusted. 'He said he has a master who gives him orders.'

'Who is it?' demanded Williamson, clearly horrified.

'I do not know. Another member of the Piccadilly Company, perhaps.'

'And there are plenty in *that* sinister organisation to choose from,' interposed Lester grimly. 'Brilliana and her brother Harley, Newell, Meneses, Margareta and Cornelis Janszoon, Jones, Pratt the architect. And those are just the ones we have identified. Most of them wear disguises to their gatherings.'

Chaloner was about to point out that 'Jones' was stupid, rather than sinister, but there was always the possibility that Williamson did not know he was Thurloe's brother-in-law, and there was no need to highlight the connection unnecessarily.

'Newell is dead,' he said instead.

Williamson's eyes opened wide. 'How do you know?'

'I have just seen his body. He was shot while showing off with a gun – an accident, apparently. It was witnessed by several people, including Leighton, Hyde, and your friend O'Brien and his wife.'

'Kitty?' Williamson was stricken. 'I must go to her at once. To comfort her!'

'What about O'Brien?' asked Chaloner archly. 'Does he not warrant comfort, too?'

Williamson glanced at him sharply, and Chaloner wished he had held his tongue. Alluding to the Spymaster's dalliance with his old friend's wife had been unwarranted and reckless. He tried to think of a way to mitigate the damage, but Lester was already talking.

'Far too many people connected to this matter have died,' he said unhappily. 'Turner, Lucas, Proby, Congett, Reyner and his mother, Elliot, Cave, and now Newell.'

'What matter?' asked Chaloner. 'Precisely?'

Williamson looked pained. 'That is the problem: we are not sure. However, we suspect that two organisations are at loggerheads: the Piccadilly Company and the Adventurers. Deaths have occurred in both.'

Chaloner played devil's advocate. 'The Adventurers cannot be involved in anything untoward. The King is a member, and so is the Queen and half the Privy Council.'

'I doubt whatever is underway involves the entire corporation,' explained Williamson shortly. 'However, there are rumours that something terrible will unfold next Wednesday—'

'St Frideswide's Day,' put in Lester helpfully.

'—and it *must* be stopped,' Williamson finished. 'Unfortunately, we cannot do it with the resources currently at our disposal.'

'Doines is Williamson's best man, and you saw what *he* is like,' elaborated Lester, oblivious to the Spymaster's irritated grimace. 'So if we are to thwart it, we shall need other help. Yours.'

'No,' said Chaloner, standing abruptly and wondering whether he would be allowed to walk out. As he did so, his eye fell on a pile of letters on a table, and he recognised the signature of the one on top. It raised another question, but it was not one he would be able to ponder until he was alone again.

'Please wait,' said Williamson softly, and Chaloner suddenly became aware of the lines of strain in his face. 'I could use your family to coerce you, as I have done in the past – and as I am currently doing to Lester – but I would rather you helped me willingly.'

'I am sure you would,' said Chaloner. 'Swaddell is gone, so you are desperate to replace—'

'Swaddell has not gone anywhere,' interrupted Williamson tiredly. 'The tale of our break is a canard, so he can inveigle himself into the confidence of those we believe to be plotting. At great personal risk, I might add. The only people who know this are Lester, and now you.'

Chaloner was horrified on Swaddell's behalf. 'Sharing such information is hardly—'

'Swaddell is my friend, and I have put his life in your hands by confiding in you. If there was another way to make you trust me, I would have taken it, believe me. But I am faced with a crisis, and I need the help of an experienced operative with the right connections.'

'I have no connections,' said Chaloner truthfully.

'At least listen to what we have to say before turning us down,' said Lester reasonably.

'You are uncomfortable here in my office,' surmised Williamson astutely. 'Would it help if we went somewhere else? We could sit in my carriage and ride around London.'

'A coffee house,' determined Chaloner. They were public places, which meant Williamson was less likely to try to harm him. 'The Paradise by Westminster Hall.'

Williamson scowled. 'Certainly not. It will be busy, and we need to converse in private.'

'It has private booths at the rear,' said Lester quickly, as Chaloner stepped towards the door to indicate the interview was over. 'And we are all in need of a medicinal draught.'

'Very well,' conceded Williamson reluctantly. 'But you are paying.'

'I cannot be long,' warned Chaloner, supposing there was no harm in listening. He might learn something useful with no obligation to reciprocate. 'I have an audience with the Queen.'

'And you say you have no connections,' said Lester wonderingly.

The Paradise was one of three establishments – the others were Hell and Purgatory – that sold food and drink in Westminster's Old Palace Yard. They were sometimes taverns, sometimes ordinaries and sometimes coffee houses, depending on the whims of their owners. The Paradise was currently a coffee house, although in keeping with the eccentricity of the place, the upper floor was given over to selling fishing tackle and an assortment of patented medicines.

Inside, it was hazy not only with smoke from the coffee beans, but from a badly swept chimney. It was dominated by a large oval table with a slit up the centre that allowed the owner to walk inside it and refill his customers' dishes. His patrons were a mixture of the black-gowned lawyers who worked in the Palace of Westminster, and the ruffians who inhabited the slums that surrounded it. They were discussing the Post Office, an institution notorious for opening any letters entrusted to its care. The lawyers were of the opinion that anyone who committed words to paper without hiring one of them to make sure they could not be misinterpreted had only himself to blame; the rest thought a man's correspondence was his own affair, and that the Post Office had no right to pry.

Chaloner started to sit at the main table, but Lester

grabbed his arm and pointed to a secluded cubicle at the back.

'We cannot discuss our problems in front of an audience. You know that. The booth is private, but in full view – Williamson cannot do anything untoward without at least a dozen men seeing.'

Williamson shot Chaloner a reproachful glance as he led the way towards it, although Chaloner felt their past encounters gave him the right to be wary. Lester placed several coins on the table, and coffee was brought. Chaloner sipped it, surprised to discover it was almost palatable. He set the dish back on the table, and indicated that Lester and Williamson were to begin their explanations.

'I suppose we must start with Lester's sister,' Williamson obliged. 'She lives in the Crown on Piccadilly, and was the first to notice that something untoward was happening.'

'Not Ruth?' asked Chaloner, startled. 'She is Lester's sister as well as Elliot's wife?'

Lester nodded. 'I thought you knew. She said you have been to visit her twice, and I know she would have mentioned me. I assumed you went to pick her brains.'

'Such as they are,' muttered Williamson acidly.

Something snapped clear in Chaloner's mind when resentment suffused Lester's face. '*She* is the reason you are working with Williamson! He said he was using your family to coerce you.'

'He threatened to commit her to Bedlam otherwise,' said Lester. He glared at the Spymaster. 'There was no need to resort to such tactics – I would have helped anyway. I am a patriotic man, which is why I joined the navy.'

Williamson ignored him. 'Ruth told Lester that

something peculiar was happening in the Crown, and rather rashly, he decided to investigate.'

'I did not know there was anything *to* investigate at first,' elaborated Lester. 'Ruth is given to imagining things, you see. But I soon realised she was right – it is the Piccadilly Company's headquarters. I managed to eavesdrop once, although I am not very good at that sort of thing, and they hired Brinkes to stop it happening again.'

'What did you hear?' asked Chaloner.

'A discussion about a plot to kill one of their members. The Queen wants Pratt dead, apparently.'

Chaloner shook his head firmly. 'She would never embroil herself in such an affair.'

'I agree,' said Williamson. 'But that will not stop people from accusing her, should the tale become public. People dislike her, and it provides an opportunity to send her back to Portugal in disgrace. Or worse. Our country does have a habit of lopping the heads off unwanted monarchs.'

'And if that happens, Portugal will break off diplomatic relations with us,' added Lester. 'We shall have to return her dowry, which includes the ports of Tangier and Bombay, jewels, money, and all manner of trading rights. It will cripple us for decades.'

'In other words, it will be an enormous disaster,' summarised Williamson. 'The French and Spanish will leap to take advantage of our weakened state, and the Dutch will declare war on us.'

'Pratt does not seem overly worried by the plot, though,' said Lester, while Chaloner's mind reeled at their revelations. 'He probably thinks Fitzgerald can protect him.'

'Protect him from whom?' asked Chaloner. 'Who is behind this plot? The Adventurers?'

'We do not know,' replied Lester. 'However, Fitzgerald may think so – it would certainly explain why he roasted Turner and Lucas, and may also account for Proby's "suicide" and Congett's "accident". We cannot forget Captain Pepperell of *Eagle*, either. Brinkes killed him, and Brinkes is Fitzgerald's henchman. Perhaps Pepperell was an Adventurer, too. He did sail to Africa a lot, after all.'

Chaloner frowned. 'So Fitzgerald has declared war on the Adventurers?'

'We suspect he has taken against *some* of them,' said Williamson. 'However, if we are right, then they are fighting back. Reyner and Newell are dead, and Pratt may soon follow . . .'

'I am still hoping that the relationship between Pepperell and Elliot will provide answers,' said Lester. He shrugged at Williamson's dismissive expression. 'You think I am wasting my time, but we have no other leads to follow, and I would like to know the truth about their deaths.'

'Are you *sure* Elliot is dead?' Chaloner asked him.

Lester looked startled. 'Of course! The wound he received was mortal. He died the same day.'

'Were you with him?'

'No. The surgeon was drunk, so I left to see whether Wiseman was available. Unfortunately, I could not find him, and by the time I returned, Elliot had expired.'

'What was this surgeon's name?'

'Jeremiah King of Axe Yard.' Lester was puzzled. 'Why do you want to know?'

'Because Cave's "brother" buried him rather hastily, thus depriving him of his elaborate funeral, and the descriptions of Jacob sound remarkably like Elliot.'

'Then it is coincidence,' said Lester firmly. 'Because Elliot is buried himself. I saw him laid to rest in St Giles-in-the-Fields yesterday.'

'That was Friday,' said Chaloner. 'But Cave was collected from the charnel house on Monday night, and buried on Tuesday. Elliot could have done it.'

'He *died* on Monday,' said Lester shortly. 'Besides, he had no reason to tamper with Cave's funeral arrangements. What a terrible accusation to make!'

'His reason for tampering would be the same as the one that led him to fight Cave in the first place,' replied Chaloner. 'Brilliana.'

'Well, he is innocent,' stated Lester uncompromisingly. 'I am sure of it.'

'I understand why Cave's brother acted as he did,' said Williamson quietly. 'The Chapel Royal choristers were organising a wildly expensive affair, and Cave was not wealthy. Payment would ultimately have fallen on Jacob, and I do not blame him for declining to be beggared.'

Lester nodded agreement, but Chaloner thought he would reserve judgement until he had visited 'Jacob' in Covent Garden and heard the tale from his own lips.

Unsettled and confused by the connections that were emerging, Chaloner followed Williamson and Lester out of the coffee house, hearing the bells of Westminster strike three. The day was passing, and he still had much to do. He took a deep breath. The air reeked of soot and blocked drains, but its coolness was refreshing after the fug of the shop.

'So, to summarise,' he said, 'you believe there is a plot underway to discredit the Queen by implicating her in

284

the murder of a prominent architect. The result will be a diplomatic crisis, resulting in the loss of Tangier, untold money and trading rights. Meanwhile, the Piccadilly Company and the Adventurers are at each other's throats, and members of both are dead.'

'*Some* Adventurers are involved,' stressed Williamson. 'Not all of them.'

'The Piccadilly Company includes Fitzgerald, Meneses, Brilliana, Harley, the Janszoons and Pratt,' Chaloner went on. 'And Brinkes is their henchman.'

'Among others,' acknowledged Williamson. 'It also includes a number of upstanding merchants, and several knights. They are not all sinister, and some may very well think their sole aim is to export fine glassware to New England and bring gravel back.'

'Meanwhile, the Adventurers also boast dozens of rich and influential people,' Chaloner continued. 'Leighton, the Duke of Buckingham, the King—'

'And four members of your employer's household,' interjected Williamson pointedly. 'Brodrick and Hyde are open about their association; Dugdale and Edgeman keep it quiet.'

'Kipps is not a member, though,' said Lester. 'I cannot imagine why, because he is exactly their kind of fellow – rich, brash and interested in extravagant parties.'

'He was rejected, although I have been unable to ascertain why,' said Williamson. 'I would say it is because he works for Clarendon, whom most Adventurers hate, but if that were true, then Hyde, Brodrick, Edgeman and Dugdale would not have been accepted, either.'

Chaloner addressed his next question to Lester. 'Have you heard of a ship called *Jane*?'

Lester nodded. 'She is a privateer trading out of

Tangier. A smuggler, in essence. I remember her well, because she has a peculiarly curved bowsprit. Why?'

Chaloner hesitated, but was acutely aware that he and Thurloe could not thwart what was happening alone, and the Queen was in danger. 'Harley may have a connection to *Jane*. It has been suggested that I use it to blackmail him for answers.'

'Then do it: smuggling is a hanging offence, and the threat may loosen his tongue.' Williamson smiled, although it was not a pleasant expression. 'Does this reluctant sharing of information mean you have decided to work with us?'

'I will think about it,' said Chaloner, reluctant to capitulate too readily.

'Very well,' said Williamson stiffly. 'You know where to find me.'

The discussion over, Lester accompanied Chaloner along King Street, while Williamson returned to his offices. Chaloner glanced at the sky as they went, and saw it was too late to question Addison, Jacob, Harley or the witnesses to Newell's death before visiting the Queen. And he dared not be late lest Hannah took umbrage and declined to let him in. Irritably, he supposed he would have to postpone his other enquiries until afterwards.

'I really am sorry about the way you were brought to us,' said Lester, seeing his annoyed grimace and misunderstanding the reason. 'Doines is a lout.'

Chaloner glanced at him. 'Are you happy working with Williamson?'

'Not at all! However, I shall continue to do so until this crisis is resolved – it is my duty as a sea-officer. Yet I cannot rid myself of the notion that he might incarcerate Ruth in Bedlam anyway, just for spite. And she does not belong there. She may be fey-witted, but she is not insane.'

'Was she fey-witted when she married Elliot?'

Lester shrugged uncomfortably. 'She has always been a little . . . unworldly. I did not want her to wed him, but she was in love, and I did not have the heart to withhold permission. I wish I had, though, because he did not make her happy.'

'My wife tells me you play the flute.' Chaloner would have liked to express his sympathy, but was unsure what to say, so he changed the subject to one he thought Lester might prefer instead.

Lester smiled. 'Williamson was waxing lyrical about your skill on the viol today, so perhaps we should try a duet. We shall do it after we have saved England from that damned pirate Fitzgerald. It will give me something to look forward to.'

Chaloner met Kipps when he arrived at White Hall, but the Seal Bearer looked him up and down in horror when he heard he was bound for the Queen's quarters – the scuffle with Doines had taken its toll on his finery. There was also a coffee stain on his cuff, although he could not recall spilling any. Kipps whisked him into his office, and set about polishing his shoes and brushing the muck from his coat. He also lent him a clean shirt and a pair of white stockings.

'I have been hearing about the Adventurers today,' said Chaloner while he changed, intending to find out what Kipps knew about them. 'I understand they—'

'Thieves and scoundrels,' declared Kipps uncompromisingly, scrubbing so vigorously at a sleeve that Chaloner feared he might make a hole. 'What gives *them* the right to sequester an entire continent for themselves, forbidding anyone else to trade there?'

'Presumably the fact that the King is a member, and he can do what he likes.'

'I thought that was why we had Parliament,' snapped Kipps, uncharacteristically revolutionary. 'So monarchs cannot make decisions based on brazen self-interest. What have you been doing to get yourself into such a mess? Surely a conversation about the Adventurers was not the cause?'

'Commerce is a dirty subject,' replied Chaloner wryly.

'It is where the Adventurers are concerned,' agreed Kipps. 'I am glad they rejected my application to join, because they are treasure-hunting aristocrats, not businessmen, and their venture will founder from lack of fiscal acumen.'

'What about the Piccadilly Company?' probed Chaloner. 'Would you join that?'

'Never heard of it,' replied Kipps briskly. 'You have one stocking inside out, by the way. God's blood, Chaloner! No wonder Dugdale considers you slovenly. And if you will not wear a wig, then at least remove the blades of grass from your hair.'

He fussed until he was satisfied, unwilling for the spy to leave in anything less than pristine condition. Aware that the process had taken some time, Chaloner set off across the Great Court at a run, but was obliged to skid to a halt when he heard someone calling his name.

It was Hyde, the Earl puffing along in his wake with Frances on his arm. Dugdale was behind them, nose in the air and looking more regal than his master. From the other side of the courtyard, Buckingham aped the Earl's portly waddle, and his rakish companions burst into peals of laughter. Hyde glowered, but it was Frances's admonishing look that shamed them into silence.

'Will you let them mock our employer so, Chaloner?' demanded Dugdale indignantly. 'Why do you not draw your sword and punish them for their effrontery?'

'Because the King will not be happy if I slaughter his oldest friend, his mistress and several of his favourite barons,' replied Chaloner shortly. He did not have time for this sort of nonsense.

'There is no need for impudence,' said Dugdale mildly, although his eyes showed his anger.

'I suggest we incarcerate him in the palace prison for a few days,' said Hyde, eyes narrowing. 'That will teach him to mind his manners.'

'That is a good idea,' nodded Dugdale. 'They are cold, dark and full of rats.'

Chaloner regarded him sharply. Was it coincidence that he should mention rats and dark places, or did the Chief Usher know what had transpired in Clarendon House the night before?

'Your incautious tongue keeps bringing you trouble, Chaloner,' said the Earl, raising his hand to prevent his son from adding more. 'I understand you accused Pratt of stealing, too. I wish you had not. What if he takes umbrage and decides not to finish my home?'

'He will do no such thing, dear.' Frances patted her husband's arm soothingly. 'His pride will not let him abandon a half-finished masterpiece.'

'And architects *are* vain,' agreed Hyde. 'I know, because I trained as one, and met lots of them.'

'It was hardly *training*, Henry,' remarked Frances. 'A few months on a—'

'We were discussing Chaloner's claims,' interrupted Hyde sharply, clearly furious at being put in his place by his mother. 'I do not believe he saw these thieves. I think he invented them, to encourage us not to dismiss him.'

'We will never do that,' said Frances vehemently. 'I feel much happier now he is home, looking after our interests.' She turned to her husband. 'And so do you, dear. You said so only last night.'

'Well, yes, I did,' acknowledged the Earl. Then he scowled at Chaloner. 'But that was before he failed to lay hold of these villains.'

'I can find someone better,' said Hyde stiffly. 'Someone who will follow orders *and* keep a civil tongue in his head. Of course, he will not be a spy, but espionage is sordid anyway, and—'

'It *is* sordid,' interrupted Frances. 'But it is also necessary. And no one will dismiss Thomas, because he is better at it than anyone we have ever known.'

She took the Earl's arm and pulled him on their way, inclining her head to Chaloner, who was not sure whether he had just been complimented or insulted. The twinkle in her eye led him to hope it was the former. Dugdale followed, leaving Chaloner alone with Hyde.

'I am glad we met,' said Chaloner, although he chafed at the passing time, and hoped Hyde would not prove awkward to interview. 'I understand you witnessed Newell's death today.'

'I decline to discuss it,' said Hyde curtly. 'And you cannot make me.'

Chaloner was sure he could. 'I only wanted to ask who else was there.'

'Lots of people,' snapped Hyde. 'Men often demonstrate new weapons in St James's Park on a Saturday morning, and I was there with Leighton and the O'Briens. It is one of London's favourite pastimes. Well, favourite among *respectable* people. I doubt you have ever been.'

'How close were you when it happened?'

'Quite close – touching distance.' Hyde's expression was suddenly bleak, and Chaloner realised that distress, not mulishness, was the reason for his reluctance to discuss the matter. When Hyde next spoke, it was more to himself than the spy. 'The weapon was a type I had never seen before – and not one I am inclined to purchase, either, given *that* demonstration of its capabilities.'

'I am sorry,' said Chaloner sympathetically. 'It cannot have been easy to witness.'

Hyde shuddered, and his manner softened slightly. 'No. But never mind Newell – I have something much more important to tell you. I declined to mention it in front of my father, because I do not want him worried, but I found another letter this morning.'

'Where?' asked Chaloner.

'In the Queen's purse again,' replied Hyde. 'Which means *she* must have put it there, because no one else goes in it. It was in a different one from last time – that was red, and this one was yellow.'

'*You* went in it,' Chaloner pointed out. 'So logic dictates that someone else could, too.'

'Yes, but I am her secretary,' countered Hyde haughtily. 'I am different.'

'What did the letter say?' asked Chaloner, declining to argue. 'And where is it now?'

'It reiterated all the same nonsense as the first three. I put it on the fire.'

'Good,' said Chaloner, pleased Hyde had done

something right at last. 'Are you sure the whole thing was burned? No readable fragments were left?'

Hyde shot him a look of pure dislike. 'Of course I am sure. But I cannot waste time chatting to you. I have an important Adventurers' meeting to attend.'

The Queen's quarters comprised a suite of rooms that were cold in winter and hot in summer, and while a few chambers afforded a nice view of the river, most overlooked a dingy courtyard near the servants' latrine. Chaloner went through the formalities of admission with Captain Appleby, then climbed a staircase that was nowhere near as fine as the one that led to the Earl's offices.

'There you are, Tom,' said Hannah, emerging from a plain and rather threadbare antechamber. 'I was beginning to think you might have forgotten. Where have you been?'

'Hyde found another letter today.' Chaloner ignored the question and said what was on his mind. 'In the Queen's purse. Does he often rummage around in those?'

Hannah gaped. 'He certainly should not! I would not appreciate a man rifling through mine, not even you. They are personal.'

Chaloner was thoughtful. Had Hyde gone where no man should dare to root because he wanted to protect the Queen, or because he was eager to see her in trouble? And there was the question that kept nagging at him: had Hyde planted the letters there himself?

'He said it was in a different purse from last time,' he went on. 'Yellow, rather than red.'

Hannah stared at him. 'The Queen never uses the red and yellow ones – she does not like them. Her favourites are the green and white.'

Chaloner smiled. 'Which is indicative of her innocence – if the letters *were* hers, they would have been in the purses she uses, not in the ones she dislikes.'

'All well and good,' said Hannah worriedly. 'But it means someone villainous has access to the Blue Dressing Room – the chamber where she keeps such accessories. I shall have to work longer hours, to see if I can catch him.'

'Please do not,' begged Chaloner, alarmed. 'It might be dangerous.'

'It would be worth it.' Hannah raised her chin bravely, reminding Chaloner of why he had married her. 'The Queen is worth ten of anyone else in White Hall – except the Duke and you.'

Chaloner supposed it was a compliment, although he was not flattered to be likened to Buckingham. 'I have a number of clues,' he lied. 'So there is no need to risk yourself just yet. But we had better make a start before Hyde comes back.'

'He has gone for the day. Why do you think I suggested you come now? I wanted to show you how Her Majesty gets letters without him leaning over my shoulder and contradicting me at every turn. He really is the most frightful bore, and I wish she had a different secretary.'

So did Chaloner. He followed her through another grimly barren chamber, to one that was luxuriously appointed, with paintings by great masters and a wealth of fine furnishings.

'Hyde's office,' explained Hannah disapprovingly. 'He has far nicer things than the Queen.'

Chaloner searched it, going through the standard procedures to identify secret hiding places, aiming to discover anything that might prove Hyde was the author of the letters. He was aware of Hannah watching some of his checks in astonishment, no doubt wondering how he had come to learn them, but she grinned her delight when he located a secret drawer in a bureau. It was not a novel hiding place, but one in keeping with Hyde's unimaginative but overconfident character.

Unfortunately, it contained nothing but sketches of Lady Castlemaine *sans* clothes. The Earl would be unimpressed to think of his son poring over such images, but it was irrelevant as far as Chaloner was concerned. Hannah picked up one of the drawings and studied it disparagingly.

'Her knees are too big.'

'If Hyde is responsible for writing the letters, then he has left no evidence here,' said Chaloner, replacing all as he had found it. 'Who else has access to Her Majesty's wardrobe?'

'All her ladies-in-waiting, along with a host of maids, laundresses and seamstresses – some twenty or thirty women in all. No men, of course – that would be unseemly. You interviewed them when you were last here. Clearly none struck you as sly, or you would have said something.'

'What happens when letters arrive for the Queen?' While Chaloner did not believe the staff would have initiated such a plot of their own volition, most would have planted the missives in exchange for money. Loyalty was cheap at White Hall, where wages were low and often paid late.

'They are given to Captain Appleby downstairs, and he brings them to Hyde.'

'And Hyde reads them all?'

'He *opens* them all, but the ones that are personal he

is supposed to pass on without perusing. Of course, he is a nosy fellow and scans the lot. Except the ones in Portuguese, which are beyond him.'

'Then what?'

'Then, if he thinks she should see them, he places them on this silver platter, and conveys them to her. He deals with the routine correspondence, of course – petitions, bills and so forth.'

Chaloner had learned nothing helpful, and was about to leave when a door opened and the Queen stepped through it. Meneses was with her, along with several ladies-in-waiting, who scampered away with indecent haste when they saw that Hannah was available to take over as chaperon.

'I hope he does not stay long,' Hannah whispered resentfully to Chaloner, 'because there is nothing more tedious than listening to conversations in a language you do not know.'

'Hannah tells me you have been in Tangier, Thomas,' said Katherine pleasantly. She spoke Portuguese, and Chaloner suspected the pleasure she always exhibited when she met him derived from the fact that she was not obliged to struggle in English. 'I hope you liked it. It was part of my dowry, and the King says it will soon become one of England's most prized possessions.'

'Perhaps, Your Majesty,' Chaloner replied evasively, wanting neither to lie nor hurt her feelings.

Meneses regarded him through narrowed eyes. 'Who are you? You speak our language like a Spaniard, but you do not look like one.'

'He is Hannah's husband,' explained Katherine. 'I suppose he does sound like a Spaniard, now that you mention it. I have never noticed that before.'

As Spain and Portugal were mortal enemies, speaking Portuguese with a Spanish accent was clearly undesirable, and Chaloner would have to remedy the matter when he had time.

'Meneses has been to Tangier, too,' said Katherine conversationally. 'In fact, he was one of its governors, before it was handed to the English. I am sure you will enjoy talking to each other.'

Meneses' smile was tight. 'Alas, my sojourn there was brief, so I have little to say about it.'

'Come, My Lady,' said Hannah, taking the Queen's arm and clearly intent on separating her from the man she did not like. 'You promised to show me the new dances you have learned – the ones you will use at tomorrow's ball.'

The Queen laughed, a pleasant sound that was rarely heard, and allowed herself to be led away. She loved dancing, and could nearly always be diverted by it.

'The Queen is a dear, sweet creature, but easily confused,' said Meneses, when they had gone. 'You will ignore her chatter. She does not know what she is talking about.'

'You mean you were not Governor of Tangier?'

'I have never been there,' replied Meneses smoothly. 'But if it amuses her to think I held the title of governor, then where is the harm in letting her dream?'

He bowed and set off after her before Chaloner could ask more. The man was lying, but about what? Had he awarded himself fictitious titles to gain her favour? Or was he reluctant for anyone other than her – whose poor English did not permit her to gossip – to know of his Tangier connections, especially given his association with Fitzgerald and the Piccadilly Company?

As Meneses turned to close the door behind him, he caught Chaloner staring, and a combination of unease and anger flitted across his face. Chaloner looked away, but too late. Meneses knew he was suspicious, and Chaloner had a very bad feeling that might prove to be dangerous.

The next day was Sunday, and Chaloner awoke long before dawn when two cats elected to hold a brawl under his bedroom window. The moment he opened his eyes, he was aware of an immediate sense of frustration.

He had collected Thurloe after leaving the Queen's lodgings, and the two of them had spent the evening being thwarted at every turn. First, Reverend Addison had been out. Second, Harley had declined to answer his door and Thurloe had baulked at breaking in. Third, they had been unable to locate Jacob's house in Covent Garden. Fourth, Leighton had taken a number of Adventurers for a jaunt on the river; his guests included Kitty and O'Brien, so none of the three were available to describe what had happened to Newell. And finally, enquiries in the Piccadilly taverns had failed to yield a single shred of useful information.

Hannah had not been home when Chaloner had returned, and he was not sure how long he had been asleep before she had arrived. He had snapped awake with a dagger in his hand when she slid into bed beside him, although he had managed to shove it under the pillow before she saw it. Exhausted, he had dozed again, and had not woken until the cats had started yowling.

He rose quietly and went into the dressing room to hunt for fresh clothes. Then, because his stomach was tender and acidic from days of missed or hastily snatched

297

meals, he went to the kitchen, to see whether there was anything nice to eat.

'It is far too early for breakfast,' stated Joan, the moment she saw him. She was still wearing nightclothes, although Nan was dressed. There was no sign of George or Susan. 'The mistress gave strict instructions that nothing was to be served before ten o'clock on a Sunday.'

'Well, I am not the mistress,' replied Chaloner coolly, going to the larder. There was a pie, but remembering his injunction to George about the possibility of poison, he settled for a cup of milk instead.

'Do not drink that,' ordered Joan. 'Cold milk is dangerous.'

Chaloner took a larger gulp than he might otherwise have done, and stalked past her, wishing he had stayed in Long Acre. He went to the drawing room and retrieved the singed document he had hidden in the skirting board – the one he had found in the Piccadilly Company's rooms in the Crown. Then he opened his pen-box, and was unimpressed to note that it had been searched a second time – a pot of violet ink, which he liked for its unusual colour, had been moved. There was nothing significant in the box for the culprit to find, but it was unsettling nevertheless.

He settled down to work, trying all manner of exotic formulae, and using reams of paper in the process, but he met with no success. Bored, he leaned back in his chair to ease the cramped muscles in his shoulders, and his eye lit on his second-best viol, which he had neglected to put away the last time he had played it. He walked over to it and ran his fingers across its cool, silky wood. Then he took a sheet of music and began to go through it in his mind. A draught on the back of his neck told him someone was watching. He whipped around to see Nan.

'Joan sent me to tell you not to make a noise,' she said boldly. 'It disturbs the neighbours, and the mistress is still resting.'

Chaloner had not been going to play, but the directive prompted him to bow a rather tempestuous fantasy by Henry Lawes, which expressed his feelings far more accurately than words ever could. It was not long before Joan appeared.

'You will wake the mistress,' she snapped, going immediately to the table where the cipher still lay. Chaloner stood quickly and went to put it in his pocket. 'And she worked very late last night. She needs her sleep, and you are disturbing her.'

It was difficult to argue with such a remark, so Chaloner burned the useless decrypting notes in the hearth, then went to stand in the garden, craving fresh air and peace.

He was not sure of the time, but the sky was lightening in the east, and London was coming awake. It was too early for bells to summon the faithful to church, but there was a low and constant hum as carts, carriages and coaches rumbled their way along the capital's cobbled streets. Dogs barked, a baby cried, someone was singing and there was a metallic clatter from the ironmonger's shop three doors down. It was hardly restful, but he breathed in deeply, relishing the cool, earthy scent of the open fields that lay not far to the west.

He was not left alone to enjoy it for long. George appeared, carrying a lamp – a luxury Chaloner had certainly not considered claiming for himself. Clearly, the footman had not taken long to make himself at home in Tothill Street.

'A smoke is the only way to start the day,' he said, blowing great clouds of it towards the last of the season's cabbages. He was wearing a curious combination of clothes to ward off the early morning chill, including what looked suspiciously like Chaloner's best hat. 'Clears the mind.'

'Does it?' Chaloner glanced at him, and as the footman's fingers closed round the bowl of his pipe, he saw a smudge of violet ink on his hand, starkly visible in the lamp light. He grabbed it and inspected it more closely.

'An accident,' said George, freeing himself with more vigour than was appropriate between master and servant.

'Explain,' ordered Chaloner curtly.

'I was cleaning the pens in your box,' replied George, not looking at him. 'And the ink spilled.'

'None of my pens appeared to be clean.'

George looked him directly in the eye. 'Then it seems I am no better at that duty then I am at most others in the stewarding line. No wonder Fitzgerald dismissed me.'

'Speaking of Fitzgerald, did you ever sail with him on *Jane*?'

'*Jane*? Never heard of her.'

'Then were you with him when he traded in gravel?'

George shrugged, and produced so much smoke that it was difficult to see his face. 'He never told me what was in his holds. And I never asked.'

A sudden screech from the kitchen made Chaloner run back inside the house in alarm, although George ignored it. He arrived to find Joan had cornered a massive rat in the pantry.

'Fetch your gun and shoot it!' she ordered. 'I know you have one, because I have seen it.'

It was a brazen admission that she had been through

his belongings, because he had taken care to hide the weapon at the bottom of a drawer. He stared at her, wondering whether all servants considered it their bounden duty to pry into their employers' affairs.

'Do not just stand there!' she shrieked. 'Fetch the pistol and make an end of the beast.'

'The neighbours will complain about the noise,' he objected. 'Chase it out with a—'

He stopped in disgust when she swooped forward and brought a broom down on the rodent's head. The resulting gore was far worse than death from a gun, and he was sorry for Nan, who was given the task of cleaning it up.

When he went to resume his discussion with George, the footman had gone. Was he already on his way to report the conversation to Fitzgerald – or whoever else had ordered him to spy? Chaloner finished the milk, took more because he knew it would annoy Joan, and retired upstairs, sure Hannah would be awake by now.

She was only just beginning to stir, which was impressive given the racket that had been made by the duelling cats and by Joan over the rat. He was glad *he* did not sleep so soundly, certain he would have been dead long ago if he had.

'Did I hear you scraping on that horrible viol?' she asked accusingly.

Chaloner said nothing, but wondered why his playing should have disturbed her, when all the other sounds had not.

'I wish you had learned the flageolet instead,' she went on. 'Those are much nicer.'

He changed the subject quickly: they would fall out

for certain if they debated the relative merits of flageolets and viols. 'Could Meneses have hidden those letters in the Queen's purses?'

Hannah blinked, startled by such a question out of the blue. 'No. He is a man, and we do not allow those in Her Majesty's dressing rooms. It would not be decent. Where are you going?'

'Church,' replied Chaloner, suddenly seized with the desire to be out of the house.

'Good. You can take the servants. I want people to know we have an exotic footman.'

'For Christ's sake, Hannah,' snapped Chaloner, unable to help himself. 'He is not a performing bear. He may not even be Christian.'

Hannah stared at him. He rarely lost his temper with her, not even when he was seriously angry. Her expression darkened. 'If you cannot be civil, Thomas, it is wiser to say nothing at all.'

Chaloner rubbed his head, itching to retort that she should heed her own advice, especially in the mornings, but he was not equal to the argument that would follow. 'You were home late last night,' he said, changing the subject again in the interests of matrimonial harmony.

'Because Meneses would not leave. Perhaps he did plant those letters, although I cannot imagine how. Or why, come to that – he will not gain anything if the Queen is accused of plotting to kill the vainest man in London. Incidentally, I caught Susan poking about in your pen-box when I came home last night. I hope you do not keep anything sensitive in there.'

Chaloner frowned. 'Did she explain what she was doing?'

Hannah looked away. 'It seems you were right to

distrust her. She has been accepting money from someone to spy on you. She would not say who.'

Chaloner aimed for the door. 'Where is she?'

'Gone. I ordered her out of the house immediately, never to return.'

Chaloner smothered a sigh. 'It would have been better to question her first.'

'I *did* question her. And I just told you all she said. Besides, I did not want her in our home a moment longer.'

There was no point quarrelling over a fait accompli, so Chaloner bowed in an absurdly formal manner and took his leave, pausing only to hide the scrap of cipher in one of his old boots, an article so grimly shabby that he was certain no one would ever be inclined to investigate within. Perhaps such a precaution was unnecessary now Susan was exposed, but he had not forgotten George's suspicious behaviour *or* the fact that Joan had made a beeline for the document when it had been left on the table. As far as he was concerned, he trusted no one in his house. Not even, he realised with a pang, his wife.

Because London was terrified of religious fanatics – defined as anyone who did not follow traditional Anglican rites – Chaloner had no choice but to go to church that Sunday. The vergers made lists of absentees, and he did not want to draw attention to himself by playing truant. He could not afford to lose two hours that day, though, so he exchanged friendly greetings with the sexton in St Margaret's porch until he was sure his name had been recorded in the register, then escaped through the vestry door before the ceremonies began.

Yet he resented the fact that such deception was necessary, feeling he had fought a series of wars to end such dictates. The injustice of the situation gnawed at him as he walked to Worcester House – exacerbated by his irritation with Hannah, George and Susan – so that by the time he arrived to ask the Earl whether Meneses had been Governor of Tangier, he was in a black mood.

He stalked past the guards and rapped on the study door with considerable force. It was opened cautiously by Edgeman, who sighed his relief when he recognised the visitor.

'It is all right,' the secretary called over his shoulder. 'It is only Chaloner.'

'It was such an imperious knock that I thought it was Parliament come to impeach me,' said the Earl, putting his hand on his chest to indicate he had been given a fright. He was sitting by the fire, and Oliver and Dugdale were standing to attention in front of him.

'It is unbecoming for an usher to pound on his master's doors,' admonished Dugdale. He looked seedy that morning, so his rebuke lacked the venom it would usually carry. 'You made us all jump.'

'My apologies,' said Chaloner insincerely. He glanced at Oliver, thinking he had never seen the assistant architect in Worcester House before. It was the Earl who explained.

'Pratt has gone to view the Collection of Curiosities that is the talk of all London, so Oliver has come to give me my daily report instead.'

'The Earl refers to the exhibition near St Paul's Cathedral,' Oliver elaborated, although Chaloner recalled Farr telling him about it and reading the advertisment for it in the newsbook, so needed no explanation. An expression of gloom settled over the assistant architect's long face as he continued. 'And everyone who is anyone will be there today. Except me – I am the only man in the city who is not invited.'

'That is untrue,' said the Earl kindly. 'I have not been asked to attend, and neither has anyone else from my household.'

Dugdale and Edgeman exchanged a smug glance that said he was wrong.

'The rich and the famous,' Oliver went on morosely. 'Earls, barons and fêted merchants. Great people like Leighton, O'Brien, Kitty, Meneses and Brodrick. And Pratt, of course. But I shall be at Clarendon House, dusting banisters before the labourers return to work tomorrow.'

'Being in Clarendon House is not that bad,' objected the Earl, offended. 'It is a fine place to spend a Sunday morning. Indeed, I shall be there myself in an hour.'

Oliver brightened. 'Will you, sir? Some company would be nice.'

'I shall bring a jug of wine, and you can show me around,' elaborated the Earl graciously. Oliver cracked what was almost a smile. 'So go and make everything ready. My wife and I will join you as soon as she is ready. We are expected at church this morning, but we shall attend this afternoon, instead. No sacrifice is too great where my house is concerned.'

'You should not have yielded, sir,' chided Dugdale, after Oliver had shuffled out. 'It is not your responsibility to create a merry workforce. I never make any concessions in that direction myself. Indeed, I keep my ushers in line by ensuring that they are as unhappy as I can possibly make them.'

He had certainly done that, thought Chaloner,

305

watching the Earl's eyebrows shoot up in surprise at the bald confession. Dugdale started to add something else, but the Earl flapped a pudgy hand to indicate he should leave. The Chief Usher grimaced his indignation at the curt dismissal, and the bow he gave as he left was shallow enough to be impertinent. Edgeman scurried after him.

'Well?' asked the Earl, when the door had closed. 'Who is stealing my bricks? And have you identified the villain who wants to kill Pratt? You are fast running out of time.'

Chaloner did not need to be told. 'I have uncovered a lot of connections between the cases,' he hedged. 'And Williamson is worried about what will happen if the plot to harm the Queen succeeds – concerned for our future relations with Portugal.'

'It would be awkward, to say the least. Moreover, I do not want Pratt to die before he has finished my home. Are you *sure* you saw the thieves yesterday? Henry thinks you were mistaken.'

'Of course I saw them.'

'There is no need to snap,' said the Earl sharply. 'I believe you. It is a wretched shame you did not catch them, though. Was there anything that might allow you to identify them?'

'They were disguised.' Chaloner moved to what he considered more important matters. 'I need some information, sir: the names of the last Portuguese governors of Tangier.'

The Earl regarded him askance. 'What an odd request! But it is one I can grant, as it happens. The fellow with whom I had most correspondence – as I negotiated that part of the Queen's dowry – was Fernando de Meneses. He was later dismissed for dishonesty.'

'What does he look like?'

'I never met him. However, I imagine he looks Portuguese.'

It was not helpful, and left Chaloner none the wiser as to whether the Queen's new friend was an impostor. Of course, if Meneses stood accused of corruption, and so was unable to secure a post at home, then perhaps he *had* come to London to try his luck with a countrywoman who might not have heard of his shortcomings.

'I am glad you came,' said the Earl, when there was no response. 'Because I want you to spend the afternoon at Clarendon House. It is the workmen's day off, so it needs guarding. Frances and I will be there this morning. You can take over at two o'clock, and stay until Wright arrives at dusk.'

Chaloner struggled to control his temper. 'I thought you wanted me to catch the brick-thief, expose the plot to kill Pratt, and find out what happened to Teviot. All before Wednesday. How am I supposed to do that when—'

'You have had days to make enquiries,' snapped the Earl. 'It is not my fault you wasted them.'

'I have *not* wasted them,' countered Chaloner in something of a snarl. 'You ordered me to Woolwich and the Tennis Court, both of which were stupid, futile exercises.'

'You go too far!' cried the Earl, shocked. 'Perhaps Henry is right, and I should dismiss you in favour of someone more amenable. Or at least, someone who does not rail at me.'

Chaloner took a deep breath, knowing he had over-stepped the mark. He was also aware that it would not have happened if he had not been troubled by his home life and its attendant problems.

'I am sorry, sir. But something deadly *is* planned for three days' time, and we need to discover the identity of the man who is giving Fitzgerald orders before it is too late. It may involve Pratt, and—'

'Then you can do it this morning and tonight,' said the Earl, unappeased. 'Protecting my new home is far more important than rumours of vague plots. It is the reason I brought you home from Tangier, after all. This is not negotiable, Chaloner. You will do as I say.'

Chaloner had no choice but to agree. His temper was even blacker as he bowed and took his leave. As he hauled open the door, Kipps tumbled inside. The Seal Bearer's expression was distinctly furtive.

'I was not eavesdropping,' he blustered. 'I just wanted to know if you had finished.'

'Yes,' said Chaloner brusquely. 'He is all yours now.'

He walked to Chancery Lane Inn amid a cacophony of bells, as churches advertised their Sunday rites. The roads were full of people flocking towards them, along with those street vendors who declined to acknowledge that there were laws prohibiting Sabbath trading, and sought to provide for those who had time and money to spare. Other services had finished, disgorging congregations into the streets, while still more were in progress, so that singing drifted through their windows.

Chaloner reached Lincoln's Inn and ran up the stairs to Chamber XIII.

'There is a Collection of Curiosities near St Paul's,' he said, opening the door and speaking without preamble. 'We should visit it, because a lot of people we need to

308

interview will probably be there. We might even be able to determine which of the Adventurers wants the Queen accused of plotting to kill Pratt.'

'Good morning to you, too,' said Thurloe drily. He was sitting at the table, and Chaloner saw he was working on the same cipher that continued to defeat him – they had made a copy the previous night. 'Do you expect me to come with you? Before my devotions in the chapel?'

Chaloner felt the business at hand was rather more urgent than religious ceremonies, although he knew better than to say so outright – Thurloe was devout. 'You can go this afternoon. The Earl will be doing the same, so he can mind Clarendon House instead.'

'He is reduced to guarding his own property, is he?' Thurloe rose with a sigh. 'Very well, we shall go to St Paul's, although I shall have to don a disguise. The Court is unlikely to appreciate being watched by an old Parliamentarian spymaster.'

Chaloner sat by the fire as Thurloe changed his appearance with a range of pastes, powders and an exceptionally unattractive orange wig.

'The more I think about it, the more I am sure that Elliot is alive and masquerading as Cave's brother,' Chaloner said, staring into the flames. 'Both the curate and Kersey mentioned an unusually black wig – which Elliot had. And both said "Jacob" was large and loutish.'

'But anyone can don a hairpiece,' Thurloe pointed out. 'While I could write you a list as long as my arm of "large and loutish" men. Lester would be on it – and we know for certain that *he* is alive.'

'Why would Lester want Cave buried without a grand funeral?' asked Chaloner impatiently.

Thurloe turned away from the mirror to regard him

soberly. 'To avenge Elliot – his shipmate and brother-in-law.'

'No,' said Chaloner irritably. 'Lester is not Jacob.'

Thurloe went back to perfecting his disguise. They were silent for some time, Chaloner gazing moodily at the fire. Eventually, Thurloe indicated that he was ready.

'Have you given consideration to Williamson's request?' he asked, as they walked across Dial Court towards Lincoln's Inn's main gate. 'Will you work with him?'

'No. I do not trust him, and the notion of taking orders from such a man . . .'

'Take them,' instructed Thurloe. 'This is far too grave a matter to be affected by your pride. He has swallowed his by asking for your help. Do likewise, and help him.'

'Then when I fall foul of him – an inevitability, given his prickly temper and our past quarrels – will you rescue me from his dungeons?'

Thurloe raised his eyebrows, and it was clear that he was thinking that Williamson was not the only one prone to bad tempers. 'He would not dare incarcerate you. Clarendon would not stand for it.'

Chaloner recalled the hot words that had been spoken earlier. 'I think he might.'

'He is all bluster, but he appreciates what you do for him. His son does not, though. You should be wary of Hyde.'

'You have warned me to be wary of a lot of people lately – Hyde, Lester, Fitzgerald. Indeed, half of London seems to be swirling with deadly villains according to you.'

Thurloe regarded him sharply. 'They *are* dangerous, Thomas, and you are a fool if you discount my advice. You think Fitzgerald is less deadly than I have portrayed, and Hyde is too feeble to be a threat, while you like Lester.'

'Yes,' admitted Chaloner. 'I do.'

'Then continue to like him. Just do not *trust* him. That should not be difficult – you repel overtures of friendship from everyone else you meet. And I cannot say it is healthy.'

'You trained me to do it,' retorted Chaloner, nettled. 'Besides, it means I am rarely disappointed when they transpire to be villains.'

'Speaking of villains, you might want to watch Kipps, too,' said Thurloe. 'He professes a powerful dislike of Adventurers, but that does not stop him from hobnobbing with them.'

'He is just friendly.' Chaloner was becoming tired of Thurloe's suspicions. Then a thought occurred to him. 'Did you ever harbour misgivings about Hannah's maid Susan?'

'I told Hannah she was sly and untrustworthy, but she – like you – declined to listen. Why?'

'She was dismissed for spying this morning. God knows who paid her to do it. Unfortunately, she had been sent packing before I could question her.'

'That is a pity,' said Thurloe.

Chapter 9

Thurloe talked all the way to St Paul's, and his calm voice and rational analyses of the information they had gathered did much to lift the dark mood that had descended on Chaloner. By the time they arrived, all that remained was an acute sense of unease, arising partly from the fact that they had less than three days to prevent whatever catastrophes the Piccadilly Company and their rivals intended to inflict on London, but mostly because he had finally come to accept the realisation that it had been a mistake to marry Hannah.

He was fond of her – he supposed it might even be love – but they had nothing in common, and he knew now that they would make each other increasingly unhappy as the gulf between them widened. But these were painful, secret thoughts, and he doubted he would ever be able to share them with another person. Not even Thurloe, who was as close a friend as any. He pushed them from his mind as they neared St Paul's, and tried to concentrate on the task at hand.

Because it was Sunday, the cathedral was busy. Canons, vicars and vergers hurried here and there in ceremonial robes, and a large congregation was massing. It was a fabulous building, with mighty towers and soaring pinnacles that dominated the city's skyline. Unfortunately, time had not treated it well: there were cracks in its walls, its stonework was crumbling, and several sections were being held up by precarious messes of scaffolding. Ambitious architects – Pratt among them – clamoured for it to be demolished, but Londoners loved it, and strenuously resisted all efforts to provide them with a new-fangled replacement.

'The exhibition is at the Mitre,' said Chaloner, as they walked. 'At the western end of the cathedral.'

'The Mitre,' said Thurloe disapprovingly. 'Even in Cromwell's time it was a place that catered to the bizarre. We should have suppressed it.'

The tenement in question was sandwiched between a coffee house and a bookshop. Its ground floor was a tavern, while the upper storey had a spacious hall that was used for travelling expositions. It was virtually deserted when Chaloner and Thurloe arrived, with only one or two clerics poring over the artefacts, killing time before attending to their religious duties.

'We are too early,' murmured Thurloe. 'But it does not matter – there is much to entertain us while we wait. I have never seen a tropic bird. Or a remora, come to that.'

'What is a remora?' asked Chaloner.

Thurloe shrugged. 'I imagine we shall know by the time we leave.'

Chaloner wandered restlessly, intrigued by some exhibits and repelled by others. The Egyptian mummy held pride of place, although moths had been at its bandages, and some of its 'hieroglyphicks' had been

313

over-painted by someone with a sense of humour, because one of the oft-repeated symbols bore a distinct resemblance to the King in his wig.

'Apparently, the tropic bird has not survived London's climate,' reported Thurloe, having gone to enquire after its whereabouts. 'I am sorry. I would have liked to have made its acquaintance.'

At that moment the door opened and Lady Castlemaine strutted in, a number of admirers at her heels. Immediately, the atmosphere went from hushed and scholarly to boisterously puerile. The exhibits were poked, mocked and hooted at, and the situation degenerated further still as more courtiers arrived. Soon, the place was so packed that it was difficult to move.

'There is your brother-in-law,' said Chaloner, nodding to where Lydcott was peering at the moon fish, a sad beast in a tank of cloudy water that looked as if it would soon join the tropic bird and become a casualty of London's insatiable demand for the bizarre.

'I cannot greet him,' said Thurloe. 'I am in disguise, and he is the kind of man to blurt out my name if I speak to him and he recognises my voice. I shall attempt to engage the Janszoon couple in conversation instead, to see what I can learn about the Piccadilly Company.'

He moved away, although he was not in time to prevent Margareta from informing the entire room that English curiosities were 'a deal more meretricious' than ones in Amsterdam.

'She means "meritorious",' explained Thurloe quickly. 'An easy mistake, even for native English speakers. She intended a compliment, not an insult.'

'I do not need interpolation,' she objected indignantly. 'My English is excellent.'

'It is excellent,' said Lady Castlemaine, regarding Thurloe coolly. 'Which means she knew exactly what she was saying – and it was nothing polite.'

Thurloe bowed to her, then took Margareta's arm and ushered her away, aiming for the giant's thigh-bone, an object that clearly had once been part of a cow. Janszoon followed, and so did the three guards. Chaloner thought the couple was right to ensure that someone was there to protect them, given that they seemed unable to speak without causing offence.

'What an extraordinarily ugly creature,' said Lydcott, glancing up at Chaloner and then returning his gaze to the moon fish. 'Do you think God was intoxicated when He created it?'

'Is Fitzgerald here?' asked Chaloner. God's drinking habits were certainly not something he was prepared to discuss in a public place. Men had been executed for less.

'No – he came last week.' Lydcott turned to him suddenly, his expression earnest. 'Thurloe says the Piccadilly Company is being used to disguise some great wickedness engineered by Fitzgerald, and I have been thinking about his claims ever since. Indeed, I spent most of last night doing it.'

'And what did you conclude?'

'That he is mistaken. I admit that I am sent more frequently than anyone else to fetch refreshments, but I cannot believe they use the opportunity to plot terrible things. He is wrong.'

'Have you ever heard them discussing an event planned for this coming Wednesday?'

Lydcott shook his head. 'Not specifically. Why?'

'It might be a good idea for you to leave London,'

said Chaloner, suspecting Thurloe's gentle wife would be heartbroken if anything were to happen to her silly brother. 'For your own safety.'

'No,' stated Lydcott emphatically. 'For the first time in my life I am involved in a successful venture, and I am not going to abandon it just because Thurloe dislikes Fitzgerald. Besides, if he is right – which I am sure he is not – then staying here will allow me to thwart whatever it is. It is still my business, so I have some say in what happens.'

Chaloner doubted it. 'It is too risky to—'

'Pratt is coming our way,' interrupted Lydcott. 'We had better talk about something else, because he has invested a lot of money with us, and I do not want him to withdraw it, just because my brother-in-law is a worrier. Pratt! Did you find the key you lost?'

'What key?' asked Chaloner in alarm.

'The one to Clarendon House,' replied Pratt, reaching inside his shirt and producing it. He glared at Lydcott. 'And it was not *lost*. It was mislaid – dropped between two floorboards.'

'What if you had lost it?' asked Chaloner. 'Would you cut a copy from the Earl's?'

'Certainly not! More keys mean decreased security. I argued against there being more than one in the first place, but the Earl overrode me. Still, it is his house, so I suppose he has a right to two if he wants them.'

'I am sure he will be pleased to hear it,' said Chaloner.

Pratt and Lydcott did not stay with Chaloner long – they went to talk to the Janszoons. Thurloe bowed and left quickly, unwilling to risk being unmasked by his foolish brother-in-law. Chaloner retreated behind the tank

316

holding the eel-like remora to watch the gathering, noting that two other Piccadilly Company members had gravitated towards each other, too – Harley was with Meneses.

Lester had also arrived, apparently hoping for an opportunity to further his investigation. Chaloner winced when Thurloe homed in on him, and could tell by the bemused expression on the captain's face that he was being interrogated with some vigour.

Meanwhile, a clot of Adventurers clustered around Leighton, listening politely as he pontificated. Swaddell was among them, but there was a distance between him and the others, and it was clear that he would never be fully trusted. He was wasting his time, and Chaloner thought he should cut his losses and return to Williamson.

Then O'Brien and Kitty appeared, at which point Leighton abandoned his companions and scuttled to greet them. O'Brien was all boyish enthusiasm for the exhibits, although Kitty's eyes filled with compassionate tears at the plight of the hapless moon fish.

'If you join the Adventurers, you will receive many invitations like this one,' Chaloner heard Leighton whisper to them. 'You will spend *all* your time in high society.'

'That would be pleasant.' There was real yearning in O'Brien's voice. 'But Kitty says we cannot join an organisation that profits from slavery. And she is right. It is unethical to—'

'Mr O'Brien!' The speaker was Lady Castlemaine, who swept forward with a predatory smile. 'Do come and inspect the salamanders with me. You can tell me all about them, I am sure.'

'It is astonishing how our wealth makes us instant experts with opinions worth hearing,' Kitty remarked to

317

Leighton as she prepared to follow. 'Last year, when we had less of it, no one was very interested in what we thought.'

Leighton opened his mouth to respond, but Kitty had gone, leaving him alone. Chaloner started to move away too, but suddenly Leighton was next to him. The Adventurers' secretary gestured to the remora, which floated miserably in water that was every bit as foul as that of the moon fish.

'We should all take a lesson from this sorry beast,' he said softly. 'It ventured into a place where it should not have gone, and it is now a thing to be laughed at by fools.'

Chaloner was not entirely sure what he meant. Had he just been warned off? Or informed that the Court comprised a lot of idiots? He realised that one of the most unsettling things about Leighton was the fact that he was near-impossible to read. Was he dangerous, as so many people believed, with ties to the criminal world in which he was said to have made his fortune? Or was he just a clever courtier with hidden depths?

'Is it dead?' asked Leighton, still staring at the fish. 'Or just pretending?'

'Speaking of dead things, I understand you witnessed an accident,' said Chaloner. 'Newell.'

Leighton's eyes bored into Chaloner's with such intensity that it was difficult not to look away. 'Apparently, the trigger needed no more than a breath to set it off, and he had a heavy hand.'

'Do you think someone ordered it made so?' asked Chaloner, recalling the conversation in the gunsmiths' shop, where Leighton had gone to have his own weapon adjusted in just such a manner.

318

'I imagine its owner did not want to be yanking like the devil while his life was in danger. But Newell was a professional soldier, who should have been more careful. Incidentally, Harley was so distressed by his companion's demise that he hurled the offending weapon into the river. It was unfortunate, because now no one can examine it.'

He scuttled away, leaving Chaloner with a mind full of questions. Chaloner looked for Harley, and saw him studying a device that claimed to launch arrows so poisonous that the victim would be dead before he hit the ground. Fortunately, it was encased in thick glass, because the devil-eyed colonel looked as though nothing would give him greater pleasure than to snatch it up and launch a few into the throng that surged around him.

'I was sorry to hear about Newell,' said Chaloner, watching him jump at the voice so close to his ear. 'You must feel uneasy, now you are the only Tangier scout left alive.'

Harley glowered. 'Newell and Reyner were careless. I am not.'

Chaloner raised his hands placatingly. 'I am not the enemy. And if you had let me help you last week, you might not be missing two friends now.'

Harley sneered. 'I am not discussing Teviot, so you had better back off, or your corpse will be the next Curiosity to attract the attention of these ghouls.'

Chaloner was unmoved by the threat. 'You threw the gun that killed Newell in the river. Why?'

Harley's scowl deepened. 'I should have kept it, to identify the bastard who gave it to him, but I was angry. The trigger had been set to go off at the slightest touch, and not even an experienced soldier stood a chance. But

I am not discussing that with you, either. It is none of your affair.'

'Perhaps we can talk about *Jane* instead, then,' said Chaloner softly. 'Carrying gravel.'

Harley stared at him, eyes blazing. 'Do you *want* to die? Is that why you insist on meddling with matters that do not concern you?'

'They do concern me,' argued Chaloner. 'I am interested in gravel. And fine glassware.'

'Then buy a book about them,' snapped Harley curtly. 'And—'

They both turned at a shriek from the Lady, who had managed to slide her hand inside the case that held the 'Twenty-foot Serpent' to see whether it was alive. It was, and objected to being poked. Her fast reactions had saved her from serious harm, but the creature had drawn blood. Harley escaped in the ensuing commotion, after which there was a general exodus as the Court moved on to its next entertainment. It was not long before only those genuinely interested in science remained. They included Kitty and O'Brien, so Chaloner went to see what they could tell him about Newell.

They were inspecting the 'Ant Beare of Brasil', a sleek creature with a long snout and three legs, although there was nothing to tell the visitor whether all members of that species were tripedal, or just that particular individual.

'Have you ever been to Brazil, Chaloner?' asked O'Brien amiably.

'It is full of plantations,' said Kitty in distaste. 'Run on slave labour – which is wicked.'

'Leighton is still trying to persuade us to become Adventurers,' said O'Brien unhappily. 'The irony is that

320

we were keen to join last year, but our copper sales had not made us rich enough, and we were rejected. Now we have ample funds, but have learned that it is an unethical venture – although their social events are certainly enticing.'

'Leighton pesters us constantly to join,' said Kitty. 'Horrible man!'

'I understand that you had another unpleasant experience recently, too,' said Chaloner. 'You saw Newell killed in St James's Park.'

Kitty paled, and her husband put a protective arm around her shoulders. 'It was dreadful,' he said weakly. 'Leighton was with us, but he said and did *nothing*. In fact, he looked like the serpent that just tried to eat Lady Castlemaine – evil and dispassionate at the same time.'

'Do you think he knew what was about to happen?' asked Chaloner.

Kitty and O'Brien looked at each other. 'I would not have thought so,' said O'Brien eventually, although without much conviction. 'How could he have done?'

'Yes,' agreed Kitty cautiously. 'It must have been an accident. But let us talk about something else. Newell's death was horrible, and we shall all have nightmares if we persist.'

'We have been invited to a soirée tomorrow and a reception on Tuesday,' said O'Brien, forcing a smile. 'The soirée is at Brodrick's house, and he promises us a memorable time.'

'I am sure you will have it,' said Chaloner, knowing from experience that Brodrick's parties usually began well, but degenerated as the night progressed and the wine flowed.

'Tuesday's event is a pageant to welcome the Swedish

ambassador,' O'Brien went on. This time the grin was more genuine. 'I *do* love a good ceremony, and London is very good at them.'

'Will you be there, Mr Chaloner?' asked Kitty. 'Joseph says he will need to be in disguise, to spy on people with wicked intentions. It means he cannot talk to us, lest he gives himself away.'

'He told us he will be in pursuit of traitors and scoundrels,' said O'Brien, laughing at the notion. 'But I cannot imagine there are many of those at White Hall.'

'You would be surprised,' murmured Chaloner.

Soon, even those of a scientific bent took their leave, and Chaloner and Thurloe adjourned to a nearby coffee house to discuss their findings. It did not take them long to know that they had uncovered very little in the way of clues, and that most of what they had learned was no more than rumour and speculation.

'In other words,' Thurloe concluded grimly, 'we still do not know who is giving orders to Fitzgerald, or what he intends to do on Wednesday. We also have no idea who wants the Queen blamed for plotting to kill Pratt, although we suspect the culprit will transpire to be an Adventurer.'

'Yes,' said Chaloner, troubled. 'But the Queen is an Adventurer, too. So much for loyalty.'

'She signed the charter and invested money, but that is all. She will never be part of them – at least, not until she produces an heir. My chief suspect is Leighton, on the grounds that he is a sinister individual who may have brought about Newell's demise with a faulty gun.'

'Which Harley promptly tossed into the river.' Chaloner was thoughtful. '*My* chief suspect for the letters remains Hyde – also an Adventurer. And you did tell me to be wary of him.'

'I did,' acknowledged Thurloe. 'However, he would never do anything to endanger his father – and Clarendon *would* suffer if the Queen is accused, because he is the one who recommended her as a bride for the King. Of course, there are other members of the Earl's household . . .'

'Dugdale and Edgeman,' said Chaloner, nodding. 'They would betray the Earl in an instant if they thought it would benefit them.'

'So would Kipps.' Thurloe held up his hand to silence Chaloner's objections. 'We will not argue about this, Tom, because there is no point – neither of us has the evidence to prove or disprove our beliefs. All we have is suspicion and conjecture.'

Chaloner accepted his point, and returned to their list of unanswered questions. 'We still do not know why Fitzgerald took over the Piccadilly Company, either.'

'I cornered the Janszoons, Meneses *and* Pratt, but they all claimed a passion for glassware prompted their interest in Lydcott's business. However, none of them know the first thing about it, which tells me they were lying.'

Chaloner was beginning to feel despondent. 'We have less than three days before some diabolical plot swings into action, but how are we to prevent it when we are thwarted at every turn? Or worse, locked in vaults with chests of hungry rats.'

Thurloe regarded him sympathetically. 'My favoured suspect for that piece of nastiness remains Fitzgerald, on the grounds that he is famous for inventing unusual ways to dispatch his victims. Or perhaps the savage imagination is his master's.'

'Or Leighton's, whose indifferent reaction to Newell's death suggests he is used to gore. Or a brick-thief, because my enquiries are becoming a nuisance. The list is endless.'

Thurloe finished his coffee and stood. 'I am going to visit a few old haunts in and around Piccadilly, then I shall prod Wallis over decoding Mrs Reyner's list. Will you come with me?'

'I wish I could, but I am condemned to spend the afternoon at Clarendon House. I hate the place. If it burned down, do you think the Earl would know I did it?'

'No, but he would order you to investigate, which would be awkward, to say the least. Do not commit arson just yet, Tom – if you fail to save the Queen and she falls from grace, Clarendon will tumble with her. It is possible that he may not survive to inhabit his mansion.'

'Is that meant to make me feel better?' asked Chaloner, shocked.

'It is an outcome you should bear in mind,' replied Thurloe soberly. 'Along with the possibility that Fitzgerald might win this contest. He bested me on innumerable occasions when I was spymaster, and there is no reason to assume he will not do so again.'

'No,' said Chaloner with quiet determination. 'I will not stand by while the Queen is used in so vile a manner. Or the Earl. He may not be much of an employer, but he is all I have.'

Thurloe smiled briefly. 'Then let us see what we can do to protect them.'

They took a hackney carriage to Piccadilly, where Thurloe disappeared into the dark recesses of the Feathers, and Chaloner walked to Clarendon House.

Oliver was just leaving for the day, his dusting completed, while the Earl was still wandering about inside with Frances.

'I shall spend the rest of the day at home,' said Oliver, his gloomy face a mask of dejection. 'Alone, with only my ferret for company. Being an architect's assistant is a lonely occupation, because the unsociable hours prevent me from meeting ladies . . .'

'You have a ferret?' asked Chaloner, not sure how else to respond to the confidence.

Oliver nodded, and arranged his morose features into what passed as a smile. 'They are cheaper to feed than dogs, and more affectionate than birds. They also keep a kitchen free of rats, and I cannot abide rats.'

'No,' agreed Chaloner unhappily, as he turned to enter Clarendon House, his mind full of the strongroom and what had happened to him in it.

It was not easy to step inside the mansion, and he was uncomfortably aware of the vast emptiness of the place as he walked through it, treading softly to prevent his footsteps from echoing. He found the Earl and Frances in the Great Parlour, a huge room in one of the wings that was accessed by a set of double doors that were as grand as any in White Hall. It was lit by windows in the ceiling, which would be almost impossible to clean, and there was a ridiculous number of marble pillars and plinths.

'I do not like it, dear,' Frances was saying, looking around in dismay. 'This is the chamber where you and I will spend cosy evenings together, but it is about as snug as a tomb. It does not even have a fireplace. Perhaps we should have hired a different architect.'

'We shall be very happy here,' declared the Earl firmly.

'Ah, there you are, Chaloner. I was beginning to think you had decided to spend the afternoon elsewhere. Have you seen my vault, by the way? You should approve, being mindful of security.'

'Mr Kipps spent a lot of time inspecting it on Friday,' said Frances, smiling a greeting at the spy. 'He was greatly admiring of it, and said it is the safest depository in London.'

'On Friday?' asked Chaloner uneasily. He had been locked in on Friday.

'We shall be late for church if we stand here chatting,' said the Earl briskly. 'My house is in your hands, Chaloner, although you will have to mind it from the garden, because I must lock up.'

When they had gone, Chaloner let himself back in with his own key and prowled, trying to learn how the thief he had chased the previous day – assuming it was not Pratt – had disappeared. But although he paced corridors and tapped on walls, he could find no hidden doorways that the fellow might have used.

He considered the stolen bricks. The conversation he had overheard on the portico told him that the thieves were known to the Earl. But who were they? Someone from his household, such as Edgeman or Dugdale? He refused to think it might be Kipps – working for Clarendon would verge on the intolerable if the one man who was friendly towards him was dismissed as a villain.

The discussion had also indicated that there might be more to the matter than the removal of materials, although he could not imagine what. Moreover, he was still sure they were disappearing during the day rather than at night, although the conviction did nothing to help him with answers.

He turned his mind to his other enquiries. First, Cave. What had induced him to fight Elliot? *Did* he have a brother named Jacob, or had Elliot recovered sufficiently from his wound to invent him? Lester had not seen Elliot die, and Chaloner doubted he had looked in the coffin before it was buried in St Giles-in-the-Fields.

Second, there were the letters. He was inclined to accept Thurloe's contention that an Adventurer was responsible – Pratt was a member of the rival Piccadilly Company, after all. Moreover, the Queen was unpopular at Court, and many Adventurers were eager to secure His Majesty a fertile Protestant bride in her place. Was Secretary Leighton one of them? Or Edgeman and Dugdale?

And finally, there was the Tangier massacre. It was clear that Harley, Newell and Reyner had sent Lord Teviot into the ambush deliberately, and that the reason was tied up with the Piccadilly Company. But what was of such importance that the lives of five hundred men were seen as an acceptable sacrifice?

Of course, the soldiers were not the only casualties of whatever war was raging. Proby, Turner, Lucas, Congett, Reyner and his mother, and Newell were victims, too. And what was the significance of gravel? Was it just a convenient cargo to transport on return voyages, as Lydcott claimed? Or was it code for some other commodity?

Frustrated when no answers came, Chaloner descended to the basement, prowling the kitchens, laundries and pantries. He paused at the top of the cellar stairs and listened, but the place was silent, and wild horses would not have induced him to go down there again.

He left the house to walk outside, carefully locking

the door behind him. The site was deserted, and he kicked his heels restlessly as the afternoon crept by, fretting at the hours that could have been used more profitably.

Predictably, it was late before Wright and his men arrived, although they were unrepentant when he complained. The clocks were striking eight before he was able to leave, and it had been dark for some time.

Sure the answers to almost all his questions lay in Piccadilly, Chaloner took up station in the shadows surrounding the Gaming House and began to watch the Crown tavern. It did not take him long to realise that someone else was doing the same. He drew his dagger and crept forward.

'Tom!' exclaimed Thurloe, once Chaloner, recognising his muffled cry of alarm, had released him. 'What are you doing here?'

'The same as you.' Chaloner slipped the knife back up his sleeve. 'Is anything happening?'

Thurloe nodded. 'The Piccadilly Company is gathering. Robert knows nothing of it, though, because he told me only an hour ago that they will not meet again until the end of next week.'

'Who has arrived so far?'

'Fitzgerald, Meneses, Harley, Brilliana and others who have disguised themselves so well that I cannot recognise them – about a dozen in all. Brinkes and his henchmen have ousted the drinkers from the tavern, which says something sensitive is about to be aired, because he should not need to clear a downstairs room when they meet on an upper floor.'

'Then we had better eavesdrop.'

'Yes, but how?' asked Thurloe impatiently. 'Brinkes will be watching the stairs.'

'Stairs are not the only way to gain access to upper floors.'

'You mean I should climb up the back of the house and listen at a window?' asked Thurloe, raising his eyebrows. 'I doubt I could do it, not with my fragile constitution. Besides, Brinkes has posted two guards there, and he checks them every few minutes. He is nothing if not thorough.'

'Then create a diversion while I try.'

Thurloe's eyes gleamed. 'It will be dangerous, but worth it. Standing out here is a waste of time.'

Chaloner made his way to the rear of the tavern, and after a few moments something began to happen. There was a lot of girlish laughter, and suddenly three near-naked prostitutes burst into the Crown's garden. It went without saying that the guards hurried towards them and demanded to know what they were doing. The men's voices were angry, but their eyes said they were not averse to the interruption. Chaloner began his ascent.

It was easier than he had expected, because the building was old, and crumbling bricks provided plenty of handholds. He was soon outside the first-floor window, where he peered through the glass to see Fitzgerald sitting at the table and his associates gathered around him. The pirate's soprano voice was clearly audible, and Chaloner was under the impression that he was in a sulk.

'. . . do not see why it cannot be done. Our master will not be impressed, and neither am I.'

Chaloner tensed when Brinkes came to find out what was happening in the garden, but the henchman stormed straight towards the girls, and did not once look up at the window. In case he did, Chaloner eased to one side, using darkness and the ivy that grew up the wall to conceal himself. He turned his attention back to the meeting.

'. . . rumours of our plans,' Harley was saying. 'I am not saying we—'

'*Jane* will arrive on Wednesday, and that is that,' snarled Fitzgerald. 'The plan *will* go ahead – on St Frideswide's Day, just as we have intended from the start.'

'Yes,' said Harley, clearly struggling for patience. 'I am not saying we should delay. I am merely reiterating the need for caution, because half of London knows something is afoot.'

Down below, Brinkes had declined the prostitutes' offer of a free session in the bushes, and was ordering his men back to their posts. The women were shoved unceremoniously through the gate, while he began a systematic search of the garden, using his sword in a way that said he would have no problem skewering interlopers.

'*You* advise caution?' Fitzgerald demanded, the anger in his voice reclaiming Chaloner's attention. 'I expected you to dispatch Teviot quietly, and what did you do? Send him into an ambush with hundreds of men! If you had shown a little caution then, our business might have been able to proceed more smoothly.'

'It was not *my* idea,' snapped Harley. 'I was under orders, too.'

No one at the table looked as though they believed him, and Chaloner was not sure he did, either.

'That escapade obliged us to rein back for weeks,' said Meneses, in heavily accented English. 'And now you say there might be an official inquiry.'

'The next time Chaloner offers to influence matters, hear him out,' said a man whose back was to the window. His voice was familiar, although the spy could not place it.

'No,' countered Brilliana sharply. She looked especially lovely that night, in a low-cut gown with a simple but expensive pendant at her throat. 'It would not surprise me to learn that *he* killed Newell and Reyner, to make my brother think he has no choice but to reveal what he knows. But his tactics will not work. We shall weather this storm, just as we weathered Teviot.'

'The gravel will make everything worthwhile,' said Meneses. There was a gleam in his eyes that was immediately recognisable as greed, and it was echoed in every person around the table.

Then disaster struck. The windowsill to which Chaloner clung gave a sudden creak, and although no one in the parlour seemed to have heard it, Brinkes and the guards immediately gazed upwards. They could not see him, but they knew something was amiss.

'It must be that damned Ruth,' said Brinkes. 'She is always spying on us. Well, this time will be her last. You two take her to the woods and cut her throat. I shall stay here. They must be almost finished by now – they told me they would not be long tonight.'

'Why not kill her here?' asked one of the men.

'Because it will be messy, and we do not want Lester making a fuss,' replied Brinkes shortly. 'This way, he will assume that she wandered off. God knows, she is lunatic enough.'

Chaloner knew he had to act fast if he wanted to save her. Unfortunately, he could do nothing while Brinkes was standing guard – he would be shot or stabbed long before he reached the ground. Agonising minutes ticked by, but the henchman showed no sign of moving. In the end, Chaloner took one of his daggers and lobbed it, heaving a sigh of relief when Brinkes hurtled after the sound like a bloodhound. It kept him occupied just long enough to allow Chaloner to slither to the ground and slip unseen through the gate.

'I doubt my ladies gave you long enough to learn anything useful,' said Thurloe, appearing suddenly out of the shadows in the street. 'They were ousted too soon, and—'

'I made a noise, and Brinkes thinks it was Ruth,' interrupted Chaloner tersely. 'He has sent men to kill her.'

Thurloe was too experienced an operative to ask questions when a life was at stake. He ran with Chaloner to the Crown, but the attic was already empty. Stomach churning, Chaloner set off along Piccadilly, hoping the guards had not taken her to some other dark road to carry out their grisly orders. Then he saw them some distance ahead. When Ruth tried to pull free, one slapped her.

Chaloner charged forward, and cracked him over the head with the hilt of another of his daggers. The fellow dropped to the ground senseless. The second henchman hurled Ruth away, and drew his knife. He lunged, but Chaloner parried the blow with his arm, simultaneously driving his other fist into his opponent's throat. The guard collapsed, gagging and struggling to breathe.

'Did I teach you to do that?' asked Thurloe in distaste. 'Or is it something you learned yourself?'

'She cannot go back to the Crown,' said Chaloner, wrapping his coat around the terrified, shivering woman.

'I will take her to Long Acre. Will you send word to Lester? I have no idea where he lives, but Williamson will.'

Chaloner spent a long and restless night in his garret, although Ruth seemed none the worse for her experiences. She curled up on the bed and went to sleep almost immediately, instinctively trusting him to look after her. Lester did not arrive until dawn. He flew to his sister's side, then closed his eyes in relief when he saw she was unharmed.

'I thought you would come sooner,' said Chaloner, irked to have spent the entire night playing nursemaid. He had not liked to leave Ruth, lest she woke and was frightened by her strange surroundings. Or worse, wandered off. He had not even been able to use the time to work on the cipher, because it was in Tothill Street, concealed in his boot.

'Williamson did not know where to find me – I was out all night, monitoring courtiers. I can scarcely credit their capacity for merriment. Indeed, Brodrick and Buckingham are still at it, although Grey and Kipps are finally unconscious. What happened to my sister?'

Chaloner told him, half tempted to include what he had overheard in the Crown, too. He resisted, but because of his habitual reluctance to share intelligence, not because of Thurloe's warnings.

'I should have taken her away from that place the moment she told me there was something amiss,' said Lester, reaching out to stroke her hair. 'It was obvious that her fascination with its comings and goings would bring her trouble.'

Chaloner agreed. 'So why did you leave her there?'

'Because Landlord Marshall and his wife are kind to her,' Lester explained. 'And she finds comfort in familiarity. If I took her to my own home, she would be alone and miserable.'

'What will you do with her now? She cannot go back.'

'I shall hire a woman to sit with her. Here, if you would not mind, just until this mischief is over. It is as safe a place as any, and it will not be for more than a day or two.'

Chaloner nodded acquiescence, feeling he owed Ruth something, given that it was his fault she had almost been murdered.

'I would stay myself,' Lester went on. 'But Williamson has ordered me to White Hall, where the Adventurers are holding one of their meetings – it will be followed by a reception to which he has inveigled me an invitation, so it is a unique and valuable opportunity to spy. But I shall come and play my flute tonight. That will soothe her.'

'What time?' asked Chaloner. Ruth was not the only one in need of calming music.

'As soon as I finish. Perhaps we can play her a duet.'

Chaloner nodded keenly. 'I am going to visit the surgeon who tended Elliot today – Jeremiah King. I want to be sure your brother-in-law is really dead.'

'Of course he is dead,' said Lester impatiently. 'Do you think that I, a sailor who has weathered numerous battles, am incapable of identifying a corpse?'

'How did you identify it? Did you put a glass to its mouth to test for breath? Touch its eyes to see if it flinched? Feel for a heartbeat or a pulse?'

'Well, no, but Elliot's face was waxen, and he looked dead.'

'So does half the Court first thing in the morning. It means nothing.'

'You are wrong, but talk to the surgeon if you must. He will confirm my tale.'

Chaloner wanted to go immediately, but there was another delay while Lester hired a nurse, and it was nearing ten o'clock by the time Ruth was settled. Chaloner and Lester set out to Westminster together. It was a glorious day, although frost dusted the rooftops and the red-gold leaves of trees.

'Tell Williamson that whatever mischief is planned for the day after tomorrow may involve *Jane* and gravel,' said Chaloner, deciding suddenly that it was time to demonstrate a little trust. He was sure Thurloe was wrong about Lester, and they needed all the help they could get. 'The Piccadilly Company believe it will make them very rich.'

Lester nodded his thanks, then strode off towards New Palace Yard, while Chaloner entered the little court named Axe Yard, which comprised some very smart houses and some extremely shabby ones. Jeremiah King was home, sewing up a fearsome wound in the leg of someone who had fallen under a speeding carriage. Even at that hour of the day, he was far from sober.

'Elliot,' he mused, swaying unsteadily, needle and thread clutched in his bloody hand. 'Was he the man who was really a woman?'

'I would not have thought so,' said Chaloner, regarding him askance. 'He had a knife wound.'

'Oh, him. He was brought here by a sea-officer – a burly, bossy fellow who accused me of not knowing my trade. But his friend was past Earthly help anyway, and died.'

'Are you sure?' asked Chaloner.

King fixed him with a bleary eye. 'Do you think I cannot tell the difference?'

'Very possibly.' Chaloner nodded at the patient on the table. 'You have been stitching him with infinite care, but he has been dead ever since I arrived.'

King peered down at the victim. 'Oh, damnation! When did that happen?'

Chaloner left even more convinced that Elliot was still in the world of the living, and headed for Covent Garden, where a helpful urchin was more than happy to earn a penny by taking him to the rooms occupied by a loutish man with an unusually black wig. Chaloner rapped on the door, but there was no reply.

'He is dead,' said the elderly woman who emerged from the garret above to see what was happening. 'A week ago now.'

'What was his name?' asked Chaloner tiredly.

'James Elliot,' replied the woman. 'He was a sea-captain, although he gambled and had debts. I am not surprised that someone made an end of him.'

'Have you heard of a man named Jacob Cave?'

'No, and I have lived in this area all my life. There is no one in Covent Garden of that name.'

Chaloner thanked her and took his leave. He was now certain Jacob did not exist, and that Elliot had invented him in order to bury Cave without a grand funeral. So where was Elliot now? Had he taken the opportunity afforded by his own 'death' to disappear and start a new life? Or was he still in the city?

Chaloner's next task was to ask Reverend Addison what he knew about Tangier. His eavesdropping at the Crown had told him that Harley had been under orders

– presumably from the same 'master' who commanded Fitzgerald – to orchestrate the massacre, but he still needed to know *why* Teviot had warranted such a fate.

Addison had rented a house near the Maypole, a landmark demolished to a stump by Cromwell, but restored to its full splendour by the King. Somewhat typically, people had complained bitterly when it was not available, but rarely used it now it was.

'Chaloner!' exclaimed Addison. 'I did not think we would meet again. On *Eagle*, you were more interested in making music with Cave than in talking to me, which was a pity, because I am very interested in military engineering, and I suspect you are, too. You certainly asked a lot of questions about Tangier's splendid sea wall – the mole – when you were there.'

'Only because I wanted to know why it is costing the tax-payer so much money.'

Addison's smile faded. 'Unfortunately, the opportunity to cheat the government is too great a temptation for those in authority. It is a shame, because the project is ingenious and daring. However, it should cost a fraction of what is being demanded, and every governor we get seems worse than his predecessor for dishonesty and greed.'

'Was Teviot corrupt?'

Addison sighed unhappily. 'I have no idea why you should ask me this now, but I cannot lie. He amassed himself a fortune by stealing the funds intended for the mole.'

'Could it have had a bearing on his death?'

Addison nodded slowly. 'I strongly suspected so at the time. Along with *Jane*.'

'The privateer ship? How does she fit into it?'

'Teviot refused her permission to dock, although her

captain was adept at bribing the soldiers who had been ordered to repel her. But even so, she only managed to put in occasionally when he was in charge. Now Bridge is governor, *Jane* regularly trades in Tangier.'

'I am confused. Was Teviot killed because he was corrupt, or because he declined to let a privateer do business in Tangier?'

'Why should they be exclusive? Banning a ship from port is a kind of corruption – you should ask yourself *why* he did it. Before you ask, I do not know the answer but I can tell you that he will have been motivated by money.'

'I was in Tangier for almost three months, but I never heard talk of a vessel called *Jane*.'

Addison shrugged. 'That is no surprise. She would not have been there legally, so her arrival was never blared from the rooftops.'

Chaloner stared at him, the germ of a solution beginning to unfold in his mind. 'The Adventurers own a monopoly on African trade, but *Jane* is a privateer. Perhaps Teviot's reason for refusing her a berth was because he did not want to anger a wealthy and influential group of courtiers.'

'It is possible, although I imagine he would have yielded if *Jane* had paid him enough.'

'Not if he was an Adventurer himself, and *Jane* was stealing custom that would have made him richer. Do you know what cargo she carried?'

'No idea, although I did once hear that she carried a quantity of gravel.'

Chaloner sighed. 'I was afraid you might say that.'

'Well, the mole needs a lot of it. But Africa is full of valuable goods, and Tangier is strategically placed at the end of caravan routes, along which gold, ivory, cotton, kola nuts and even slaves are transported.' Addison's expression darkened. 'Slavery is a despicable business. Were you there when *Henrietta Maria* went down? That cost the Adventurers a pretty penny, I can tell you.'

'So I have been told,' said Chaloner, wondering what would happen to him if the likes of Leighton ever discovered his role in the affair.

'They were livid,' Addison went on gleefully. 'They blamed a corporation called the Piccadilly Company, but they have no evidence. I know who did it, of course.'

'You do?' asked Chaloner uneasily.

Addison nodded. 'Harley, Newell and Reyner. And do you know why? Because they slunk away from Tangier within hours of the sinking.'

'So did you,' Chaloner pointed out, not adding that he had, too.

'Yes, but I am not the type to commit criminal damage,' said Addison. 'Of course, I have since learned that Harley and his cronies are members of this Piccadilly Company, so I imagine it will not be long before the Adventurers exact revenge.'

'Perhaps they already have,' said Chaloner, uncomfortably realising that here was another reason why he was responsible for what had happened to Newell and Reyner. 'Because two of them are dead.'

Addison stared at him. 'Then I wager you my treasured copy of Harbottle Grimston's *Duties of a Christian Life* that Harley is the one who is still alive.'

'Why do you say that?'

'Because he is the most unscrupulous of the three, and the one most dedicated to himself.'

* * *

His mind a whirl of questions, Chaloner aimed for Lincoln's Inn, hoping Thurloe might have learned something useful, and was just crossing Dial Court when he was intercepted by William Prynne. Prynne was the inn's most repellent resident, a pamphleteer with deeply bigoted opinions, and someone to be avoided by decent people. He was pulling down the long cap he always wore, to hide the fact that his ears had been lopped off as punishment for 'seditious libel' – not that it had taught him to moderate his thoughts. If anything, it had made him more poisonous than ever.

'They are Satan's spawn,' he snarled, launching into one of his tirades without preamble. 'And the dissolute and unhappy constitution of our depraved times made me wonder whether to sit mute and silent over these overspreading abominations, or whether I should lift up my voice like a trumpet and cry against them to my power.'

'I assume you opted for the latter,' said Chaloner drily, certain the opportunity to bray like a trumpet was one Prynne would not have been able to resist. When he started to move away, the old man snatched his sleeve with a claw-like hand of surprising strength and kept him there.

'It occurred to me to bend my pen against them, as I have done against other sinful and unchristian vanities, but my thoughts informed me that I would only earn the reproach and scorn of the histrionic and profaner sort, whose tongues are set on fire of Hell against all such as dare affront their infernal practices.'

'I have no idea what you are talking about,' said Chaloner, trying again to escape. He could have broken the grip on his arm, but he was not in the habit of using force against the elderly, not even loathsome specimens like Prynne.

'I am talking about that Dutch pair,' shouted Prynne, having worked himself into a frenzy. 'Cornelis and Margareta Janszoon. You must hunt them down, or the mischievous and pestiferous fruits of hellish wickedness that issues from their noxious and infectious nature will—'

'Please, Mr Prynne,' said Chaloner tiredly. 'I really do not understand what you are saying.'

'Then I shall speak in simple terms,' said Prynne, calming himself with an effort. 'Although I expected more of you – Thurloe tells me you are highly intelligent. The Janszoons are saying terrible things, and you must stop them.'

'Me? Why? I have no jurisdiction to—'

'You must,' cried Prynne. 'I do not know who else to ask, and you are often at Court. Silence this couple before they do serious harm. Do you know what they said in church yesterday? That the Dutch will send a plague to kill us all.'

'You misunderstood. Or, more likely, they said something they never intended.'

Prynne scowled. 'Rubbish! How else can you interpret "we ply you with boils"? And right in the middle of an innocent discussion about games, too!'

'Then I imagine what they meant was "we play you at bowls",' said Chaloner.

Prynne stared at him. 'I suppose you might be right – it would certainly explain the sudden change in topics. But people took offence and damage was done anyway. You *must* make them curb their tongues, or they will have the entire city baying for war, and I am currently fond

341

of the Dutch – they have decent Protestant views about religion.'

'You oppose war?'

'I do,' declared Prynne, although Chaloner could not help but wonder whether he had taken that particular stance because almost everyone else would disagree; Prynne was famous for expounding opinions that few others held. 'It would be contrary to the will of God.'

'The Janszoons have hired henchmen to protect—'

'To protect *them* from harm. But what about the damage they *cause* with their silly remarks? Other Dutchmen will pay the price, and we shall have a bloodbath. Not to mention a war.'

Sympathetic to anyone struggling with the vagaries of spoken English, Chaloner promised to explain the situation when he next saw them. He resumed his journey to Chamber XIII, where he found Thurloe sitting at a table surrounded by paper. The ex-Spymaster had been working on decrypting both the half-burned letter from the Crown and Mrs Reyner's list.

'Any luck?' asked Chaloner hopefully.

'None whatsoever, and neither has Wallis,' replied Thurloe. 'But I have decided that they must be broken as a matter of urgency, and I shall sit here all day if necessary. What are your plans?'

Chaloner removed his coat and dropped it on to the back of a chair, before rolling up the sleeves of his shirt. 'To help you.'

Chaloner worked with Thurloe until well past midnight, by which time he was stiff from sitting hunched over the table, and his head ached. With a pang of regret, he recalled the tentative plan to play a duet with Lester, but did not mention it to Thurloe, sure he would disapprove.

He tossed down his pen and went to the tray of food Thurloe's manservant had brought some hours before. The bread had gone hard and the cheese had been left too near the fire, so was molten, but he ate some anyway. Thurloe opted for several pills that he shook from an elegantly enamelled pot. Chaloner rubbed his eyes, trying to summon the energy to return to his labours.

'Yes!' the ex-Spymaster exclaimed suddenly. 'God be praised! I have made sense of the scrap of paper you found in the Crown.'

'What does it say?' demanded Chaloner, darting to the table, weariness forgotten.

'It is really very simple,' said Thurloe in satisfaction. 'As I predicted, it was a substitution code, where a code of one-two-three means you move the first letter of your message one place to the right, the second letter two places, and so on. So 'cat' becomes 'dcw'.'

'I know that,' said Chaloner impatiently, trying to see Thurloe's translation. 'We have been struggling over different combinations for hours.'

'In this case, the sequence is three-five-four-eight, repeated again and again.'

Chaloner regarded him blankly. 'What is the signifi-cance of that number?'

'It is the latitude of Tangier.'

'I see,' said Chaloner, thinking that he could have worked on the cipher for years and not tried that particular combination. 'What does the message say?'

Thurloe read it. '*From ye Governour of Tanger to ye Pikadilye Companye our ship will sayle with a fulle complimente of gravelle*

343

in three dayes and wille be in Londonne by Saynte Frydswyds Daye at last we . . .'

Chaloner stared at it in dismay. 'It tells us nothing new!'

'On the contrary, it informs us that Governor Bridge sends coded messages to the Piccadilly Company, which is evidence that Fitzgerald and his cronies *did* dispose of Teviot so that a malleable successor could be appointed. Reverend Addison said *Jane* is more often in Tangier now that Bridge is in command, and here is more proof of it.'

'So "our ship" refers to *Jane*, and she left Tangier carrying gravel.' Chaloner was becoming despondent, feeling he had wasted time he could ill afford. 'But we already knew she trades in that particular commodity. And that she was due to arrive here on St Frideswide's Day – I heard the Piccadilly Company say so when I eavesdropped.'

'Yes, but we did not know she was coming from Tangier. No wonder Fitzgerald and his cronies burned the letter! It is a valuable clue.'

'It is?' asked Chaloner doubtfully.

'Yes! You must make enquiries along the river and ascertain where *Jane* will berth,' said Thurloe urgently, handing Chaloner his coat. 'Someone will know at which wharf she is expected. And then we shall go and inspect this gravel for ourselves.'

'Now?' asked Chaloner without enthusiasm. 'In the middle of the night?'

Thurloe glanced at the window, startled to see it was dark outside. He snatched the coat back again. 'Rest for an hour or two, and then go.'

'What will you do while I trawl the docks?' asked

Chaloner, daunted by the task he had been set – the Thames was thick with them, all the way from Wapping to Westminster.

Thurloe pointed to the Reyners' list. 'We must decode it as soon as possible.'

Chaloner did not think he would sleep, given that his mind was full of worries and questions, but he did. Thurloe prodded him awake when it was still dark, although the rumble of traffic said London was coming to life. The ex-Spymaster's face was pale, and he shook his head tiredly to Chaloner's raised eyebrows – the cipher continued to elude him.

Even at that early hour, the air was full of soot as fires were lit all over the city. The Thames had produced a heavy fog that mingled unpleasantly with it, making breathing difficult. It enveloped shops and warehouses, and gave them an eerie, other-worldly appearance.

Feeling he had been set an impossible challenge, Chaloner began at Black Friars Stairs, where lamps had been lit to illuminate a frenzied scene – its work was driven by tides, not clocks, so it was often busy during the hours of darkness. Meeting with no success, he went to Puddle Wharf, because it was famous for dubious transactions. It required a hefty bribe before he learned that *Jane* was not expected.

He approached Queenhithe next, fighting down his rising agitation – it was all taking far too long, and he was acutely aware that whatever atrocity Fitzgerald's master had planned might well take place in less than twenty-four hours. He asked his question distractedly, not expecting an answer, and so was astonished when the harbour-master nodded.

'Tomorrow afternoon,' the fellow replied, pocketing the coins Chaloner had offered for a moment of his time. 'The Bridge is scheduled to open for ships at midnight tonight and noon tomorrow, and *Jane* is expected at noon. She has booked a berth here at three o'clock.'

'What will she be carrying?'

'We shall not know that until she arrives, but it will not be anything heavy. She is a dog, and too much weight would take her under.'

'Not gravel, then?'

The harbour-master shrugged. 'If so, then there will not be very much of it.'

Chaloner hurried back to Lincoln's Inn. Assuming that the Piccadilly Company's plan would coincide with *Jane*'s arrival – or at least, not swing into action until she was safely moored – it meant they had a day and a half to work out what was happening and stop it.

'I may not have cracked this cipher, but our mysteries have been simmering in the back of my mind,' said Thurloe, after listening carefully. 'Fitzgerald is powerful and dangerous, but he has no money – he was obliged to dismiss all his servants after his gold-laden ship sank.'

'Yes,' agreed Chaloner impatiently. 'Everyone says he is in London to recoup his losses after the disaster. What of it?'

'Hiring Brinkes and his henchmen will require cash. So will investing in a struggling glassware business. Ergo, it is his master who has money at his disposal. We can eliminate the Adventurers as suspects, because they are on the opposing side.'

Chaloner was thoughtful. 'Your brother-in-law told us that some of their thirty members are wealthy merchants or nobles. And he said Pratt has invested heavily.'

'Pratt might be the master,' conceded Thurloe. 'He is earning a fortune from your Earl, so he will have plenty of funds at his disposal. Of course, it would mean that the threat against his life is a ruse, to throw us off his scent. Another candidate for arch-villain is Lester—'

'No! There is nothing to say he is a member of the Piccadilly Company – indeed, Williamson has charged him to monitor them. Besides, his sister was almost murdered by Fitzgerald's henchmen. I doubt that would have happened if he were their leader.'

'His sister was taken along a dark lane to be rescued by you,' corrected Thurloe. 'Perhaps she was never in any danger. And I have never liked his role in all this – he just *happened* to be there when Cave and Elliot fought; he just *happens* to have a mad sibling whom Williamson uses to secure his services. I have not forgotten that he and Fitzgerald were once shipmates, either.'

'Who else?' asked Chaloner, declining to argue.

'Meneses. He was Governor of Tangier, and we all know how talented they are at making themselves rich – and *he* was so brazen about it that he was dismissed. I am bothered by Leighton, too. He is the Adventurers' secretary, but he has criminal connections. It would not surprise me to learn that he is pitting two powerful and greedy organisations against each other for his own ends.'

'What about Dugdale and Edgeman?' suggested Chaloner. 'They are Adventurers, but both are treacherous types who would think nothing of betraying friends. They serve the Earl, yet they consort with his enemies. It is suspicious.'

'Possible but unlikely – I doubt the Earl pays them enough. Of course, they may have access to a source of wealth that we do not know about. Kipps is rich, too, but his application to enrol as an Adventurer was rejected. I imagine he bears them a grudge . . .'

'Yes, but that does not mean he would act on it,' said Chaloner defensively.

'Then there are those who are openly villainous,' Thurloe went on. 'Brilliana, the wealthy courtesan; her brother Harley, who must have been well paid to carry out the Tangier massacre; and the Janszoons, who know nothing about the glassware that their Company exports . . .'

'And whose shaky English is stirring up anti-Dutch sentiments,' finished Chaloner. 'I am not surprised that they never go anywhere without guards to protect them.'

'We cannot dismiss Ruth as a suspect, either,' Thurloe went on. 'She lives in the Crown, is sister to the sinister Lester, and wife to Elliot – who is said to be dead but is probably alive. Most men do not marry lunatics, so you must ask yourself whether she is as fey-witted as she would have us believe. After all, it would not be the first time a devious plot was masterminded by a lady.'

Chaloner shook his head. 'She is not wealthy. Neither is Lester.'

'On the contrary,' argued Thurloe. 'Lester did very well for himself in the navy, and captured several enemy ships that were later sold for princely sums. He is extremely rich, and would certainly share his good fortune with a much-loved sister.'

Chaloner regarded him uneasily. Lester did not give the impression of being well off, while Ruth's lodgings in the Crown were hardly palatial. Of course, he had no idea where Lester lived – it might be a mansion on The Strand, for all he knew. But he *liked* the man, and his instincts still told him to ignore Thurloe's reservations.

'And finally, I am not happy with Kitty O'Brien,' Thurloe went on. 'She has seduced Williamson, perhaps to distract him from her crimes. Her husband is more interested in inveigling himself into high society than in plotting, and he certainly does not need more money – his copper sales have made him fabulously rich already.'

'Then the same applies to Kitty,' argued Chaloner.

'Only if he lets her into the family purse. She may as well be poor if he ekes out every penny. Incidentally, I received a report from one of my old spies when you were out. It seems Fitzgerald is not the only one who has plans for tomorrow.'

'Yes?'

'Leighton has arranged for the Adventurers to dine aboard *Royal Katherine* at dusk. It will be a glittering occasion, and several dozen Adventurers and their spouses are expected to attend.'

'In Woolwich?'

'Yes – that is where *Royal Katherine* is moored.'

'Do you think he arranged it so that he and his cronies will be away from the city when Fitzgerald strikes?' asked Chaloner uneasily. 'Or, if Leighton is Fitzgerald's master, that he plans to keep the Adventurers alive, because he cannot be secretary if there is no corporation?'

Thurloe sighed tiredly. 'Who knows? We have too many questions and too few answers.'

'There is one thing we can do,' said Chaloner suddenly. 'Williamson refuses to arrest Fitzgerald of his own volition, so we must persuade the Earl to *order* him to do it. Perhaps the plan will founder without Fitzgerald to see it through.'

'Perhaps,' said Thurloe, although he did not look convinced. 'What then?'

'The Swedish Ambassador is visiting White Hall at noon, and all our suspects are likely to be watching the ceremonies. It will afford me a final opportunity to eavesdrop.'

'Then I shall join you,' determined Thurloe.

'No!' Chaloner was horrified. 'It is not a good idea for ex-spymasters to invade White Hall.'

'Credit me with some sense, Thomas,' said Thurloe irritably. 'I shall go in disguise. And do not say it is a risk I need not take, because I was doing it before you were born.'

Chapter 10

Chaloner arrived to find White Hall in turmoil, because preparations for the ambassadorial visit had been left until the last minute. The Banqueting House was full of frantic servants, and there was an air of emergency as they tried to make everything ready in time. The situation was not helped by the number of courtiers who had appeared to 'help'. They included the King, who seemed to know what he was doing, and a vast array of earls, dukes and lords, who did not.

Chaloner walked inside, dodging around six footmen who were struggling to carry an enormous painting of a Turkish bordello. It had been used for the play that had been performed there recently, but it was too large to hide with ceremonial cloths – and was hardly a suitable backdrop for diplomatic ceremonies – so the King had ordered it removed. Judging by the strained expressions on the men's faces, this was easier said than done.

'The *blue* ones, man!' Buckingham was shouting to another minion, who had been charged with hanging flags. 'We keep the red for the Russians, and today's visitor is Swedish.'

'I shall ensure the ambassador does not take umbrage,' drawled Lady Castlemaine. '*I* can think of something that will make him feel welcome.'

Chaloner glanced at her once, and then looked again because he could not quite believe what he had seen. She had donned a flimsy shift that did nothing to conceal her elegant curves, and had adopted a posture to show them to their best advantage. He was not the only one whose attention had been snagged: virtually every other man was staring, too.

'She was wearing a gown over that when she first arrived,' said Kipps, making no effort to disguise his admiration. 'But she gave it to the Queen, who said she was cold.'

Chaloner looked to where he pointed, and saw Katherine standing forlornly to one side. The robe was too long, and trailed rather ridiculously on the floor. Hannah, who was with her, beckoned Chaloner over.

'I see someone caught your eye,' she said frostily.

'She caught Hyde's, too.' Chaloner gestured to where the Earl's son was hurrying towards the Lady, divesting himself of his coat as he went.

'What is he doing?' asked Hannah, amused. 'Does he intend to ravage her? The King will not appreciate that. Not in front of all these witnesses.'

They watched Hyde drape the garment around the Lady's shoulders. Irritated, she shrugged it off, but the King happened to glance around at that moment, and was patently furious to see his mistress sharing herself with the world. He surged towards her and had it buttoned around her in a trice. He muttered something to Hyde, who flushed with pleasure.

'Hyde will be even more unbearable now,' said Hannah in disgust. 'Smug little b—'

'Why all the fuss?' asked Chaloner quickly, looking around at the chaos. The Queen was within earshot, and he did not think she would approve of a lady-in-waiting calling her secretary names. 'The Swedish ambassador's reception has been planned for weeks. I read about it in *The Newes*.'

'Yes, but no one reminded the Court, and it was only remembered this morning,' explained Hannah. 'So the King roused everyone out to make ready in time. The Queen and I have been asked to make sure all the paintings are hung straight. I am sorry I did not come home last night, by the way. I was at Brodrick's soirée until dawn.'

'I missed you,' lied Chaloner, not bothering to mention that he had not been home either.

'Brodrick had invited a lot of Adventurers,' said Hannah disapprovingly. 'They do nothing but party these days – they are having another one tomorrow, on *Royal Katherine*. O'Brien is going, too. He is flattered by the invitation, but it will not induce him to join – Kitty is too strongly opposed to slavery. But here comes the Queen. Be nice to her, Tom: she is in low spirits today.'

'Meneses has abandoned me,' said Katherine bitterly in Portuguese. 'Hannah said his interest would last only as long as he thought I had money to give him, and it seems she was right. I should have listened to her.'

'But Meneses is here, ma'am,' said Chaloner, puzzled. 'I saw him when I came in.'

'Yes, but he has shifted his affections to Kitty O'Brien. Of course, he will make no headway there, because her heart belongs to Joseph Williamson. Breaking sacred wedding vows seems to be the way of this horrible Court.'

Chaloner was not sure what to say, given that the King was nearby, laughing heartily with his paramour. He was, however, aware that such remarks were dangerous for both of them, even when spoken in a language that few, if any, courtiers would understand.

'Please, ma'am. Someone might hear—'

'Why should I not say what I think?' she flashed, tears sparkling in her eyes. 'People accuse me of undermining the English throne by refusing to produce a baby. So why should I not speak treason, since people believe it of me anyway?'

'Who believes it of you?' asked Chaloner gently. Hannah was glaring at him, assuming he had introduced whatever subject was upsetting her mistress.

'Everyone!' whispered Katherine miserably. 'Someone went into my favourite purse yesterday, and left me a terrible letter. It said the murder I had commissioned will occur tomorrow. I have commissioned no murder, but who will believe me when I deny it?'

'Burn it,' said Chaloner urgently. 'As soon as possible. And make sure nothing remains, not even ashes. Do you have any idea who might have put it there?'

'I do not think my ladies-in-waiting would stoop so low, not even Castlemaine. And the only men to have set foot in my apartments recently are my husband, Hyde and Meneses.'

'Meneses,' said Chaloner, a solution snapping into his mind. 'And now he shuns you?'

Katherine bit her lip, and he saw he had been overly blunt. 'I suppose Meneses might have done it,' she admitted unhappily. 'Revenge, because I cannot repay his friendship with gold and titles.'

More tears glittered, but Chaloner was spared the

354

need to make some comforting remark by the unlikely figure of Dugdale, who approached with a patently false smile. He bowed elegantly to the Queen and turned to Chaloner. The grin stayed in place, but his eyes were hot with anger.

'How dare you approach the Queen,' he said. He spoke mildly, to disguise the hostility in his words. 'If you wish to speak to royalty, you request an audience through *me*. The protocol is perfectly clear on this point.'

'Thomas is being told he cannot talk to you,' explained Hannah icily, when the Queen turned questioningly to her. She shot Dugdale a glare of dislike, not a woman to stand by while her husband was being unjustly attacked. 'In future, he must ask this gentleman first.'

'It is protocol, ma'am,' reiterated Dugdale defensively. 'And he has no right to break it.'

'Does that mean he must request your permission to talk to his wife, too?' asked Hannah archly. 'Because that it what he was doing when you stormed over and interrupted us. There are protocols about that, too – and you have just broken them. Now go away, before I complain to Clarendon about your shabby manners.'

Dugdale stared at her in astonishment, but Hannah glowered at him until he bowed to the Queen and left, muttering under his breath that the Earl wanted to see Chaloner at once. Chaloner grinned, delighted to see him put so firmly in his place.

'Vile man!' exclaimed Hannah, watching him go. 'He makes my skin crawl.'

Chaloner left her blackening Dugdale's name to a Queen who barely understood, and went to see what the

Earl wanted. Dugdale intercepted him, his face dark with anger.

'And do not address her in that foreign tongue, either,' he snarled. 'The King issued express orders that she is to be spoken to only in English or French. How dare you defy him!'

'I did not know,' said Chaloner, supposing he should not be surprised. No monarch would want a wife who gabbled away to people in a language he did not understand.

'Well, you do now,' snapped Dugdale. 'And if you do it again, I will tell him, and it will bring you more trouble than you can possibly imagine.'

Chaloner was sure it would, and was equally sure that Dugdale would relish every moment of it.

Clarendon's contribution to the preparations was overseeing the refreshments. He strutted up and down the tables, adjusting a bowl here and a platter there, sampling as he went. Hyde was with him, screening his father's antics from the other courtiers by placing himself in their line of vision. Chaloner did not blame him: Buckingham and the Lady would have ridiculed Clarendon's comically gluttonous behaviour for months if they could have seen what he was doing.

Dugdale and Edgeman were smirking, amused both by the Earl's brazen greediness and by Hyde's efforts to conceal it. Brodrick was slumped in a chair, his face grey and his eyes more bloodshot than usual. He was careful to look away from the mounting piles of food.

'You cannot *still* be unwell?' the Earl was saying to him. 'Are you sure it was because you spent so long at your prayers this morning? Not because of your soirée last night?'

'Yes,' said Brodrick tightly. 'Spending hours on one's knees takes its toll.'

'Perhaps you should sit down to pray in future,' said the Earl kindly. 'God will understand.'

Brodrick had the grace to wince.

'Tell me, cousin,' said Hyde maliciously. 'Who joined you in this holy marathon?'

'Friends,' replied Brodrick curtly. 'Why? Would you like an invitation next time? I have never imagined you to own sufficient mettle, but if you think you can handle the challenge . . .'

'I can handle any challenge issued by you,' stated Hyde sneeringly. 'And I—'

'Chaloner,' interrupted the Earl, bringing an abrupt end to the burgeoning spat, 'are you here to say you have foiled these devilish plots? Tomorrow is when the sky will come tumbling down, according to the letters Henry intercepted, so you must have answers by now.'

'Some, sir,' replied Chaloner, itching to say that he might have had more if his employer had not sent him on so many fool's errands. 'But not enough to prevent a crisis.'

'I have a snippet that may help,' said the Earl. 'You asked about Meneses yesterday, and I happened to run into the Portuguese ambassador last night. I mentioned Meneses, and he said the fellow is in London at the moment. Apparently, he has been visiting the Queen.'

'So it is his real name,' breathed Chaloner. 'But why did he deny being Governor of Tangier?'

'Does my intelligence help?' asked the Earl, straining to hear what he was saying. 'Are you assailed by a blinding light that will allow you to see answers to everything?'

'Not quite,' said Chaloner. 'But it *is* helpful. Thank you, sir. However, there is one thing you can do to avert a catastrophe: issue a warrant to arrest Fitzgerald.'

'Why? Is he the one who plans to murder Pratt?'

'Possibly,' hedged Chaloner, unwilling to say more with four Adventurers listening. He did not want Hyde, Brodrick, Dugdale or Edgeman to repeat his suspicions to their cronies.

'I need more than "possibly",' said the Earl. 'He has powerful connections, and I have too many enemies as it is. Unless he is the one stealing my bricks?'

'You will never lay hold of *that* villain, father,' interjected Hyde. 'So you may as well tell Chaloner to stop wasting his time. Or—'

'Look at Kipps!' exclaimed the Earl suddenly, pointing to where the Lady had shrugged off Hyde's coat, and was parading around in her indecently flimsy shift. 'His eyes are all but hanging out of his head! Such brazen lechery is inappropriate, and I shall have words with him later.'

'I will do it,' offered Dugdale eagerly. 'The man has ideas above his station, and—'

'Many courtiers do.' The Earl glanced at his son. 'Including these reprehensible Adventurers. They are not good company, and I would certainly dismiss any member of my staff who had the temerity to join them. I wish you had not accepted their invitation to enrol, Henry.'

'I accepted because it is a good way to win the friendship of men who have been our enemies,' replied Hyde tightly, as Dugdale and Edgeman exchanged a brief but uneasy glance. 'It is politically expedient, *and* it represents a chance to make some easy money.'

The Earl did not deign to debate the matter, and

addressed Chaloner instead. 'You have less than a day to find answers, because I *will* have these brick-thieves by tomorrow. No one steals from me and evades justice!'

At that point, it was discovered that the painting of the Turkish brothel would not fit through the door, and the Earl and his retinue were among those who hurried to tell the hapless footmen what to do about it. Brodrick made no effort to follow, and as he looked so ill, Chaloner took a piece of bread from one of the baskets and handed it to him, indicating that he would feel better if he ate. The Earl's cousin nibbled the offering without enthusiasm.

'I must be getting old,' he muttered. 'I do not recall feeling like this after a late night ten years ago. And other events are lining up relentlessly, when all I want is a quiet evening in. There is this affair, which is likely to drag on until the small hours, and then Leighton has organised a feast with a nautical theme aboard *Royal Katherine* tomorrow. I hope I am not seasick.'

'How far will you be sailing?' asked Chaloner.

Brodrick shuddered. 'Nowhere! She will be tied to a bollard at Woolwich. But I know from my last visit that she rocks horribly, even when fastened to a pier.'

'How well did you know Cave, the singer from the Chapel Royal?' asked Chaloner, recalling that Brodrick's love of music had earned him many connections in such quarters.

Brodrick blinked at the sudden change of subject, but answered anyway. 'Not well, although I am sorry he came to such an ignoble end. Of course, he was a fearful liar.'

'What did he lie about?'

'He claimed he was commissioned to organise music for the troops in Tangier, but it cannot have been true

– I doubt they are interested in Italian arias. Ergo, he went there for some other purpose.'

Chaloner stared at him. He had also been sceptical of Cave's declared mission, and Kitty O'Brien had expressed reservations, too. 'What other purpose?'

'Personally, I believe he was one of you – an intelligencer. Sent to Tangier to spy.'

'What evidence do you have?'

'None whatsoever,' replied Brodrick airily. 'But what else could he have been doing?'

'Perhaps he went there for business. A lot of men are making themselves very rich from Tangier, as you will know from being an Adventurer.'

Brodrick shook his head. 'We *are* thriving, but we have a monopoly. No one else is licensed to trade there – it would be illegal – and Cave was not one of us. However, I suppose he might have gone to capitalise on all the corruption surrounding the building of the sea wall.'

'That would not be easy. You do not simply arrive and demand a cut of the profits.'

'Well, then,' said Brodrick, tossing the half-chewed piece of bread back into the basket as he stood. 'My point is proven. Cave was an intelligencer. After all, he was killed when he returned by one James Elliot. And who is Elliot? Spymaster Williamson's creature!'

Chaloner gazed after Brodrick as he shuffled away. Was that the real reason for the duel? To prevent Cave from telling anyone what he had learned in Tangier? But Cave had died more than a week after his return, by which time he would already have made his report to whoever had sent him. And who *had* sent him? As Elliot had done the killing, it was unlikely to have been Williamson. Did that mean the Spymaster had ordered Cave's murder?

But from what Chaloner had seen of the spat, it had been Cave who had engineered the quarrel. He shook his head slowly, not sure what to think.

It was not easy to convert the Banqueting House into a state room after its interlude as the King's personal play-house, and the difficulties were compounded when the ambassador arrived early. The King, pursued by valets still fussing with his ceremonial finery, rushed into the Great Court to greet him, hoping to gain the frantic servants and their noble helpers a few more minutes to prepare.

Lady Castlemaine was hot on his heels, clad in a robe that accentuated her ample frontage and narrow waist. She expected to be admired, and her jaw dropped in astonishment when the ambassador barely spared her a glance. It was the Queen who saved the day, by engaging him in a discussion about herring, a subject that made his eyes light up. As every remark needed to be translated, the ensuing conversation took some time.

'She is a great diplomat,' whispered Hannah proudly. 'She took care to learn about his interests, you see. Unlike the Lady, who assumes a display of bosom will keep him transfixed.'

'It seems to have transfixed the King,' said Chaloner, aware that His Majesty was far more interested in the Lady than his guest's ramblings about salting processes.

But even the Queen could not maintain a discussion about fish indefinitely, and when it eventually faltered, the ambassador began to move towards the Banqueting House again. The King heaved a sigh of relief when Buckingham winked to say all was more or less in order, and if the emissary noticed that the interior décor was somewhat unusual, he was too polite to show it.

The occasion was a large one, and guests included virtually everyone Chaloner had met since returning from Tangier. Both Adventurers and members of the Piccadilly Company were present, rubbing shoulders with naval and military officers, clerics, courtiers, merchants, servants and even local shopkeepers. Chaloner was startled to see Joan and George there, having apparently persuaded Hannah to get them in. There was a pipe clamped between George's teeth, and his eyes were everywhere. Chaloner watched him, thinking that while it may have been Susan who had been caught spying, there was still something very questionable about the footman.

'Fitzgerald has been invited,' came a voice in his ear. Chaloner turned, and it took him a moment to recognise that the choleric churchman in the orange wig was Thurloe. 'When he arrives, leave him to me – along with Lester, who is currently talking to Kipps.'

Chaloner had not known that Lester and Kipps were acquainted, but said nothing, unwilling to fuel Thurloe's suspicions about the captain.

'I will corner Meneses,' he said instead. 'I think he was the one who planted the letters in the Queen's purses, and he has turned cool towards her now we are on the eve of Pratt's so-called murder. Moreover, he was strangely eager for me to be disabused of the notion that he has a connection with Tangier.'

'But he is not an Adventurer,' Thurloe whispered. 'And it seems to me that they are the ones who want the Queen implicated in a treasonous plot.'

'Perhaps he infiltrated the Piccadilly Company in order to spy. It seems Cave may have been an intelligencer, too, and I cannot help but wonder whether he was sent to discover what really happened to Teviot.'

'I doubt it,' said Thurloe. 'He was not the kind of man *I* would have entrusted with such a difficult and dangerous mission. Who else will you monitor, besides Meneses?'

'Leighton,' replied Chaloner promptly. 'And I will listen to as many Adventurers and Piccadilly Company members as I can. I do not suppose you have cracked the cipher, have you?'

'No, but Wallis did.' Chaloner started to smile in surprise, but the ex-Spymaster's expression was bleak. 'Reyner told his mother that it was a list of his enemies, but either he lied to her or he was mistaken. It was actually a description of Jews Hill in Tangier – the kind of report that a scout might send to his commanding officer, detailing dips, rises and the number of trees.'

'So it was nothing?' asked Chaloner, acutely disappointed. 'All that time we spent on it . . .'

'Was wasted,' agreed Thurloe grimly. 'We *must* learn something today, Tom, or Fitzgerald will succeed tomorrow, and we shall all be the losers.'

Chaloner's reply was drowned out by a sudden blast of trumpets. The King sat down on his great throne, his courtiers clustered around him so tightly that Buckingham's face was full of Clarendon's wig, and the Lady was pressed hard against the Bishop of Winchester. She gave the prelate a long, slow wink, and he recoiled in alarm.

There was another fanfare and the speeches began, unusually brief because no one had had time to prepare anything. The ambassador opened his mouth to remark on it, clearly interpreting the brevity as a diplomatic snub, but the King invited him to dine before he could do so, steering him towards the tables and chatting about the dancing that had been arranged for later. The Earl

363

was one of the first to take his place at the table, knife in one chubby hand, and spoon in the other.

Only the elite had been asked to eat, and O'Brien's face was a mask of disappointment when he realised he was not to be one of them. Kitty patted his hand consolingly, and led him away.

'We were sorry you did not attend Brodrick's soirée last night,' she said, when their route took them past Chaloner. 'We were hoping for some decent music, but there were only flageolets and drums. Moreover, the occasion became rather wild as the evening progressed.'

'It was unruly,' agreed O'Brien, in what was almost certainly an understatement. He started to add something else, but stopped when a shadow materialised at his side. It was Leighton.

'I have just heard a rumour,' said the Adventurers' secretary silkily. 'About Cave's brother.'

'I hope you do not intend to criticise him for burying Cave in St Margaret's Church,' said Kitty, regarding him with dislike. 'The Chapel Royal choir had arranged a very expensive ceremony without consulting him, so I do not blame the fellow for taking matters into his own hands.'

'Nor do I,' agreed O'Brien stoutly. Then he grimaced. 'Although I was rather looking forward to attending a funeral in Westminster Abbey. The music would have been fabulous.'

'Actually, I was going to tell you something else entirely,' said Leighton, a little coolly. 'Namely that James Elliot – the man who killed Cave in the swordfight – pretended to be Jacob, and buried him early for spite.'

Chaloner stared at him. How had he heard that story? The only people *he* had told of his suspicions were

Thurloe and Lester. Thurloe would never have gossiped, so did that mean Lester had spread the tale? But why would he do such a thing when it reflected badly on a man who was his friend and brother-in-law? Or had someone else reached the same conclusion, and was more inclined to chat about it?

'Well, that cannot be true,' said Kitty stiffly, 'because Elliot is dead, too. Joseph Williamson told us so. Elliot was buried on Friday.'

'Well, if he has been buried, then he must be dead,' said Leighton slyly. 'We are not in the habit of interring people alive in London. I cannot imagine it would be pleasant. Rats might come.'

Chaloner glanced at him sharply. Was it a random remark or one that carried a greater meaning? But Leighton's face was impossible to read, as usual.

'I am *not* discussing this,' said Kitty firmly. 'It is repugnant. Mr Cave was our friend.'

'You are quite right,' said O'Brien, taking her arm. 'Come, we must pay our respects to Buckingham. He is having a dinner next week, and has intimated that we are to be invited.'

'I shall put in a good word for you,' Leighton called after them. 'And do not forget the Adventurers' event tomorrow at dusk. You will not be disappointed with *that*, I assure you.'

When they had gone, Chaloner saw a number of Adventurers had gathered together. Swaddell was with them, dark eyes alert and reptilian. His companions had been drinking, and their loud, self-congratulatory discussion was generating considerable distaste among those near enough to hear.

'Personally, I believe their monopoly on African trade is unpatriotic,' said Kipps, coming to stand next to Chaloner and glaring at them. 'It means that *Dutch* ship-owners are growing fat on Gold Coast slaves, whereas if Africa was open to everyone, *I* could reap some of this profit.'

'Are you saying you would invest in the slave trade if the Adventurers' charter did not forbid it?' Chaloner was shocked, because he had expected Kipps to be more principled.

'Of course. Slaves are no different from any other commodity, and I predict they will be more profitable than gold in time.'

Chaloner itched to tell him what he thought of people who dabbled in that particular business, but Kipps's voice had been loud, and a number of people were looking at them. They included Adventurers and several members of the Piccadilly Company. Kitty and O'Brien had also turned, while Leighton was watching the scene unfold with aloof amusement.

'What about gravel?' asked Chaloner. It was a reckless question in front of so many people, but he was desperate enough for clues to take the risk.

'There is plenty of that in the Thames,' drawled Leighton, his expression curiously bland. 'So we have no need to import it from Africa.'

There was a hoot of mocking laughter from the Adventurers, and a meaningful exchange of glances between members of the Piccadilly Company.

'That was an idiotic remark, Chaloner,' said Kipps, scowling at the still-snickering merchants. 'Gravel indeed! Have you been drinking?'

'I hear many idiotic remarks at White Hall,' brayed

Margareta Janszoon. Her henchmen exchanged uneasy glances, and Chaloner recalled his promise to Prynne to suggest that she and her husband refrained from joining discussions they did not understand. 'I have never heard English spoke with such greasy charm.'

'Yes,' said Janszoon, nodding gravely. That evening, his scar was less pronounced, slathered as it was with fashionable face pastes. 'Everyone here is a champion at greasy charm.'

There was an angry murmur from Adventurers and Piccadilly Company members alike.

'She is praising our command of the English language,' explained Brodrick quickly. 'She meant "idiomatic", and the smooth way in which we courtiers can—'

'Actually, I think she intended an insult,' interrupted O'Brien, troubled. 'She called us "greasy".'

'She did,' agreed Leighton softly. 'And I shall be glad when we go to war and defeat the Dutch at sea. They are all arrogant, impertinent and untrustworthy.'

Neither Janszoon nor Margareta had any trouble understanding that remark, and both paled. Their soldiers closed around them, hands on the hilts of their swords.

'You call us names?' asked Janszoon indignantly. 'When the English leave much to be desired?'

'How dare you!' cried O'Brien, incensed. 'We are the greatest nation in the world!'

'Let us see if there is any more wine, O'Brien,' said Brodrick loudly. He lowered his voice as he hauled his friend away. 'Easy, man! We do not want the Swedes to think us barbarians.'

The Adventurers were more than happy to avail themselves of liquid refreshment, and followed eagerly, Leighton scuttling among them. Janszoon opened his mouth to yell something to their retreating backs, but Thurloe was suddenly in front of him.

'Your wife has dropped her fan,' he said, bending to scoop it up. 'And you are quite pale. Allow me to escort you both to a place where there is more air.'

'We do not—' Margareta began angrily, but there was something in Thurloe's steely gaze that made her accept the proffered arm. The guards and Janszoon followed, and so did Chaloner.

'Your English is very good,' Thurloe began politely, once they were outside. 'But there are nuances in our language that are difficult for foreigners to comprehend. You might be advised to keep quiet until you are sure you understand them.'

'We understand them,' began Janszoon, outraged. 'We are fluent in—'

Thurloe's baleful eye silenced him abruptly. 'It might be time to leave London and return home. It cannot be comfortable here for you, with our two countries on the edge of war.'

'No,' agreed Margareta sullenly. 'We shall go as soon as we find a suitable ship. London is a hateful place, and we will be glad to leave it.'

'Where in Amsterdam do you live?' asked Chaloner in Dutch, more to placate them than for information. 'I know it well, and—'

'It is rude to use foreign languages here,' snapped Margareta in English. She indicated Thurloe. 'He did not understand what you said. My mother was right: London is full of unmannerly savages.'

'Go home,' said Thurloe shortly. 'And I do not mean to your lodgings – I mean to Holland. The situation here will only grow more uneasy as we inch towards a conflict.

You know you are in danger, or you would not have felt the need to hire guards.'

'It does feel dangerous,' agreed Janszoon, still nettled. 'And I grow to hate the English. They are stupid if they think they can win the war.'

He took Margareta's arm and led her towards the gate. They held their heads high, but people shot them unfriendly glances as they passed, and their guards were tense and alert.

'Prynne was right,' said Chaloner, watching them. 'They *are* a danger to peace.'

'I imagine any Hollander in London is a danger to peace at the moment, regardless of the quality of their English. London is itching to lynch one.'

Chaloner was bemused. 'Why do they not learn from their experiences and keep quiet at these courtly gatherings? Or do you think they are actually clever Dutch spies, sent to needle us into war before we are ready? Shall we follow them, and demand answers?'

'Not unless you feel equal to dispatching their guards first – I imagine they will be under orders to prevent such a situation. No, Tom, we must look to others for our answers.'

'Fitzgerald?'

'He has sent his apologies, saying he is unavoidably detained and cannot be here. It is bad news, because it means he is working on his plans for tomorrow. I only hope we overhear something that will allow us to thwart him, because time is fast running out.'

The heat and crowded conditions in the Banqueting House had driven many people out into the Great Court, where they congregated in groups. It was a clear autumn afternoon, and the sun was shining, so it was pleasantly warm. Thurloe slipped away to eavesdrop on Harley, who was engaged in urgent conversation with Kipps, so Chaloner aimed for Lydcott in the hope that *he* might have learned something useful. He was intercepted before he could reach him.

'Today, I decided to arrest Fitzgerald and damn the consequences,' said Williamson in a low voice. He had attempted to disguise himself, but was instantly recognisable by his haughty strut. Lester was at his side, resplendent in a fine blue coat that made him look every inch the successful sea-officer. 'But he must have had wind of it, because he has disappeared.'

'He will be busy making arrangements for tomorrow,' predicted Lester soberly. 'The threat of incarceration is not responsible for his flight, because he considers us an irrelevancy.'

Williamson glared at him. 'But we have made some progress in learning what is to happen. Swaddell overheard a conversation between Leighton and some of his Adventurers today – they plan to attack and burn *Jane*. Unfortunately, he did not catch where or when.'

'Queenhithe,' supplied Chaloner. 'She will dock there at three o'clock tomorrow afternoon, but arson is better managed in the dark than in daylight, so I imagine they will strike tomorrow night.'

Williamson nodded his thanks for the information. 'Then at least we shall prevent one crime. Obviously, I do not condone piracy, but we cannot allow *Jane*'s crew to be roasted alive. Or a conflagration set that might destroy half of London – Queenhithe has wooden warehouses.'

'I understand you sent Cave to spy in Tangier,' began Chaloner. 'And—'

370

'I did nothing of the kind,' interrupted Williamson sharply. 'I have intelligencers there, of course, but they are soldiers. What use would a musician be in such a place?'

'*Who* hired him, then?' mused Chaloner, more to himself than the others. 'The Adventurers?'

'Possibly,' replied Williamson, although Chaloner had not expected an answer. 'But here is Swaddell, come to make his report. We shall ask him.'

Chaloner was horrified. 'He will tell you his findings here? With half the Court watching? I thought you wanted everyone to believe that he has broken with you.'

'I do,' replied Williamson. 'But if we do it in full view of everyone – ensuring we look strained and angry – it eliminates the need for meeting secretly. It is safer for him.'

Chaloner would not have been fooled by such a ruse, and doubted others would, either, but it was too late to say so, because the assassin was there. He bowed stiffly to Williamson.

'Nothing,' he said, pointing as though he was remarking on the Banqueting House's roof. It was patently transparent, and Chaloner cringed. 'All they ever talk about is money. However . . .'

He paused as several people walked past, and resumed when they had gone. Chaloner winced a second time. He did not like Swaddell, and thought London would be a better place without him, but the man was risking his life with such reckless amateurism.

'. . . they certainly plan to sink *Jane*. Or rather, hired hands will. The Adventurers themselves will be on *Royal Katherine* in Woolwich, so they can later claim ignorance of the affair.'

'You must have heard something else,' said Williamson in exasperation. 'For God's sake man!'

Swaddell glared at him. 'I am doing my best. Unfortunately, they still do not trust me.'

'Have you heard anyone mention gravel?' asked Chaloner.

Swaddell frowned. 'Leighton said Teviot had wanted some. I assume it was for the mole. Why?'

'Do you know whether Cave was spying for the Adventurers?' asked Williamson.

'He was not,' replied Swaddell with conviction. 'He worked for the Piccadilly Company. I know, because I heard Congett tell Leighton so. He also said that he was glad Elliot had killed him.'

'I wish we had known that sooner,' said Lester with an irritable sigh.

'I did not think it was important,' snapped Swaddell. 'But I should go or they will be suspicious.'

He bowed again and moved away, although Chaloner saw the exchange had been observed by several Adventurers, including Leighton, all of whom were smirking: they knew perfectly well that Swaddell had been sent to infiltrate them. Chaloner felt a surge of exasperation that Williamson should have employed such clumsy tactics to tackle a group of powerful and intelligent people.

'I want your help later, Lester,' he said, when Swaddell had gone. 'Meet me by the Great Gate at eight o'clock.'

'Why?' asked Lester. 'To play the duet we missed last night?'

'No. We are going to solve the riddle of Elliot, Cave and Jacob once and for all.'

*   *   *

Leaving before Williamson could ask questions, Chaloner resumed his walk towards Lydcott. Thurloe's errant kinsman was half-hidden behind a fountain, watching Pratt and Oliver. The pair were trying to converse with Meneses, who was pretending not to understand them.

'This is hilarious,' Lydcott whispered gleefully. 'Fitzgerald has asked Pratt to keep Meneses away from any Adventurers today. Apparently, he is afraid that Meneses will tell them how successful our glassware venture has become.'

'Why should that matter?' asked Chaloner.

'If they hear how profitable we are, they might decide to do something similar,' explained Lydcott. 'And we do not want the competition.'

Chaloner stared into Lydcott's wide, guileless eyes, staggered by the man's credulity. 'Why should Meneses be a greater risk than the other members of the Piccadilly Company?'

Lydcott waved an airy hand. 'Who knows, but I trust Fitzgerald to look after us. Four of the Adventurers – Turner, Lucas, Proby and Congett – said nasty things about us, and Fitzgerald predicted that God would disapprove of such malice. Sure enough, within days they were dead. He has an uncanny knack for prophecy.'

'Very uncanny,' agreed Chaloner drily. 'I do not suppose it has occurred to you that he might have killed them himself?'

Lydcott stared at him in distaste. 'You are just like Thurloe – so twisted by your profession that you cannot see the good in people. Fitzgerald is a decent gentleman, as I have said before.'

'Right,' said Chaloner. 'Where is he tonight? It is unlike him to miss a glittering occasion.'

'*Jane* will arrive in London soon, and he has a lot of paperwork to complete. We are all pleased. Her coming means money for us – another voyage successfully completed.'

'Has he mentioned any plans for tomorrow?' asked Chaloner, declining to inform him that *Jane* was coming from Tangier, not New England, and that any profit would not be derived from fine glassware. 'Anything might help. Even where he intends to eat his breakfast.'

Lydcott shook his head. 'He is a private man, and keeps his personal life to himself. But I had better not spend any longer lurking behind a statue – I do not want folk to think me odd. Good day, Chaloner. Give my regards to Thurloe when you see him.'

He sauntered away, whistling, and Chaloner turned his attention to Pratt, Oliver and Meneses. He needed to speak to Meneses anyway, so he abandoned his hiding place and walked to where the architect and his assistant were speaking ever more loudly in an effort to make Meneses understand them, clearly of the opinion that all foreigners would comprehend English if it was bellowed at sufficiently high volume.

'I have heard that Lisbon is very nice,' Oliver was yelling. The finery he had donned for the occasion had turned green with age, which did nothing to dispel the aura of mournful shabbiness that hung about him. Moreover, he had stuffed his pockets with pens and papers, which made him oddly bulky around the hips. 'It is by the sea, I believe.'

Meneses shook his head blankly, although the gleam in his eyes indicated he was enjoying himself at the Englishmen's expense.

'Perhaps you can help us, Chaloner,' said Pratt. He

looked pained as he lowered his voice. 'I have been charged to entertain this fellow, but he does not understand a word we are saying.'

'Ask whether he enjoyed himself at Temperance North's brothel the other night,' suggested Chaloner. 'Perhaps that will remind him that he can speak perfectly good English when he wants.'

'Can he?' asked Pratt doubtfully, as a flash of irritation crossed Meneses' face. 'I have never seen evidence of it – he always looks confused at Piccadilly Company meetings, too. But the Earl tells me you have a talent with languages, so you speak to him.'

'We meet again,' said Chaloner in Portuguese, while Meneses scowled.

'Oh, dear,' muttered Pratt. 'You seem to have vexed him. Say something nice – such as that his coat is very becoming.'

'You are a liar, Meneses,' said Chaloner, still in Portuguese. 'You told me you had never been to Tangier, but you were its governor. Dismissed for corruption, so I am told.'

Meneses was furious. 'I resigned because it suited me, and the missing money was coincidental. Now go away. I am not obliged to tell you my business.'

'What business? Sharing Piccadilly Company details with the Adventurers? You are playing a dangerous game, because men from both sides have died—'

'And you will be next, if you continue in this vein,' snarled Meneses.

'He does not seem very happy talking about his coat,' breathed Oliver in Chaloner's ear. 'Discuss London's weather instead.'

'You realise that Fitzgerald knows what you have done,

do you not?' asked Chaloner. 'Pratt has been ordered to mind you, almost certainly to keep you here until an accident can be arranged. Like Turner, Lucas, Proby, Congett and God knows how many more.'

'Now you have frightened him,' whispered Pratt. 'What did you say? That it rains all the time?'

'What do you want from me?' demanded Meneses, not bothering to deny the charge.

'Tell him we have lovely summers,' suggested Oliver. 'Well, I remember a lovely one once.'

'I know why you came,' said Chaloner. 'You still have connections in Tangier – the dubious kind. You have been helping the Piccadilly Company trade there, even though it is illegal under the Adventurers' charter. But because you are a greedy man, you decided to hedge your bets and throw in your lot with the Adventurers, too.'

'It was expedient,' said Meneses stiffly. 'Neither organisation is competent, and it was difficult to decide which was the better option. So I elected to support both. And everyone should be pleased with what I have done for the Piccadilly Company – my reports have given them an edge over the Dutch, a country with which England will soon be at war.'

'You are in a desperate fix, Meneses,' said Chaloner softly. 'Fitzgerald will kill you for betraying him, and Leighton will not protect you now your usefulness to him is over. Moreover, Spymaster Williamson does not take kindly to men who try to harm our Queen.'

Meneses gazed at him. 'I had nothing to do with planting those documents in her purses. I—'

'Very few people know where those letters were found,' pounced Chaloner. 'Your own words have condemned you. How did you do it? Men are not supposed to have access to her wardrobe.'

Meneses swallowed hard. 'Captain Appleby is a conscientious guard. He would stop anyone from entering the Blue Dressing Room, so I cannot be guilty of what you accuse me.'

'You have just damned yourself a second time – only Her Majesty's servants should know the name of that particular chamber. And Appleby guards the entrance to her apartments, but anyone can roam around once he is inside. However, I will not stop you, if you want to escape.'

Meneses was wary. 'In return for what?'

'The name of the Piccadilly Company's master,' replied Chaloner. 'And do not say Fitzgerald.'

Meneses was alarmed. 'But I do not know it – I know virtually no one's name. Why do you think I turned to the Adventurers? Because I am mistrustful of men who decline to show me their faces.'

Chaloner suspected he was telling the truth, because he had seen the members' penchant for disguise himself. 'Then tell me about the gravel *Jane* will bring to London tomorrow.'

'It will make us very wealthy, and it is coming from Africa. And do not ask why grit should turn us all into nabobs, because they did not share that particular detail with me.'

Chaloner was beginning to be exasperated. 'If you cannot tell me why someone wants the Queen blamed for plotting to murder Pratt, I am taking you to Spymaster Williamson.'

'What are you saying about me?' asked Pratt immediately. 'I am not building *him* a mansion, because everyone knows all the money he acquired in Tangier was confiscated by his government. He is as poor as a church mouse.'

And there was Meneses' motive for travelling to England and playing such a deadly game, thought Chaloner: poverty. Meneses regarded Chaloner in alarm.

'But they did not trust me with that information, either! I was only told to befriend her and leave the letters in places where she could not deny that she had received them. It was not easy, because she is distrustful of strangers, and it took me a long time to win her confidence. It was tedious work, because she is a bore, with her convent manners and lack of clever conversation.'

'You do not deserve a chance to escape,' said Chaloner coldly, reaching out to grab his arm. Pratt and Oliver gaped at the sudden show of force, so he said in English, 'It is the Portuguese way of saying goodbye. Permanently.'

'All right!' squawked Meneses. 'It is part of a plan to return Tangier to Portugal. If the Queen is accused of plotting to kill . . .' – he glanced uneasily at Pratt – 'someone, then diplomatic relations will be severed, and Portugal will demand the dowry back.'

'Why should anyone here be interested in that outcome?'

'Because then Tangier will no longer be in the hands of the Adventurers, and *Jane* can trade there again. It was impossible under Teviot, so he was deposed. Governor Bridge is more amenable, but he is greedy and demands too hefty a slice of the profits. However, if I am reinstated . . .'

Chaloner stared at him. 'The *Piccadilly Company* is behind the plot? But I thought it was the Adventurers – Pratt is one of the Piccadilly Company's own members . . .'

Meneses shrugged. 'That is what anyone inclined to meddle was supposed to think. Our master – whoever he might be – is nothing if not clever. Do not underestimate him. He will stop at nothing to smash what he sees as an inconvenient monopoly.'

'At the expense of damaging relations between two friendly countries? Perhaps permanently?'

'He does not care about Britain, Portugal, the Dutch or anyone else. All he is interested in is making himself rich. At any cost.'

His mind a whirl of unanswered questions, Chaloner watched Meneses run towards the stables; the man was obviously intending to make his escape before his interrogator changed his mind.

'Damn it, Chaloner,' snapped Pratt. 'I said to entertain him, not drive him away.'

'We were discussing the plot to kill you tomorrow,' said Chaloner, turning his gaze on the architect.

A flash of alarm crossed Pratt's face, but it was only fleeting, and then he looked smug. 'The news is all over London, and has made me England's most celebrated artisan.'

'*I* should not like to be threatened with death,' said Oliver, his expressive face full of gloomy foreboding. 'I know you say your friends will protect you, but what if they prove unequal to the task? I would rather be a nonentity and alive, than dead and famous.'

'That is because you lack greatness,' declared Pratt haughtily. 'Unlike me, who is awash with it. But I had better stop Meneses, or Fitzgerald will be cross.'

He hurried away, and Chaloner looked around for Thurloe. The ex-Spymaster was nowhere to be seen, and rather than waste time hunting for him – it was nearing the time when he was to meet Lester – Chaloner asked Oliver if he had a pen and paper.

'I do, as a matter of fact,' replied Oliver, rummaging in his bulging pockets. 'Mr Pratt has architectural inspirations at peculiar times, so I always have writing paraphernalia to hand – he gets vexed if his flashes of genius are forgotten for the want of a scrap of paper. But how is your enquiry into the missing bricks? Have you solved the mystery yet?'

Chaloner shook his head, and indicated Oliver should turn, so he could use his back as a desk. Employing a cipher known only to him and Thurloe, he quickly outlined all he had learned and asked the ex-Spymaster to pass whatever he deemed appropriate to Williamson. He concluded by saying that he would visit him at three o'clock the next morning in Lincoln's Inn, sure that would give him ample time to complete everything he needed to do first. As he worked, a small pink nose poked from under Oliver's collar. He jumped in alarm.

'Christ! Is that a rat?'

Oliver's mournful eyes were reproachful. 'It is my ferret – I have mentioned him to you before. He was unwell this morning, so I brought him with me.'

He glanced around furtively before pulling the animal from his coat and affectionately stroking its silky fur. It was a pretty creature, but hardly something that should have attended a diplomatic reception. While he petted it, Oliver continued to pontificate on the Earl's supplies.

'Personally, I think he is making a fuss over nothing. All wealthy people should expect to lose a few bricks on occasion. It is the way builders work.'

'Do you have a list of what has gone missing so far?'

Oliver rummaged again. 'Yes – the Earl is in the habit of asking for it.'

'Did you write it yourself?' asked Chaloner, scanning the neat figures before passing it back. The losses were heavier than he had thought, and he did not blame the Earl for objecting.

'Hyde did. He started to keep a tally at his father's request.'

'How will you spend the rest of your evening?' asked Chaloner conversationally, going back to his note to Thurloe.

'At home with my ferret,' replied Oliver glumly. 'Unless you happen to know any nice young ladies who might keep a lonely Westminster man company? In fact, I had better go now – he is getting restless, and I should not like him to escape. Someone might keep him.'

Chaloner was thoughtful as he and Oliver parted, aware that he now had more than enough clues to solve one of his mysteries. He walked towards the gate, where a number of black servants had assembled. George was among them, taller than most by a head, and a sullen, looming presence that inhibited the friendly chatter that would normally have characterised such a gathering. Chaloner beckoned him out, noting the relieved glances that were immediately exchanged. George was as unpopular there as he was in Tothill Street.

'I want you to deliver this note to a choleric minister who wears an orange wig,' said Chaloner, passing it to him. 'He should be here somewhere, so there is no need to leave White Hall.'

'Good,' said George. 'Because I have just heard that there is to be dancing in the Banqueting House later.

And there is nothing so entertaining as watching white men dance.'

'Really,' said Chaloner coolly. 'And how do you do it?'

'With passion. And colour and noise.'

'Well, do not do it here. Hannah might not like it, especially if you invite Joan to take the floor with you.'

Amusement gleamed briefly in George's eyes at the notion. 'When I was on *Jane*—' He stopped suddenly, disgusted at the inadvertent slip.

'*Jane?*' asked Chaloner mildly. 'You told me you had never heard of her.'

George shrugged and looked away. 'I was mistaken. She is not a memorable ship.'

'And what about the gravel she carried? Is that forgettable, too? What is it? Another word for diamonds? Or perhaps for some exotic spice? Or sugar from the plantations?'

'It is *gravel*,' replied George sullenly. 'Stones and dirt.'

'Fitzgerald may well have transported gravel *to* Tangier,' acknowledged Chaloner. 'The mole will need a lot of it. But what did he transport *out?*'

'You will have to ask him. Although I would not recommend it. He has a temper.'

'So do I,' said Chaloner shortly. 'And it is beginning to fray with you. You cannot have sailed with Fitzgerald and not known what he carried in his holds. You are neither blind nor stupid.'

'No,' agreed George. 'But I did not choose to pry.'

'You pry when it suits you,' Chaloner retorted. 'Did you translate the cipher you found in my pen-box, by the way, or would you like me to help you?'

George regarded him with steady eyes. 'You confuse me with Susan. She was the spy.'

Chaloner threw up his hands in exasperation. 'Fine! Can I trust you to deliver that message or shall I hire one of these others?'

'You can trust me,' said George. He looked offended, and perhaps it was the suggestion that he was unreliable that encouraged him to attempt an explanation. 'There was always gravel in *Jane*'s holds. Even in Tangier, when Fitzgerald could have sold the lot, he kept some back. Thus any customs official boarding her will find gravel at any time in her voyage. As is written in her log.'

Chaloner stared at him, struggling to understand what he was being told. 'Fitzgerald lost a ship carrying gold, which is valuable but that does not require much space. It could have been concealed under a pile of gravel . . .'

George gave a brief smile. 'Well, then. Perhaps that is all you need to know.'

He bowed and walked away, leaving Chaloner with the glimmer of another solution as facts came together in his mind. If the Piccadilly Company's business was trading small but highly valuable items, then it was not surprising that Teviot had objected to *Jane*'s presence in Tangier – as an Adventurer, he would have preferred the profits to go to himself and his friends. It made sense, therefore, that the Piccadilly Company would want a more amenable governor, although Chaloner was appalled that nearly five hundred men had to die to make it happen. Meneses was right: Fitzgerald and his master *would* do anything to smash a powerful monopoly.

Chaloner was hovering by the Great Gate as the clocks struck eight. It was moonless, but clear, although the stars were invisible because plummeting temperatures were beginning to produce another thick fog. Chaloner did

383

not mind. It would conceal him, and make his next task easier.

'We should be listening for rumours about tomorrow,' said Lester, arriving a few moments later. 'Not wasting time with this errand. What is it, anyway?'

'We are going to St Giles-in-the-Fields.'

'Why? To look in the register of burials to convince yourself that Elliot is dead? I assure you, I did not imagine attending his funeral. It would be better to stay here, and—'

'Williamson can eavesdrop without us. Of course, there is a reason why his enquiries have been so spectacularly unsuccessful: there was a spy in his organisation.'

'Almost certainly,' agreed Lester, matching the brisk pace Chaloner set. 'He is not a man who commands loyalty, and I imagine a lot of his agents take the traitor's penny. But what does this have to do with Elliot? Or do you think *he* was such a fellow?'

'Yes, and I believe that is why Cave challenged him.'

'I suppose it is possible.' Lester looked troubled. 'Elliot was an excellent man to have at one's back at sea, but he became a different fellow once on land. I should never have let him marry Ruth. He gambled, which made him greedy for money, and that led him down dark paths. My enquiries have revealed that he was definitely involved in Pepperell's murder.'

The stabbing of the *Eagle*'s captain the day she had docked at Queenhithe seemed a long time ago, although it was only a little more than two weeks. Chaloner recalled what he had seen.

'Brinkes murdered Pepperell. I watched it happen, and so did several other—'

'Brinkes did the deed, and the Piccadilly Company

384

ordered it,' interrupted Lester. 'Of that I have ample proof. But someone *helped* Brinkes strike the fatal blow, and that man was Elliot.'

Chaloner frowned. 'Brinkes was with someone who wore a red uniform and a Cavalier hat that hid his face . . .'

'Elliot's ceremonial naval regalia – I have an identical set. It was what enabled him and Brinkes to stroll past the port guards. Once I had your sketches, I was able to find several people who can confirm that there was bad blood between Elliot and Pepperell. Of course, I still do not know *why* Elliot wanted Pepperell dead. They did not like each other, but that is no reason to kill.'

'I can answer that,' said Chaloner, recalling what he had deduced from Pepperell's sometimes odd behaviour aboard *Eagle*, and the letter he had seen in Williamson's office – the one penned in the sea-captain's distinctive scrawl. 'Pepperell was Williamson's man, too – paid to monitor passengers travelling to and from Tangier. The Piccadilly Company were aware of this, and decided that his report on Harley, Newell and Reyner should never be delivered. And how did they know what Pepperell did to boost his income? Because another of Williamson's spies betrayed him.'

'Elliot?' asked Lester unhappily.

'Elliot,' agreed Chaloner. 'The man who had been charged to watch the Piccadilly Company, and who moved his addled wife into rooms in the Crown to enable him to do it – keeping lodgings for himself in Covent Garden lest it transpired to be too dangerous. He used Ruth mercilessly, and did not care that his antics put her at risk.'

'Fitzgerald must have guessed what Elliot was doing, and realised how easily he could be turned into a traitor,' said Lester bitterly. 'Which explains why Williamson's knowledge about the Piccadilly Company was always so scanty – Elliot had been paid to tell him nothing of value.'

Chaloner nodded. 'Pepperell tried to communicate two clues before he died: Piccadilly and trade. He must have learned from eavesdropping on the three scouts that the Piccadilly Company is involved in smuggling goods from Africa, and wanted Williamson to know.'

'It is a pity he did not have the breath to be more specific,' said Lester ruefully. 'Because we could have done with this information days ago. Who else heard him speak?'

'Besides the three scouts? Reverend Addison, Cave and Captain Young, who promptly seized command of *Eagle* and sailed her away on the evening tide.'

'Young?' asked Lester sharply. 'There is an Anthony Young who sails for the Piccadilly Company. Williamson told me. Did he know Pepperell was going to be murdered? Is that why he was so quick to grab the ship?'

'I doubt it – not in advance. But I imagine he would have understood who had ordered the murder when he saw Brinkes.'

'And then Cave, whom we now know was a Piccadilly Company spy, was ordered to start a quarrel with Elliot and kill him,' finished Lester. 'Presumably, to ensure that Elliot never told anyone what he had done – no traitor can be trusted, after all. But Cave also died in the fracas . . .'

Chaloner did not bother to reiterate his conviction that Elliot was still alive. For all he knew, Elliot might be the villain who gave orders to Fitzgerald – his actions certainly showed him to be ruthless and unprincipled.

*   *   *

St Giles-in-the-Fields was a handsome, red-brick building not forty years old. Unfortunately, its brash splendour had attracted the attentions of the Puritans during the Commonwealth, and many of its best features had been smashed or stolen. Moreover, it had a much smaller churchyard than its pastoral name suggested, and was tightly hemmed in by houses. It was eerie in the shifting mist, and Lester jumped in superstitious alarm when a cat slunk across their path.

There was a small shed at the far end of the grave-yard. Chaloner broke the lock with a stone and emerged with two spades and a lamp. 'Show me Elliot's grave.'

Lester's jaw dropped. 'You mean to dig him up? Christ God, Chaloner, no!'

'We will find a box filled with stones or soil. Elliot will not be in it.'

'Of course he will be in it!' Lester was aghast. 'I told you – I attended his funeral.'

'Did you look in the coffin?' demanded Chaloner. Lester shook his head reluctantly. 'You were not with him when he died, and the surgeon you hired is incapable of telling the difference between the living and the dead. I *know* Elliot is alive and still causing mischief. Exposing his empty casket will be proof of it.'

'Then we shall ask the sexton to do it tomorrow – with a priest on hand to say whatever prayers are appropriate when desecrating tombs. We will not burrow like ghouls—'

'It might take weeks to obtain the necessary permissions,' argued Chaloner. 'And we need answers tonight. Besides, think of Ruth. Surely, she has a right to know whether she is a widow?'

Lester glared, but Chaloner's words had the desired

effect. He took a deep, unhappy breath, and led the way through the wet grass to a mound of recently dug earth. Fortunately, it was shielded from the surrounding houses by a dense yew.

'There must be a better way to find out than this,' he muttered. 'If we are caught . . . I am sure this sort of thing is illegal. And I doubt Williamson will speak for us.'

Chaloner was sure he would not, and began to excavate as fast as he could, eager to be finished as soon as possible. It was not long before there was a hollow thud: fortunately for them, lazy gravediggers had not bothered to make the hole very deep.

Lester scraped away the remaining soil, but then hesitated uncertainly, so it was Chaloner who inserted a spade between coffin and lid, and levered. The two men exchanged a brief glance as the wood splintered, and then Chaloner took the lamp and brought it close to the coffin.

Elliot's dead face stared out at them, an unusually black wig on his head.

Chapter 11

'You owe him an apology,' said Lester, his voice low with anger and revulsion. 'And me, too. Elliot *did* die when I said he did. Surgeon King was not mistaken: *you* are.'

Chaloner gazed at the body in disbelief. He had been so certain he was right. 'But if Elliot has been dead since last Monday, then who buried Cave?'

'His brother,' replied Lester curtly. 'You have been a spy too long, and see treachery where there is none – Jacob buried Cave to avoid funeral costs that would have crippled him. You say the descriptions of him matched Elliot, but lots of men are large and own black wigs.'

'Then why did he tell Kersey that he lived in Covent Garden?' demanded Chaloner defensively. 'Elliot lived there, but Jacob never has.'

'Because he did not want vengeful courtiers after him for depriving them of the "social event of the month",' snapped Lester. 'I might have done the same in his position. And given that you are so spectacularly wrong over Elliot, are you sure your conclusions about Cave are correct?'

'Yes,' said Chaloner firmly. 'He *was* a spy. Brodrick

and Reverend Addison said so, as did Swaddell. The Piccadilly Company employed him – you were there when Swaddell confirmed it.'

Yet Thurloe had said *he* would not have hired a man like Cave for espionage, and so had Williamson. Was it possible that the Piccadilly Company had not, either?

'And their claims are based on what?' asked Lester archly. 'Actual evidence or supposition?'

Chaloner said nothing, because the captain had a point. Moreover, Thurloe's words were echoing loudly in his mind: that the descriptions of Jacob applied just as well to Lester as to Elliot. He glanced at the captain, taking in his bluff, hearty face and kindly eyes. Thurloe must be wrong!

'If Ruth ever learned what we have done, she would hold it against me for the rest of my life,' Lester was saying, as he replaced the coffin lid and grabbed a spade. 'I hope to God she never finds out.'

Chaloner hoped no one would. He clambered out of the grave. 'Can you finish this alone?'

Lester gaped at him. 'You are leaving? Christ God, man! I thought we were in this together.'

'I am sorry, but there is something I need to do. And time is short.'

'Then help me rebury the man *you* exhumed, and I will assist you with whatever it is.'

'There is no time.' Chaloner brushed mud from his clothes. 'I need to go now.'

'For pity's sake!' cried Lester, dismayed. 'It is hardly comradely to abandon me here.'

It was not, but Chaloner did not want company when he made his next port of call. Muttering a hasty but sincere apology, he aimed for Clarendon House. It was time to resolve the business of the stolen bricks, so there would be one less matter to explore the following day, when *Jane* would arrive, the Adventurers would destroy her, and some diabolical plot would swing into action.

As he walked, a stealthy, solitary figure in the mist, he pushed Elliot and Lester from his mind and considered all he had learned about the Earl's missing materials – from his visits to the site, and from what his suspects had inadvertently let slip. He knew the culprits would be at Clarendon House at that very moment, confident that they would not be disturbed while the celebrations at White Hall were in full swing. He smiled grimly. They were going to be in for a shock.

He could hardly believe his luck when he bumped into Wright outside the Crown. A knife to the throat persuaded the sergeant to answer questions that confirmed Chaloner's suspicions, and a knock on the head ensured that he would not warn the villains before they could be confronted.

The mansion was an imposing silhouette in the blackness when Chaloner arrived. There were no guards, but he had expected that: Wright had already admitted that he and his cronies had been paid to sit in the tavern all night. He approached it silently, and aimed for the library.

Voices emanated from it, and Chaloner nodded to himself when he recognised them: all his reasoning had been correct. The only thing he did not know was *why* they had seen fit to steal from the Earl. He advanced silently, and saw two men there, poring over a sheaf of plans. He drew his gun, wanting them frightened into making a confession, because he did not have time for a more leisurely approach.

'I assume those are the papers that changed hands

the day I chased you,' he said, stepping into the room and pointing the dag at its startled occupants. 'The Earl's son and Pratt's assistant: two men who have betrayed a trust.'

There was a silence in the library after Chaloner had made his accusation, the two culprits regarding him in astonishment – although at his claim or his unanticipated appearance it was impossible to say.

'How did you get in?' demanded Hyde, startled. 'I borrowed my father's key, and Pratt owns the only other one in existence. And I doubt *he* lent it to you.'

'Never mind keys,' snapped Oliver, glaring accusingly at Hyde. 'You told me you had not been followed. You damned fool! You should have been more careful.'

Hyde bristled. 'Do not call me names! And no one followed me. You, on the other hand—'

'I followed no one,' interrupted Chaloner. There was no time for a silly spat. 'Although I was certainly suspicious when Oliver told me he was going home to Westminster, but then promptly set off in the opposite direction.'

'I did not know he was watching,' objected Oliver, when he received an accusing scowl in his turn. 'I am not the distrustful type.'

'Then you are in the wrong business,' murmured Chaloner.

'How did you guess it was me you chased through the house the other day?' asked Hyde. Chaloner blinked his surprise at the question – he had expected at least some declaration of innocence – while Oliver's gloomy face was a mask of disbelief at his associate's easy capitulation. 'I disappeared without a trace.'

'Yes,' acknowledged Chaloner. 'But that in itself is a clue – it meant there had to be secret rooms or tunnels. And *that* is where the "stolen" materials have been going – they have been used to build these devices. It explains why no one has ever seen them carted away: they are still here.'

'You cannot prove that,' warned Oliver. 'You will never find—'

Chaloner tapped on a panel that glided open to reveal a space behind it, large enough for a man to stand. 'Of course I will. I have been locating these contrivances for years. It will be easy.'

It was a bluff, because he still had no idea how Hyde had disappeared near the library. He walked to the desk and glanced briefly at the plans. Then he rolled them up and slid them inside his coat. They would help him understand what had been constructed where.

'You reckoned without Wright, too,' he went on. 'He did not hesitate to say that he had been paid to stay away tonight. He also explained how he has been taught to arrange the supplies so that Pratt will no longer notice what is missing.'

'You paid him to stay away?' asked Oliver of Hyde, unimpressed. 'That was a waste of money – he is rarely here anyway. And then he betrayed you! I told you he could not be trusted.'

'I admit to teaching him how to re-stack bricks and wood,' said Hyde stiffly. 'But I certainly did not give him any money tonight. The man is a liar and a villain.'

Chaloner regarded him in disgust, thinking that a son who put his father through such torments was hardly a saint himself. He resumed his analysis.

'You have been on my list of suspects since the

393

morning of the chase,' he said, 'because you opened the door with a key. Pratt's was around his neck, so the man I dashed after must have had the Earl's. You are in a better position to borrow that than anyone else.'

'Yes, but there must be *more* than two of them,' said Oliver, looking hard at Chaloner. 'Because otherwise you could not have gained access to—'

'Most of the workmen are in your pay,' interrupted Chaloner, loath to pursue that particular line of thought. 'Which is why the materials disappear during the day – your tunnels and passages are constructed during normal working hours, when Pratt is away on other business. No wonder I did not see anything vanish when I stood guard at night.'

'We were able to work in the evenings, too, before you appeared,' said Hyde sullenly. 'It was a damned nuisance when my father summoned you back from Tangier.'

'It is an impressive achievement,' said Chaloner grudgingly. 'Especially as I imagine Pratt is unaware of what is being done to his creation. I suppose your architectural training came in useful?'

'Very,' said Hyde smugly. 'My artifices are a masterpiece in their own right.'

'Perhaps so,' said Chaloner. 'But I do not understand *why* you built them. What possible advantage is there in having your father's house riddled with such devices?'

'So he can spy on his enemies, stupid!' said Hyde in sneering disdain. 'He would never have agreed to these measures himself – you know how conservative he is – so I decided to install them for him. You will doubtless take advantage of them in time. Assuming you are still in his service, of course, which is looking increasingly unlikely at the moment. He will dismiss you when I tell him you held me at gunpoint.'

Chaloner eyed him contemptuously. 'How will these contrivances benefit him? He does not entertain enemies in his own home. And I doubt he spies on his friends.'

Hyde opened his mouth to reply, but then closed it again, indicating that this notion had not occurred to him. 'We shall see,' he hedged stiffly.

'There was another clue, too,' Chaloner went on. 'The note that enticed me into the strongroom was in your handwriting. I recognised it when Oliver showed me the inventory of missing materials you had made. It was a nice touch: small jaws, death and darkness.'

'I *did* write those words,' acknowledged Hyde, puzzled. 'I have an elegant hand, and Oliver asked me to pen them as part of an anonymous love poem to his woman. Curious phrases to express passion, but each to his own. However, I doubt he left such an intimate item in the vault.'

'Oliver does not have a woman,' said Chaloner, recalling how the assistant architect had twice alluded to being at home with no one but his pet. 'And then there were the muddy footprints on the cellar stairs that same night. Most were human, but there were an animal's, too. They told me that Oliver had been there with his ferret shortly before I was locked inside.'

Oliver scowled when he saw he was cornered. 'I only wish you had died there, as I had intended,' he snarled. 'Then we would not be having this ridiculous conversation.'

'Died?' echoed Hyde, shocked. 'No one is supposed to die! And no one is meant to be shut in the strongroom, either. It is designed to be airless.'

'It would have been deemed an unfortunate accident,' said Oliver, malice suffusing his gloomy face. 'If the lack of air had not killed him, the rats would have done.'

'*Rats?*' cried Hyde in bewilderment. 'What are you talking about?'

'Hyde's note would have suggested otherwise,' said Chaloner, ignoring him.

Oliver sneered. 'It would have been eaten. Along with most of you. But if not, no one could have proved it came from me. Hyde wrote it, after all.'

'Stop!' shouted Hyde, increasingly appalled. 'Murder has no part in our plans. We will come to an arrangement with Chaloner. Every man has his price, and my father is a wealthy man.'

Oliver smiled, but his eyes were icy cold. 'You think we can let him go, do you?'

'It may have escaped your notice, but I am the one holding the gun,' said Chaloner, while Hyde gaped at the assistant architect in disbelief.

Oliver's grin widened. 'And it may have escaped yours, but I have workmen at my disposal.'

He gestured around him, and Chaloner was horrified to see the barrels of several weapons jutting through holes in the panelling. He counted at least four. Reacting quickly, he darted across the room and grabbed Hyde around the neck, putting the dag to his temple and using the younger man's body as a shield.

'I still have the advantage,' he said. He would have preferred Oliver as a hostage, but the man had been too far away. 'Order your people to stand down, or I will kill your accomplice.'

Oliver had predicted his move, and had ducked behind the desk, out of Chaloner's line of fire. 'Do it, then,' he said viciously. 'I do not care. And then we shall dispatch *you*. You have been nothing but trouble ever since you came back from Africa. It will be a delight to end your life.'

Hyde had been thrashing about furiously, trying to free himself from Chaloner's grasp, but he went rigid with shock when he heard Oliver's words.

'What?' he gasped. 'We are in this together, Oliver, so you *will* care if I am harmed. And you can put me down, Chaloner. You will not shoot me: you would not dare.'

'He might not, but *I* shall,' called Oliver from under the table. 'We do not want anyone else knowing what we have installed here. And as you gave me your original drawings the other day, the only other record is in your head. In other words, you have gone from helpmeet to liability.'

'Liability?' squeaked Hyde in confusion. 'No! I am your *partner*. And Chaloner has the plans, anyway – he put them in his coat. He will give them to you in exchange for my life.'

'We shall take them from his corpse,' said Oliver disdainfully. 'You cannot bargain with them.'

Chaloner released Hyde abruptly. 'You should choose your associates more carefully – you are about to become the victim of your own deceit.'

'What do you mean?' Hyde's voice was unsteady with rising panic.

'I cannot imagine these secret passages and spyholes were your idea,' said Chaloner, thinking him a fool. He took a step towards Oliver's table, but the click of more guns being cocked stopped him from taking another. 'Did

Oliver come to you with the notion, claiming they would work to your father's advantage?'

'Well, yes he did,' conceded Hyde. 'But—'

'Who commissioned you?' Chaloner asked of Oliver. 'Buckingham? Lady Castlemaine? Which of the Earl's enemies is so determined to harm him that he went to all this trouble?'

'You will just have to wonder,' replied Oliver, keeping his head well down. 'Now drop the gun. You cannot hit me from where you are standing, and if you try, my friends will shoot you.'

More men had gathered in the doorway; Chaloner recognised the sullen woodmonger Vere and the labourers who worked under his supervision. All were rough, ruthless individuals who would happily commit murder for money. He knew he was unlikely to survive the encounter, so with nothing to lose, he aimed at where he thought Oliver's chest would be and pulled the trigger. There was a loud report, and splinters flew from the table, but it was a sturdy piece of furniture, and Oliver's startled yelp said he was unharmed.

Immediately, there was answering fire from the spyholes, which had the men at the door wheeling away in alarm. Fortunately for Chaloner, the angle of the apertures prevented them from aiming properly, and most missed, although one nicked his shoulder, causing him to drop to his knees. Hyde hurled himself to the floor and covered his head with his hands.

'Stop!' shouted Oliver, as there came the sound of weapons being reloaded. 'You will damage the panelling, and Pratt will demand to know what happened. We cannot afford questions. Come in here and grab them – without bloodshed, if possible. We do not want stains on the floor.'

Men poured into the library to lay hold of Chaloner and Hyde, but although Chaloner managed to club one with the now-useless dag and disable another with a kick, it was not long before he was subdued. Then Vere relieved him of gun, sword and daggers. Wiseman's scalpel went undetected, though, tucked as it was in his cuff.

'You cannot do this to me!' shrieked Hyde. 'We have been working together for months, and—'

'Shut up,' snarled Vere. He looked at Oliver, who was inspecting the shattered desk, obviously amazed that he had escaped unharmed. 'What do you want us to do with them?'

'Put them in the strongroom.' Oliver dragged his attention away from the table. 'And this time, mount a guard outside to ensure they do not escape. While they suffocate, we shall concoct evidence that proves Hyde has been stealing his father's bricks, and that Chaloner locked him in there to teach him a lesson.'

'And became trapped himself at the same time?' asked Vere doubtfully.

'When they are dead, you can bury him in the woods. Everyone will assume he fled London when he realised his antics had brought about Hyde's demise.'

'No!' whispered Hyde, while Chaloner went cold at the thought of being shut in the vault a second time. 'Please, Oliver. I will not tell anyone what . . . There is no need to kill me.'

Oliver laughed, and Chaloner was stunned by the change in the man. Gone was the glum, shambling fellow, replaced by something far less attractive.

'You were never going to be allowed to live, Hyde,' he said pityingly. 'What would be the use of these devices if you blab about them to your father? It means my employer would have wasted his money. Use the wits you were born with, boy!'

His gloating voice, coupled with a determination not be to incarcerated again, served to concentrate Chaloner's mind, and a plan began to form. He went limp in his captors' hands; they swore when he suddenly became a deadweight.

'What is wrong with him?' demanded Oliver impatiently.

'He has passed out from the pain of his wound,' said Vere. 'He will not be any trouble now.'

'Then I will deal with him and Hyde,' said Oliver briskly. 'Green and Berry can help. Vere – take everyone else to the Room of Audience and start work. It is imperative that we finish tonight, because the house will be crawling with people once Hyde's corpse is found.'

Hyde started to cry, while Chaloner contrived to make himself as difficult to carry as possible. Green and Berry soon grew exasperated, and frustration turned them careless. The moment their guard dropped, he plunged the scalpel into Green's arm. The man's eyes widened in shock, but Chaloner was already spinning away, and had knocked Berry senseless with a punch.

'Run!' he hissed to Hyde, whipping around to deal with Oliver. Unfortunately, the assistant architect's reactions were faster than he had anticipated, and he had already snatched a gun from the reeling Green, his face full of enraged fury.

At such close range, Oliver could not miss, and Chaloner braced himself for the shot that would end his life. But he had reckoned without Hyde. With a screech of passion, the Earl's son grabbed a sledgehammer that was leaning against a wall, and swung it with all his might. It caught Oliver on the back of his head, and Chaloner knew from the sound it made that it had shattered his skull. The gun went off at the same time, and Chaloner had no idea how it had missed him.

Hyde raised the hammer again, but Chaloner grabbed his arm and pulled him away. The gunshot and Green's shrieks would have warned the others that trouble was afoot, and sure enough he heard a distant shout. Grateful that his explorations had familiarised him with the house's layout, he hauled Hyde along a corridor towards a chamber where there was a defective window. Hyde was sobbing hysterically, slowing them both down.

They reached the room and Chaloner forced open the shutter. He shoved Hyde through it, acutely aware of footsteps coming ever closer. Hyde was clumsy, and took longer than he should have done, so by the time it was Chaloner's turn to escape, the workmen were almost at the door. Forced to hurry, he jumped badly, jarring his lame leg as he landed. The resulting limp slowed him down. Hyde was making good time now, though, sprinting towards the woods as fast as his feet would take him. He was soon invisible in the fog.

Chaloner was not so fortunate, and his pursuers were so close behind him that he could hear the rasp of their breath. He also aimed for the woods, in the hope that the trees would prevent them from all attacking at once – he might stand a chance if he could fight them in twos or threes.

He reached the copse, then whipped around with the scalpel. The fellow at the front of the mob reeled away with a howl of pain, but others jostled to take his place, and the ferocity of their assault made Chaloner stumble. His lame leg buckled, and he crashed to the ground.

With grim purpose, Vere stepped forward, a gun in his hand.

Chaloner was not sure what happened next, except that there was a sudden yell and a ragged volley of shots. Then other men appeared, weapons at the ready, although it was too dark to see their faces. Vicious skirmishing followed, and rough hands hauled him to his feet.

'Run! We cannot hold them off for long.'

Chaloner did not need to be told twice. He followed his rescuer through the woods, staggering along twisting paths in the misty darkness until he was wholly disoriented. Behind him, he heard more shots and the continued clash of steel.

Just when he was beginning to think it was time to stop and demand answers, they reached a row of houses, and he knew they were on the northern end of the Haymarket, because he could see the distinctive form of the windmill looming out of the fog. Then he saw his rescuer's silhouette.

'Lester!'

'Pratt saw lights in Clarendon House when all should have been in darkness,' explained Lester. 'So he ran to White Hall to tell Williamson, assuming the brick-thieves were at work. I went with Doines and his men to lay hold of them, and we were about to pounce when you raced out with that horde on your heels. I thought we had better intervene.'

'Thank you,' said Chaloner sincerely.

'Well, you did save Ruth. I shall always be in your debt for that. Of course, I am not quite so ready to forgive you for abandoning me in a graveyard with my brother-in-law's exhumed corpse.'

'Where is Hyde?' asked Chaloner, not wanting to dwell on his ill-judged notions about Elliot. He stopped walking abruptly. 'I will have to go back for him.'

'He is here, with me,' came a soft voice from the darkness. Chaloner jumped, disconcerted that Williamson should have been listening to their conversation. 'And I think an explanation is in order, but not here. Lead the way to the Gaming House, Lester. We all need a drink.'

As they walked, Chaloner was aware of Hyde conversing in an urgent hiss to the Spymaster. He could not hear what was being said, but was disinclined to demean himself by telling his own side of the story. Williamson would believe what he pleased, and nothing Chaloner could say would make any difference. Doines caught up with them just outside the Gaming House.

'Most of them got away,' he reported. 'But we shot two and caught Vere. He has agreed to give the others up in exchange for his freedom. Shall we take him up on his offer?'

'Yes.' Williamson indicated Hyde. 'This gentlemen says they tried to kill him, and we cannot have earls' sons assassinated. I want them all in my cells by the end of the day. And Vere can join them there once he is no longer of use to us. I dislike traitors.'

Doines saluted and disappeared, while Chaloner thought that if these orders were followed, Vere would die at his accomplices' hands, because they would not appreciate traitors, either. He followed Williamson into the Gaming House, where the Spymaster commandeered a private room and ordered a jug of claret. He sat on a bench and allowed Lester to inspect his shoulder.

'Just a scratch,' the captain declared, dabbing at it rather roughly. 'You were lucky.'

Chaloner accepted the wine Williamson poured him, resisting the urge to swallow the lot in a single gulp. His hands were unsteady and his stomach churned, mostly a reaction to the thought of being locked in the vault again – being dispatched in the woods had not been nearly as terrifying a prospect. Meanwhile, Williamson watched Hyde like a cat with a mouse.

'You have regaled me with quite a story,' he said. 'About thieves stealing bricks to build secret passages in your father's house, and how you discovered their villainy and confronted them. You had better tell me again, and this time fill in the details. Such as why you elected to challenge them all by yourself, and how Chaloner came to be involved.'

Hyde had the grace to look sheepish, but it did not prevent him from recounting a tale that put him firmly in the role of hero. He declared he had always been suspicious of Oliver and Vere, and Chaloner's conclusions about them being in the pay of the Earl's enemies were presented as his own. He even claimed to have saved them both from being locked in the strongroom.

'Chaloner fainted,' he said in conclusion. 'And I was obliged to carry him from the house with one hand, while fighting off Vere with the other.'

'Really?' asked Lester coolly. 'Because I saw you racing away to save your own skin, leaving him to the mercy of—'

'You are mistaken,' interrupted Hyde curtly. He turned to Williamson. 'My only regret is not forcing Oliver to tell me the name of the man whose orders he was following.'

'And now Oliver is dead,' said Lester flatly. 'Killed by Chaloner with a sledgehammer. Was that before or after

404

Chaloner passed out, by the way? Or did he do it while he was insensible?'

'Unfortunately, Vere and his cronies will be minions,' said Williamson, while Hyde glowered at Lester. 'I doubt they have been trusted with the name of the man who paid their wages, although I shall certainly ask. But what will the Earl do about it, Hyde? Destroy these spyholes?'

'They are of no use to his enemies now, because *I* know about them,' Hyde declared. 'And as from today, so will he: I shall tell him exactly what happened. But I think the situation can be turned to his advantage. He can use them to monitor his guests.'

He shot Chaloner a glance that warned him not to reiterate his earlier remarks about the Earl not entertaining the kind of person who warranted being put under surveillance.

'Well, he has paid for them by inadvertently providing the necessary materials,' sighed Williamson. 'So they are his to deploy as he sees fit.'

While Lester proceeded to interrogate Hyde, tying the younger man in knots over his lies and inconsistencies, Williamson turned to Chaloner and spoke in a low voice.

'I am not a fool, Chaloner – I know who unravelled this mess. So why do you sit back and let Hyde take the credit?'

'I do not care about him. I am more worried about the plans of Fitzgerald's master.'

'Then you had better tell me everything you have learned. Thurloe confided some of it, but there is a great deal I still do not understand, and we need to work together if we are to thwart these villains. Neither of us can do it alone.'

405

It was not easy to forget his dislike of the Spymaster and share his findings, but Chaloner knew he had no choice. When he had finished, Williamson was sombre.

'There was an accident at White Hall after you left.'

Chaloner regarded him in alarm. 'What kind of accident?'

'The fatal kind – Meneses was trampled by a horse. No one knows how it happened, although there is some suggestion that he may have been borrowing it to go for a ride.'

Chaloner closed his eyes. Who had killed Meneses as he had tried to escape? The Piccadilly Company for his betrayal? Or the Adventurers, because he was no longer useful?

He dragged his thoughts back to the problems they would face the following day – or rather, that day, because although he had no idea of the time, he sensed it was long after midnight, and approaching the hour when he was supposed to meet Thurloe. He had not anticipated that confronting the brick-thieves would transpire to be such a deadly business, or so time-consuming.

'From the start, I have considered the plot to kill Pratt as a bluff,' he said. 'That the real aim was to damage the Queen. But now I am not so sure. I think someone might actually do it.'

'I shall arrest Pratt, then,' said Williamson promptly. 'They cannot kill him if he is in custody.'

Chaloner nodded approvingly. It was as good a way as any to prevent the architect from being used to harm Her Majesty. 'Meanwhile, *Jane* will dock at three o'clock in the afternoon, almost certainly carrying a valuable

406

cargo hidden beneath gravel. The Adventurers have hired men to attack and burn her, and the Piccadilly Company will resist.'

'They will,' agreed Williamson. 'And the resulting mêlée could be very bloody.'

'And finally, Leighton has arranged for his Adventurers to enjoy some sort of nautical feast aboard *Royal Katherine* at dusk. I have an awful feeling that a large gathering of opponents may be too great a temptation for the Piccadilly Company . . .'

Williamson regarded him in horror. 'You think that is the nature of the atrocity Fitzgerald has planned? But the Adventurers comprise some of the wealthiest and most influential men in the country – members of the Privy Council, of Parliament, and of the royal family! If anything were to happen to them en masse . . . well, there would be chaos!'

'I do not think the Piccadilly Company will care. They are more interested in the fact that it will leave a massive void in African trade – one they will be eager to fill.'

Williamson was silent for a moment. 'Then our duties are obvious. First, we shall confine Pratt until he is no longer in danger. Second, troops must be sent to Woolwich, to ensure no member of the Piccadilly Company goes anywhere near *Katherine*. And third, someone must prevent *Jane* from docking at Queenhithe: she cannot be attacked if she is not there.'

'No,' argued Chaloner. 'The best way to defend the Adventurers is to cancel their feast. Contact Leighton and tell him to—'

'Impossible,' interrupted Williamson shortly. 'There have been threats against the Court ever since the King reclaimed his throne, and he refuses to defer to them

407

– the Adventurers will never postpone their feast. If I suggest it, I will likely be arrested myself.'

Chaloner sighed irritably, but suspected the King was right – he and his government would never get anything done if they allowed lunatic plots to dictate their actions.

'How many men do you have?' he asked.

'Not enough, especially now Doines has gone after those damned brick-thieves. Still, it cannot be helped. I shall send the rest to Woolwich, because protecting the Adventurers is paramount. Swaddell can take charge until I arrive.'

'Why him? What will you be doing?'

'Locating Pratt. Meanwhile, perhaps you will manage Queenhithe. Go now, though, because ships are notorious for not arriving on schedule. You will doubtless have a tedious time of it, but so will I – when he came to warn me about the brick-thieves, Pratt mentioned going out for the night. I have no idea where to start looking for him.'

'Try the gentleman's club on Hercules' Pillars Alley.'

Williamson smiled. 'Thank you. Perhaps working with you will not be as grim as I feared.'

Chaloner was grudgingly impressed when he saw Williamson swing into action, forced to admit that he was not as incompetent as he had always imagined. The Spymaster dispatched his men to Woolwich with cool efficiency – half in boats and half in coaches, lest one form of transport should prove problematic.

When they were safely on their way, ears ringing with impassioned imprecations not to waste a single second, Chaloner started to walk towards Queenhithe. He had not taken many steps before Hyde grabbed his arm. He

408

was released abruptly when the expression on his face indicated that while he might have lost most of his weapons and been shot, he was still not someone to manhandle.

'Contradict me at your peril,' Hyde hissed, trying to sound menacing. 'My father will not appreciate you calling me a liar, and neither will I.'

'Is that so?' said Chaloner shortly.

Seeing intimidation was not going to work, Hyde tried another tack. 'If you will not consider my feelings, then think of him. His enemies will use my . . . my *errors* to harm him, and if he comes to grief, you will be unemployed. It is better for you if you tell the story as I have constructed it.'

'Very well,' said Chaloner. He started to walk away, but Hyde stood in front of him.

'Do I have your word? Now Oliver is dead, you are the only one who can argue with my version of events – no one will listen to Vere and his helpmeets.'

'What about the man who hired them?' asked Chaloner, thinking him a fool. 'He will know who designed the devices. And who helped Oliver steal the necessary materials.'

Hyde smiled coldly. 'Yes, but he is hardly in a position to say anything, is he? By exposing me, he reveals his own role in the affair, and that is something he will never do.'

Chaloner tried to pass Hyde a third time, and was irritated when he was stopped yet again.

'I mean it, Chaloner,' said Hyde, confidence returning as he felt himself to be gaining the upper hand. 'You will do as I say, because you do not want powerful enemies.'

Chaloner's patience snapped. 'No, I do not. I am more than happy for you to have them instead.'

Hyde regarded him uneasily. 'What do you mean?'

'I mean that Oliver's employer probably *won't* contradict you publicly. However, there are other ways to express his displeasure. You are wealthy and can hire guards to protect yourself, whereas I cannot. You are right: it *is* better this way. Thank you.'

Chaloner was rewarded with the satisfaction of seeing alarm fill Hyde's face.

'He would not dare harm me!' Hyde swallowed hard. 'Would he?'

Chaloner regarded him dispassionately. 'At least I know now why you have been so keen for your father to dismiss me. You were afraid I would stumble across the truth at Clarendon House.'

'I wanted you gone because I abhor your dubious skills,' countered Hyde, although he would not meet Chaloner's eyes. 'Dugdale is right: they are unseemly in a gentleman.'

'They prevented you from being murdered tonight.'

'Rubbish! I would have extricated myself, given time.'

Chaloner did not dignify that claim with a response. He changed the subject. 'You are an Adventurer, are you not?'

'What of it?' snapped Hyde. 'Or do you want me to inveigle you an invitation to join? I suppose it can be arranged, if that is the price of your silence.'

'No, thank you,' said Chaloner in distaste. 'But tell me what you know about the event that is to be held in Woolwich tomorrow at dusk. Why did Leighton organise it?'

'Today,' corrected Hyde. 'It is already well past

midnight and so . . .' He faltered when he saw Chaloner's steely glare, and hastened to answer the question. 'Because arranging interesting treats for us is the way he keeps our favour.'

'Is he unpopular, then? He needs to bribe you to be allowed to continue as secretary?'

'Not exactly, but our members are wary of him. There are rumours that he made himself rich by criminal means, you see, although he denies it, of course. And you are wrong, by the way – the event will not be in Woolwich. We all said it was too far to travel, so Leighton changed it.'

'Changed it to where?' asked Chaloner uneasily.

'Oh, still on *Royal Katherine*, but she will be moored at Queenhithe instead.'

Chaloner stared at him in horror. 'Are you sure?'

'Of course – he lives in Queenhithe, and has friends who will help with the arrangements. It will not be at dusk, either. We were all disappointed by the Swedish ambassador's reception, because too many common folk had been invited and there was not enough food. So Leighton brought our event forward. He says there is nothing so memorable as breakfast on a ship at dawn—'

'Dawn?' echoed Chaloner in disbelief. 'No one will attend a function at that hour of the day!'

'Of course they will. Most of the Court will not have been to bed, and they will be perfectly happy to round off the evening at Queenhithe. Lady Castlemaine hosts breakfasts all the time.'

Chaloner was appalled. 'But how can Leighton change everything at such short notice? His staff will not be ready!'

411

'They would not dare fail him,' said Hyde grimly. 'But what is the problem with—'

'Do not go,' said Chaloner urgently.

Hyde regarded him with dislike. 'I most certainly shall! It will be fun.'

'There are rumours that something terrible will befall the Adventurers on St Frideswide's Day. And then there is *Jane*. Queenhithe will not be safe—'

'I know about our plan to destroy *Jane*,' said Hyde casually, as though looting and burning a ship was nothing special. 'But she is not due to arrive until three o'clock in the afternoon. Queenhithe will be perfectly safe for hours yet.'

But Chaloner's churning stomach told him that the change of time and venue were significant. Had Williamson's decision to issue an arrest warrant for Fitzgerald driven the Piccadilly Company to act sooner than it had planned? And what of Leighton's role in the affair? Was he, like Meneses, playing one side against the other, and his allegiance was actually to the Adventurers' rivals? Chaloner thought about the man's sly smiles and unreadable expressions – he had been an enigma from the start.

'Stay well away,' he urged. 'Better still, cancel it. Tell your colleagues not to go.'

Hyde scowled. 'Is this how things will be from now on? You will use my little indiscretion to bend me to your will?'

'No! I am trying to save your life. And those of your friends.'

Hyde relented. 'Unfortunately, you overestimate my influence,' he said, although it clearly pained him to admit it. 'I could scream warnings all night, but no one would take any notice.'

'Well, try,' Chaloner snapped. 'And now I need to find Williamson.'

As the Spymaster had used every available carriage to transport his men to Woolwich, he had been reduced to walking to Hercules' Pillars Alley. Chaloner caught up with him on Fleet Street. Lester was with him. Gasping for breath – he had run as hard as he could – Chaloner told them what Hyde had said. The blood drained from Williamson's face.

'But I have dispatched all my officers down the river, and Doines is off God knows where rounding up thieves! There is no one left to go to Queenhithe and protect Adventurers!'

'Perhaps they no longer need protecting,' said Lester hopefully. 'Fitzgerald may even now be standing at Woolwich, scratching his head at an empty berth.'

'No!' whispered Williamson, shocked. 'Chaloner is right. The plot is swinging into operation early, and we shall be found lacking.'

'Then tell Leighton to cancel his dawn feast,' said Lester practically. 'It is a stupid time for a soirée anyway. At sea, we would never—'

'We have already been through this!' snapped Williamson. 'It cannot be done.'

'Then perhaps they deserve whatever is coming to them,' muttered Lester. 'If they are unwilling to forgo entertainment in the interests of their own safety, then they are too stupid to—'

'Pratt will have to fend for himself,' determined Williamson, regaining his composure as he began to make decisions. 'Because the death of a conceited architect pales into insignificance when compared to the murder

413

of fifty nobles and their wives. Lester, hunt down a hackney and send a message after the other carriages, ordering them back immediately. I will do the same for the boats.'

'If you say so,' said Lester doubtfully. 'Although it seems to me—'

'There is no time for debate,' the Spymaster snapped. 'Chaloner, go directly to Queenhithe. Lester and I will join you there as soon as we can. Wait! You are going in the wrong direction!'

'We need all the help we can get,' called Chaloner over his shoulder. 'I am fetching Thurloe.'

Williamson seemed relieved. 'Yes – he is a good man to have at one's side in a crisis. But we must hurry. Lives depend on our actions tonight, and so does the future stability of our country.'

'No pressure, then,' mumbled Lester.

When Chaloner arrived at Lincoln's Inn, panting hard from what had been another furious dash, it was to find Thurloe with company. Lydcott was lounging by the fire.

'You are late,' said Thurloe curtly. 'It is almost four o'clock, and I have been worried.'

'I told you he could look after himself,' drawled Lydcott, standing and stretching lazily.

Chaloner limped to the cupboard where Thurloe kept his weapons. He grabbed a sword and a knife, struggling to outline all that had happened while still catching his breath. Never a man to waste time with needless questions, Thurloe armed himself, too, then led the way down the stairs at a brisk trot. Lydcott followed uninvited, his face a mask of confusion, although every time he attempted to ask a question, Thurloe waved him to silence.

414

'There are no hackneys,' said Thurloe tersely, when they reached Chancery Lane. 'We shall have to go on foot.'

'Go where?' demanded Lydcott, running after them. 'Stop! Wait! I do not understand!'

'So Elliot did die in the swordfight,' concluded Thurloe, ignoring his kinsman as he set a cracking pace through the dark streets. 'Which means Cave's brother really did bury him early in order to save money. And you have caught the brick-thief, although you will never be able to tell Clarendon the truth.'

'Pratt knew nothing about it,' gasped Chaloner. His lame leg ached, his shoulder throbbed, and he was not sure how much longer he could continue to race all over the city. 'Of course, that does not exonerate him – as Clarendon House's architect, he should have noticed there was something amiss with the place's proportions, especially as he was so proud of them.'

'Do you think the threat to murder Pratt came from Oliver?' asked Thurloe, also beginning to pant. 'So he could have Pratt's duties and his handsome wage?'

'No – Oliver had no reason to want the Queen implicated in a plot that will shatter diplomatic relations between us and Portugal. That is the Piccadilly Company's doing.'

'You are wrong,' declared Lydcott, snatching at Thurloe's arm to make him slow down. Thurloe shook him off impatiently. 'Listen to me – I shall explain! Fitzgerald told me and Pratt to be at St Paul's at dawn. He said he has a surprise for us.'

Thurloe skidded to a standstill at this remark. So did Chaloner, and although he chafed at the wasted seconds, he was grateful for the respite.

'He must be planning to kill Pratt there, then,' said Thurloe worriedly. 'Another accident that will be impossible to place at his door. And he plans to dispatch you at the same time, Robert, because you have outlived your usefulness to him. Like Meneses.'

'No,' argued Lydcott, exasperated. 'Fitzgerald is *not* a villain. How many more times must I say it? He has changed since he opposed you during the Commonwealth. He is a different man now.'

'Go to my rooms and stay there,' ordered Thurloe, not bothering to address the claim. 'We shall send word of this to Williamson, and he can detail a few henchmen to rescue Pratt.'

'He does not have any left,' said Chaloner tiredly. 'He is trying to recall the ones he sent to Woolwich, but I doubt he will succeed – he ordered them to go there as fast as they could travel.'

'Then *I* will save Pratt,' declared Lydcott. 'You are wrong about this, but I shall go anyway.'

'You will do as I say and return to Lincoln's Inn,' ordered Thurloe. 'Ann would never forgive me if anything were to happen to you.'

'And she would never forgive *me* if I sat by your fire while a man was murdered,' countered Lydcott. 'If you are wrong – which I know you are – then no harm will have been done. But if you are right, I shall be a hero.'

'You will be a dead hero if you do not take proper care,' warned Thurloe.

'I shall be perfectly all right,' said Lydcott, although there was a flippancy in the reply that said he still did not accept the seriousness of the situation.

'Pratt will die if you do not reach him first,' said Chaloner, speaking forcefully to make him understand the danger he was courting. 'It is not just your life that will be forfeit if you blunder.'

'Then I had better hurry,' said Lydcott, giving a jaunty wave before trotting away to where the cathedral was almost invisible against the black night sky.

Chaloner and Thurloe reached Queenhithe, both breathing hard from what had been a desperate sprint. Thurloe had stumbled in a pothole and was limping, while Chaloner felt every step was draining resources he did not have.

The fog grew denser as they neared the river. It caught the feeble glow of the lamps that had been left to illuminate the pier, softening the edges of the ramshackle warehouses that lined it. Two ships were moored there, bobbing gently on the ebbing tide, and transformed by the mist into a ghostly lace of spars and rigging. The smell of the Thames was strong – mud, seaweed and wet wood. The quay appeared to be deserted.

Chaloner edged towards the ships, noting that they were tethered so close together that the stern of one overhung the other. One was *Royal Katherine*, tall, proud and elegant, while the other was a smaller, shabbier affair, with a wide beam, stubby masts and crooked bowsprit. There were lights and movement aplenty aboard *Katherine*, but the other vessel was dark and still.

'Oh, no!' he breathed in horror. '*Jane*! She has arrived early.'

'How do you know?' Thurloe whispered back. 'Her name is too weathered to read.'

'The bowsprit – Lester said it was strangely curved. She must have sailed in on the midnight tide. She looks

417

abandoned, but I imagine crewmen will appear if we try to board.'

He was about to add something else when he saw a flash of light in the window of the nearest warehouse. He tensed, imagining it to be one of the Piccadilly Company, but then he recognised Lester's distinctive silhouette. Wondering how the captain had completed his errand to recall Williamson's carriages so quickly, he crept towards it, indicating Thurloe was to follow.

The door to the building had been forced, presumably so Lester could monitor the ships without being seen – although lighting a candle was hardly the best way to go about it. Thurloe apparently thought so, too, and regarded the sea-officer with open suspicion, which Lester appeared not to notice. Hastily, Chaloner indicated the light was to be doused.

'There you are at last,' came Williamson's uneasy voice from the resulting gloom. 'I was beginning to think you had deserted me. Lester found a hackney in record time, although I doubt it will catch up with my men before they reach Woolwich – and neither will the boat I dispatched. We are on our own, gentlemen.'

'There is a lot of activity on *Katherine*,' said Lester, peering out of the window. 'The Adventurers are definitely expected.'

'If I had the manpower, I would arrest the entire Piccadilly Company,' said Williamson bitterly. 'And sort everything out later. The plot cannot unfold if its perpetrators are behind bars.'

'Yes, but unfortunately, while you might lay hold of the minions, the master would almost certainly escape,' Thurloe pointed out. 'Besides, I would not recommend a mass detention of wealthy merchants. You would never hear the end of it.'

'But *who* is the master?' said Williamson in anger and frustration. 'We know it is not Fitzgerald, and Harley is not clever enough.'

'It must be someone closer to home,' replied Thurloe, and Chaloner rolled his eyes when he saw his friend look meaningfully at Lester.

Williamson nodded, although he had not understood the significance of Thurloe's glance. 'My favoured suspect at the moment is Kipps.'

'Kipps?' echoed Chaloner warily.

'He has a habit of appearing in unexpected places,' explained Williamson. 'Such as in the Tennis Court at an Adventurers' gathering, even though he is not a member. And he is very rich, yet they refuse to enrol him. Why, when he seems exactly their kind of man?'

And that was not all, Chaloner thought but did not say. Kipps had pretended not to notice while Dugdale and Edgeman had rifled through the Earl's office in search of God knew what, and he had known about the letters to the Queen, even though Clarendon and Hyde had kept them secret. Moreover, Frances had mentioned Kipps' interest in the vault the day Chaloner had been locked in, and he had eavesdropped when Chaloner had made one of his periodic reports to the Earl. Chaloner was aware of Thurloe looking at him – he had also voiced suspicions about the Seal Bearer – but he ignored him, not yet ready to consign the affable Kipps to the role of villain.

'I thought the culprit might be Meneses,' said Thurloe, when Chaloner declined to speak. 'But if he is dead, then I suppose he must be innocent. He *is* dead, is he not? You are certain?'

Williamson nodded. 'Personally, I am suspicious of Dugdale and Edgeman. The Adventurers comprise many of their employer's enemies, and I never did understand why they joined.'

'I think it might be Leighton,' said Chaloner softly. 'He lives in Queenhithe, and he does sinister business with the gunsmiths in St Martin's Lane.'

'Leighton is high on my list of suspects, too,' agreed Williamson. 'He is too smug by half.'

Thurloe suddenly addressed Lester. 'Do you know the latitude of Tangier?'

Lester blinked. 'Of course. It is thirty-five degrees and forty-eight minutes. Why do you ask?'

'No reason,' replied Thurloe, although he glanced at Chaloner and there was a world of meaning in the look. Lester saw it.

'Or is it forty-five degrees and thirty-eight minutes? It has been a while since I sailed there.'

It was not long before something began to happen. Secretary Leighton appeared, wearing a thick cloak, but identifiable by his scuttling gait. He approached *Katherine* silently, and stood staring at her for a moment, a sinister figure in the swirling mist. Then he clapped his hands and suddenly the quay was alive with activity.

Servants hurried from *Katherine* bringing torches, some of which they held aloft, while others were set into sconces along the walls. These formed bubbles of yellow light, which did little to illuminate matters, and a good deal to reflect the fog. Then a veritable cavalcade arrived, a chaos of prancing horses and rattling hooves. Within moments, the hitherto silent wharf was transformed into a riot of movement and noise. Lights began to burn in the nearby houses, as residents roused themselves from their slumbers to see what was happening.

'The Adventurers,' whispered Williamson, although Chaloner and Thurloe did not need to be told. 'They are early, damn it! Is there *nothing* that will not conspire against us today? I was hoping for more time, to give my men a chance to return.'

'No hope of that,' said Lester grimly. 'As you said, we are on our own.'

Chaloner watched helplessly as half the Court disgorged from the coaches and aimed for *Katherine*'s gangway. Leighton scurried forward to greet O'Brien and Kitty, who were both clearly looking forward to what promised to be an unusual occasion. Brodrick was there, too, although there was no sign of Hyde. After them came Grey, Dugdale, Edgeman, Buckingham, Lady Castlemaine and other wealthy and influential people. They assembled in a noisy, chattering throng before being assisted aboard by men in uniforms. The escorts' unsteadiness on the gangway said they were not sailors, but White Hall servants dressed to emulate them.

'Was *Jane* here when you arrived?' Chaloner asked Williamson. There was no answer, and he looked to see the Spymaster transfixed by the sight of his friend's wife.

'Should I go to her?' the Spymaster asked in a whisper, more to himself than the others. 'Warn her that mischief is afoot, and that she should leave without delay?'

'Yes,' replied Chaloner. 'And tell her to take everyone else with her.'

'Tom is right,' said Thurloe, after a moment. 'I know it is not for mere spymasters to cancel such occasions – I faced similar restrictions when I held your post – but this is too grave a matter to take chances with. Go to Leighton, explain your concerns.'

'And what if *he* is the master?' asked Williamson wretchedly. 'It will tell him that we are suspicious, and we will have lost our only advantage – the element of surprise.'

'True,' nodded Lester. 'So we had better hold off until we have a clearer idea of their plans.'

'What about Tom's question?' asked Thurloe, giving the captain a glance full of dark suspicion. 'Was *Jane* here when you arrived?'

'Yes,' replied Lester. 'I went aboard briefly, but she was deserted.'

'Surely that is odd?' asked Chaloner. 'I would not leave a ship without a guard in Queenhithe.'

'Neither would I,' said Lester. 'Perhaps the crew had wind of the Adventurers' attack, and decided to scarper. I do not blame them – I would not give *my* life protecting a wreck like *Jane*.'

'Maybe we are worrying over nothing,' said Williamson in sudden hope. 'The Adventurers will not attack her now – not while they are enjoying themselves on the boat next door.'

'True,' acknowledged Thurloe. 'However, the Piccadilly Company's plan is still set to unfold, and that has always promised to be the more deadly.'

'Perhaps not even that will happen if Fitzgerald's master fails to kill Pratt,' persisted Williamson. 'You say you sent a man to warn Pratt – that may be enough to retard the entire scheme.'

It was a pleasant thought, but Chaloner did not believe it. He took a deep breath in an effort to summon some energy. 'Regardless, we are doing no good in here.

We need to go aboard *Katherine* and find out what is happening.'

'I will come with you,' offered Lester immediately.

'No,' said Thurloe sharply. 'He does not need your help.'

'He does,' countered Lester sharply. 'I know my way around ships. He does not.'

'Quite,' murmured Thurloe in Chaloner's ear. 'He will have an unfair advantage.'

'Perhaps we should all go,' suggested Williamson worriedly. 'Two of you will not be able to do much, but four . . .'

'You should stay here and be ready to deploy your men, should they return,' said Lester practically. 'Besides, it is only a reconnaissance mission. We do not intend to do anything.'

'Very well,' said Williamson. 'But be careful.'

'Yes,' said Thurloe pointedly, his eyes boring into Chaloner's. 'Be *very* careful.'

Chaloner followed Lester towards the ships, acutely aware of being watched by Thurloe and Williamson. Or was it other eyes that made the hair stand up on the back of his neck, as it always did when he was in danger? Fitzgerald, perhaps, or his master? Because whatever Lester said, Chaloner was certain the pirate would *not* have left *Jane* unprotected, especially given that a heavily armed warship containing a lot of Adventurers was moored next to her.

There were two gangways attached to *Katherine*. The one the Adventurers had used boasted streamers and carpets, and led to the aft end of the upper gun deck. The other was a narrow service entry through a gunport at the bow, intended for crew. A footman had been stationed at the top of the former to deter gatecrashers, and when his back was turned, Chaloner aimed for the second.

'There is something odd about *Jane*'s trim,' said Lester, pausing halfway up the plank to study her. Chaloner grabbed his arm and pulled him on, horrified that he should dawdle when they might be being watched. 'She is strangely heavy in the bows.'

'Perhaps only the back half of her has been unloaded.'

Lester smirked at this lack of nautical knowledge. 'It is more likely that she is taking on water.'

'The Adventurers will be pleased, then,' said Chaloner, squeezing through the gunport. 'If she sinks, they will not have to worry about burning her.'

Once on board, he paused to gain his bearings. *Katherine* was rich with the scent of new wood and tar, and he was immediately aware of the rhythmic creak of her timbers as she rocked on the ebbing tide. The guests were in the stern, and there was already a lot of noise – the clink of goblets, the plummy laughter of men who were well pleased with themselves, and the banter of lively conversation. Lester caught Chaloner's arm.

'They will be in the Great Cabin – that is the big room at the other end of the ship. It is the only space large enough for a party their size. Go there, and see what is happening.'

'Where will you be?'

'Looking at the rest of the vessel to see whether there is anything unusual. You will appreciate that I am better qualified to do it than you.'

Chaloner felt a twinge of misgiving, but nodded anyway. His unease intensified as he travelled the whole length of *Katherine* without encountering another person. Surely there should be servants present, managing matters behind the scenes as their masters socialised? Men to broach casks of wine, or prepare refreshments? Or sailors to ensure that ignorant landsmen did not tamper with something that might later cause problems at sea?

He reached the Great Cabin and peered around the door, expecting at any moment to be grabbed and an explanation demanded for his presence. Inside, the Adventurers were enjoying themselves. Leighton was serving rum – familiar to sailors, but still a rarity in London – from a large barrel in the centre of the room, and although there were winces at the taste, all were willing to endure it for the sake of novelty.

There was an atmosphere of jollity, which intensified when O'Brien picked up a fiddle that had been left lying artistically on a chest and began to play a medley of sea-jigs. A few people started to sing, while others spoke more loudly to make themselves heard. Drink was spilled as sloppy toasts were made, and the reek of it was strong in the crowded room.

Not everyone had given themselves over to rowdy entertainment, however. Dugdale and Edgeman stood near the door, their faces taut and expectant. Were they waiting for something to happen, or were they just uneasy after the Earl's earlier words about dismissing members of his staff who were Adventurers? Grey was another who seemed ill at ease, and so was Swaddell, while Brodrick was clutching his stomach, claiming he was seasick.

Chaloner was about to leave when Dugdale happened to glance in his direction. Their eyes locked. The Chief Usher opened his mouth and an accusatory finger started to rise. Chaloner did not wait to find out whether anyone would be interested to hear that interlopers were aboard. He turned and ran back the way he had come. There were raised voices behind him, but he could not tell whether they were simply those of men – and women – made boisterous by the consumption of strong drink, or whether some sort of chase was in progress.

Unwilling to be ejected before he had learned anything useful, Chaloner aimed for the lower decks, sliding down three ladders in the hope that any pursuers would assume he had aimed for the gangway, and would not expect him to move deeper inside the ship. When he was sure the ruse had worked, he began to walk forward, intending to find a different set of steps to take him back to the Great Cabin's level.

He was surprised to see lamps had been left burning at regular intervals, and wondered whether Leighton planned to open the entire vessel to the Adventurers later – and whether they would treat it with the same careless abandon that they treated Temperance's club. Regardless, it was risky to leave unattended flames in a structure that was made of wood.

He whipped around suddenly when he heard a click behind him. It was Lester, and he was holding a gun.

'That is far enough,' the captain said softly. 'It is time this matter was ended.'

Chapter 12

Chaloner gaped at the dag that Lester held. Then he saw it was not pointing at him, but at someone hiding in the shadows behind him. He turned to see Fitzgerald. The pirate stepped into the circle of light cast by the lamp, moving with a haughty confidence that immediately set alarm bells ringing in Chaloner's mind. Before he could draw his own weapons or shout a warning to Lester, Brinkes and his henchmen emerged from the darkness, too. All carried guns and daggers.

Undeterred, Lester took aim at Fitzgerald, intending to shoot him anyway, but ducked when a knife hurtled towards him. It missed by the merest fraction, and the gun flashed in the pan. Without waiting to see what happened to Lester, Chaloner hauled his sword from its scabbard and launched himself at Brinkes, hoping the speed of his attack would catch the henchman off guard.

But Brinkes was no novice in the art of skirmishing. He feinted away and brought his gun down hard on Chaloner's wrist, forcing him to drop the blade. Chaloner was reaching for his knife before the sword hit the floor, but the others also reacted with commendable speed, and it was not long before he was overwhelmed. Powerful hands grabbed him, and when he finally stopped struggling, he saw that Lester had been similarly secured.

'Do not bother to shout for help,' said Brinkes, his face bright with the prospect of violence to come. 'You will not be heard, not above the racket the Adventurers are making.'

'Hold them tight,' ordered Fitzgerald in his piping treble. His single eye glittered. 'We do not want them to interfere with our plans.'

'What plans?' demanded Lester.

'I am not inclined to discuss them with you,' replied Fitzgerald coldly.

Although it was not the first time Chaloner had been in the pirate's presence, it was the first time he had seen him commanding troops. Fitzgerald's manner was calm and self-assured, and the men he had hired were professionals who followed his orders unthinkingly. With a growing sense of alarm, Chaloner finally began to understand why Thurloe considered him such a formidable adversary.

Footsteps caused everyone to glance towards the stairs. It was Harley, whose eyebrows shot up in surprise when he saw that prisoners had been taken.

'The man who has been asking questions,' he said, regarding Chaloner with contempt. 'You have been a nuisance ever since you realised the Piccadilly Company might make you rich.'

'Will it?' asked Chaloner innocently. 'How?'

Harley sneered at him. 'I am no more inclined to answer questions now than I was a week ago.'

'Then let me answer them,' said Chaloner quickly, when Harley nodded to Brinkes, who cocked his pistol and aimed it at Lester. 'You want the Queen discredited, so Tangier will return to Portugal – away from the hands of the Adventurers. You have a sympathetic governor in Bridges, but he is greedy and demands too much—'

'Enough,' snapped Harley. 'Shoot them, Brinkes. We do not have time to deal with captives, and these two are too dangerous to leave alive.'

'No!' countered Fitzgerald, as Brinkes prepared to obey. 'Their yells may not carry, but gunshots will, and we do not want any alarms. I know how to dispose of them with no risk to ourselves.'

He gave Harley a significant look, causing the colonel to smile slowly as understanding dawned. Chaloner suppressed the unsettling images that immediately flooded into his mind, and forced himself to concentrate.

'Murder,' he said, looking hard at Harley. 'But that is no stranger to you, is it? I know it was you who killed Reyner and Newell. And Reyner's mother, too.'

'Liar!' snarled Harley, although the alarm in his eyes told anyone who saw it that the accusation was true. He turned to Fitzgerald. 'He is just trying to make trouble. Ignore him.'

'Reyner was beginning to weaken,' Chaloner went on. 'So you gave him a paper written in the Vigenère cipher, which you said was a list of enemies and would protect him. But it did nothing to reduce his agitation, so you killed him, lest he cracked.'

'Reyner would not have cracked,' said Harley, although his voice lacked certainty.

'Vigenère cipher?' asked Fitzgerald rather dangerously. 'Not a letter from our master?'

'Of course not,' said Harley quickly. 'It was a copy

429

of one I once sent to Teviot, describing Jews Hill. I do not know why Reyner agreed to meet Chaloner in the Gaming House, but it would not have been to reveal all.'

'Reyner made an assignation?' asked Fitzgerald. 'Then it seems you were right to dispatch him.'

Harley had evidently not anticipated approval, because his expression was one of confusion. 'I did not . . . It was . . . But never mind this. Brinkes, bring the prisoners over here.'

'Newell suspected you were Reyner's killer, so you murdered him, too,' said Chaloner, as Brinkes moved to obey. He was guessing, but the immediate anger in Harley's face said he was right. 'You went to a gunsmith, and ordered a dag with special modifications. It killed him as he demonstrated it in St James's Park.'

'How very interesting,' said Fitzgerald flatly, fingering his enormous beard.

'And you strangled Reyner's mother because—'

'Because she could not keep her mouth shut,' snarled Harley, cutting across him and addressing Fitzgerald. 'Reyner confided in her, but she gossiped, especially when she was drunk. It was necessary, and I would do the same again.'

'You *have* been busy on our behalf,' mused Fitzgerald softly. 'Very busy.'

Chaloner continued his attack on Harley, aiming to widen the rift that was beginning to open. 'I know why you murdered Teviot, too – he was an Adventurer who made it difficult for *Jane* to trade. But was it really necessary to slaughter his soldiers as well?'

'Of course,' said Harley, continuing to speak to Fitzgerald. 'Because if we had poisoned or shot him, eyebrows would have been raised – our master made that perfectly clear. His plan saw Barbary corsairs blamed instead.'

'Not true,' countered Fitzgerald softly. 'There are rumours of an official inquiry. I told him he could not trust the corsairs not to blab about the arrangement you made with them, and I was right.'

'They did not blab.' Harley pointed an accusing finger at Chaloner. '*He* started those tales to frighten Reyner and Newell. There is no truth in them.'

He snatched the firearm from Brinkes and there was murder in his eyes as he pointed it at Chaloner. But before he could pull the trigger, Fitzgerald stepped forward and brought the butt of his own gun down on Harley's head. The sound it made was unpleasant, and the scout dropped to the floor, where he lay twitching.

'I *said* no gunfire,' declared Fitzgerald, with a marked lack of emotion. 'Open a gunport and tip him out, Brinkes. We do not want the Adventurers finding him if they wander down here.'

Brinkes hasted to oblige. Lester's face was white with shock, although Chaloner was not sure whether it was because a murder had just been committed in front of him, or because he had just realised the extent of the danger he was in.

Once Harley had been unceremoniously dumped overboard, Fitzgerald became businesslike. He turned to leave, indicating that the captives were to be brought, too.

'Why take the risk?' asked Brinkes. 'Hit *them* over the head and toss them out.'

'One corpse might be overlooked,' explained Fitzgerald shortly. 'But three will cause consternation among our

431

enemies if they are seen. Do as I say, please, or we shall have words.'

Brinkes obeyed with alacrity, although he took the precaution of tying the prisoners' hands first, and of searching them for weapons. Chaloner lost three knives, and Lester one.

When Brinkes was satisfied, Chaloner and Lester were shoved towards *Katherine*'s stern, some two decks below where the Adventurers were carousing. On any other night, they would have been seen from the warehouse – it was now fully light – but the fog had thickened, and nothing of the quay was visible. Lester opened his mouth to yell, but was silenced by a slap from Fitzgerald.

'You will make me angry if you try to raise the alarm,' the pirate said mildly. 'Come quietly, and we might still be friends. You and I were once shipmates, after all.'

But Chaloner knew he planned to kill them. He also knew that shouting would be futile: the Adventurers would not hear over the racket they were making, and even if Thurloe and Williamson did, it would take more than a word or two to explain what was happening – and he and Lester would be dead long before they could accomplish that. He turned his mind to escape, but Brinkes and his henchmen were watchful, and he knew any attempt to run would fail.

Brinkes slid through a gunport and landed lightly on *Jane*'s afterdeck, which was no more than the height of a man below them. He indicated Chaloner and Lester were to follow. It was not easy with their hands tied, and both landed awkwardly. Lester sniffed as he struggled to his feet.

'There is an odd stench on this ship. Alcohol and—'

'You will find out soon enough,' said Brinkes, shoving him forward. 'Now move.'

Chaloner was also aware of the peculiar smell. He looked around for the source as he stumbled after Lester, but could see nothing amiss. To gain more time, he exaggerated his limp.

'Hurry,' snapped Brinkes, giving him a push. Chaloner fell to his knees in order to earn a few more seconds, causing Fitzgerald to glare and Brinkes to swear under his breath.

'He was shot last night,' explained Lester quickly, stepping between Chaloner and Brinkes's fist. 'He cannot move quickly.'

'That did not stop him earlier,' said Fitzgerald, 'when he was racing around *Katherine* with a view to learning our plans. He might have discovered them, too, had we not been expecting him.'

'Expecting me? But how . . .' And then Chaloner understood. 'You knew we were coming! You were waiting for us, and we walked directly into your arms.'

Fitzgerald smiled coldly. 'We were expecting a better show, to be frank. Williamson and Thurloe should have managed something a little more impressive than a bumbling sea-officer and a worn-out Parliamentarian spy.'

'What is he talking about, Chaloner?' whispered Lester. 'How did he know we were coming?'

'Because he was warned,' replied Chaloner. He nodded to where a flash of red ribbon indicated that someone was watching from behind a hatch. 'Lydcott did not go to St Paul's to save Pratt from being murdered – he ran straight to Fitzgerald, the man who has turned his paltry glassware business into a lucrative concern.'

* * *

There was a pause, and then Lydcott stepped into the open. He shrugged apologetically, and his expression was sheepish as he addressed Chaloner.

'I had to think of myself,' he said. 'I owe more to Mr Fitzgerald than I do to Thurloe, who never does anything but criticise me. I am sorry you must die, but it cannot be helped—'

'Has there been any activity?' asked Fitzgerald, cutting across him impatiently.

Lydcott shook his head. 'Williamson came past, pretending to be drunk as he surveyed us, but he did not linger. No one suspects anything – although that might change if Thurloe thinks Chaloner is taking too long. They are friends, and he will come to find out what has happened to him.'

'Let him,' said Fitzgerald. 'Come with us, Lydcott. Yorke can stand guard now.'

'Come where?' asked Lydcott uneasily.

'To view *Jane*'s holds,' replied Fitzgerald smoothly. 'They are quite a sight.'

He led the way to one of the hatches, with Lydcott following and Chaloner behind them. Then came Brinkes, Lester and three henchmen. Chaloner hesitated, aware that once he stepped off the open deck he might never escape, but Brinkes fingered his dagger, and Chaloner sensed there was nothing he would like more than to use it. Reluctantly, he did as he was told.

'I should have known you were a villain,' he said to Lydcott as they went. He spoke softly, so Fitzgerald would not hear; the pirate was humming to himself, which helped. 'At the Banqueting House, you pretended to laugh at the way Pratt was monitoring Meneses. But the reality was that it was you who was minding him – as Fitzgerald had no doubt ordered you to do.'

'He did ask me to ensure that Meneses stayed out of mischief,' acknowledged Lydcott.

'And then you killed him. Thurloe and Pratt both praised your skill with horses, and Meneses was trampled by one. You knew exactly how to arrange an "accident" without risk to yourself.'

Lydcott shrugged. 'He was selling our secrets to the Adventurers. Fitzgerald had no choice but to order his execution.'

Chaloner wondered what it was about Fitzgerald that compelled people to do what he asked – Lydcott committing murder and betraying a kinsman who had never been anything but kind to him; Brinkes to look the other way while Harley was clubbed to death; all manner of people to join the Piccadilly Company. He could only suppose it was the promise of riches to come.

'Did you kill Pratt, too?' he asked. 'At St Paul's?'

'I lied,' said Lydcott, rather proudly. 'I was not summoned to St Paul's, and neither was Pratt. I came straight here instead. And you and Thurloe did not suspect a thing!'

'No, but we should have done.' Chaloner was as disgusted with himself as with Lydcott. 'The clues were there to identify you as a villain. For example, you told Thurloe that the Piccadilly Company would not meet until next week, but there was a gathering on Sunday. You were there, but in disguise – I recognised your voice. You were sitting with your back to the window.'

Lydcott's jaw dropped. 'You spied on us? My God! I was right to warn Fitzgerald: you *are* a danger! Just wait until I tell him! He will be sure to give me the little bonus I requested now.'

'You are demanding a bigger share of the profits?' asked Chaloner. 'Then you will die tonight, too. I wondered why he wanted you below decks, but it is obvious now.'

'You understand nothing!' said Lydcott, loudly and angrily. 'He appreciates my skills.'

Fitzgerald whipped around. 'No talking, or I will cut out your tongues. Both of you.'

Chaloner could see he meant it, and thought that while Lydcott was not quite the empty-headed fool he had assumed, he was still unspeakably stupid.

It was dark inside *Jane*, and the lamp Fitzgerald lit was the kind that was used during storms at sea – one that would not break if it fell over, spilling fuel that would cause a fire. The odd aroma was much stronger, but there was no time to analyse it as they were ordered to descend a series of stairs. Then all that could be smelled was bad water and rotting wood.

'They have not kept her seaworthy,' murmured Lester. 'She is taking on water, and will sink in the next serious blow. No wonder she looks heavy in the bows.'

He was proven right when they reached a flooded hold. Brinkes jumped in, and indicated that Chaloner and Lester were to follow, while Fitzgerald, Lydcott and the three henchmen watched from the ladder. The waist-deep water was bitingly cold, and as they waded forwards, Chaloner felt something crunching under his feet: gravel. When they reached a post, Brinkes secured them to it.

'It will be over soon,' called Lydcott sympathetically. 'You do not have long to suffer.'

Fitzgerald moved fast, and before Chaloner could

shout a warning he had brought the butt of his gun down hard on Lydcott's head. Lydcott swayed for a moment, then plummeted into the water.

'Another risk eliminated,' announced Fitzgerald with chilling blandness. He began to hum again.

It was completely silent in *Jane*'s hold, and not even the carousing from the Adventurers could be heard. Lydcott floated face down in the water, his arms out to the side, and Fitzgerald and his men watched Brinkes finish tying Chaloner and Lester to the post. When it was done, the henchmen moved away, but Fitzgerald lingered, nodding approvingly from his dry perch on the stairs as Brinkes gave his knots a final check.

'You will be next, Brinkes,' whispered Lester. 'Fitzgerald is singing, and he always does that before dispatching someone. You—'

'Let him go, Lester,' said Chaloner. He tried to sound calm, but his stomach churned with agitation. 'We have nothing to say to the likes of him.'

'Fitzgerald will kill you, Brinkes,' Lester went on, ignoring him. 'You are a risk, too, no matter what he tells you now.'

'Lies,' whispered Brinkes. 'You do not know what you are talking—'

'What are you muttering about down there?' called Fitzgerald, causing Brinkes to leap away from the prisoners in alarm and begin to wade back towards the steps.

'If we are going to die, then at least tell us the name of the man who is behind all this,' shouted Lester, boldly defiant as he glared at the pirate. 'We know it is not you.'

'Do you indeed?' Fitzgerald sounded amused. 'How?'

'Do not answer him,' warned Chaloner. 'Or he will race down the ladder and beat *your* brains out.'

'Better that than whatever else he has planned,' Lester muttered back. 'Besides, I want answers.'

'We do not need them,' said Chaloner, wanting Fitzgerald gone from the hold so he could think about how to escape while there was still time. 'It is—'

'Because you are not clever enough, you damned pirate,' yelled Lester. 'Or rich enough. And do not say that Lydcott's glassware venture gives you funds, because we all know that is untrue.'

Chaloner tensed, expecting swift and brutal retaliation, but Fitzgerald only laughed. 'Then you will die in ignorance, because I am not inclined to confide in you. And I am not a pirate, by the way, I am a privateer.'

'Tell us what you plan to do,' shouted Lester, as Brinkes reached the ladder and began to ascend. 'It involves alcohol and something else . . .'

'For God's sake, Lester!' hissed Chaloner urgently. 'Just let them go, so we can turn our minds to escape. You are wasting time with your banter.'

'Poor *Jane*,' said Fitzgerald, leaning down to give a beam an affectionate pat. 'She has served me well, but her timbers are rotten, and it is time to put her to another use.'

'Gunpowder!' yelled Lester in sudden understanding, although Chaloner had grasped the significance of what he had smelled the moment they stepped aboard – along with the fact that Fitzgerald was willing to sacrifice a ship that was a virtual wreck anyway.

'Yes, he intends to blow her up,' Chaloner snarled. 'And I imagine there are enough explosives on board to

438

destroy *Jane*, *Katherine*, and half of Queenhithe. Now just shut up and let him—'

'My master will be rid of the Adventurers once and for all,' called Fitzgerald gloatingly. '*And* a pair of irritating spymasters into the bargain. Thurloe and Williamson will perish in the blast, too.'

'You cannot!' cried Lester in horror. 'There must be two hundred people on *Katherine*, including women and servants. It would be a terrible massacre!'

'But not our master's first,' said Fitzgerald with a cold smile. 'As Lord Teviot could attest, were he still in the land of the living. Are we ready, Brinkes? Is everything in place?'

Brinkes nodded. 'All that remains is to set the fires. Shall I remove the gangways, to ensure no one can get off *Katherine*?'

Fitzgerald laughed, and the shrill, mad sound of it filled the hold. 'Do not bother: our explosion will obliterate Queenhithe, and it will not matter if our enemies are aboard or on the quayside. They will die regardless.'

There was a thump and sudden darkness as Fitzgerald disappeared through the hatch and slammed it closed. Chaloner willed his footsteps to retreat, knowing that he and Lester did not have much time.

'What are we going to do?' asked Lester brokenly. 'I do not care for myself – I have cheated death too often already in my years at sea. But all those innocents in the Great Cabin . . .'

'Hardly innocents,' said Chaloner, listening to ensure their captors had gone before making his move. 'They are wealthy Adventurers, who intend to make themselves richer by trading in slaves.'

439

'But their wives are with them,' cried Lester. 'Besides, I am sure we could make some of them see reason. Grey, for example. He would condemn the slave trade if he understood what it entails – he is not a bad man.'

Chaloner thought Lester was deluded if he believed he could persuade a lot of very rich people to forgo an easy way to make more money. But there was something refreshingly decent about Lester's optimism, and he respected him for it.

Then there was a series of scrapes and rattles.

'What is that?' Chaloner asked in alarm.

'Someone climbing down the side of the ship,' explained Lester. 'The scoundrels must be making their escape by river. The fog will help – Williamson and Thurloe will never see them.'

But Chaloner was more interested in trying to avert an atrocity than in Fitzgerald's movements.

'Quickly!' he urged. 'Up the stairs.'

'How? My hands are tied so tight that I can barely move . . . but I can! We are free! How in God's name did you manage that?'

'With Wiseman's scalpel,' explained Chaloner, grateful that Brinkes had missed it. He shoved Lester towards the ladder. 'Why do you think I wanted you to stop talking? Now, hurry!'

Lester was gone in a trice, feeling his way in the darkness much more efficiently than Chaloner, and running up the ladder with the ease of the experienced seaman. Fortunately, Fitzgerald had not deemed it necessary to bar the hatch, and it opened easily. Beyond was nothing but darkness.

'The gunpowder will be on the upper deck,' whispered Lester, grabbing Chaloner's sleeve and leading him unerringly along a companionway and then up another flight of steps. It was there that the reek of the bilges gave way to the sharper, cleaner scent of explosives.

'At least we know why Fitzgerald used storm lamps,' said Chaloner. 'He did not want to blow himself up with stray sparks.'

The moment he spoke, he became aware of smoke and the crackle of flames: fires had been lit. He began to move faster, but stopped abruptly when they reached the upper deck and the dim light of another lantern revealed just how many barrels of gunpowder Fitzgerald had acquired. There were more than he could count, and would certainly destroy the quay. Worse, sparks from the resulting explosion might set the surrounding buildings alight, and the conflagration could easily spread. Lester darted to several separate hatches, then swore as he turned to face Chaloner.

'Fires have been set in three different parts of the ship, all splashed with alcohol to make them spread.' His face was white. 'All will need to be doused if we are to prevent the kegs from igniting. But by the time we have one under control, the others will be beyond us.'

Chaloner ran to the nearest gunport and peered at the water below. It moved sluggishly as the current tugged it towards the sea. He whipped around, grabbed the nearest barrel and hurled it overboard. It sank, but then bobbed to the surface a moment later, where, half-submerged, it began to drift away. Would it be enough? He hoped so. He reached for another but it was heavy and his injured shoulder prevented him from throwing it as far as he would have liked.

'I will not be able to lob them all overboard before the fires take hold,' he explained quickly, reaching for a

441

third. 'But I should be able to manage enough to reduce the impact. Go and warn the Adventurers. Hurry!'

Lester did a quick survey. 'You are right! We can foil these evil bastards and save the quay!'

Chaloner heaved the barrel overboard. 'Yes, now raise the alarm.'

'No.' Lester snatched up a keg and pitched it through the hole. It fell much farther out than Chaloner's had done, and was towed away more quickly. 'I know which part of the deck to clear first – you do not, as evidenced by the barrels you have chosen to grab. Moreover, I have not been shot, and can work more efficiently. *You* warn the Adventurers.'

'It is only a scratch,' said Chaloner, struggling to lift the next cask. 'You said so yourself.'

'I lied,' said Lester, snatching it from him. 'Now go and save those people before it is too late.'

'I left you once. At Elliot's grave. I cannot do it again.'

'It is hardly the same.' Lester gave him a vigorous shove, then smiled lopsidedly. 'Look after Ruth for me, because if Williamson puts her in Bedlam, it will be you I come back to haunt. It has been an honour serving with you, Tom. Now go before I toss *you* overboard.'

Chaloner could think of no trite declaration of friendship to make in return. With a final, agonised glance, he turned and clambered up the final set of stairs, sickened by the knowledge that he was exchanging the life of a good man for a lot of ruthless merchants who traded in slaves.

In *Katherine*'s Great Cabin, the Adventurers had finished the rum and were looking for something else to drink. There was a lot of discontented mumbling, because

442

Leighton had gone to fetch wine some time ago, and had not returned. Also notable by their absence were Dugdale and Edgeman.

'I will look for Leighton,' Brodrick was offering, transparently grateful for an excuse to be back on *terra firma*. 'He cannot have gone far. Play the fiddle again, O'Brien. It is—'

Chaloner burst among them, urgently enough to make Kitty issue a squeal of alarm. He supposed he did look desperate – dirty, sodden and reeking of bilge-water.

'The ship next to you is going to blow up,' he gasped. 'Everyone needs to leave. Now!'

'*Jane?*' asked O'Brien in surprise. 'I seriously doubt anyone would waste powder on that old tub. Indeed, I am surprised she survived her voyage up the Thames.'

There was a chorus of agreement, but Brodrick knew Chaloner well enough to see that he was not in jest. He took command and ordered everyone out. Unfortunately, his uncharacteristic display of authority caused immediate panic, and it took him and Swaddell at the stairs, and Chaloner at the gangway, to ensure there was not a stampede. As many Adventurers were drunk and others were weak with terror, the evacuation took far longer than it should have done. Williamson and Thurloe, quick to comprehend what was happening, hurried to direct people to a safe distance.

'Where are you going?' shouted Thurloe, as Chaloner fought his way through the last Adventurers waiting to disembark and began to run towards *Jane*.

'Lester needs help,' yelled Chaloner over his shoulder. 'He—'

'No!' Thurloe raced after him and grabbed the flying tails of his coat. 'It will be too late.'

Chaloner struggled free, but Thurloe stuck out a foot that sent him sprawling. Even as he started to rise, there was a tremendous explosion. Heat washed over him, and had he not been protected by the mass of *Katherine*, he would certainly have been blown to pieces. When he was able to look up, it was to see *Jane*'s masts toppling with a series of tearing groans. Every timber and sail was a bright cluster of flames.

He whipped around in alarm, fearing for Thurloe, but the ex-Spymaster had thrown himself to the ground, and was covering his head with his hands as fragments of burning wood began to rain down. When the treacherous fallout had finished, Chaloner scrambled upright on unsteady legs. *Jane* was a mass of blazing stays and spars that made the fog glow amber, while *Katherine* was battle-scarred and alight in a dozen places, but still afloat.

'He did it,' he whispered. 'Lester saved *Katherine* and Queenhithe.'

Williamson arrived, looking around wildly. 'Did you see Kitty leave? And Swaddell?'

'I am here.' Swaddell materialised out of the fog like a spectre. He shot his master a pained glance. 'It seems we infiltrated the wrong group – it was not the Adventurers I should have been watching, but the Piccadilly Company.'

'You did your best.' Williamson's face was a mask of agitation. 'Kitty?'

'I saw her escape,' said Swaddell soothingly. 'Do not worry. O'Brien will look after her.'

'So is this the atrocity Fitzgerald and his master plotted?' asked Thurloe, while Williamson winced at the blunt reminder that the object of his affections was married to his friend. 'The murder of half the Court and the upper echelons of government?'

'Yes, and they did not care that it might destroy Queenhithe, too,' said Swaddell in disgust. 'But where is Lester? I did not see him leave *Katherine.*'

Chaloner did not reply, and only stared at the burning remnants of *Jane.*

Williamson's face fell, and he closed his eyes. 'Damn!' he whispered. 'Damn!'

For a long moment, no one did anything except stare at Jane's blazing masts and spars. Then Thurloe grabbed Chaloner's arm and shook it.

'We must avenge Lester's sacrifice by laying hold of Fitzgerald and his master. They will not get away with this – we will not let them.'

'Fitzgerald escaped by boat,' said Chaloner numbly. 'He could be anywhere by now.'

'Would he go to the Crown?' asked Swaddell.

'Too obvious,' said Thurloe. 'He is not a fool. Yet I imagine he *will* be with his Piccadilly Company cronies. They will want to gloat over the triumph they think they have won.'

'If it is of any help, I just saw Pratt leap on a horse and gallop off at a colossal speed,' said Swaddell. 'I wondered what he was doing here, because he is not an Adventurer. However, he *is* a member of the Piccadilly Company . . .'

'Fitzgerald summoned him to St Paul's earlier,' said Thurloe, bemused. 'To be murdered.'

'It was a lie.' Chaloner was still too stunned by Lester's death to give details. 'Lydcott never went to St Paul's, and Pratt did not, either. In fact, I think *he* might be Fitzgerald's master.'

'Pratt?' asked Williamson in patent disbelief. 'What

reason could he have for wanting courtiers dead? He will view them as potential clients.'

'Besides,' added Thurloe, more gently, 'he is the one whose murder was—'

'There *is* no plot to kill him.' Chaloner jumped when a dull roar indicated that a stray spark had caught one of the wooden warehouses. 'There never was – the Piccadilly Company just wanted the Queen accused of it. Pratt was never in any danger, which explains why he was never very concerned.'

'Chaloner has a point,' said Swaddell to Williamson. '*I* would not have been happy if *I* had been threatened with death and the likes of Sergeant Wright had been hired to protect me. Yet Pratt was indifferent. Indeed, I heard him tell people he was flattered by it.'

'I suppose he might be the master,' conceded Williamson. 'He is wealthy enough to finance the Piccadilly Company's activities. But we can examine motives later, when he is arrested. The question we should be asking now is: where has he gone?'

There was a sudden yell from Brodrick: flames from the burning warehouse were threatening to spread to its neighbours.

'Clarendon House,' said Chaloner, as all became clear. 'I wondered how he had come to raise the alarm earlier, when Hyde and I were doing battle with Oliver. I imagine he went there to ensure that all was ready, and found it full of brick-thieves instead.'

'To ensure all was ready for what?' asked Thurloe.

'To receive the cargo *Jane* brought,' explained Chaloner. 'They will need to store it somewhere safe, and Clarendon House has a lockable vault.'

'What cargo?' demanded Williamson.

'Something that was concealed in *Jane*'s consignment of gravel,' explained Chaloner. 'Jewels or precious metals from Tangier, perhaps. It will not be bulky – she could not have coped with that – so I imagine it is no more than a chest or two. Fitzgerald took a risk, though. He has already lost one fortune on a ship that could not withstand a storm.'

'He had no choice,' said Swaddell. '*Jane* is the only vessel he has left.'

'But Clarendon House is too public, surely?' objected Williamson. 'It will be full of workmen.'

'Not in the small hours of the morning, which is when *Jane* arrived.' Something else became clear to Chaloner, too. 'Hyde and Oliver denied paying Wright to linger in the Crown tonight, but someone did. It was not Pratt, because Wright would have told me, so one of the other Piccadilly Company members must have done it – Fitzgerald or another of his accomplices.'

More shouting drew their attention. A second warehouse was alight, and although people were rallying to douse the flames, their efforts were disorganised and ineffectual.

'My instincts scream at me to go to Clarendon House,' said Williamson, agitated. 'Yet I cannot leave courtiers to fight this inferno. I doubt they will contain it, and half the city could be lost.'

'Stay and do your duty,' instructed Thurloe. 'Tom and I will deal with Fitzgerald and Pratt.'

'I will send help if my men return from Woolwich,' promised Williamson. 'In the meantime, take my sword and dagger, Chaloner. You should not attempt this unarmed.'

*　　*　　*

447

Thurloe set off at a run, Chaloner at his heels. A number of private coaches had parked in Thames Street, and loath to miss any of the excitement, their wealthy Adventurer-owners and their drivers had not fled the scene, but had lingered. Some were helping with the fire, but most were there as ghoulish spectators, eager to witness first-hand what promised to be a serious conflagration. With cool aplomb, Thurloe commandeered one of the carriages, and they were soon galloping towards Piccadilly at a speed that was far from safe when fog meant that neither the driver nor the horses could see where they were going.

Thurloe closed his eyes when he heard what had happened to Lydcott, but opened them to listen without interruption as Chaloner told him everything he had seen, heard and deduced on *Jane*.

'I am not sure you are right about Pratt,' the ex-Spymaster said when he had finished. 'I know you have good reasons for accusing him, but I remain unconvinced.'

'We might have known for certain if you had not forced me to make that ridiculous promise,' said Chaloner bitterly, clinging to the carriage's side as it lurched across a pothole. 'I could have tackled Fitzgerald and had answers directly.'

'You would have been dead,' said Thurloe harshly. 'He is not in the habit of revealing all to anyone who asks. But never mind recriminations: we need a plan of attack, because if we charge into Clarendon House without one, he will kill us. How many helpmeets will he have?'

Chaloner swore when the coach swerved so violently that he was almost hurled out. 'Brinkes and his men number about a dozen. Then there are thirty members of the Piccadilly Company . . .'

'I doubt all of them are involved,' said Thurloe. 'Some will have been recruited to provide a veneer of respectability and funds for investments.'

'Even so, you were reckless when you offered to confront them. I doubt we will succeed.'

'Of course we will,' said Thurloe with quiet determination. 'We shall use our wits. Now think of something – *anything* – that might give us an edge over them.'

Chaloner racked his brains. 'The secret passages . . .'

He reached into his coat and retrieved the roll of plans he had taken from Oliver. Fortunately, they had been tucked high enough to avoid a soaking when he had been forced into *Jane*'s flooded hold. He handed them to Thurloe, then clung on for dear life as the coach rounded a corner. For a moment, only two wheels were on the road, but then the others came down with a bone-jarring thump, and they picked up speed again.

It was not easy to read when the carriage was pitching about like a ship in a storm. Chaloner glanced out of the window once and hoped the driver knew where he was because he could tell nothing from the occasional flash of building through the mist. Then he glimpsed the familiar line of the Gaming House walls. They were almost there.

'The Crown is all shut up,' said Thurloe, who was looking in the opposite direction. 'I am sure you are right to predict that these villains will go to Clarendon House.'

'Have you thought of a plan yet?' Chaloner banged on the ceiling to make the driver stop. It would not be a good idea to hurtle up to the front gates and warn their enemies of their arrival.

Thurloe regarded him sombrely. 'No, and all I can

hope is that these secret passages will work to our advantage. If not, God help us, because Fitzgerald will have no mercy, and neither will his master.'

The fog was so dense along Piccadilly that Chaloner was obliged to hold Thurloe's wrist to ensure they did not lose each other. Fine droplets of moisture glistened on their clothes and caught at the back of their throats. The urge to cough was strong, but they resisted, not knowing who might be nearby.

Eventually, they reached Clarendon House's distinctive gateposts, where the winged pigs looked almost evil in the shifting mist. Following the ruts made by the labourers' wheelbarrows, Chaloner aimed for the portico. He climbed the steps, aware that the silence was absolute, because the fog deadened all the usual noises, so there was not so much as a twitter from a bird or a bark from a dog. There were certainly no human sounds.

'Most of the workmen will be under arrest,' whispered Thurloe. 'Or still running away from Doines. The Piccadilly Company will have the house and grounds to themselves.'

Chaloner pulled out his key and opened the door to reveal darkness within. All the window shutters were closed, and what meagre light did filter inside was dull and did little to illuminate the place. He secured the door behind them, and began to move stealthily towards the Great Parlour, which seemed the obvious place for a large group of people to gather.

'I can hear something,' whispered Thurloe, stopping abruptly. 'Voices.'

'Brinkes and his men. Step carefully – the builders leave their tools lying around.'

450

Chaloner's heart thudded as they crept forward. How many villains would they have to confront? Would Pratt and Fitzgerald be there, or were they in another part of the house?

Eventually, he detected a glimmer of light, which grew stronger as he and Thurloe inched towards it. They reached the Great Parlour, and heard voices. The handsome double doors stood open to reveal Brinkes inside, serving ale to his cronies.

'It is almost over, lads,' he was saying encouragingly. 'And then we shall be rich.'

'Good,' said one fervently. 'It has been a dirty business, especially Turner's children. Our employers are too brutal for me, and I shall not weep if I never see them again.'

The others growled assent, even Brinkes, which did nothing to ease Chaloner's growing anxiety. If callous louts like them thought Pratt and Fitzgerald too ruthless, then what chance did he and Thurloe stand against them? But it was no time for faint-hearted thoughts, and he turned his attention to neutralising Brinkes and his henchmen.

The windows in the Great Parlour were so high as to be unreachable, which meant there was only one way in or out of the room – through the thick, heavy doors that opened outwards into the hall in which he and Thurloe were standing. He glanced at his friend, and saw the ex-Spymaster understood exactly what he was thinking: that if they could shut and lock them, imprisoning Brinkes and his friends inside, it might even the odds while they tackled Fitzgerald and Pratt.

The left-hand door would have to be closed first, because it contained a lever – located near the doorknob

– which snapped bolts into the ceiling and floor. Then the right-hand door could be shut and locked with the key. Chaloner pulled the key from his pocket and inserted it soundlessly, testing it to make sure it turned. Thurloe took the side with the key, Chaloner the one with the lever.

His inclination was to slam it shut and yank on the lever as quickly as possible, but Brinkes and his men were too near – they would be out and fighting before Thurloe could manage his side. With agonising slowness, he eased it closed little by little, relieved to discover that its hinges did not creak. He had almost succeeded when Brinkes happened to glance at it.

There was no time to hesitate. Chaloner leaned all his weight on it, so it cracked into place, then grabbed the lever, aware as he did so of Thurloe beginning to shove his side. Brinkes leapt forward, hauling out his dagger. The lever was stiffer than Chaloner had anticipated, and took all his strength to tug. While he wrestled with it, Thurloe's door moved faster and faster towards him, threatening to crush him.

Just when he thought he was going to be squashed between the two doors, an unmoving target for Brinkes to stab, the bolts clicked into place, and he was able to twist away. The door slammed shut an instant later, and he saw Thurloe reach for the key. But the door had banged so hard that it had popped partly open again, just enough to prevent the key from turning.

Chaloner hurled himself at it, and pushed with every fibre of his being, hearing the blood roar in his ears. Brinkes was doing the same on the other side. The henchmen were yelling, and Chaloner was sure they were racing to help Brinkes – and when they did, the door would fly open and he and Thurloe would die. The thought of losing his friend was just enough for a final, massive effort. The door closed and the locks snapped into place. They had done it.

'Come,' said Thurloe urgently, hauling Chaloner to his feet. 'We must tackle the others before Brinkes escapes – these are sturdy doors, but they will not hold him for long.'

Chaloner's legs were unsteady as they ran back the way they had come. There was only one place Pratt would be – the Lawyers' Library, the room he had been using as an office. Behind them, Brinkes and his men were pounding on the doors furiously, sending hollow booms reverberating through the entire house.

Chaloner reached the library and paused to listen. The door was closed, but someone was murmuring within. Unfortunately, the voice was too soft to recognise. Then he saw a flicker of movement under the door – someone was coming to investigate the racket Brinkes was making.

It was too late to hide, so he whipped out Williamson's sword and dagger and kicked the door open with as much force as he could muster. It flew against the wall with a resounding crack, and the person who had been about to open it stumbled back in alarm.

'Janszoon,' said Thurloe flatly, standing next to Chaloner with his own gun drawn. 'And Margareta. Whose remit in this nasty plot is to whip up ill-feeling towards Hollanders in the hope of encouraging a war. Prynne was right to want you stopped.'

Chaloner stepped inside quickly, but there was no sign of Pratt or Fitzgerald. Margareta smirked, not at all discomfited to find herself at the wrong end of a dag. Chaloner was immediately uneasy, and edged to one side, so as not to come under fire from the peepholes again.

'You are right,' she said carelessly. 'But I doubt you know why.'

'Of course we do,' said Thurloe disdainfully. 'Your country owns the best shipping routes, but war will disrupt them. And that will be to the Piccadilly Company's advantage.'

'They are not Hollanders,' said Chaloner, aware that Margareta had spoken without the merest trace of an accent. 'I have known it ever since they refused to speak Dutch to me at White Hall last night. Moreover, no learner of English would use complex grammatical structures one moment, and make basic vocabulary mistakes another. Their ridiculous choice of names is another clue to their real identities.'

The man's eyes narrowed. 'There are many Janszoons in Holland. I researched it very carefully.'

'So who are they, Tom?' asked Thurloe. 'More greedy merchants? Or pirates, perhaps?'

Chaloner pointed to the scar on the man's face. 'Whose cheek was cut in a public swordfight recently? And who was then given a hasty funeral – not to avoid an expensive send-off as we all assumed, but to explain why his "corpse" was removed from the charnel house within hours of his very public "death"?'

'Cave?' breathed Thurloe. 'He is not dead and buried in St Margaret's churchyard?'

Chaloner nodded, then turned to the woman. 'And who was his lover, a manipulative courtesan who is also a member of the Piccadilly Company and sister to the dangerous Harley?'

'Brilliana!' exclaimed Thurloe in understanding. 'It all makes sense now.'

When Brilliana gave a brief, cold smile, the pastes on her face cracked, revealing a glimpse of the beautiful but deadly woman underneath. 'Well done. Unfortunately for you, your deductions have come too late to make any difference to what has been set in motion.'

'It has failed,' said Thurloe harshly. 'Your brother is dead, and the Adventurers are still alive.'

'My brother is not dead, so do not think you can frighten us with lies,' said Brilliana coldly.

Chaloner looked around uncomfortably, unable to escape the conviction that something was very wrong. Why were they not more concerned at being exposed?

'We should leave,' he said in a low voice to Thurloe. 'I do not like this.'

'We should have guessed days ago,' said Thurloe, ignoring him to glare at Cave. 'You either paid or coerced Elliot to start a fight, so you could disappear and become Janszoon. You were good. Your "death" convinced Tom, and he is not easily misled.'

Guiltily, Chaloner recalled how he had berated Lester for not checking Elliot's body. Now it seemed he had done the same thing with Cave, but with far graver consequences.

'I confess I was alarmed when he tried to inspect my "wound",' admitted Cave. 'But I stopped him, and then he was kind enough to hire a cart to take me to the charnel house. The original arrangement had been for Elliot to do it, but that changed when I was obliged to stab him.'

'And then another Piccadilly Company member – or, more likely, Brinkes – collected your "body" later the same day,' surmised Thurloe.

455

Cave grimaced. 'He should have arrived sooner. I had to spend hours in that terrible place, in constant fear that someone would come and inspect me. He used the excuse that he was perfecting his disguise, but I think he did it for malice.'

'Brinkes made himself look like Elliot,' Thurloe went on. 'And told Kersey that he lived in Covent Garden – where Elliot had rented rooms.' He glanced at Brilliana. 'And you claimed it was Elliot who had encouraged "Jacob" to give Cave a hasty funeral – to make Tom waste time looking for a man who was dead and buried.'

Chaloner glanced behind him again. Why did Cave and Brilliana seem so relaxed? Because they expected Fitzgerald or their master to rescue them? He looked hard at the spyholes in the panelling, but could detect nothing amiss. Cave smirked at his wariness, making him even more certain that something was about to happen.

'Enough,' he said softly, tugging on Thurloe's arm. 'We should—'

'It worked,' Brilliana said gloatingly, ignoring Chaloner and addressing the ex-Spymaster. 'Everyone was so easy to deceive. Chaloner should have drunk the chocolate I provided, though – then we would not be having this discussion.'

'You "die" in operas all the time,' Thurloe said to Cave, freeing his arm from Chaloner's hand. 'I suppose you wore a sack of animal blood under your clothes, which gushed out when it was jabbed. That is how it is managed on stage, I believe. Then you both donned disguises, testing them on cronies at the Piccadilly Company first . . .'

'They were impressed.' Brilliana's smile was smug with satisfaction. 'And it gave us the confidence to step into that most auspicious of circles – White Hall.'

456

Chaloner was barely listening. Every nerve in his body screamed that something was wrong, although he could still hear the distant boom of Brinkes and his henchmen hammering on the Great Parlour doors, so he knew they had not yet managed to break free.

'But why kill Elliot?' Thurloe was asking. 'He did what you asked.'

'Barely,' said Cave coldly. 'Lester told him he would hang for murder if he "killed" me – an outcome that had not occurred to the fool, because I could see him having second thoughts before my very eyes. I was obliged to goad him to fulfil his end of the bargain by attacking Lester.'

'Who was unarmed,' said Chaloner, recalling the crowd's murmur of disapproval. 'I suppose you were afraid that Elliot would tell the truth about the deception to save himself from the noose.'

'Yes.' Cave touched a hand to his scarred face. 'And I was angry because he hurt me. That was certainly never part of the arrangement.'

'What is in this for you?' Thurloe asked. 'It means your old life is over for ever – your voice will be recognised if you ever sing in public again. There can be no going back.'

The besotted expression on Cave's face as he glanced at Brilliana answered that question, although Chaloner could see just by looking that the devotion was not reciprocated. When he had outlived his usefulness, Cave would be dispatched, like so many others.

'I am sorry, Chaloner,' he said, and he sounded sincere. 'I enjoyed singing to your viol when we sailed on *Eagle*. You have a rare talent, and it is a pity to silence it. But it cannot be helped.'

Chaloner was about to remark that he had no intention of being silenced when he heard the merest of rustles behind the door. A faint smile tugged the corners of Brilliana's mouth, and he knew her deliverance was at hand. Reacting instinctively, he hurled himself to the floor, dragging Thurloe with him. And then the room was full of noise as bullets ripped into the oaken panels and smashed the windows.

Before the gunmen could reload, Chaloner kicked the door closed and struggled to his knees to lock it. Immediately, someone started to batter it from the other side. It began to splinter, not being as robust as the ones in the Great Parlour. Chaloner glanced fearfully at Thurloe, expecting him to be shot, but the ex-Spymaster scrambled to his feet and hurried to Brilliana, who was gazing at the shattered remains of her right arm in shocked disbelief. Cave was dead.

'Open the window,' hissed Thurloe. 'We shall escape through that. Hurry!'

Obediently, Chaloner ran towards it, but could see shadows moving in the fog outside. When one of them fired a musket at him, he whipped around and began prodding the panels instead.

'The plans said Hyde installed a passage in this wall,' he whispered urgently. 'Help me find it.'

There were voices in the hallway – Fitzgerald's piping treble ordering someone to hurry. The pirate sounded deranged, and Chaloner knew he and Thurloe would not live long once they were caught. Whoever was kicking the door intensified his assault, and Chaloner's hunt for the hidden passage became more frantic, too.

It was Thurloe who found it – a tiny knob disguised

as a carving of a pineapple. Chaloner followed him inside, then pressed the mechanism that closed it. A little light filtered through the holes that had been placed for spying, but it was still difficult to see where they were going.

'Fitzgerald did not care who was shot just then,' Thurloe whispered, shocked. 'Indeed, I cannot help but wonder whether he wanted Brilliana and Cave dead anyway.' His voice was unsteady, stunned by the ruthlessness of the onslaught.

'Probably,' agreed Chaloner. 'It is more loose ends tied.'

'Do you accept *now* that I was right to keep you away from him? And understand why I could never find witnesses to speak against him when I tried to bring him to trial? How could I, when he murders his accomplices?'

They were passing the last of the peepholes when the door burst open and Fitzgerald flew in. Chaloner stopped to watch. The pirate did not so much as glance at the writhing Brilliana, and instead issued a piercing scream of frustration when he saw his enemies had escaped. His master entered more calmly.

'They seem to have gone,' said O'Brien softly. 'Find them, or you will die, too.'

Chaloner gaped at the man who had been the author of so much carnage, then clenched his fists as rage consumed him. It was *O'Brien's* fault that Lester had died saving worthless Adventurers, and in the darkness of Hyde's secret passage, he vowed the man would pay. Unfortunately, his dive to the floor to avoid the deadly hail of gunfire meant he had dropped his weapons, so the odds of him fulfilling that promise were remote to say the least. But he determined to do his best.

'*He* was never among my suspects,' whispered Thurloe. He sounded disgusted and stunned in equal measure. 'I underestimated him – and his capacity for greed, because he is already rich.'

'Rich enough to have funded the Piccadilly Company all these months,' replied Chaloner. 'No wonder he refused to join the Adventurers. I believed him when he said it was because he opposed the slave trade – he was convincing. But it was a lie, a ruse to conceal his real intentions.'

'And what are his real intentions? What can he gain, other than to make yet more money?'

Chaloner was about to repeat the reply he had given when Rector Thompson had posed the same question the previous week – that money was one of those commodities of which those who owned it never felt they had enough – when O'Brien crouched by the dying Brilliana. She tried to move away but he made a sudden movement and she went limp, head lolling to one side.

'I thought I told you to find our unwanted guests,' he snarled, when he saw Fitzgerald watching him. The pirate took an involuntary step backwards at the force of the words. 'Hunt them down and kill them. They have done immeasurable harm with their meddling.'

'I said it was a bad idea to bring the Adventurers to Queenhithe,' Fitzgerald snapped back. 'If you had let me blow them up in Woolwich, as we originally planned—'

'How?' snapped O'Brien. 'You could not have smuggled gunpowder on board *Royal Katherine*, and using *Jane* was a stroke of genius.'

Fitzgerald scowled. 'Modestly put. But how did you

persuade Leighton to change the time and venue of his party? It cannot have been easy.'

'It was, actually – I told him I would join the Adventurers if he did as I asked. Unfortunately, now our plan is foiled, he will know that I am behind the plot to massacre them all, so I will have to kill him today, too. But not before I have dispatched Thurloe and his helpmeets, to teach them what happens to those who cross me.'

'*I* did not cross you,' said Fitzgerald immediately. 'I was on my way to warn you that we had to set the explosion early, but then I saw you on the quayside, so obviously I did not risk our venture by exposing myself to recognition by approaching you.'

'Obviously,' said O'Brien flatly, while Chaloner recalled that O'Brien had been one of those whose life had been saved by the timely evacuation. However, he was sure O'Brien was right to be sceptical of Fitzgerald's intentions.

Beside him, Thurloe released a soft sound of disgust. 'If he trusted Fitzgerald not to betray him, then the man is deranged,' he said softly.

'He *is* deranged,' Chaloner whispered back. 'Look at his face. And what he did to Brilliana . . .'

'Well, do not just stand there!' O'Brien was snapping to his accomplice. 'Our enemies cannot be allowed to escape, so find them and kill them. Now!'

Fitzgerald was an intelligent man, who knew his quarry could not have left through the window while there were guards outside, so he immediately turned his attention to the panels. He began tapping and poking, and Chaloner knew it was only a matter of time before he found what he was looking for.

He and Thurloe moved as fast as they could along

461

the passage, but it was difficult in the dark. Thurloe gave him a vigorous shove when Fitzgerald screeched his triumph, sending him stumbling down a flight of steep stairs. When he had finally regained his balance, he saw a flare of light close behind him. Thurloe had a tinderbox and had lit a candle.

'Douse it!' Chaloner hissed in alarm. He glanced up to see a second gleam at the top of the steps. 'They are coming!'

'They know we are here,' Thurloe snapped back. 'And it is better to see, than to blunder blindly.'

Chaloner snatched the candle and ran along a corridor that – according to Hyde's plans – led to the kitchens. He was acutely aware of footsteps behind them. Then he reached a dead end.

'I sincerely hope we have not gone past the exit,' gulped Thurloe, groping frantically along the wall. Chaloner did likewise, noting that the mortar was still damp.

Chaloner gasped his relief when he detected a knob. He pulled and twisted, but nothing happened. He did it harder, then gaped in horror when it came off in his hand. Calmly, Thurloe reached past him and pushed the exposed metal. There was a soft sigh, and a stone slid to one side. Aware of Fitzgerald's lamp coming ever closer, Chaloner crawled out quickly, and when Thurloe had followed, he stood by the hole with a brick in his hand.

'The next person out will lose his brains,' he said grimly.

Thurloe cocked his head. 'Fitzgerald may be in the tunnel, but O'Brien is coming down the stairs. They separated!'

'Then we will fight them,' said Chaloner with quiet determination. 'One each.'

'We cannot combat bullets with a stone,' hissed Thurloe. 'Run! It is our only chance!'

He was right, so Chaloner did as he was told, racing through sculleries, laundries and pantries, sure-footed again now he was in familiar territory. Suddenly, the basement began to echo with a metallic, grating sound that echoed eerily. Fitzgerald was humming to himself. Chaloner winced: not all the notes were true.

'Whoever told him he could sing was lying,' he whispered, wishing it would stop.

'He warbles before making a kill,' muttered Thurloe. 'He thinks he has defeated us.'

Chaloner looked around desperately, but saw nothing that would help them survive. Then his eye lit on the stairs that led to the cellar. It was the last place he wanted to go, but he felt a surge of hope as a plan began to form in his mind.

'The vault,' he said in a low voice. 'If we can do to Fitzgerald and O'Brien what we did to Brinkes, we might yet avenge Lester. This way – run!'

The cellar steps were dark and uninviting, and Chaloner's chest tightened when he recalled what had happened the last time he had ventured down them. But there was no time for squeamishness. He descended them quickly and made for the strongroom. It was locked, but this time he had Wiseman's scalpel, which proved to be a much better instrument for dealing with the mechanism.

'Why do they not release Brinkes and his men to hunt for us?' he asked as he worked, aware that on the floor above, O'Brien and Fitzgerald were conducting a

463

systematic search. 'Or summon their other Piccadilly Company cronies? Pratt, for example.'

'Arrogance,' replied Thurloe shortly. 'They believe they can best us alone.'

'Then pride will be their downfall,' muttered Chaloner. 'Find a lamp and light it. Quickly!'

Thurloe obliged, and it was not long before he was back. 'I recommend you hurry,' he said tensely, 'because I hear footsteps on the cellar stairs.'

The words were no sooner out of his mouth when the vault's lock clicked open. Fighting down his nausea, Chaloner tugged open the door and entered. The chest that had contained the rats was gone, and in its place were two more, both sturdy items with metal bands. There was no time for finesse, so he smashed the locks on one with the brick he had brought from the kitchen.

'Tom!' pleaded Thurloe nervously. 'Are you sure we have time for this?'

Chaloner lifted the lid to reveal a mass of gold and silver ingots, with a good smattering of jewellery and precious stones. Thurloe gasped at the sheer volume of it.

'Is this what came on *Jane*?' he breathed.

Chaloner nodded. 'And it is time to put it to good use.'

He grabbed two large gold bars and shoved them into Thurloe's hands, then took two himself. Leaving the chest open, and the lantern illuminating it, he dived into the room opposite, flinging the ingots away as soon as he and Thurloe were concealed in the shadows. He slipped his hand into his pocket, hunting for Wiseman's scalpel. He could not find it, but his fingers located something else. It was the packet of Tangier dust George had given him days ago, which he had all but forgotten.

O'Brien was the first to arrive. He held a gun, and his boyish face was lit by a viciously cruel expression. It showed his true nature as the pitiless villain who had ordered the deaths of Teviot and his garrison, Proby, Lucas, Turner, Congett, Meneses and all the others who had died since he had taken exception to the Adventurers' monopoly on African trade.

His eyes lit on the open chest, and he released a strangled cry of disbelief before running towards it. Fitzgerald arrived moments later, also armed with a dag. Chaloner tensed, willing him to step inside too, but the pirate only leaned against the doorframe.

'The treasure!' shouted O'Brien furiously. 'You said it would be safe here – that you stole the only key from Pratt, and no one else would be able to get at it. But some has been stolen!'

'Impossible,' countered Fitzgerald. 'No one knows it is here except you and me. Unless *you*—'

O'Brien's eyes blazed as he leapt to his feet. 'Are you accusing me of cheating you?'

'It is not an unreasonable assumption,' Fitzgerald flashed back. There was a tremor of fear in his voice but he held his ground. 'Our venture was more costly than we anticipated, and the returns so far have been disappointing. Of course you might try to—'

He took several steps back as O'Brien stalked towards him, and Chaloner knew he had to act now or they would both be out in the corridor – at which point he and Thurloe would die. He leapt forward, shoving Fitzgerald as hard as he could. The pirate cannoned into O'Brien, and Chaloner started to close the door.

But Fitzgerald recovered quickly, and hurled himself against it.

Chaloner's strength was all but spent, and he felt the door begin to open, even when Thurloe raced forward to help – fury had given the pirate a diabolical might. It was then that he realised he was still holding George's powder. With nothing to lose, he flung it in Fitzgerald's face, hoping the footman had not been lying when he claimed it would render his former master helpless.

The pirate jerked away in surprise, and for a moment nothing happened. Then he sneezed. He blinked furiously and sneezed again. And again. Chaloner and Thurloe leaned all their weight on the door, which slammed shut, allowing the lock to click into place.

Suddenly, there was a yell from the stairs. Chaloner and Thurloe exchanged a glance of horrified dismay. Brinkes must have battered his way free at last. Weaponless, they turned and stood shoulder to shoulder, bracing themselves for the onslaught.

'There you are!' said Williamson, skidding to a standstill. 'When we found Brinkes locked up but no sign of you two, we feared the worst.'

'Fitzgerald and his master are safely secured,' said Thurloe, indicating the strongroom with a nonchalance Chaloner was sure he could not feel. 'However, I recommend you leave them there for a while. You may find them less feisty once the air has grown thin.'

Epilogue

It was a fine, clear morning when Williamson married Kitty O'Brien in St Margaret's Church. It was a small ceremony, with only Swaddell and Doines to act as witnesses. Chaloner slipped into the shadows at the back and watched, thinking that he had never seen the Spymaster look so pleased with himself, although Kitty's expression was more difficult to read.

'Congratulations,' he said, as the happy couple walked up the aisle together.

Williamson inclined his head. 'I was shocked to learn that my oldest friend was complicit in that vile affair – especially as he was already rich and had no need for more money. But before he hanged himself in my cells, he told me to look after Kitty. Today is the fulfilment of that promise.'

'I was shocked, too,' said Kitty, while Chaloner struggled to determine whether Williamson had had a hand in O'Brien's alleged suicide. 'But that is all in the past, and we must look to the future. I shall accept Leighton's

467

offer to join the Adventurers tomorrow. My husband . . . my *first* husband spent too much of our money on his wild schemes, and I must recoup my losses.'

'But the Adventurers still trade in slaves,' Chaloner pointed out. 'That has not changed.'

'No, it has not,' said Kitty. She smiled, an expression that did not touch her green eyes. 'But perhaps I shall be able to change them from within.'

They walked away, leaving Chaloner staring after them unhappily. Since the events that had culminated at Piccadilly, he had been in low spirits. He had recurring nightmares about the strongroom, his home life continued to be a trial, and he felt guilty for abandoning Lester. Thurloe pointed out patiently that any attempt at rescue would have meant his own death, but that was of scant comfort.

His work for the Earl did nothing to help, either. As there were no mysteries to investigate, he was obliged to pass the time in routine duties that put him in the company of Dugdale and Edgeman. The Earl had been furious when he had learned they were Adventurers, and they blamed Chaloner for their exposure: they set out to make his life miserable, and they succeeded.

One morning, as Dugdale railed at him for wearing a grey coat instead of the blue one he had stipulated, Kipps appeared. His fist shot towards the Chief Usher's face and there was a dull smack as the two connected. Chaloner stared at the Seal Bearer in astonishment.

'What did you do that for?' howled Dugdale, hand to his nose. 'Are you insane?'

'A maid called Susan was just here, asking after you,' replied Kipps, eyeing him with dislike. 'She told me you paid her to spy on Chaloner. In his own home.'

Dugdale swallowed uneasily. 'I did it to protect the Earl. And I would not have had to do it at all if Chaloner had been cooperative. I asked him for progress reports, but he fobbed me off with half-answers and lies. What else was I to do?'

'Why were you so desperate to know what I—' began Chaloner.

'Because he is jealous of the Earl's faith in your abilities,' snapped Kipps. 'But that does not excuse him from corrupting a silly girl to spy on a colleague. It is not the act of a gentleman, and I shall ensure all White Hall knows it. Moreover, if I catch him doing anything like it again, I shall hit him even harder. That goes for you, too, Edgeman. I know you were in it together.'

'You do not care about Chaloner,' sneered Edgeman, although he took refuge behind Dugdale as he spoke, unwilling to suffer a similar fate. 'The reason you punched Dugdale is because he told Leighton not to let you join the Adventurers. You have always resented that.'

'I would never enrol in that band of scoundrels,' declared Kipps, although the flash of anger in his eyes said Edgeman was right. 'I do not approve of monopolies. However, if he recommends against me joining anything else, a bloody nose will be the least of his problems.'

'I am not sure that was wise,' said Chaloner, when Edgeman had helped Dugdale away. 'The Earl does not approve of his retainers thumping each other. Why do you think I have never hit the man myself? It is not because of my superior self-control, I assure you.'

'What is he going to do about it?' shrugged Kipps. 'Tell the Earl? If he does, he will be sorry. But they have learned their lesson. They will not bother you again.'

Chaloner suspected they would just be more subtle in

their hounding of him, and doubted Kipps's intervention had done him any favours. But the punch had been a declaration of allegiance and he was heartened by it – it meant he was no longer alone and that there was someone he could call a friend in the unsettled, unpredictable world that was White Hall. Kipps's next words promptly reversed any improvement in his mood, though.

'Have you heard the news? Governor Bridge has been dismissed and a new man hired to rule Tangier in his place. Fitzgerald the pirate has been honoured with the post.'

Chaloner stared at him. 'Fitzgerald? But he is in the Tower, charged with the attempted murder of most of the Adventurers and half of Queenhithe.'

'That was ages ago,' said Kipps. 'It has all been forgotten now, especially as Fitzgerald has offered to bring another chest of treasure to London later in the year.'

'So yet again the wicked prosper,' muttered Chaloner. 'Is there *never* justice in this rotten city?'

'Fitzgerald will travel to his new domain on *Royal Katherine*,' said Kipps, straining to hear what Chaloner was mumbling. 'The damage has been repaired and she looks as good as new again. She sails from Queenhithe on the afternoon tide.'

Chaloner went home, but the news of Fitzgerald's freedom troubled him, and he was restless and angry. Bemused by his sullen mood, and exasperated when he declined to discuss it, Hannah sent him out for a walk, no doubt afraid that he might use his viol to settle his mind if he were allowed to stay. She need not have worried: Chaloner had not played since the events at Clarendon House, and felt no desire to do so.

'Take George with you,' she said. 'I dislike being in the kitchen when he is there, and I feel like baking a cake. It will be ready on your return.'

Even more dejected, because he would be expected to eat it, Chaloner walked to Queenhithe to see for himself whether Kipps was right about Fitzgerald. George trailed at his heels.

When he arrived, he found scant evidence of the chaos that had ensued after it had almost been blown into oblivion. The warehouses that had been burned were already rebuilt, and the wharf was its usual hive of activity. Boats rocked gently as they were tugged by the ebbing tide, and *Katherine* stood tall and proud among them, like a graceful swan amid a flock of ducks.

Suddenly, there was a clatter of wheels on cobbles, and a convoy arrived. Chaloner clenched his fists in impotent fury when Fitzgerald alighted. Even from a distance, he could hear the high-pitched voice, laughing jovially. It seemed to be mocking him, but, short of darting forward and plunging a dagger into the man, there was nothing Chaloner could do.

'I would not mind a berth on that ship,' said George.

Chaloner jumped. They were the first words the footman had spoken since leaving Tothill Street. 'You want to return to Fitzgerald's service?' he asked, bemused.

'I meant as a sailor. Work my passage to Tangier.'

'Then go,' said Chaloner.

George stared at him. 'I am your servant. I cannot leap on a ship.'

'You can if I tell you to,' said Chaloner, wondering whether he would be spared the ordeal of Hannah's cake if he went home with the news that he had solved the problem George had become.

471

Once the captain had been assured that George was an experienced seaman, willing to work, he happily agreed to take him on. Chaloner gave George all the money he had with him, plus his coat; George took them without a word of thanks. Chaloner watched him stride up the gangway, then went to tell Thurloe of Fitzgerald's good fortune.

'What?' exploded the ex-Spymaster. 'How can they let such a dangerous man go free? And to promote him into a position of power into the bargain! Are they *insane*?'

'No, they are corrupt,' replied Chaloner. 'He bribed them with promises of more gold bars.'

'So the profits from mismanaging the mole will go into *his* pocket now,' fumed Thurloe. 'He not only has his liberty, but he is given licence to prosper at the tax-payer's expense.'

'It is a sorry business, and all about money as usual,' said Chaloner despondently.

Thurloe nodded grim agreement. 'And it all began with O'Brien objecting to the monopoly on African trade held by the Adventurers, and deciding he was going to smash their hold on Tangier. He did not care that it would destroy the Queen and take all manner of lives in the process. But some justice was served, at least.'

'Was it?' Chaloner could not think of any.

'All those greedy people who hoped to profit were hit where it hurt them most – in the purse. The Piccadilly Company lost all the treasure they had spirited to Clarendon House after *Jane* docked – it was confiscated by the government. And it was decided that the Adventurers should pay for the repairs to *Katherine*, because they were fooling about on her when *Jane* exploded.'

'I suppose so,' said Chaloner. 'But most of them are so rich that they will barely notice the loss.'

'Well, we should not be too downcast. Fitzgerald murdered all those members of the Piccadilly Company who were involved in the plot, while the remainder are too relieved by their narrow escape to dabble with dubious characters again. And war with the Dutch will destroy the Adventurers – their ships will be unable to trade, and their venture will go bankrupt.'

'Temporarily perhaps. Do you know, when I scuttled the slave-ship *Henrietta Maria* in Tangier, I believed I had made a difference – that it might make these unscrupulous merchants think twice about the trade. But the reality was that it accomplished nothing at all.'

'It enabled dozens of people to escape life on the plantations,' countered Thurloe. '*They* will not think it was nothing. But you are right in that the filthy business will flourish. You may have to hone your scuttling talents. Let me know if you ever need an accomplice.'

Chaloner gave him a wan smile.

Thurloe sighed. 'Fitzgerald may have bested me yet again, but at least some of the villains met a fitting end. Brinkes and his louts are in Williamson's tender care, while O'Brien, Harley, Brilliana, Cave, Meneses and my brother-in-law are dead.'

'Harley was the worst. He murdered his friends and Reyner's mother.'

'Fitzgerald was the worst,' corrected Thurloe. 'He brained two men in front of you, and he was responsible for Turner, Lucas and even children burned to death, as well as Proby being hurled from the roof of St Paul's Cathedral, Congett poisoned and Meneses trampled by a horse.'

'It was O'Brien who issued those orders.'

'Perhaps, but the wicked imaginativeness tells me that Fitzgerald decided how to execute them. He ordered Brinkes to kill Captain Pepperell, too, before his report on the three Tangier scouts could be delivered to Williamson.'

'Poor Pepperell,' said Chaloner. 'I doubt he knew much that could harm Harley, Newell and Reyner, and there was no need to kill him. However, I think you will agree that the slaughter of the garrison on Jews Hill was by far the worst outrage in this miserable affair, and while it was O'Brien's idea, it was Harley who put it into action.'

'True,' acknowledged Thurloe. 'Of course, the Teviot affair has been vigorously suppressed. The government does not want it known that its own scouts brought about that tragedy.'

Chaloner was not surprised, being well acquainted with the fact that governments all over the world had ways to keep people from finding out about their mistakes.

'But Pratt was not guilty of anything except making bad friends,' he said. 'And of naively believing that members of the Piccadilly Company would hire him to design houses for them once *Jane* had made them rich. He was so shocked when he learned he had been used in a plot against the Queen that he has retired from public life. He has gone to live in Norfolk.'

'That is extreme: I have been to Norfolk.' Thurloe sighed again. 'However, we saved the Queen from embarrassment and persecution. That was worthwhile.'

'It was, but she remains vulnerable until she produces an heir.' Chaloner glanced at Thurloe. 'I am sorry about Lydcott, by the way. He was not a bad man, either. Just lacking in judgement.'

474

Thurloe pursed his lips. 'I beg to differ – he sacrificed you and me to Fitzgerald without a second thought. I was wrong about him, just as I was wrong about Lester, although Ann mourns his loss, of course. Still, at least I did not underestimate Fitzgerald, so I have not lost my touch completely.'

'Far from it.' Chaloner stood. 'I had better go. The Earl asked me to meet him in Clarendon House this evening, and he will be angry if I am late.'

'I have no desire to set foot in that place ever again,' declared Thurloe with a shudder. 'I shall always associate it with evil dealings.'

So would Chaloner, but *he* did not have the luxury of declining the Earl's summons.

Clarendon House stood silent and imposing in its sea of mud and winter-brown trees. The site was deserted because the Earl had dismissed all the workmen, being uncertain which ones were involved with Oliver, and unwilling to take chances. More had yet to be recruited, although it would not be long before the place rang with the sounds of industry again.

As Chaloner walked up the drive, he regarded it with dislike, and began to formulate plans to burn it down. No one would miss it, except the Earl – even Hyde would be grateful to lose this monumental reminder of his gullibility. It took considerable willpower to open the door and step inside, and he could not repress a shudder as he passed the stairs that led to the basement.

He found the Earl standing in his Great Parlour, which was still scarred from Brinkes's efforts to escape. He looked short and insignificant in its lofty grandeur, more like an interloper than its owner.

'Hah!' he exclaimed as Chaloner approached. 'There is an unforeseen advantage to this place.'

'What is that, sir?'

The Earl grinned. 'You cannot mask the sound of your footsteps in this echoing chamber, so you will never be able to creep up on me. I am safe from frights at last.'

Chaloner had made no effort to approach quietly, but was sure it could be managed, especially in the dark. The Earl's grin faded as he looked around him.

'It was a pitiful business,' he said softly.

Chaloner nodded, and stared at the floor. Lester had died saving people who continued to profit from the slave trade, and one of the greatest villains he had ever encountered was currently sailing down the Thames on his way to a new and prosperous life. Even Kitty, whose role in the affair was far from certain, was happily married to the man she had taken as her lover while her husband still lived.

'I am sorry so many people died,' he said quietly.

The Earl stared at him. 'Actually, I was thinking about my stolen bricks. The other business was far from pitiful, because you presented me with four gold bars that the King's treasurers had neglected to find.'

'Oh,' said Chaloner. 'I had forgotten about those.'

'You are a curious fellow! Anyone else in my household would have kept one for himself, but you gave me the lot.'

'I did not want anything to do with them.'

'Luckily for me.' The Earl cleared his throat. 'Henry has shown me every one of these sly secret passages, but they are all in the wrong places.'

Chaloner frowned. 'I do not understand.'

The Earl waved a sheaf of papers at him. 'They are

in the main reception rooms, but these are large chambers, and experiments have shown that if you stand in the middle and mutter seditious remarks, a spy cannot hear you.'

Chaloner took the plans and studied them. 'There are no devices in the bedrooms – other than yours – either. That is where most confidences will be whispered. You are right: I doubt they will serve you very well. Hyde . . . whoever designed them did not know what he was doing.'

'Speaking of my son, Williamson came to see me yesterday. He had information that indicates Henry lied – that it was one of my enemies who arranged to have these spyholes installed, not him. I asked Henry about it, but he says Williamson is mistaken. What do you think?'

'That you should never invite Secretary Leighton here for dinner.'

The Earl stared at him. 'These spyholes were *Leighton's* idea?'

'Yes – because he dislikes your opposition to the Adventurers, although when I confronted him, he claimed he never intended the matter to end in the attempted murder of your son.'

'Did you believe him?' asked the Earl, round-eyed.

'No. Had his plan worked, he would have wanted the devices kept secret – but Hyde knew about them, so of course he would have killed him to ensure his silence.'

'I shall issue a warrant for his arrest,' said Clarendon. 'And see what he has to say for himself once he is in the Tower. You can lay hold of him tomorrow.'

'Yes, sir.'

The Earl sighed softly. 'So Henry *did* lie to me. I

thought as much. He is not a brave boy and I was scep-tical of him tackling gun-wielding villains. But we shall say no more about it. His mother thinks him a hero, and I would rather not distress her with the truth.'

'Very well, sir.'

'But the affair will not be entirely forgotten, either. I shall send him to Sweden on a diplomatic mission soon. You will accompany him.'

'Are you punishing him or me?' asked Chaloner, appalled by the notion of spending what might be weeks in the company of such a man.

'Do not look so gloomy, lad,' said the Earl, rather more kindly than was his wont. 'I have some news you might find cheering. From Williamson.'

Chaloner doubted it, but listened politely.

'It involves a fellow called Lester. Apparently, he managed to jump overboard before the flames caught *Jane*'s gunpowder. A Queenhithe family nursed him until he regained his wits, and he is now well on the road to recovery.'

Chaloner stared at him. 'Lester is alive?'

The Earl smiled. 'Williamson said you would welcome the news. He is being tended by his sister in the Crown tavern, and says he would like to play his flute to your viol, if you have time.'

Chaloner felt his spirits lift at last. 'May I . . .'

'Go,' said the Earl, waving a chubby hand.

Tangier, April 1665

George breathed in deeply, relishing the scent of sun-baked earth, the stew that was cooking, and the familiar, dusty odour of the cows he had purchased with the money Chaloner had given him. He stared up at the vast night sky, millions of stars flickering like diamonds suspended in nothingness.

He was content for the first time since Fitzgerald had enticed him to sea with promises of easy wealth and a life of adventure, and knew he had made the right decision to return home. He had not liked London's filthy, crowded streets, and nor had he enjoyed life as a servant. Moreover, he had certainly not appreciated being hired because it was fashionable to employ black retainers.

He remembered the ones he had met at White Hall – not free men like him, but slaves taken from the Gold Coast. They had been resigned to their lot, telling him it was a better fate than the plantations in Barbados, but he had railed on their behalf, silently and bitterly, deploring the vile trade in human souls.

An evening in Tothill Street flashed into his mind, when he had eavesdropped on a discussion between Chaloner and Wiseman. Chaloner had said little, but the surgeon had made it clear who had been responsible for the infamous attack on *Henrietta Maria*. George had decided then that he would repay the good deed one day, although he had not been sure how – devoted servitude was certainly not on the cards. He was not a deferential man.

Then news had come of Fitzgerald's promotion, and Chaloner had taken him to watch the pirate strut about on Queenhithe. Seeing him had angered George on two counts: because of the callous way Fitzgerald had abandoned him in a foreign city after ten years of loyal service; and because he knew Fitzgerald would dabble in the slave trade again when he reached Africa. He had vowed not to let that happen.

479

It had not been possible to tip him overboard on the voyage, as he had intended, because Fitzgerald had kept to his cabin, only emerging when *Katherine* had docked in Tangier. And after that, George had been more concerned with adapting to his new life than in monitoring his former master. But the day had come when he had gone to town to sell some livestock, and then he had made his move.

He had acquired more of the yellow dust he had used in the past, and it had not been difficult to gain access to Fitzgerald's bedroom: the man was so certain that no one would dare move against him that security was minimal. He had blown the powder into Fitzgerald's face, and when the pirate had been blinded by the sneezing that followed, he had plunged a knife into his black heart.

As he stared at the stars, George thought about Chaloner. Would he know who had delivered the fatal blow, or would he assume that robbers were responsible, which was the tale that was flying around Tangier? George smiled. Chaloner would guess, and perhaps sleep a little easier at night because of it. George hoped so.

Historical Note

When the Portuguese Infanta Katherine de Braganza married Charles II in 1662, she brought with her a dowry that included the ports of Bombay and Tangier. Tangier was thought at the time to have the greater significance, and the Navy Board intended to develop it as a base from which to fight the pirates that infested the north African coast. In the event, it was Bombay that transpired to be the real catch – it was developed into a major commercial centre, and played a pivotal role in the later British Empire.

Tangier, on the other hand, proved to be expensive. A fortune was poured into making it a viable port, mostly by constructing a mole. This was the biggest marine engineering project attempted by the British to date, and comprised a sea wall that was a quarter of a mile long. Contemporary engravings show houses and other buildings on it, as well as guns and their embrasures.

Twenty years later, the government decided to cut its losses and abandon the port. The diarist Samuel Pepys was there to supervise its evacuation; his 'Tangier Diary' recalls his horror at a town that was dirty, corrupt and full of vice. The mole was blown up, although parts of it can still be seen at low tide today.

Tangier had a number of governors. One of the last Portuguese colonial heads was Fernando de Meneses, Conde de Ericeira (he left in 1661, by which time discussions to pass it to the British were well underway). Lord Teviot was governor in 1664. He was not an effective leader, and was probably corrupt. On 3 May 1664, he went out to inspect his defences and cut wood, having been assured by his scouts that the area was free of Barbary corsairs. But either the scouts lied or were inept, because a much larger enemy force (some accounts say it was ten thousand strong) was lying in wait, and Teviot and all but thirty of his five hundred men were massacred.

His post was taken by Tobias Bridge, notable for being one of Cromwell's major generals. Colonel John Fitzgerald was appointed to succeed Bridge, although he held power only until April 1665. As a rule, good people did not want to go to Tangier: it was a long way away from any political power, and its climate was considered unhealthy.

The Company of Royal Adventurers Trading into Africa was founded in 1660, and its charter granted it a complete monopoly of any goods coming out of Africa, including precious metals, ivory and slaves. The vast amount of money poured into Tangier would have suited the Adventurers, who would have benefited from a British-controlled harbour near the Mediterranean – and what they wanted went, as its members included the King, his Queen, his mother, his sister, his brother, the Duke of Buckingham, several earls, Peter Proby, Sir Edward Turner, Lord Lucas, James Congett and Thomas Grey. Its secretary was Ellis (or Elisha) Leighton, a brazenly villainous character who was known to be devious and dishonest.

The Adventurers' corporation did not survive long. It suffered during the Second Anglo-Dutch War, and was deeply in debt by 1667. Its successor, the Royal African Company, was founded in 1674 with a new charter – and fewer courtiers and more merchants as investors – and by the eighteenth century it was making a fortune in the slave trade.

Most of the people in *The Piccadilly Plot* were real. Reverend John Addison was chaplain to Tangier in the 1660s. John Dugdale, William Edgeman and Thomas Kipps were the Earl of Clarendon's Chief Usher, secretary and Seal Bearer, respectively. The Earl's (second) wife was called Frances, and she was the mother of Henry. Henry Hyde, Viscount Cornbury, became the Queen's private secretary in 1662, a post he held until he was appointed her chamberlain in 1665.

John Oliver, first mentioned in documents of 1667–8, was Master Mason to the King. John Vere was a woodmonger in the 1670s, and was convicted of theft. William Prynne was a pamphleteer in Lincoln's Inn, who hated virtually everything about the world in which he lived, and Robert Lydcott was John Thurloe's brother-in-law, and did indeed take advantage of his kinsman's influence during the Commonwealth, when Thurloe was Secretary of State and Spymaster General. Thurloe often used cipher to communicate with his spies, and hired John Wallis, a famous mathematician, to decode documents for him.

Early in 1664, John Cave, a gentleman of His Majesty's Chapel Royal, was killed outside the New Exchange by one James Elliot. The argument was said to be about who was to take the wall.

The Collection of Curiosities, on display at the Mitre near St Paul's Cathedral throughout 1664, really did contain a mummy, a moon fish, a torpedo, a remora and other objects and animals that were virtually unknown to London at the time.

Records show that at the Restoration, Piccadilly was a hamlet set in open countryside. It comprised a few cottages, a windmill and the famous Gaming House. A survey of 1651 shows local residents to include William Reyner and Robert Newell. John Marshall owned a tenement called the Crown, which boasted 'drinking rooms' on the ground floor. Brilliana Stanley and her brother Colonel Edward Harley had moved to Piccadilly by 1658.

Joseph Williamson, one of those who stepped into Thurloe's shoes as Spymaster, really did marry Catherine O'Brien (here called Kitty to avoid confusion with Queen Katherine), who was the wife of a friend from his Oxford days. The speed of their marriage after Henry O'Brien's death has led to the speculation that they had been lovers beforehand. Documents in Williamson's handwriting dating to the 1660s show he made payment to spies called Captain Lester, William Doines and Josiah Brinkes.

Royal Katherine was launched on 26 October 1664 in Woolwich, an occasion that was attended by the King, the Queen and Samuel Pepys, who records the bad weather and the King's teasing of the Queen's ladies over their seasickness. I have taken the liberty of moving it forward a few months for *The Piccadilly Plot*. *Henrietta Maria* was a slaving ship, and *Eagle* was a merchantman trading to and from Tangier in the 1660s; one of her captains was Anthony Young. Captain Pepperell was the master of an Adventurer-owned ship; he fought and seized a privateer vessel called *Jane*.

Clarendon House was designed by Roger Pratt in 1664. It was a massive H-plan structure costing some £40,000 to build, plus the cost of interior furnishings. This was wildly extravagant, even by Restoration standards, and Londoners resented it. It stood roughly where Albemarle Street is today, and faced down St James's Street. It was said to have led the way in English domestic architecture, and stood in an eight-acre site amid open countryside.

The house contributed to the Earl's downfall, and was demolished less than twenty years after its completion. Pratt retired to his country estate in Norfolk, where he built himself Ryston Hall. He was awarded a knighthood, and lived in quiet obscurity for the rest of his life, playing the role of a country squire. Only two of the five houses he designed still survive – Ryston Hall and Kingston Lacy – although both were extensively remodelled in the nineteenth century.

A CONSPIRACY OF VIOLENCE

The first Thomas Chaloner adventure

Susanna Gregory

The dour days of Cromwell are over. Charles II is well established at White Hall Palace. London seethes with new energy, freed from the strictures of the Protectorate, but many of its inhabitants have lost their livelihoods.

One is Thomas Chaloner, a reluctant spy for the feared Secretary of State, John Thurloe, and now returned from Holland in desperate need of employment. His erstwhile boss, knowing he has many enemies at court, recommends Thomas to Lord Clarendon, but in return demands that Chaloner keep him informed of any plot against him.

But what Chaloner discovers is that Thurloe had sent another ex-employee to White Hall and he is dead, supposedly murdered by footpads near the Thames . . .

978-0-7515-3758-1

DEATH IN ST JAMES'S PARK

Susanna Gregory

Five years after Charles II's triumphant return to London there is growing mistrust of his extravagant court and of corruption among his officials.

When a cart laden with gunpowder explodes outside the General Letter Office it is immediately clear that such an act is more than an expression of outrage at the inefficiency of the postal service. As intelligencer to the Lord Chamberlain, Thomas Chaloner discovers that the witnesses he needs to interview about the poisoning of birds in the King's aviary in St James's Park have close links to the business conducted in the General Letter Office, activities more firmly centred on intercepting people's mail than delivering it.

Then human rather than avian victims are poisoned, and Chaloner knows he has to ignore his master's instructions and use his own considerable wits to defeat an enemy whose deadly tentacles reach into the very heart of the government: an enemy who has the power and expertise to destroy anyone who stands in the way . . .

978-1-84744-434-9